MW01224486

WISH ME FROM THE WATER

2nd Edition May 2104
Printed in USA

2nd Edition Copyediting by Kathrin DePue, The Writing Mechanic

Wish Me from the Water is a book of Fiction.   All characters involved in the story are from the imagination of the author, and any resemblance to anyone living or dead is purely coincidental.

The Spy Hill Correctional Centre for Young Offenders is a real place. Life inside the Spy Hill Correctional Centre and all physical details associated with this facility as described in this book are fictional creations by the author and are not factual nor representative of this facility.

ISBN-13: 978-1482095975

ISBN-10: 1482095971

Wish Me From the Water

WISH ME FROM THE WATER

CHAPTER 1

Jason brushed his dark bangs away from his eyes as he raced along the path to the high school. He was late, and he was supposed to meet his brother Tommy by the bike rack on the west side of the gym. He looked at his watch and was sure the game had already started. He was really looking forward to tonight.

Tonight was the season home opener for the Bluffington Shadows' High School girls' basketball team. He didn't care to watch the game, but there was a girl he wanted to ask out after the game ended. Patricia Mackie was her name. She played guard for the Bluffington basketball team.

Jason didn't play basketball. Hockey was his game, and hockey took up nearly all of his, and his older brother Tommy's, spare time. Tonight was one of the few nights the Midget Triple-A hockey practice didn't overlap with the basketball schedule.

He first spotted Patricia at the hockey camp tryout in early September. She sat up in the bleachers with the other girls. There were always girls in the stands at the Triple A tryouts and games. Patricia kept pointing at him, giggling to the other girls when he made another save. After each session was over, the girls swarmed the entrance to the rink, desperate to say hi to all of the boys they liked as they left the building. It took all of the nerve Jason had to open his mouth and say "hi" back to Patricia as he passed by her each time. He liked her, but he had no idea how to talk to a girl.

He finally decided tonight was the night he was going to ask her out on a date. That was the reason he desperately wanted his older brother Tommy to be there with him at the game. If any guy knew about girls, it was Tommy. He was the centre on the hockey team. Tommy never had a problem attracting girls. Tommy's star status as the league's leading goal scorer was a huge girl-magnet everywhere he went.

Jason was almost out of breath, having run from across town. He brushed his long hair off to the side and turned onto the shortcut that was cut into the small ridge below Simon's Flattened Frog Bistro. The path started below Simon's and ran exposed along the hillside before it suddenly cut deep in through the dense trees. The shortcut dropped off a good quarter mile to the school as the main road swung out away from the bottom of the hillside, running parallel to Pinhole Creek. The patch of forest here was thick with old growth spruce, jack pine, and poplars. It was a common hangout area for kids; it only took a few paces into the brush to be out from under the wandering eyes of downtown Bluffington.

Patricia was still on his mind as he rounded a bend in the trail and spotted movement off to his left in a small clearing. It was Doogie Fisher and Willie Wahnkman holding someone down in the dirt, laughing and teasing him. Doogie was seventeen, the same age as Jason's older brother Tommy. Doogie always seemed to find trouble wherever he went, and Willie always followed right behind. Willie was a few French fries short of an order, as they say, and he always did what Doogie told him to do. Right now, Doogie was Willie's teleprompter.

"Tell him! Tell him what he is!"

"You're a faggot, Tim," Willie said and laughed. He looked smugly at Doogie for approval.

Tim struggled to sit up, but Doogie and Willie kept one foot each firmly planted onto his skinny back.

"I'll let yous up but first yous gotta tell me what yous is," Doogie demanded.

"No," Tim yelled spitting out dirt-spotted saliva.

"Tell me, and I'll let yous up."

"No!" Tim said again, determined not to give in. He struggled some more, but it was useless. Doogie took his foot off Tim's back for a moment, flicked more dirt into Tim's face, and dropped with both knees hard onto his back. Tim yelled out in agony, and again tried to wiggle his way out. Doogie pushed down on the back of Tim's head making him eat dirt again before letting go.

Tim coughed and spit out more dirt. He opened one eye and tried to look around. The other stung with grit.

Jason stopped running when he recognized his small friend Tim. Tim lived on the east side of town in an area known as Townhouse Row. He played triple A hockey with Jason and Tommy. He was the youngest on the team and was small in stature, but he was fast and had very good hands.

Jason had his own run-ins with Doogie and Willie in the past, and he was not about to back away when one of his closest friends was on the receiving end. He charged through the trees into the clearing and tackled Doogie before Doogie had a chance to defend himself. Jason swung hard and quick. His fists pounded down, splitting Doogie's lower lip wide open. Jason got in as many swings as he could before Doogie could turn things around and fought back. The only thing that always kept Jason safe from Doogie's beat-down attempts was Jason's persistence. He would never give up in any fight, and for every three or four punches Doogie landed, Jason always got at least one good one back. Doogie wasn't used to taking punches, and he didn't like it at all when he took one to the face.

Willie took his foot off Tim and turned his attention to Jason and Doogie rolling about on the ground. Tim used the opportunity to scamper away to the side of the clearing where he stood up and wiped the dirt from his face with his sleeve. He watched uneasily as Jason and Doogie continued to exchange blows.

The two boys wrestled in the dusty earth and continued to throw punches. The two kept trading blows until they stood chest-to-chest across from each other. Doogie shoved Jason away hard with both hands. Jason staggered back a few steps but managed to keep his balance while keeping his eyes on Doogie.

Both boys were exhausted from the short scramble. Doogie pressed his fingers to his lips and pulled them away seeing blood.

"Yous're dead, Jason," Doogie said, flustered. Doogie always talked with a slur, and there was a noticeable deficiency in his sentence structure.

"We'll c'mon then," Jason replied. He lifted his hands and beckoned with his fingers.

Doogie wiped his mouth again.

"C'mon, big man. It takes two of you to pick on someone Tim's size? He's half your size, Doogie!"

"Tim's a faggot," Willie said from the side and laughed. He looked first at Tim and then over to Doogie and Jason.

This seemed to settle Doogie, and he looked back at Willie approvingly. "He is a faggot. You knows it, Jason."

Tim stood at the side of the clearing. Colour drained from his face.

"You're the faggot," Jason responded, standing his ground.

Doogie pointed his finger at Jason. "Yous better watch your back because this ain't done yet."

Jason moved to the side of the clearing towards Tim and ignored Doogie. He asked Tim if he was okay. Tim nodded while spitting out another clump of dirt.

"Sometime, somewhere I will get you!" Doogie shouted. He touched his lip and felt it beginning to swell. "And yous too, Tim. Yous're both dead. Next time when yous doesn't have Jason here to protects you." He stared at Tim. "Fricking faggot," he mumbled, and motioned to Willie. The pair quickly left the clearing in the direction of downtown.

Jason stepped up close to see if his friend was all right. Tim immediately shoved Jason away hard. "Back off!" he shouted angrily.

Jason stumbled backwards. "It's okay, Tim, they're gone," he said. He tried to calm Tim down, but Tim stood there shaking his head side-to-side violently. He stared at Jason with a distant and vacant expression.

Jason approached Tim again, but Tim stepped back, extending his hands out in front of him ready to push Jason away if he came any closer. Tim continued his shuffle away from Jason until he stumbled and fell backwards into a small shrub at the edge of the clearing.

"What's the matter with you?" Jason asked. He was very concerned about his friend's odd behaviour, but Tim said nothing. He lay spread-eagle upon the shrubs shaking his head.

"Let's go home. I'll walk with you," Jason offered. His friend was more important than any girl or basketball game. He reached his hand out towards Tim.

Tim shook his head. "No! I'm not doing that." He scrambled back up on to his feet. "I can't do this anymore," he cried out. He turned and ran off through the forest towards town. Jason watched him leave, not sure what he was supposed to do. He eventually chased after his friend. Jason was extremely fit and caught up to Tim easily. He walked next to Tim through the dense trees keeping a good eight feet between them. He wasn't sure what had set his friend off.

"What was all that back there about?" Jason asked.

Tim stopped walking, and kept his stare straight ahead without looking at Jason. "It's too much. I just don't want to do this anymore."

"Do what anymore?"

Tim slowly turned to Jason. "Live," he blurted out.

Jason shook his head slowly from side to side. "You don't mean that. Those guys are just assholes and you know it. They get me all the time too, so you can't give up because of them. Look at my face from Doogie's punches," he said, pointing to his own swollen lip and dirty, bruised cheekbone.

"You don't understand. It's not them." Tim stared at Jason as tears fell down his face. "Do I look like a fag to you?" he asked.

Jason snickered, "What do you mean? Those guys call everybody a fag."

"I asked you a question, and it's not funny. Do I look like I'm gay?"

Jason hesitated. He didn't know what he was supposed to say. "You look like everyone else."

Tim began to sob. He sat down on the leaves and twigs and gestured Jason to come near. "I gotta tell you something, and you can't tell a soul. You hear me? Not a soul."

Jason nodded and sat down next to Tim on the moss that covered the forest ground.

"I never told anyone this yet, but..." Tim wiped away a few tears that had fallen down his face. He sniffled and caught his breath. "And I'm not gay."

Jason shook his head, "It didn't matter if you were, Tim."

"It's just..." He hung his head and sobbed. "I've been buggered."

Jason frowned. He didn't quite believe what he heard. He asked Tim to repeat what he said.

"I've been buggered, Jason, and I want it to stop... and I don't know what to do."

"Who?" was all Jason could ask. He found it inconceivable that his friend Tim was being molested. Tim only shook his head, and Jason prompted him to tell him more. "Who's doing this?"

Again, Tim shook his head. He wouldn't say who it was. The two boys sat in the forest. Neither one said anything else for some time. Jason's cell phone rang. He saw it was his brother Tommy, and he pressed the ignore button. Tommy was probably still waiting outside the school and wondering where he was.

Jason seriously wanted to know more. Who could possibly do such a thing to his friend, and what was actually done to him? Thoughts raced through his mind. Where and when? He wondered how long Tim had suffered. Was it an adult in Tim's home? Someone else he knew? Doogie? He suddenly shouted out before he could stop his voice. "Doogie? Was it Doogie?"

"No!" Tim shouted back. "It wasn't Doogie. Nor Willie, or anyone our age."

"Oh, sorry." Jason knew it was an adult. "So you're not going to tell me who it was?"

"I can't, Jason. I can't. You wouldn't understand." He stared firmly at Jason as if he wanted to say more and then looked away dejected.

"Try me," Jason pushed, but Tim wasn't going to say more. Over an hour passed as the two sat in the forest. Tim refused to talk about who it was, and Jason did his best to offer only his ears. He didn't ask any more questions about what went on, but he hoped Tim would open up with more on his own. Tim cried and Jason told him that it was okay to cry. The sun eventually settled behind the mountains to the west, and darkness fell by the time the boys walked out of the forest. They discussed nothing more.

Jason offered to walk Tim home, but Tim insisted he needed some time to himself before he went home. Jason didn't like the thought of leaving Tim on his own, but relented. Tim turned and headed back into the forest along the path down towards the high school alone, while Jason followed his own way home through the centre of town.

Jason walked away but was deeply bothered. He wanted to turn around. Part of him shouted deep down inside and insisted he must turn around and follow Tim. The conversation amongst the twigs and darkness of the forest wasn't finished. He finally stopped when he was about halfway home. He looked across town in the direction of Simon's Bistro and the path Tim had followed back into the trees. In his heart, he felt a terrible darkness he never knew he could feel: His friend was in trouble, and he didn't know what to   do.

CHAPTER 2

Sarah glanced out the kitchen window, turned to check on the salmon that baked in the oven, and watched for Gerald's truck to arrive. The sun had already set, and the last of the blue glow had long since faded behind the mountain peaks. Gerald still was not home from work. She knew what she was in for, and it was going to be all her fault again. The salmon was all dried out. The baked potatoes were shrivelled and began to collapse inward. The only thing salvaged was the peas, and that was only because she had not yet thrown them into the microwave.

She poured herself another glass of wine. It was her third as she waited for Gerald. *Waited* was the right word. She always *waited*. What Gerald wanted, Gerald always got. Supper: hot and ready on the table when he walked in the door. A cool beer ready for his consumption in the fridge. Her legs wide open whenever he wanted them there.

She was tired of this game.

The lights of Gerald's truck suddenly shined through the front window onto the wall as he pulled into the front drive. Sarah dumped the remains of her wine quickly into the sink and placed the empty glass in the back of the dishwasher. She had to be quick. She popped the peas into the microwave, opened the oven and began to plate the food for both of them. She had to be sure not to forget a cold one from the fridge.

She heard the truck door slam as she rushed to set the two plates down onto the table. She sat and then straightened her dress and hair. She looked across the table at the two plates and cutlery. Something was missing.

Gerald's beer! It was still on the counter in the kitchen.

The front door opened as Sarah rushed back out from the kitchen with Gerald's beer in hand. She caught Gerald's stare as she placed the beer next to his plate and sat back down. She swallowed hard and read his eyes immediately. They said, "Let's get it started."

CHAPTER 3

Tommy waited at the bike rack for his younger brother, Jason, for more than half an hour. It was uncharacteristic for Jason to be late. He called him on his cell, eager to get inside the gym after hearing the shouts and cheers from the spectators inside, but the call went to voice mail. He didn't leave a message. He finally went inside and searched for his friends, Bobby and Ricky. He spotted Bobby waving at him from the back of the seats near the top. Ricky sat next to him with his eyes pointed downward at the play down on the court.

Tommy gave a quick wave back and worked his way through the crowd. It wasn't easy for someone like Tommy to walk through a crowd unnoticed. He was the star of the Midget AAA team. Tommy was tall and lean. His light blonde hair was short, almost military in style. He was the league-leading scorer, and it seemed that everyone knew who he was. He worked his way towards the bleachers and acknowledged the comments from fans as he passed through. "Great start to the season, Tommy!" "Way to go, Tommy." "Good game last Sunday!" "Going all the way this year, eh, Tommy?"

He maneuvered his way through the crowd, smiling and acknowledging everyone who commented. For Tommy, his responses just came naturally: a handshake back to an outstretched hand; a "thank you" here and there; a big smile or simple nod. He had his fans. The entire town loved Tommy, and he accepted his minor celebrity status graciously. "The one to watch for in Junior A," the papers wrote.

Tommy was already more than good enough to play Junior A and was invited to camp tryouts, but Tommy's dad, the coach and trainer of the Midget AAA wouldn't let him. He wanted Tommy to bask in the limelight for one more season. He could be the league-leading scorer for one more year, and the MVP for one more year. There were still more records to be broken. He wanted that feeling of being "the best" buried deep inside Tommy so he wouldn't forget what it was like when he played Junior A next year.

"Where's Jason?" Ricky asked knowing he was the reason Tommy waited outside.

Tommy just shrugged, looked down towards the girls on the court and smiled. Ricky shook his head, rolled his eyes and nudged Bobby on the arm. "Look at him. Already at it with the girls."

The boys watched the rest of the game. The Shadows won, easily beating the South Calgary Cheetahs ninety-two to sixty-eight.

The crowd cleared quickly, and the boys lingered outside the back exit of the gym. It was late and they all had school in the morning. They were just about to head back along the path through the forest to town when Tommy spotted their teammate, Jason's friend Tim, sitting alone on the post-and-rail fence on the far side of the parking lot. He stopped and stared at Tim for a moment. Something didn't look right. Tim was alone, his hair was mussed and his clothes looked dirty and disheveled.

"Hey guys, you go on ahead," Tommy said. "I'm just going to see Tim over there for a sec. I'll catch up with you." Ricky and Bobby looked over to see Tim backlit by the street light. Bobby turned away and began to shuffle himself down the path alone before he realized Ricky wasn't following.

"Ricky, c'mon. I gotta get home. I'm late already."

20

Ricky played hockey with Tommy, Jason and Tim, but quit at the end of last season. He was in grade twelve with Tommy and was a natural at hockey. He played right wing to Tommy's centre and was instrumental in helping Tommy win the scoring title last season. Ricky wouldn't offer up any reason for quitting other than he wanted to do something else.

Bobby didn't played sports like the rest of his friends. He was a year younger, in grade eleven with Jason and Tim, and he had his own problems. He was born with deformed legs, and it took years of surgery and physiotherapy for Bobby to progress to where he could walk without aid of crutches. Only a shuffle of the left leg remained, and he was told it would be with him forever. Bobby's mother still doted on Bobby. She was very strict and demanding, and she treated him as if he was made of porcelain at times. Getting home late was not on option for Bobby.

"Ricky!" Bobby yelled. "I gotta get home."

Ricky continued to watch Tommy as he reached Tim in the parking lot. Tim jumped from the fence as Tommy neared and darted out towards the street. Tommy followed close behind. As he watched Tim scamper away with Tommy chasing after him, he felt something deep inside him hurt and he swallowed hard. Ricky really wanted to follow Tommy and Tim, but Bobby yelled at him again.

"Okay, I'm coming! Just shut up already!" Ricky shouted back. He turned and ran the few paces to catch up.

"What's the matter with you, Ricky? You don't even like Tim. Why do you even care about what's going on over there?"

"I don't care," he lied to Bobby. He walked on a few minutes in silence. "Tim's okay I guess. When we played together last year, he was just an ass to me all the time... trying to check me into the boards all the time in practice, or tripping me up. Shit like that. He'd really piss me off.

Sometimes when he'd see me wide open going for the net he'd refuse to pass the puck to me.   He always seemed to have a chip on his shoulder."

"Hmm," was all Bobby replied. Bobby never talked hockey. He was always a good listener and the other boys knew it. They could say anything to Bobby without being judged and know he wouldn't repeat it. Bobby lived across the street just four doors down from Tommy and Jason. They had all become close friends over the years. Bobby bonded more with Tommy even though he was Jason's age.

"I don't know why he didn't like me," Ricky pondered aloud.

The two walked along the path through the trees back towards the centre of town. It was eerily dark in the trees, and Ricky was glad for it as he wiped away at his eyes. Bobby couldn't see he was almost crying. He felt something as he had watched Tommy chase after Tim, and it hurt inside. He knew he would have to talk to Tim eventually.

CHAPTER 4

Gerald slammed the front door and glared into the kitchen at Sarah seated at the table. Sarah forced a smile, and kept her eyes downcast; she pretended not to see the rage set on Gerald's face. She knew how to behave when he was like this. Usually when he was late from work, he was drunk, and tonight was no exception.

"Supper's ready. Come sit," she said pleasantly, and patted the seat next to her. She dared not look up at him yet. Not until he spoke. Only then would she know how intense tonight was going to be.

"Damn fucker!" Gerald shouted. "That God damned idiot Danny didn't put the load on the back of my truck properly. Lost most of it pulling on to the highway out by Baxter's garage. Spent most of the last hour picking up two by fours and shit from all over the road!"

Sarah knew better. Gerald was drinking, and he probably got into another scramble at the bar, hopped into his truck and pulled out in a tear onto the highway. It was most likely his own damned fault.

"Oh babe, I'm so sorry," she apologized. Gerald tossed his jacket onto the couch and walked into the kitchen. He left his dirty boots on. Sarah's eyes dropped to watch the muddy chunks fall onto the carpet.

"He's in for shit when I get in tomorrow! I'm telling you."

Gerald sat down at the table and caught her as she looked at the chunks of mud. "What are you lookin' at?" he yelled.

Big mistake. She knew better than to stare at the dirt that fell from his boots. Gerald raised his hand in the air, ready to backhand her. "When I'm speaking you look at me! You understand me?"

She got it. Tonight was going to be very intense. She looked immediately up at Gerald and nodded.

Gerald lowered his hand and began to eat. Sarah followed Gerald's lead, being sure not to eat faster or slower than he did.

"Salmon," he said.

"You like salmon, Gerald. I thought tonight I'd make you something special."

Gerald picked away at the salmon. He cut into a potato. "Dried out shit," he said. "You cook like your God damned mother."

Gerald slammed his fork and knife down on the table. He glared at Sarah and suddenly pushed his chair away and stood up. He reached over, grabbed Sarah by the neck, and shoved her face down into her plate. "If I wanted slop to eat, I'd a married a fucking pig farmer!"

Sarah struggled to free herself from his grasp. Her arms were outstretched, but Gerald repeatedly shoved her face down into her plate.

"I hate Salmon! I hate fucking peas! You like peas so much, well eat these!" he screamed, and shoved Sarah's face all over the plate again. The peas and potatoes mashed into her eyes and up her nose.

Sarah tried to scream but couldn't. His grasp was solid. He lifted her face off the plate and slammed it back down hard enough to split the plate in two. Sarah flailed her arms and knocked the butter and Gerald's plate to the floor. A trickle of blood dripped onto her plate from the cut on her forehead.

Gerald grabbed her by the hair and sweater and dragged her from the table down the hall towards the bedroom. Sarah tried to scream, but her sweater was pulled up high and choked off her air supply. He threw her on the bed and told her he was going to show her who was boss in this house.

"You stay right fucking there, and don't you dare move a fucking muscle!" he shouted and left the room.

CHAPTER 5

Tommy approached Tim where he sat on the fence in the parking lot. He could see something had happened; Tim's shirt was torn, his hair was a mess, and there was dirt smeared across his hands and face.

"Tim, what happened?" Tommy asked.

"Just go away, Tommy!"

Tommy moved closer, but Tim jumped off the fence and ran a few paces towards the dark street in front of the school.

"What happened?"

"Go away," Tim said again and darted towards the street. Tommy followed quickly behind. Tommy couldn't help himself; he had to follow. Not only was Tim a teammate and one of his brother's best friends, Tommy couldn't help but step in when someone, anyone, was in trouble. Tommy was that way with everybody. He certainly wasn't about to let Tim walk away without knowing what had happened.

Tim ran down the sidewalk that followed the main road towards downtown. Tommy followed and called out for Tim to stop, but Tim ran faster. Tommy followed relentlessly, block after block. Finally, Tim tired and slowed to a walk, and Tommy caught up to him. Tim was crying.

"Who did this to you?" Tommy asked.

Tim just shook his head. "You don't know nothing."

"Maybe I don't. But I want to know who did this to you."

Tim stopped sharply and took a swing at Tommy. Tommy tried to dodge to the side, but he was too slow, and took the punch solidly on his shoulder.

"Shit! What was that for?" he asked and held his shoulder with his other hand. "That frickin' hurt!"

Tim turned and walked away not answering. Tommy followed.

Tim suddenly turned back and screamed at Tommy. "Would you just leave me alone?"

"I can't do that. Not until you tell me what's going on."

Tim stopped. He was furious at Tommy, and his eyes were red and puffy from crying. "You don't know nothing," he said again and walked on. Tommy reached out and grabbed Tim hard by the shoulder. "For Christ sakes, Tim. I thought I was your friend. What did I do? I just want to help."

Tim turned back with his hand raised, and fist clenched. He was ready to slug Tommy again. His face grimaced with anger. "You really want to know who did this, Tommy? Because if you do, I will tell you, but you really don't want to know! You don't! So if you ask me again, Tommy… you should just bugger off and leave me alone!"

Tommy raised his hands in self-defense. "Whoa. But I do want to know."

"Jesus, Tommy! You just don't see it, do you? No one does."

Tommy shook his head. He didn't understand Tim at all.

Tim finally had enough. He stepped forward and shoved Tommy hard with both hands. Tommy stumbled backwards. "You don't get it!" Tim shouted. He stepped forward and shoved Tommy again with both hands. "You don't, do you?"

Tommy stumbled back again. He didn't know what to do, but he knew his friend was in serious distress.

"None of you see what's really going on. Not you! Not Jason. No one!"

Tommy looked back at Tim whose tears etched dark channels of grime down his sad face.

Tim stepped up and shoved Tommy hard with both hands one last time. "You wanna know who did this to me, Tommy?" He stared at Tommy and stuck his finger in Tommy's face. "Your dad did this to me! Your dad!"

"My dad beat you up? What are you saying?" Tommy replied defensively.

"Fuck, you're stupid!" Tim screamed. "Just like everybody else!" He kicked Tommy in the shins as hard as he could, ran off, and left Tommy to collapse on one knee and watch as Tim disappeared into the darkness.

CHAPTER 6

Sarah couldn't believe it happened again. It had been nearly four months since the last time Gerald gave her a food face wash. This time it was much worse. In the past, he always left in a rage out the front door immediately after the outburst; he wouldn't show up until the next evening, apologizing for what he had done, but he always let her know it was she who made him do this to her. She never knew where he stayed when he left, and she never dared to ask.

Tonight it was very different. He hadn't left; what did he just say before he left the room? "I'm gonna show you who's boss in this house." That cannot be good.

Sarah reached up to wipe some of the potato and peas from her face but felt a sharp searing pain strike through her right arm after hearing a "swoosh" through the air. She turned to see Gerald with intense anger on his face as he held a corn broom high in the air above her. He brought it down a second time with a fury, aiming for her skull. She instinctively raised her arm into the air to block it and felt the snap as the broom broke the bone in her forearm. She screamed as the pain soared through her body. Gerald went for another swing, and brought the broom down hard, over and over again onto her already broken arm and her head. The broom finally snapped into two pieces down the crack produced by the first swing.

The room spun away from Sarah. The pain rushed in and filled her mind with sudden blackness. She heard Gerald's voice faintly through the pain; he shouted obscenities. The words were incoherent in her semi-conscious state. She struggled to right herself on the bed, but slipped and fell hard to the floor. The pain blazed through her body again. She glanced over to see Gerald still screaming as he stood over by the closet. He was in a rage, yanking her clothes from the hangers and tossing them everywhere about the room as he spewed obscenities.

She wasn't sure how long he remained in the room, and she didn't even know if he had hit her again. Her mind descended deep into the chasm where reality was out of reach. She thought she was dead; her loving sister and her recently deceased mother and father's faces flashed in front of her. She wanted to scream, and maybe she did, but she heard nothing. She felt pain and only pain. Gerald had crossed the line, and she was beyond terrified. The horror of how far she let herself fall had finally materialized tonight. She felt herself drift away into darkness; Gerald's voice was just a distant murmur beyond the swirling agony that devoured her.

Everything went black.

CHAPTER 7

Tommy walked around to the back door of the house and let himself in. The boys always entered through the back door. The front entrance of the large house on Founders Road was for guests only, his mother insisted. He saw the lights still on in his dad's therapy office out back, and he heard the usual grunts and shouts from the late night sessions his father offered free to the top university athletes.

Peter Oliver had a doctorate in sports medicine and was the head of the Sports Training and Physiotherapy Department at the University. Eight years ago, shortly after they moved in, he started up a sideline therapy business at home. He built the physiotherapy office next to the garage in the back of their large property. Peter was very generous with his therapy; he offered one-on-one training for fitness and injury physiotherapy at his home office in the evening to fit the schedules of his top athletes.

Peter also volunteered his time as head coach and trainer of the boys AAA midget hockey team. He had coached his boys' teams since peewee, and it was the same group of boys year after year. Any of the boys were welcome to come for the extra training. Tommy and Jason used the fitness room constantly, and many of their friends came over after school to weight train. Some even took the one-on-one training Peter offered. He extended his no-fee, one-on-one offer to all of the boys on the hockey team and to many of the town's lower income, sports-playing families.

Hockey was a big thing in this town. To be a part of the Triple AAA midget team was a very big deal, and Peter

Oliver and his boys were at the centre of it. Peter had a knack for delivering success; he coached the boys to the league title and the Provincial Championship two years running. He coached his boys from the very beginning, and it seemed every team Peter coached ended up at the top of the standings. The boys easily excelled under their father's rigorous workout routine. It was obvious to everyone who watched hockey, or had the privilege of playing under Peter and alongside his boys, that this family was the real deal. How far they could go was anybody's guess.

Peter's wife Marie was the perfect hockey mom. She was always the taxi driver when Peter couldn't be there, and she was heavily involved in booking and scheduling the tournaments and road trips. She found her place organizing, fundraising, volunteering and being a part of the hockey community. Life revolved around hockey from morning until bedtime each day.

Tommy stood in the darkness and stared out at the physiotherapy office. He really wanted to talk to his dad. What Tim suggested upset him deeply. Why would Tim say such a thing? His dad roughed Tim up? It just didn't make any sense. But Tim swore it was his dad who did this, and he had never seen Tim so upset about anything. Tommy's gut ached and his head hurt as he thought about what Tim said. He continued to stare out at the shop and almost walked over, but he knew better than to interrupt one of his dad's sessions. He stepped inside the house instead. The one-on-one sessions were private, and the office door was usually locked. Interrupting his dad was an unforgivable offence.

He spotted Jason's shoes just inside the back door and knew he was home too, but sensed from the darkness and silence that Jason was already in bed. Talking to Jason about Tim would have to wait until morning.

CHAPTER 8

Gerald was long gone when Sarah finally emerged from the darkness her mind had taken her to. She lay on the floor, and her arm throbbed terribly. Her head pounded. At first she wasn't sure where she was and wondered why she was on the floor with her clothes scattered everywhere about the room. She tried to move and the pain soared through her arm once again, causing her to grimace instantly. She looked down to see her forearm swollen and badly misshapen.

She lay still on the floor for a while and let the events of the last few hours return to her consciousness. She kept her arm as still as possible. It was dark outside and she glanced up to the bedside clock to see that it was very early in the morning. Gerald was certainly gone, and she was sure he wouldn't return until late in the evening. That was how Gerald always did it. Crawling back as if what had happened the night before wasn't that big of a deal, and he would promise not to do it again if she promised not to provoke him.

Sarah was tired of the game they played. She felt certain last night that she was about to die. It was the first time she had ever felt this way with Gerald.

She tried to move up to a sitting position, but the pain was too intense. She screamed out and fell back on the floor. She cried softly and stared about the room. What was she going to do now?

Her mind drifted off to her work; what would she say to her co-workers? Sarah worked as a student counsellor a few blocks away at the Forest Lawn High School on Calgary's east side. The school was a tough one. Gang fights were common between the racial divisions of Whites, Chinese, Koreans and Blacks. The altercations happened mostly between her school and the Christian school on the opposite side of the soccer field. Stabbings in the halls and students caught with knives were common occurrences, and the odd firearm was confiscated on rare occasions.

She almost laughed as she looked down at her broken arm and knew she wasn't going to be anywhere near Forest Lawn High for a while. She was the counsellor. There was a strange irony to it all. She was the one students looked to for guidance in an adolescent environment from hell, while she secretly returned to her own hell each night.

She rolled onto her side and stared at the mess Gerald had made of her closet. Everything was upside down. Through all the pain her eyes focused on something inside the closet she had not seen for many years. Down in the right corner, barely peeking out from behind the stack of shoeboxes was the corner of a bright red suitcase.

She still had that?

She stared at the red suitcase, and remembered back almost ten years when she first left home for college. Her mother gave her this bright red suitcase and told her something she had long since forgotten. She struggled deep to remember her mother's words, and slowly they returned. She let them return and kept her eyes on the bright red suitcase.

Her mother hugged her and cried as Sarah prepared to leave home for the first time. It was only Bluffington University, just one hour's drive south, but she was leaving home. "In this suitcase are not just clothes, my darling. Inside you carry your future. Wherever you go and wherever you end up, remember where it started. The future you make yourself."

Sarah hugged her mother and never wanted to let her go. She met Gerald at college. He was a construction worker, and she was in her third year. She missed her mother so much.

Sarah knew what she was about to do. She screamed out in agony as she forced herself to her feet. She stumbled to the closet, pulled the red suitcase out from the corner with her good arm, and quickly loaded it with all she could gather. She had made her future with Gerald. She was about to unmake it and start over. It took all of her energy to fight through the pain. She nearly passed out multiple times, but it wasn't long before she made the two phone calls she needed to make and the taxicab pulled up in front of the house.

CHAPTER 9

Tim woke his little sister Amber and did what he did every weekday morning. Amber was only twelve, and it was his job to make sure Amber was up, dressed and off to school each day. Tim's mother was long gone to work already. She had a job at the Tim Horton's on the edge of town, working the five thirty AM morning shift as she did every day. Tim never did have a father, as far as he knew.

Amber was a good little sister and always listened to what Tim told her to do. The routine was the same every day. Tim woke Amber up, fed her breakfast, cleaned the kitchen, locked the house and walked her to the elementary school on his way to the senior high school.

Today was different. Tim sat Amber down and told her she had to walk to school on her own today.

"Why?" she asked. "I don't want to walk by myself, Tim."

Tim tried not to cry. "Just today, Amber. Honest."

"Why aren't you going to school?"

Tim turned his head towards Amber. He grabbed her by the shoulders, pulled her close and hugged her.

"Stop it, Tim," she said and pushed him away. "So why aren't you going to school?"

"I'm just going later," he said. "I've got stuff to do first."

"Like what?" she asked.

"Boy stuff. Just go to school already or you're going to be late."

Tim pushed Amber out the door, and stood on the steps to watch her as she walked down the road. He kept his watch until she finally turned two blocks down on Blonde Street. He went inside, closed the front door and locked it.

Tim already knew what he was going to do next. He had tossed and turned all night, thinking about nothing else. He didn't really know what else he could do. Who was out there, really, to help him? He had tried to talk to his friends yesterday and made a right mess of that. Yesterday was the tipping point, and there was only one way out of it now.

Tim ran up the stairs to the second floor of the townhouse and into Amber's room. He knew exactly where she kept it, and he pulled open the top dresser drawer. Amber always kept her favourite toys in the top dresser drawer. He knew it would be in there because he had picked it out for her, and she had hugged him and screamed with joy when she unwrapped it six weeks ago on her birthday. His heart pounded as he opened the drawer. "Please, please, be there," he whispered.

To him it had been no big deal. It was just a skipping rope, but it meant the world to Amber. She had never owned her own before and treasured it dearly.

He looked inside the drawer, and there it was, laid out perfectly, the loops all kinked together just as it had come out the package. Amber was always very particular. He grabbed the rope, walked out of her room and stood at the top of the stairs. He leaned over the railing and looked down into the small foyer at the bottom. It was a big drop. His adrenalin rushed, and his heart pounded particularly hard, nearly bursting through his chest. He took a deep breath and tossed one end of the rope over the railing into the foyer.

CHAPTER 10

Tommy awoke later than he hoped. He had a free study period first thing and didn't have to be at school until ten. The sun was already up and the house was quiet. He quickly grabbed his robe and rushed downstairs to find Jason had already left for school.

"Damn," Tommy said, disappointed that he had missed Jason. He still worried about Tim. He ran what Tim said over and over in his mind last night and just couldn't understand why Tim blamed his dad. What was he really talking about? His dad roughed Tim up?

He texted Bobby who lived just four doors down and asked if he also had first study spare.

Bobby quickly texted back that he did. Tommy told him to wait, and he would be right over to walk to school with him. He needed to talk to him about something very important.

CHAPTER 11

Brandy Sykes sat in the emergency waiting room tired and upset. She had been there for nearly four hours since she rushed Sarah over to there in the middle of the night and had still heard nothing from the doctors about Sarah's condition.

Brandy worked with Sarah as a counsellor at Forest Lawn High School. Over time, she and Sarah had become good friends. Sarah would have named Brandy as her only friend if anyone had ever asked. Gerald didn't allow Sarah to have friends. Over the years, he belittled or taunted her friends when they came over to visit until they finally just quit coming. When Sarah wanted to go out to see them, Gerald told her that she wasn't allowed out of the house to see anyone. Brandy was Sarah's little secret. She was her oasis of promise when things got tough. Gerald didn't even know she existed, and Sarah kept the three-year-long friendship close to her chest, careful to only see Brandy when Gerald was out of town or working late.

Sarah had made two phone calls after she packed up the red suitcase. The first was the distress call to Brandy. The second was the cab as she couldn't drive her five speed with her broken, swollen arm.

The doctor came into the emergency waiting room, nodded at Brandy and pointed to one of the small side rooms. Brandy got up quickly and followed the doctor inside.

"Sarah is doing okay," the doctor told her. One bone was broken and they reset it. There was a lot of bruising on her arms, legs and head but she would recover. The cut on her forehead was minor, and she would have a goose egg to deal with for the next few weeks. The doctor asked if Brandy had witnessed any of Sarah's beatings and Brandy replied "no," shaking her head, somewhat bewildered. The doctor told Brandy that Sarah had been in the hospital many times before today, each time denying that Gerald had touched her, but he had never seen anything this bad.

Brandy was shocked. Sarah's husband was a complete mystery to her. Sarah never talked about him, and Brandy never really even noticed. She told the doctor that she would bring Sarah home with her if that was all right. The doctor agreed it was best, and emphasized that Gerald should not know where she is. He made it clear to Brandy that Gerald could have killed her if she had not protected herself. No one must know where she is.

Could she really do that for Sarah, she asked herself? Could she put herself right into the middle of Sarah's troubles? Could she hide her away as the monster prowled around the city, searching for her relentlessly? Of course she could.

Brandy assured the doctor she would tell no one of Sarah's whereabouts.

The doctor sat down next to Brandy and once again put it very bluntly. Sarah wasn't going to press charges. They needed to ask patients these questions in obvious acts of violence such as this. They would have immediately called the police if her injuries had been any worse, but Sarah insisted.

Brandy's mouth gaped open in shock that Sarah would do nothing after receiving such a beating. The doctor affirmed her response, shrugged and suggested she speak to Sarah. If the damage he did to her tonight was any indication of the type of man Gerald was, Sarah's life may depend on his arrest; the sooner, the better.

He offered to take her up to see Sarah.

CHAPTER 12

Tommy was sitting in the library after lunch when he read the text on Facebook that just popped in. He stopped what he was doing and read the text again. The blood drained from his head, and he suddenly felt very dizzy.

Did u hear? Tim Guenther killed himself today! Betty Harrison.

Tommy read it again. No! It couldn't be true.

His phoned blipped. Another message.

It cus Doogie beat m up yesterday. Patricia Mackie.

Patricia hung out with Doogie and Willie, and if anyone knew what Doogie did on a daily basis, it was Patricia Mackie.

Another message. And another. The messages began to flow.

Thats so sad. I liked Tim. Simon Cotters.

Where Luke Wilson.

OMG. Not Tim! the hockey player? Andrew Fillpot.

Poor Tim. Luke Wilson.

He was good at hockey. Andrew Fillpot.

I heard he did it at home Patricia Mackie.

It was. ambulance outside rite now Betty Harrison.

u at home Betty? Andrew Fillpot.

all day. Police here 2! Betty Harrison.

Tommy put his cell phone down and looked across the library at the students that continued to press their noses deep into some book or binder. They had not yet heard the news. It was an odd, cold feeling. The room began to close in and

Tommy needed to breathe. He quickly stuffed all of his books into his backpack and walked out of the school agitated. He stopped and looked around, not sure which way to go. He was suddenly angry. Very angry.

Tommy replayed Tim's last words repeatedly in his mind.

"Fuck, you're stupid! Your dad did this to me! Just like everybody else! Fuck, you're stupid! Your dad! No one does! You don't see it, do you! No one does! Fuck, you're stupid! Fuck, you're stupid! Your dad did this to me!

Tommy turned and ran towards home.

CHAPTER 13

Breaking news had its way of travelling through the school. The school didn't allow cell phones in any of the classrooms, but there was always one student who managed to sneak one inside.

Jason was in the middle of afternoon math class when the ruckus erupted at the back of the class. The teacher, Mr. Denson, called for order. In just a few minutes, two girls were starting to cry, and the word *suicide* was repeated at least a dozen times around the back of the classroom.

Jason listened and turned towards the back like the others from the front of the class. He listened curiously, and wondered who they continued to talk about. When Tim Guenther's name was uttered, his insides turned over and he nearly collapsed in anguish. Jason listened to the words repeated from text messages as they were suddenly repeated aloud for all to hear. Jason felt strongly that those words should be private and not discussed in anything like this public forum.

Mr. Denson demanded order, but the furor continued to grow at an alarming rate, exceeding anything Mr. Denson could handle.

Jason stared around the room, not sure how he should feel. He only knew what was happening around him was wrong. The dull, routine quietness in the classroom was shattered with a strange stimulus that transformed these mates of his into something obscene and indescribable. He suddenly despised these people, and he never wanted to be friends with any of them again. Students, who only moments before were sitting bored, and even yawning periodically, had suddenly awoken and were filled with an exhilarated enthusiasm for gossip and speculation that disgusted Jason. This was his friend they were talking about! Tim was the fodder for their frenzy. He looked about at the many faces in the room. Some were crying, some smiled and a few even laughed. Laughing? Jason felt his stomach churn and the taste of bile inched its way up.

Jason stood up and ran out of the classroom. He ignored Mr. Denson's demand to sit down immediately. It couldn't be true. Not his friend Tim. He ran down the hall as fast as he could. The tears began and he wiped them away, but they wouldn't stop. He stopped at his locker and fumbled to dial in the combination. He had to try three times before he succeeded. He quickly grabbed his iPhone and scrolled through the incoming messages. He needed to see these for himself. He felt weak and slumped against the wall of lockers, and read the messages over and over. He tried to piece together what was happening, but his perspective was lost.

I didn't like that kid anyway Mike Jenkins.

He was cute. asked me out once Maria Fuccini.

:(Larry Holmes.

Who wants to go to his house as soon as they let us out? Billy Jorgeson.

I thought he was great. He was good at hockey. so sad Sarah Shelly.

I'll go Billy. c u at the dumpster Frank Polson.

He wasn't in geo class this morning Shelly Smith.

It was Doogie that drove him to it Francine Falcone.

Willie and Doogie beat him up yesterday I heard. Called him a faggot Bob Sykes.

How'd he do it? Billy Jorgeson.

In his own house. His mother found him. Betty Harrison.

Jason stopped reading. He turned and ran. He crashed through the doors of the school into the cool October air. He wanted to scream, to cry, to beat his head with his hands. None of these people really knew Tim. He was suddenly angry. He was angry at Tim for not talking. He was angry at himself for not really listening.

Why Tim? Why did you have to do this?

He raced down the same path where he found Tim yesterday and cried as he remembered the secret Tim had made him promise not to tell anyone. He didn't know it, but his brother Tommy also ran down the same path just five minutes ahead of him.

CHAPTER 14

Tommy slowed to a fast walk when he turned on to Founders Road. Founders Road was *the* place to live in Bluffington. The wealthy and important people of Bluffington owned grandiose houses, and Tommy and Jason's parents were included in that group. The Oliver home was just as large as the others. It was an older two story Victorian, and, like most of the others, it was set on a half-acre lot that reached back to the river behind it.

Tommy walked slowly up to the house, and expected that both his mother and father would be at work, but he spotted one of the garage doors in the back wide open. His father's polished, jet-black, series 5 BMW sat parked inside. His father was home? In the middle of the afternoon? Tommy quickly assumed his father was in the office attached to the garage. He slowly strolled slowly up to the open garage door, squeezed past the BMW and approached the office door.

He dropped his backpack on the cement floor and put his ear up to the inside door that led into the office but he heard nothing. Tommy remained there with his ear to the door still listening when Jason entered the garage behind him. He was still out of breath from running all the way home.

"What are you doing?"

"Shhh!" Tommy replied and waved his hand behind him to quiet his brother. He still heard nothing from the office beyond the door.

Jason wiped the last of the tears and dirt from his face and walked two steps towards his brother. He looked at Tommy. "You heard I guess."

Tommy turned toward Jason and nodded. Both boys stared at one another. Neither knew how to approach the subject.

"Dad's home," is all Tommy said.

Jason rubbed his hand across the car and walked towards Tommy. "What'd you hear?" he asked.

Tommy shrugged as tears welled into his eyes. "Just stuff." He wasn't sure what to say. He glanced again at the BMW.

"I ran into Tim last night," Jason said and stared at the cement floor in the garage. "He said some things... I..." He began to cry. Tommy stepped towards Jason, put one arm around him, and rubbed his head with the other.

"It's not your fault," Tommy said. He began to review his own recent encounter with Tim. "Fuck!" he said loudly. He let go of Jason and put his hands on his head in frustration. He suddenly pushed Jason hard. Jason fell backwards across the hood of the BMW and nearly slipped off the car onto the garage floor.

Jason scrambled about and tried not to roll off. He recovered, righted himself and sat upon the hood. He shouted at Tommy. "What did you do that for?" He could see his brother was angry.

Tommy shook his head, the rage building inside. "It's not you. Damn it, Jason! It's just what Tim said to me last night!"

"You spoke to him last night?" Jason asked. "When did you talk to him?"

"After the game. The one you never showed up to and left me standing outside waiting for you!"

"Screw you, Tommy! I came across Tim getting beat up by that shithead Doogie in the forest by the school, and I stepped in to stop it! I scrapped with Doogie. Bust his lip pretty good, too. Tim was really upset. The stupid game and meeting you didn't seem very important after that."

Tommy nodded his head repeatedly and raised his hands to calm Jason down. "Okay, okay! But Tim said some serious shit to me that I didn't understand last night. Maybe if I had I could've stopped him."

"What did he tell you? Did he tell you anything? Like why he did it?"

Tommy shouted back with frustration embedded in his voice. "You think if he had told me anything like that I'd have let him go home last night? What do you think I am, Jason?" He slammed his hand down on the workbench, kicked his backpack that sat on the floor and slowly wandered about agitated.

"So what did he tell you?"

"Damn it, I can't. I don't know really."

"Tell me!"

Tommy's eyes glazed over as his mind rolled through Tim's words again. "He said a lot of shit! Nonsense. Weird stuff."

"He told me some things too, but what he told me wasn't shit! He was scared, Tommy. Scared real bad. He told me he didn't want to live anymore."

Tommy grabbed a screwdriver off the bench, waved it in the air, and threatened to toss it across the garage. Fury set itself deep in his panicked eyes. "He actually told you he didn't want to live? Jesus, Jason!"

"I tried to talk to him, but he wouldn't talk."

"Well, Jason, he said some real nasty things to me. Said I didn't want to hear what he had to say!"

"Like what?"

Tommy gave in to his urge and threw the screwdriver across the garage as hard as he could. It bounced off something metal and fell to the floor. "I don't really want to tell you right now, okay?"

"You have to, Jason! It's important!" Jason stepped over to Tommy, shoved him hard against the workbench and stuck his finger in Tommy's face. "If Tim said anything to you, then you gotta tell me. He was my best friend!"

Tommy tried to push Jason back, but Jason grabbed his arms and held on, pinning Tommy against the bench. "Did he say a name?"

"A name?" Tommy struggled to free his arms from Jason's grip. The two wrestled. Jason demanded to know if he said a name. Any name. "He just said we knew nothing! That I knew nothing! You knew nothing! Nobody did! Fuck, Jason! Let me go!" He again tried to push Jason away, but Jason wasn't about to let up. The two wrestled against each other. "The only thing he said before he finally ran off was, well... he said that it was dad that beat him up yesterday!"

"What?" Jason replied confused. He relaxed his grip on Tommy. "I was with Tim when he was beat up, Tommy. He was beat up by Doogie, not dad. I was there. It was after the fight was over and Doogie and Willie took off that Tim finally broke down and told me what happened to him. He told me why he was upset. He even told me why he wanted to die. And it had nothing to do with getting beat up by Doogie."

"He never said anything like that to me. But he did say that dad did that to him," Tommy replied.

Jason hesitated and collected his thoughts before he spoke.

"Someone had been molesting him. He told me he had been buggered and that he didn't know what to do about it. He clammed up when I asked him who it was. He wouldn't tell me. I tried and tried to get him to tell me who it was, but he wouldn't say."

Tommy stared dumbfounded at Jason. It took only a moment, but he finally connected what Tim had been trying to tell him. Tommy never saw it. Neither did Jason. No one did. Tommy glanced to the door of his dad's physiotherapy room next to the garage, and he suddenly remembered all of the one-on-one sessions his father had with Tim in private to improve Tim's hockey performance. The new season had just started, and Tim was once again getting a lot of after school and late night, one-on-one practices with his dad these past few weeks. He received more private sessions than he normally did, it seemed, and definitely more than the other boys.

Tommy screamed like he had just died inside, and with a sudden furious explosion of rage, tossed Jason easily away from him onto the floor in a heap. He spotted an axe in the corner and rushed over, grabbed it and swung as hard as he could at his dad's BMW, crushing the right headlight in.

"What the hell!" Jason yelled as he lay on the floor of the garage. He watched confused as Tommy raised the axe for a second blow.

Tommy moved swiftly to the other side of the BMW, and swung deliberately and accurately as he grimaced hard and smashed out the other headlight. Another swing and the mirror dangled down at an odd angle; one more and the windshield was crushed.

"Tommy! Stop it!" Jason screamed. "What are you doing?"

"Don't you see it, Jason? It was..." Tommy stopped and pointed to the house. "It was..." He couldn't use the word dad. "Him!" He thrust his finger towards his dad's office, held it there and stared down at Jason.

Jason stared at Tommy in disbelief. "Dad? What...?" Then it clicked for Jason too.

Tommy turned and stomped out of the garage towards the house with the axe still in his hand. Jason stayed on the floor and cried. He now understood why Tim refused to tell him who did this to him.

CHAPTER 15

Tommy entered the house through the back door and stepped into the kitchen. He scanned the area for his dad but didn't see him anywhere. He checked the great room and the living room, but his father wasn't there. "Of course," Tommy thought to himself. He knew where he would find the bastard.

He strode quietly down the hall to his dad's study and paused momentarily at the door. The axe hung down by his leg. His father spent a lot of time in the study when he was home, usually with the door closed. Today the door was slightly ajar. Tommy listened and could hear sounds from the other side like muffled voices as if a television set was on in the background.

Tommy took a deep breath and let the anger drive him on inside.

He took one step inside and looked around. The office was large, fronted by a beveled glass bow window covered in dark shears. A large river rock fireplace covered the entire wall at the back of the room opposite the window. His father's large maple office desk sat just in front of the fireplace facing out towards the window.

Tommy moved further inside and stopped in the centre of the room. He looked all around the room in search of his father and the sounds he heard. He looked towards his father's desk and the fireplace behind it. His jaw dropped open as he stared forward. The centre of the fireplace didn't look right. It was at an odd angle with the right side pushed backwards. He continued to stare at the fireplace and he suddenly realized there was a secret room hidden behind it.

He listened, and once again heard the sound of voices. The sound came from within the darkened room behind the fireplace. His father was in there somewhere. He peered in from where he stood, but it was too dark to see anything clearly. There was only a bit of shifting light that emanated from within, but it wasn't enough to discern anything inside the room with clarity.

He crept slowly forward, the axe now clenched tightly in both his hands. He moved up to the fireplace hearth and prepared to step inside. He suddenly heard the voice of his dead friend, Tim, and he stepped back a few steps, startled by what he had heard. Tim's voice was soft, and he said things Tommy didn't want to hear. Disturbing words. Words that should never be uttered by anyone.

Tommy listened as Tim's voice continued to speak in a soft, delicate manner of horrid unimaginable things. Tommy's father suddenly burst forward from the darkness towards Tommy, and caused him to step back away from the hearth. His father stopped just inside the entrance and Tim's voice went silent with a click. His father emerged from the secret room, his ashen face contorted into a strange, horrible expression of anger mixed with surprise.

Tommy's mind began to spin away in manic chaos, and he knew he couldn't stop himself after hearing Tim's voice inside that dark room uttering those sickening words. He knew what his father was doing in that room and it angered him to a level beyond his control. His father took another step from the hearth into the room, and Tommy poised himself to react.

It was his friend and teammate that his father had violated.

His father spotted the axe Tommy was holding. He raised his arms defensively into the air as shock stretched gruesomely across his face. He sputtered out some incoherent words, but Tommy couldn't hear them. He pleaded with Tommy to put the axe down, but Tommy only heard his friend's quiet cries as his thoughts continued to spin around in a furious confusion of anger and loss.

Tim would never speak again. Tim would never smile again.

His father stepped further into the room towards Tommy and paused. One tear fell down his right cheek, but Tommy only saw Tim's many tears.

Tommy didn't even know he was doing it until he saw the axe embed itself deep into his father's chest. His father fell first to his knees, and then he slumped onto his side facing Tommy. Tommy instinctively swung again. This time, the axe sliced even deeper. The blood spewed out and sprayed onto the camel-coloured area carpet and across the desk. It left an arc of blood drops across the papers set out on the surface.

Tommy continued to swing the axe over and over; his deep rage still was not satisfied. The blood sprayed and covered Tommy, the desk, the carpet and walls. It was everywhere.

Only Jason's voice finally made him stop swinging and turn around. He looked at Jason and then down on what he had done. Blood covered his clothing, arms, trousers, and even his face. Jason ran over frantically to see for himself and then grabbed the axe away from Tommy, horrified. He stared at his father's mutilated body on the floor.

"I had to Jason," Tommy said weakly.

Jason continued looking down at his father and said nothing. Shock overwhelmed him and rendered him speechless.

Peter Oliver's chest was a mangled cavity, and his blood had already begun to pool and soak into the carpet.

"What did you do?" Jason suddenly screamed. "Tommy!" he shouted in disbelief and terror.

Tommy looked down at his father's body and shrugged.

"Tommy! You killed him!"

Jason began to pace around his father's body and he looked Tommy up and down. His mind was awash with anguish and fright. "Shit! Tommy! Holy shit! What the hell?" He ran one hand through his thick black hair in disbelief while still staring at his father's lifeless body. He began to tremble. He struggled to find some reason behind what his brother had done, but a new panic forced its way forward. "We can't stay here," he exclaimed in a shaking voice. Jason looked around quickly scanning the room and the windows and tried to comprehend the situation that now confronted them. He suddenly spotted the open cavity behind the fireplace.

"What is that?" Jason asked nervously and pointed toward the secret room.

"It's just a room. I will tell you about it later. Let's just get it closed for now."

Tommy had expelled an enormous amount of emotion and energy hacking his father to death, and a strange calmness overtook him. He moved up to the secret room and set one blood covered shoe inside the small room.

"C'mon," he said calmly. "Now."

Jason followed and stepped forward to help Tommy. Both boys grabbed onto the fireplace from the lip of the opening and pulled hard, which caused it to swing outward until it closed and latched in place, hiding the room once again. The bloody footprints of the two boys remained inside the room and on the hearth.

"Tommy, we gotta leave!" Jason shuffled over to the office doorway, still highly agitated and on edge. He began to bounce up and down and looked anxiously about the room. "Shit! Shit! Shit! Shit!" he shouted. He still didn't believe what he had just witnessed. The air was getting thin, and Jason struggled to keep it together.

"Not yet." Tommy moved around his father's body to the far side of the desk.

Jason continued to bounce up and down, and the dreadful panic etched itself deeper and deeper as he waited for Tommy to do something. Anything.

Suddenly there was a sharp creak from behind Jason. Jason recognized the sound immediately, having walked the hallway outside this room for many years. He looked up to Tommy and towards his father's body. He couldn't see the body behind the desk but the blood was clearly visible. The blood was everywhere. He wanted to say something to Tommy, but there was another yet louder creak, and then another. Somebody was only steps away from entering the room.

A shadow suddenly popped through the entrance of the doorway and crawled forward across his shoes from behind. Jason didn't know what else to do. He turned and swung the axe in the direction of the doorway as hard as could. He wasn't sure why. Years later, he would still wonder and often cry over why he responded in that way. Maybe it was from seeing his brother do the same just a few minutes before, or maybe it was just outright, bone-deep panic that held him.

The axe had not even hit its target before Jason wished the axe would stop. He saw who it was that had stumbled in. But the axe wouldn't stop. It carried forward on its arc. Jason opened his mouth to scream, but only air rushed out. He watched in horror as the axe he held onto tightly with both hands cut through the air and sliced through his mother's upheld hand. The momentum forced her hand along with the axe until it was pinned to her body. The axe carried on through her coat and dress and finally embedded itself deep into her heart. She turned to him. Her blue eyes were wide open and full of fear. Her mouth was agape in a silent scream.

Jason continued to hold the axe as his mother dropped to the floor, her eyes questioned "why" until she finally landed in the doorway with her gaze locked on Jason. He let go of the axe handle, stood up and quickly turned away from the gruesome sight of his mother on the floor with the axe embedded in her chest. He could hear the gurgle of her last breath behind him. The reality of what he had done shot another dose of adrenalin through his already energized veins.

"No! No! No!" he screamed in disbelief of what he had just done.

Jason didn't even hear his brother's screams and curses until Tommy began to beat Jason about the head from behind.

Jason turned around and the two boys faced each other, screamed, and cried while Tommy continued to beat Jason about the head. Tommy stared behind Jason at his dead mother and suddenly his punches lost their energy. The two boys collapsed into each other's arms and held each other crying and sobbing.

"I didn't know," Jason said. "Where did she come from?" Tommy hushed him and held him tight.

The boys stood there in each other's arms, neither sure how nor why it had come to this.

Jason let go of Tommy, turned to his mother, and dropped to his knees. "Oh mom. I'm sorry. I am so sorry," he cried. He buried his face into her bosom and hugged her, ignoring the blood as the last of it leaked out around her body. He cried and cried. "Why mom? Why did you have to come home? I am so sorry."

Tommy pulled Jason away from their mother after a few minutes and held him tight again. Both boys emitted body-wracking, ragged-breathed sobs. Jason pushed Tommy away and fell to his knees again. He started to retch as reality finally permeated and the seriousness of what had just happened sunk into his consciousness. He continued to retch until he brought nothing up. He glanced over repeatedly to his mother's lifeless body. He felt his heart snap inside, and he knew there was neither recourse nor reason for what he had done. He had no more words to speak and simply reached out for his brother. He was all he had left now. Tommy grabbed hold and led Jason away from their dead mother until they could no longer see her body broken in the doorway. The two stopped and stared down at their father's mutilated body. There was no happiness in what Tommy did to him, but there was neither guilt nor shame from either son.

Tommy stepped up to the desk, picked up the phone and looked at Jason.

Jason began to shake and cry. He shook his head hard, and then turned away from his father's body. His shoes tracked the blood away with each step. He pulled the axe from his mother's chest and carried the axe in both hands over to Tommy. Tears trickled out as he spoke. "Why did you do have to do this, Tommy? Why?"

Tommy wiped his eyes. "Because of Tim," he said. "I couldn't..." He looked over to the fireplace and recalled what he had seen and heard inside. He couldn't tell Jason about it. "I couldn't let him get away with it."

Jason looked down at his dead father. "He didn't," he replied simply. Jason continued to stare at the body and said suddenly, "We should leave."

"No! We can't run away. Where would we go?" Tommy still held the phone in his hand. He hoped Jason would see it was the only way.

"We'll go to jail if we stay here!" Jason cried. "I don't want to go to jail."

Tommy knew what every kid knew about the justice system in Canada. "We're both under eighteen. What can they do to us?"

"But Tommy..."

Tommy interrupted, "We're young offenders. They may lock us up for a bit, but it won't be a prison. That I know. We'll only be locked up for a while."

Jason listened to Tommy's words. He had heard about how young offenders can get away with murder and not do any time. Just a bit of lockup, and they would be free. "You sure about this?" he asked and attempted to dry his eyes.

Tommy shrugged. "It's just what I've heard." He looked down at the phone he held in his hand and then back to Jason. "And I really think it's best, don't you? I don't think running away will get us anywhere."

Jason's suffering was intense and was etched in his grimace. He really wanted to believe Tommy. An overwhelming sense of loss washed over him. Both his parents lay dead on the floor by his and Tommy's hands, and he had no idea what he should do. He nodded finally and committed himself to follow whatever Tommy suggested.

Tommy paced the room. Jason waited for Tommy to say something. The air in the room seemed to grow cold and the silence brought with it a truth and clarity that their lives were never going to be the same. There was no more happy family. There was no more future for the star hockey player. There was no more hockey of any kind. It was suddenly all gone. Erased.

After another few minutes, Tommy cradled the phone to get a dial tone and dialled 911 without saying a word.

While the two boys waited for the police and emergency crews to arrive, Tommy outlined exactly what they were going to say to the police. They agreed to admit to what occurred and then say no more. Tommy insisted it was important that they not say why this happened.

"Why not?" Jason asked. "Everyone should know why."

"Think about Tim. Think about our mother. Everyone thinks Tim killed himself because he was bullied. Let them think that. There is nothing to be gained by telling what our dad did to Tim. It would bring shame to Tim and shame on our family name. Just think about our mom!"

Jason tried not to look over to his mother's body, but couldn't help himself. "It doesn't seem right." He turned and looked at his father's body and began to cry again.

Tommy stared at the fireplace and remembered the words he heard coming from inside. "Trust me, Jason. And no one is to ever know about that room behind the fireplace."

Jason gazed at the fireplace and wiped the tears away. He was puzzled by Tommy's request to keep the small room a secret, but he nodded again. He squeezed the axe between his fingers and waited for the approach of the sirens.

CHAPTER 16

Gerald arrived home at his usual time, shortly after five o'clock. He was prepared for how it always went down after one of those crazy nights. Sarah would once again have dinner ready at the table, and he would arrive home on time. The meal would be perfect, hot and steaming. His cold beer would be set out with a glass this time, which he would use, but only as a gesture of apology. The house would be spotless, the floors and counters gleaming with a shine eliminating any evidence of the charade the night before. Gerald would set himself gently at the table across from Sarah. The conversation would remain light and stay clear of anything to do with the night before. It would only be after the table was cleared that Gerald would offer his version of the apology, promising that if she didn't provoke him so much he wouldn't have to hit her. She always agreed. The dance would be complete.

It was a shock to Gerald when he found the front door ajar. Inside, the evidence of what he had done last night was everywhere. The muddy prints across the carpet and linoleum, yesterday's supper scattered across the floor, and the busted plate still on the table with the few drops of blood and food mashed and scattered about.

Gerald's demeanour suddenly changed to one of worry. He looked down the hall towards the bedroom and remembered how he had left Sarah unconscious on the floor. Had he gone too far? He couldn't remember it clearly. It was all just a bad, fuzzy memory. Why did she have to push his buttons all the time? His worry began to tip to anger as he made his way down to their bedroom.

By the time he made it to the end of the hall and entered the room, he was outraged. "If she's not dead, she's gonna be after I'm done!" he thought to himself as he entered the room, but Sarah was gone.

Gerald punched at the wall and busted a fist-size hole through the drywall. He screamed in anger as he looked around the room. He had not yet noticed that some of her clothes were missing, nor that the little red suitcase was gone too. Gerald never would have noticed that the suitcase was gone because he never noticed it was ever there.

CHAPTER 17

News about the link between Tim Guenther's suicide and bullying traveled across the Web like wild fire. Earlier that morning, Detective Dean Daly's phone was ringing off the hook from reporters seeking any inside information they could squeeze out of him. He knew it was only going to get worse, so he had to make it look like he was taking the investigation of Tim's suicide very seriously.

School had let out, and he was on the south side of town at Willie Wahnkman's house. He was in the middle of interviewing Willie about the beating he and Doug Fisher (Doogie) gave Tim Guenther when he received the urgent call about the murders on Founder's Road.

Dean Daly was the only homicide detective assigned to the precinct in Bluffington. With the exception of the Gardener murder last year, Bluffington was a quiet community with very little crime on the magnitude of murder. Dean split time between regular patrol duty and detective work. The Gardener murder from last year was one Dean would rather forget. The prosecution's case against the defendant fell apart during the trial and resulted in an acquittal due to what was later called "a sloppy and incomplete police investigation." Dean was furious that all the blame fell on him as the lead detective. His reputation suffered considerably from the ridicule of the police chief, the mayor, the crown prosecutor, the press and the community in general. It seemed as though everyone called his abilities and competency into question after that case.

Dean felt a sudden rise in his mood. He hung up his cell phone and looked down on poor Willie. Willie still looked very upset, and his long, scraggly, red hair hung down over his skinny shoulders. He was upset mostly because he didn't understand why he was even being questioned. All it took was one look at young Willie's fingers to know why people called him dense and thick. He was missing the fleshy tips of his first two fingers and thumb on his right hand. It happened last summer: Willie and Doogie were refilling gun shells while camping with Doogie's uncle just south of town at the Mosquito Creek campground. Willie and Doogie liked to act tough. They played with guns and would shoot the shit out of anything they could find. Of course they drank and smoked every chance they got. Doogie would drag Willie into the back county a few valleys back on foot to tent for a few days just so they could blast the shit out of the forest where no one was around to tell them to stop. Doogie liked his guns, and Willie liked what Doogie liked.

Willie had lit up a smoke once they ran out of shells to fill. He didn't give it a second thought as he went to put his cigarette out in the same ashtray into which he had emptied the bag of gunpowder earlier. There was still a good mound of gunpowder waiting patiently in the ashtray for Willie, and it blew the tips of his fingers apart in an instant and scared the hell out of the surrounding campers. Doogie thought it was a riot and laughed all the way to the hospital. His uncle chewed both boys out for their stupidity, while Willie, with his hand wrapped in a blood-drenched towel cried, screamed in pain and thought he was dying.

Dean warned Willie to stay clean and said he would be back. This investigation regarding Tim Guenther wasn't finished. Willie nodded sheepishly and closed the door behind the detective.

Dean took a deep breath and let it out slowly. Founder's Road. Another murder on Founder's Road and only four houses down from where the Gardener murder took place last year. He wished it were somewhere, anywhere else. He didn't want any reminders of the hell he had been through from the last murder on this road. He would have to drive by the Gardener house, but he would push those thoughts out of his mind. This was the opportunity he needed to restore faith and trust from his community. He quickly hopped into his vehicle and headed across town to the crime scene on Founder's Road.

CHAPTER 18

Sarah expressed her deepest gratitude to Brandy for her generosity. She thanked her many times for letting her stay at her place. She had nowhere else to go to feel safe. Gerald would certainly look for her at her sister's. She had no one else. Sarah's parents had died in a car crash last summer; their deaths left her one step closer to the total isolation Gerald wanted for her. She really saw Brandy as a shining star through all of this, and Brandy vowed that she would be there for her.

Brandy was a counsellor and graduated with a degree in psychology like Sarah. The two shared the common interest in helping others. Their passion for helping others was evident in their work ethics and was the reason that they had become friends.

Some may have thought it strange that with her degree in psychology Sarah could become a victim of such serious abuse, but Brandy knew better than to judge her. No one is ever truly immune to what can happen over time in a relationship. That was the case with Sarah. It wasn't always this way with Gerald. When they met he was gentle, calm and very considerate, but he always had that macho image and that attracted Sarah when she was young. He was a nice, strong man, without a care in the world, but he always seemed to know what he wanted. He was a real decision-maker. There was nothing wishy-washy about Gerald.

"How's the arm now?" Brandy asked.

"Still aches a lot, but it is much better," she replied, and rubbed her free hand up and down the cast. "Thanks again, Brandy."

Brandy patted Sarah on the leg, "Don't you worry about it. You can stay as long as you need. I'll get your prescription for the drugs in the morning, but you need to get some rest."

"We both do," Sarah replied and smiled.

Brandy laughed and agreed. It had been a long night and an even longer day. Brandy had already pulled down the sheets in the spare room for Sarah shortly after she arrived home. She desperately wanted to know more about her relationship with Gerald and what happened last night, but she held herself back. Sarah would say what she needed to say in time.

"I heard you're not pressing charges," Brandy said.

Sarah's smile evaporated and she looked down sheepishly into her hands. She rubbed her fingers together and just shook her head. Tears began to come. "I just can't," she said.

"But why Sarah, why? He nearly killed you last night."

Sarah just shook her head. "I don't want to ever see him again." She looked up at Brandy. "I'm scared Brandy, real scared. You don't know him like I do."

"You can't let him get away with this. If it was me, I'd have his ass in jail at first chance."

"You don't get it! This is Gerald we're talking about! I ran off on him, and he's going to search for me until he finds me. I know him. He'll never stop. Never. And when he finds me, he's not going to just forget about all this, pull me back into his arms and take me home. Not Gerald. He'll never forgive me for doing this. I'm really scared that when he does find me he's going to make me pay for it. He'll kill me. I know him, and he will kill me if he finds me."

Brandy stared at Sarah in disbelief, her mouth open, at a loss for words to rebut what Sarah had just told her. Certainly, no one could be this evil. Not even Gerald.

"You're serious? Really?"

"I'm telling you, Gerald will come after me. I don't want to add more fuel to the fire by having him charged. It's you I'm worried about now, and I'm not sure if I should even be here. If Gerald finds I'm here, you're in danger too!"

CHAPTER 19

Ricky and Bobby walked home after school to Bobby's house on Founders Road. Both boys were sickened and saddened by the news of their friend, Tim. They sat on stools in the kitchen and nibbled on pepperoni sticks while they discussed what they knew.

"I walked to school with Tommy today," Bobby said. It was unlike Bobby to gossip and retell conversations, but he was deeply bothered, and he had to let it out. "Tommy was really upset."

"About Tim?"

Bobby nodded and rubbed his leg unconsciously as he did sometimes when he was nervous. "He texted me before school and said he needed to tell me something important."

"So tell me," Ricky said, his interest peaked.

"It was about Tim." He looked down at his feet, not sure if he should really say anything at all, and decided to only repeat half of the conversation. He would keep the rest inside. Maybe later he would tell Ricky the rest, or maybe Tommy would tell Ricky himself. Bobby hated to repeat things said to him in private by others.

"So tell me already." Ricky pushed Bobby on the shoulder and Bobby looked up from the floor. Ricky could see Bobby's discomfort.

"It's just... He said some things last night that upset Tommy."

Ricky frowned. "You mean when he left us after the game?"

Bobby let out a sigh. "You saw how Tim was, and how he ran off when Tommy approached."

"So what'd Tim say to Tommy?"

Bobby hesitated and decided quickly how much he would share of the morning's conversation.

"Tommy didn't tell me exactly what he said word for word," he lied. "He only told me that Tim was very upset and wouldn't tell him why he was upset. Tommy assumed it was because of Willie and Doogie again. Those two always push Tim around every chance they get. Everyone knows it. In the halls at school, in the wash room, after school..."

"Those two are bad news. I avoid em' all the time too. Your sure Tim didn't tell him anything more?"

Bobby shook his head.

"That really sucks! Tim didn't need to kill himself. I've half a mind to take a baseball bat to that fucker Doogie!" Ricky jumped off his stool and mashed one fist into the palm of the other. "I could probably take Doogie myself if I had to. Thinks he's so tough." He looked about anxiously as if he was ready to go confront Doogie immediately.

"You can't do that. What's that gonna solve? Nothing."

"If Tim killed himself because of those guys..."

"We don't know that. Maybe it was something else," Bobby said. He hated violence of any kind.

Ricky tried to read Bobby. Bobby looked back to his feet, took another bite off his pepperoni stick and only lifted his eyes momentarily to Ricky before he returned his gaze to the floor. Ricky sensed Bobby wasn't telling him everything.

"What else, Bobby? I know you. Tommy told you something else Tim said. What is it?"

Bobby shook his head and rubbed his leg again. "Nothing else. He just told me that he was really worried about Tim. That he had never seen Tim ever as upset as he was last night. Tim even slugged him and told him to just leave him alone. He kicked Tommy in the shins and ran off."

Ricky felt there was more to the story. He knew it yesterday as he saw Tim sitting under the streetlight in the parking lot. He also knew he should have followed his heart last night and gone with Tommy to talk to Tim. But that wouldn't have worked out either. Not with Tommy there. He really wanted to talk to Tim alone. The opportunity was lost forever.

"So where's Tommy now?" Ricky asked.

Bobby shrugged. "Home maybe."

Both boys turned to each other when they heard the unmistakable sound of sirens in the distance. They listened intently as the sounds grew louder and louder, finally culminating into an explosive chorus of sirens from multiple emergency vehicles. The boys rushed to the front window, Bobby a little slower because of his leg, and watched a number of emergency vehicles scream past Bobby's house with their lights flashing. The vehicles came to a sudden stop at Tommy and Jason's home.

CHAPTER 20

A small perimeter was already set up around the Oliver home when Detective Dean arrived on the scene. He stopped briefly to scan the crowd that was gathering on the street before he lifted the yellow crime scene tape over his head and walked up to the front of the house.

It was Constable Jackson Heavy Head, one of the two native officers on the Bluffington detachment, who met Dean outside the front door.

"Who's here?" Dean asked.

"You're the last. Paramedics have been inside, already." He nodded to his right at the two paramedics who stood beside their vehicle and waited patiently for further instruction. "Coroner's inside. Mike Scott is with the boys."

Dean pointed to the house surprised. "The boys are still in there?"

Officer Heavy Head nodded. "You see what's inside and you'll understand why."

"Francesca here as well?" Constable Francesca Saldarriega and Constable Mike Scott were part of Dean's crime scene team. Francesca was the photographer. A flash lit up the doorway inside before Jackson was able to reply.

Dean looked around the street one more time. He glanced down to the east and could see the peak of the Gardener house jutting high above the trees into the evening sky. He once again tucked away the events that followed the murder over there. More people gathered, and he spotted the Bluffington News van heading his way from the end of the block.

"Try and keep the press as far away as possible on this one. Maybe block the road off completely a few doors down in both directions. Push everyone back. This place is going to be crawling with people and media in the next while."

Jackson knew the drill and handed Dean a pair of booties to put on before he entered the house. "You're really going to need these."

Dean slipped on the booties and stepped inside.

The Oliver home was a large, two-story Victorian with narrow hallways and tight corners, quite the opposite of the open space concept. All of the excitement was in the study down one short hallway that connected to the front foyer off to the left by another short hallway.

Dean stopped immediately as he turned down the hall that led to the entrance. Marie Oliver's body lay sprawled across the opening to the study. She lay on her back, very dead. The blood pooled around her body and down the hall some four feet towards the kitchen at the back of the house. He tried to comprehend what it was he was seeing. It was gruesome. He moved slowly forward to her body and made a number of mental notes.

He stuck his head through the doorway and saw Francesca busy taking more photos behind a large wooden desk to his right. The coroner stood solemnly next to her. The boys sat on a small settee near the front window. Mike Scott stood beside them.

Dean stepped gingerly around Marie Oliver's body and inside the room. It was difficult to know where to step. Bloody footprints were everywhere.

"Tommy Oliver and Jason Oliver," Mike stated, and pointed at each of the boys as he introduced him.

Dean nodded and put his hand in the air to halt Mike from speaking. It was the way Dean approached every crime scene. He wanted to make his own assessment of what he saw. He didn't want to hear any opinions or statements until he visually captured what was before him. What he saw was horrific. Both boys were covered in blood. Tommy's khakis were soaked with what could only be blood. The blood was everywhere on Tommy, covering his shoes, khakis, shirt, arms and face. Jason's appearance wasn't as horrid. His hands and shirt were spotted with blood, and blood-streaked smears, now quite dry, swept down his face from crying and wiping at the tears. He wasn't crying any longer and sat without any expression of emotion.

Dean moved around the desk to where Francesca was still taking photographs. He paused and looked at Francesca as she bent down to get close up shots of the pulverized remains of Peter Oliver's chest. Her face was ashen white, and she was clearly in great discomfort. She could only manage a glance towards Dean as she pushed herself to finish up as soon as she could.

The coroner acknowledged Dean and said he would be done soon. It was a horrible scene and nothing like the Gardner murder from last year. In that murder, Donna Gardener had been strangled in her own bed. There was no blood. Only the single guitar wire remained wrapped around her tiny neck as she lay naked, face down on the bed. Her husband, Dean's very close friend, was a few hours away on a business trip when the murder occurred. All Dean had to start with on that crime scene was the guitar wire, a pair of muddy footprints at the back door and some hairs found on her body. All of that evidence pointed to someone else, but Dean knew deep inside from the outset that it was his close friend, the husband, who was responsible for her death. He just wasn't able to prove it, and every time he was reminded of that murder, it stung him like a pesky wasp.

In front of him here were two more murders. Ghastly murders with an abundance of blood everywhere, and two suspects who had supposedly already confessed to the crime. He looked at the carpet and could see that the boys had wandered back and forth around their father's body numerous times, even stepping up onto the hearth of the fireplace at one point.

Dean had his first impression sorted. "You get a statement yet, Mike?"

"The boys themselves called it in. Confessed to the dispatch operator. Confessed to me as well. What they told me was..."

Dean raised his hand and cut him off once again. "Let me," he said simply and walked over to the boys for the first time. Both boys looked up at Dean. Confusion and disbelief lurked just behind the eyes of the younger boy, as if his sanity was hanging on by a thread, and he was about to scream. His dark bangs hung down and partially shielded his eyes. The older, clean cut boy, Tommy, displayed a strange, calm acceptance in his expression, as if he were in a constant shock.

Dean looked down upon the small coffee table in front of the boys where a bloody axe lay. It had clearly visible hand and fingerprints all over it.

"Let's see. Father killed first. Probably killed in a rage by one of the boys. Tommy would be my guess." He pointed at Tommy, but Tommy didn't respond and just stared back blankly. "Mother hears the ruckus and is killed with one blow as the boys sit and wait for her to walk into the room." The boys glanced at each other and in unison returned their gaze towards the floor.

Mike nodded. "Something like that, I suppose. Jason was still holding the axe when I arrived."

Dean walked back over to the mother and looked at her once more. She looked strangely peaceful as she lay staring up at the ceiling in the hallway. Her left hand almost seemed to be reaching into the cavity of her chest to her heart, but it was just an illusion as the axe had severed her hand in half and pinned it to her body.

Dean moved over to the window, pulled back the shears and looked outside. It was as he expected. The news had travelled quickly and there were multiple media vans on the street with camera crews already filming. He could see Jackson Heavy Head still in the process of having the barriers moved out onto the street to push the media back in both directions. The crowd continued to grow out side. He really needed to get these boys out of here and down to the station.

"You got this, Francesca?" he hollered as he pointed to the two boys. She shook her head no.

Dean waved her over and instructed the boys to stand up. He had the boys turn around while she took photos of them from all angles. Arms down at their sides, and then up in the air. She took close ups of their hands, front and back, and then their faces. Dean then had the boys remove their shoes and socks on the spot and bagged them. He had booties brought over for the two of them. The rest of the clothes would be removed at the station where they would be stripped and once again photographed from head to foot.

Dean was done with the boys for now, and he ordered Mike to arrange for the boys to be moved out. A van would back up to the front door of the house as close as possible. A blanket was brought to cover the boys so no photographers could capture the bloody images as they were removed from the home one at a time.

Dean breathed a big sigh. It all looked simple enough. The boys were still here with the murder weapon and they even confessed, twice. But he just had a feeling about what he saw. The footprints on the hearth bothered him immediately. It appeared as if the boys had gone over to the hearth purposefully to stand and look down upon their mutilated father's body. But why? Why would they step up on to the hearth?

Dean walked slowly back over to the front of the fireplace and avoided stepping on any bloody prints on the floor. He studied the hearth, and finally stepped up on to it just like the boys had, but off to the side where there were no bloody tracks. He turned around, faced out, and looked down upon Peter Oliver's body. There was something wrong in what he saw. He looked again at the boys' footprints and noticed why it bothered him. He looked down to his own feet and then again at the bloody imprints. The boys had not stepped on the hearth and turned around. They had stepped up, and stepped off. They had not looked down at their father's body at all. They kept both feet planted side by side, just as he currently stood. He rubbed his chin in thought.

He studied the stones on the hearth again more carefully. He spotted a few finger prints in amongst the blood spatter on the stones. The boys had not only stepped onto the hearth, but had grabbed hold of a couple of the stones. Was it in a moment of anguish over what they had done? He didn't understand it.

He hated that he had this feeling again. The last time he had had this feeling was with the Gardener murder, and he had been right about that one right from the start. However, he had been unable to do anything about what he knew deep inside was the truth. Now, the image of the footprints of these two young boys as they stepped up and off the hearth a half dozen feet from their dead father stuck the same way in his brain, and he knew that unless he understood why they stepped up on to the hearth, the thought would fester like an untreated wound.

CHAPTER 21

Gerald hated when he felt like the fool, and that's exactly how he felt as the liquor seeped into his veins. It slowly released the dragon inside. It had been nearly five weeks since Sarah left him, and the cold of winter had crept its way in with early December. The ground had a dusting of snow, and the first of the season's Christmas lights were already hung, brightening the evening streets and walkways of Calgary. Most people appreciated the vibrant colours and decor the season always brought, but not Gerald. He hated the ceremony of what it all represented: the false hope, the fake smiles and the gratuitous well-wishers everywhere he went.

Gerald slammed his empty glass down on the counter inside Ratskeller's Pub and immediately drew the attention of Dustin Toomey, the young bartender who worked the bar at night for extra cash to put himself through college. Gerald nodded at Dustin, an indication that he wanted another whiskey on the rocks. He had already put back a number of drinks since he arrived after work. Dustin quickly set another before Gerald on the bar. Gerald had never been inside Ratskeller's before. He liked the dark atmosphere. It suited his ominous mood.

Gerald grunted his approval at the quick response. He pointed his finger at Dustin. "You got a girl there, Dusty?" he asked gruffly. He heard the waitress call Dustin by name earlier.

"The name's Dustin, and no I don't," he replied politely and turned his attention down towards the other end of the bar where one of the waitresses hailed him.

Gerald smiled, pleased that he had offended Dustin. "That's okay, Dusty. Women ain't worth a shit anyways." He thought about Sarah. "Bitches, Dusty. All of 'em."

Dustin stopped and turned back towards Gerald. "It's Dustin. I don't like being called Dusty," he said and walked down to the other end of the bar.

Gerald slugged back more of the drink and shifted off the bar stool to stand up. He leaned against the bar. He stared with devious purpose towards Dustin. "Hey, Dusty!" he shouted. "Sorry if I offended you, you little shit!" He laughed gregariously, and waited for a response.

Dustin ignored Gerald's comment.

Gerald wanted a reaction. He needed one tonight. It was what he always got at home when he wanted it, and he needed an outlet since Sarah was temporarily out the picture. *Temporarily.* He wasn't done with her yet. Not by a long shot.

The liquor felt good tonight. It burned down to his belly and warmed his veins. It slowly released the fire he thirsted for since he arrived in the pub. "Hey, Dusty! I'm speaking to you!" He called out again. He slapped his hand down hard on to the bar. "What's your fucking problem?" he shouted.

The dull murmur from the other patrons in the pub suddenly went quiet and all eyes turned up towards the bar. A few of the men near the bar caught Dustin's glance.

Dustin stopped his chat with the waitress and turned back to see Gerald staring down at him. His drunken expression shifted and deepened beyond simple intoxication. Dustin had seen this before: the drunken gaze, the eyes that wandered and could barely hold a stare as they shifted about continuously in a demon-like fashion. He knew it was imperative to control the situation immediately.

Dustin moved towards Gerald, careful to keep his manner in check. He didn't want to escalate the situation with any kind of confrontation. "Hey, let's keep it cool, hey bud?" he said as he locked eyes with Gerald. "Take a seat," he motioned, "and I'll..."

It was already too late. Gerald jumped towards Dustin and attempted to leap over the bar to grab hold. Dustin simply stepped back out of his reach. Rage etched across Gerald's face, and within seconds four men pounced on top of him. Regular patrons watched the scene unfold and immediately rushed to Dustin's aid. They grabbed hold of Gerald by the arms and neck. Gerald tried to swing and fight, but he was no match for the four men who pinned him down. They quickly wrestled Gerald from the bar and shuffled him out through the front door to the parking lot where they threw him into the snow-covered gravel. He scrambled to his feet, ready to attack, but the four men stood their ground side by side. Gerald quickly reconsidered. He wiped his arm across his mouth and pointed at the four of them.

"You all just made the biggest mistake of your lives!" he shouted and staggered a few steps to the side, trying to stay upright.

"Go home and sleep it off," one said.

"Yeah, and don't come back here. We don't want guys like you hanging around here. This is a nice place, you stupid drunk!"

Gerald stared back and thought one more time about rushing them, but his anger refocused itself. He wouldn't even be here at this bar in the first place if Sarah had not run off on him. He turned away, scrambled over towards his truck and lumbered up against it. He opened the door and attempted to step inside while the four men looked on and shouted at him. They warned him that he was too drunk to drive, and they would call the police if he dared to start that truck up.

Gerald didn't hear a word they said. The image of Sarah's defiance swelled inside and beckoned him to do something. He finally managed to pull himself inside the truck and slammed the door. He fumbled a few minutes before he was finally able to get the key into the ignition switch. He bolted like a rocket out of the parking lot. The gravel rocks and icy dust sprayed a trail of evidence of his crazed, drunken state.

Gerald drove away from the pub and knew exactly what he was going to do. He was going to find Sarah tonight, and he knew exactly where he would start. Sarah's sister would know where she was. She must know.

"Sarah!" he screamed in anger. "You're gonna be sorry you ever walked out on me!"

He punched the gas and slammed his fist hard onto the steering wheel in anger. The vehicle shunted abruptly towards the ditch on his right. Gerald tried to correct the drift, and pulled the wheel hard to the left, but it was the wrong thing to do in his inebriated state. The left wheels of his truck suddenly lurched up into the air, and the vehicle went into an immediate roll. It tumbled over a number of times, tossing Gerald about, before it crashed through a wooden fence and slammed upside down against a large fir tree only a few blocks from the pub.

Gerald found himself upside down in the truck with his head twisted and planted against the roof. His feet were up behind him, and one foot was caught under the gas pedal. He groaned and struggled to free his foot, but he quickly gave up and passed out.

CHAPTER 22

Jason lay in the top bunk, Tommy on the bottom, when the lights went out in the dorm for another night. Spy Hill Correctional Centre for Young Offenders on the outskirts of Calgary wasn't at all like the boys thought it would be. They had expected to be in a cell similar to the one they were kept in for the last five weeks until the trial began. That one, in the back of the police station behind the Bluffington courthouse, was tiny and uncomfortable with only two narrow beds. Each bed was hitched out from the concrete wall on its own. A toilet was tucked in the corner behind a small pony wall. Spy Hill was much more communal with a number of dorm rooms instead of cells. The dorms had bunk beds lined up on each side of the long rooms; this one room was capable of housing up to sixteen inmates at a time. It was luxurious compared to the police station cell.

The boys had been interrogated repeatedly. First Dean interrogated them in Bluffington at the station the entire night after the murders. Then other members of the police force questioned them periodically over a number of weeks, and now at Spy Hill they were interrogated once again. Sometimes Dean would be there and sometimes not. At each interrogation, someone tried to draw out a bit more of the truth about the murders from one of the boys. Lawyers, doctors, therapists, and still more cops came each day wanting a piece of the two boys, but they were relentless and kept their silence no matter how hard and manipulative the interviews became. The boys learned how to avoid revealing any of the truth by simply not answering any of the questions put in front of them. Many tactics were used to provoke the boys into a response, but they succeeded in frustrating every one who came to see them. They each eventually left stupefied about the reason the boys had committed the murders.

Many motives were suggested and were examined with heavy pressure to the brothers. They ranged from wanting to escape from under the thumb of a ruthless, unrelenting disciplinarian of a father to trying to escape from an endless environment of physical and verbal abuse. When those suggestions got no response, they pushed the boys even farther with wild accusations of sexual abuse and buggery. The boys took it all and neither agreed with nor denied the suggestions. Even though neither could deny what their father had done to their friend Tim, it still hurt deep down to hear such statements spoken out loud by others.

In the end, the theory the police and reporters fell back on was the simple fact that the Olivers were very wealthy. The boys murdered for the money. Many found this simply impossible to believe because the boys could never expect to be recipients of the proceeds after openly confessing to a crime such as this. However, Dean's team couldn't really find any evidence to support any other motive. It was the best motive they had, but Dean himself couldn't buy into it. It didn't explain why the boys smashed the BMW prior to the murder nor the footprints on the hearth.

What bothered Dean most of all was how the boys cried often during the interrogation and showed very real remorse for what they had done. It struck Dean that the boys would take it all back if they could, but they still didn't respond with an answer to any question along those lines. It puzzled him deeply. It fit with a crime for money, but the boy's reluctance to speak caused Dean to believe that there was more to this crime.

"Bobby's coming up again tomorrow," Tommy whispered in the darkness. The lights in the dorm may have been out, but whispered comments often wafted throughout the dorm as the boys all settled in for another night. Only eleven of the sixteen beds were occupied.

Jason leaned over the edge of the top bunk, his hair draped down over his eyes. "Ask him to come see me too this time. No one's come up to see me yet." This wasn't quite true. The boy's Aunt Meredith had made a point to see both boys separately. She had not come up to console the boys. Not Aunt Meredith. Aunt Meredith was Peter's sister and she was extremely angry about what the boys had done. She had only visited to verbally berate and scold the boys. She told them, in no uncertain terms, just how despicable they were and that she personally hoped they both rotted in hell.

Tommy nodded. "Bobby's got a car now. Got his driver's license last week."

"Really?" Jason responded. Any news from the outside about their friends was welcome. It was a change and an escape from the usual inmate conversation. "What's he driving?"

"His mom bought him a used CRV. Not sure what year."

"I wish we could go for a drive somewhere. Anywhere actually," he said and laughed. "Get out of this depressing place."

Tommy didn't laugh with him. His mind was elsewhere. "Bobby said something strange today when he was up to see me."

"Like what?"

Tommy shook his head. "I don't recall his exact words, but it was just the way he talked about what happened with you and me. He seemed really fidgety and on edge.

Before he left, he asked if it was okay to bring Ricky up next time."

"Ricky?"

"Yeah, and it seemed so odd to me that he would even ask that. Ricky hasn't been to see us since we've been locked up. Not once. Not you or me. I got the impression that the only reason Bobby came by was to see if he could get some kind of response from me when he suggested that Ricky come up. I've got a feeling that there's a real big reason Ricky hasn't visited."

"Like what?"

"I don't know. That's just the impression I got from Bobby. I mean, why did Bobby have to come all the way up here just to ask if it was okay if Ricky comes by? Why didn't he just bring Ricky? He is on our visitor list."

"Something happened since we've been locked up maybe?"

"I don't know. Anyway, Bobby is bringing Ricky up tomorrow."

"Will you guys shut the fuck up already and go to sleep!" another inmate shouted at Tommy and Jason through the darkness.

"Don't be such a pussy ass!" Tommy shouted back. "We're done talking now anyway. You can go have you're precious beauty sleep!"

"I'm gonna come over there and kick your ass, Oliver, if you don't shut your bloody trap."

"Oh yeah? You and who's army?" was the appropriate response. It was an old comeback, but a few chuckles were heard in the darkness from some of the other beds.

"Fuck you, Oliver," the response floated back through the darkness.

Jason rolled back to the centre of the top bunk and closed his eyes. He tried to put good thoughts forward as he closed his eyes to sleep, but the bad ones just rolled back like they had each night so far. He missed his mother dearly, and the image of his mother's dead body crept in again and caused Jason to cry silently into his pillow until sleep finally overtook him for another night.

Tommy lay below Jason in the darkness and continued to review Bobby's behaviour during his visit earlier in the evening. There was obviously much more to what Bobby had said. Or rather, what he had not said. Deep down, he suspected it must have something to do with what Tommy had heard in his father's study just before all hell broke loose. Memories of that moment still festered like a deep wound inside Tommy. As much as Tommy tried to put what he heard Tim say behind him, the memory would sometimes edge its way back unexpectedly. Now, it came back again as he thought over Bobby's visit.

Tommy wanted simply to close his eyes and sleep, but it was difficult once again. The words Tim spoke emanating from the secret room in the study returned. They returned each night and often led Tommy into nightmares of the horror and shame Tim endured at the hands of Tommy's father. The dreams would shift, and Tommy would be watching the evil on a small monitor in the tiny dark room as Tim or some other young friend was forced to perform unimaginable acts. He heard those awful words repeated in his dreams, over and over again. Tommy would wake up in the middle of the night and want desperately to scream out, but he always held back, turned his face into his pillow and wept. He knew the nightmares would come again tonight and again tomorrow night. He wanted to rid himself of the bad dreams, but he suspected that the dreams would continue as long as he held on to the secret of what remained hidden in that room.

What other demons rested inside that room, waiting for someone to stumble upon them? Tommy realized he was struggling with denial. He was in constant denial that his father, his own blood, could be responsible for what had taken place in the office behind the house. It was a heavy weight to carry alone. Tommy knew that since his father kept tapes of his abuse of Tim, there would likely be the same terrible, residual evidence of his abuse of other victims. It was like some sick and twisted trophy case.

There was really only one thing he could do to ever be able to sleep without the recurring nightmares. He needed to accept what was inside that room. He also knew he would have to tell Jason at some point.

Tommy stared up at the bunk above where Jason lay. He closed his eyes and wanted to sleep, but only tears came in the darkness. He sniffed and wiped his runny nose, glad no one could see him. Just like Jason, Tommy cried himself to sleep for another night.

CHAPTER 23

It was very late in the evening when Sarah called her sister, Carolyn. Sarah and Carolyn were always very close and she hoped Carolyn was still up. It wasn't unusual for many months to pass without one sister calling the other. Carolyn didn't like Gerald in the least, so she found it difficult to see Sarah with Gerald always at Sarah's side. He seemed to purposely spoil what always started out as a good get together by being a bad drunk or by just being rude and obnoxious.

Carolyn didn't answer, and Sarah left a message saying she would call Carolyn back tomorrow. "...and oh, I've left Gerald, so please don't call me at the house. I'll tell you all about it when we talk. See ya." She put the phone down and shrugged at Brandy who sat opposite on the couch.

"I really appreciate you putting up with me these past weeks."

"You really don't have to go. You can still stay longer if you wish, and you still haven't even had the cast removed."

"No, no!" Sarah insisted. "I need to get back on my feet. I've found that place in Bluffington. I really like Bluffington. It's where I started out when I graduated, and I really have to get away from Calgary. Somewhere Gerald won't find me."

Brandy nodded in understanding. "I will miss you, you know. Not just here in my home, but at work too. It won't be the same without you."

"You're okay to drive me down tomorrow then?"

Brandy nodded back. "Absolutely. And you're sure you're not going back to your house for anything?"

"No way. I can't risk it, and money's not a problem anymore with mom and dad's insurance finally coming through." It was the insurance money from when her parents were killed last summer in the auto accident. It took many months to probate the will, and the money from the estate had just been freed up. "And thanks again for taking me down to the lawyers to change all my contact info. That money is already transferred into the new account. I am so glad Gerald doesn't know about it. It really couldn't have come through at a better time. Gerald can keep what is in the joint account, and he can keep my car. In fact, he can keep everything back there."

"I bet he's fuming."

"Knowing Gerald, it's probably worse than that. I bet he's watching everything, just looking for anything to lead him to where I am."

"He won't find you in Bluffington. I know it's only an hour away, but what reason would he have to go looking for you there?"

"There is none. That's the whole point. The apartment is just up behind the Flattened Frog Bistro. Do you know where that is?"

"I'm afraid I don't."

"The landlord said it's at the south end of Main Street. Up the side of the hill behind the Bistro. It sounds like it should be easy to find. And it's just until I can buy my own place. I probably won't buy for a few months. I still need to find a job too."

"You'll find one. Get rid of the cast first," she said and laughed.

CHAPTER 24

Gerald came to laying on the icy ground. It was dark, and he was cold. There were lights that flashed all about, and two paramedics knelt next to him and shouted questions at him that he couldn't understand. He looked around, unsure of where he was as the men continued to poke and prod at him and ask him questions. He grunted something back, and looked over at his truck all beat to shit sitting upside down with the side door ripped off and tossed to the side.

It all started to come back. Gerald tried to sit up, but the paramedics quickly pressed him back down. They were not about to let Gerald go anywhere.

Gerald struggled against the medics and shouted obscenities. Two police officers appeared and helped pin Gerald to the ground while the medics continued to check him over. He tried to turn his head to see his truck, but the paramedics forced his head to the centre. They insisted on his co-operation. They asked him where he hurt and continued with the examination.

With the exception of an obvious sprained or broken ankle, Gerald seemed to be suffering only minor scrapes and bruising from being tossed about inside the cab of his truck.

Gerald was given a sedative and was soon loaded and shunted off to the hospital for further observation.

CHAPTER 25

Ricky was over at Bobby's first thing in the morning.

"So what'd he say?" Ricky asked.

"He said of course you can go see him."

Bobby shuffled over to one of the bar stools at the island in the kitchen, sat down and stared at Ricky. He wasn't sure why Ricky seemed so edgy this morning. "Have a seat already," he added and motioned for Ricky to sit and stop his bouncing around. He tossed a blueberry muffin over to Ricky and began to pick the crusty top off the one he grabbed for himself.

Ricky sat himself down opposite Bobby and gazed out the window. Bobby could see he was deep in thought.

"What time are you going up?" Ricky asked.

"*We* Ricky. *We* are going up. You and me. Just like you wanted. I didn't drive all the way up there yesterday for nothing. I told Tommy we'd be up at four and the guy at the security desk said it was okay since you're on the list."

Ricky only nodded his head and continued to look blankly out the window. He unconsciously peeled the paper cup away from the muffin.

"Are you going to tell me what this is really all about?" Bobby asked directly.

Ricky turned to Bobby. A solemn expression covered his face. "We talked about this already. About Tim. You know what I mean."

Bobby grinned. "No, I don't know what you mean. About Tim? What about Tim? What really are we talking about?"

Ricky didn't grin back. "I'm talking about Tim and why he killed himself. That's why I want to see Tommy. You were the one that told me what Tommy said about Tim and why he did it."

"What Tommy told me about why Tim did it? That was weeks ago, and Tommy never told me why Tim took his life," Bobby replied dumbfounded. He quickly recalled what he had told Bobby about what Tommy said the morning Tim committed suicide. "I only told you what Tommy told me the night he followed Tim after the game. Tommy only said that Tim was upset. That's all I told you. I don't know where you're getting this other shit from."

Bobby recalled Tommy also said Tim said he blamed Tommy's dad for roughing him up, but he hadn't told Ricky any of that part. He still didn't understand it himself.

Ricky shook his head and pinched at his eyes as tears began to surface. "I know that's what you said. I know that. But there's other stuff I know myself that I never told you."

"Like what stuff?" Bobby replied, quite agitated. "What more is there to tell? Tim's dead, and Tommy and Jason are in jail for killing their parents. I still don't even know why they did that."

Ricky began to cry and wiped at his eyes. "I know why, Bobby. I know why Tim killed himself. I also think I know why Tommy and Jason killed their parents."

Bobby rubbed his leg, confused why Ricky would know anything at all about why they killed their parents. He popped some of the muffin into his mouth and gestured for Ricky to continue, still disturbed and affronted by Ricky's sudden display of emotion.

"Why do you think I quit hockey?"

Bobby shrugged. "I dunno. I thought you just wanted a change. That's what you told us."

"I loved hockey!" He jumped off the stool, slammed his fist on the table, and dropped the muffin on the counter. He ran his hands through his hair. "I never wanted to quit! You don't know what it is like to quit something you love so much. I cried and cried at night when the hockey season started because I couldn't play anymore. My dad was so pissed at me for quitting, and he still won't talk to me. If it wasn't for mom, I'm sure my dad would have taken me out back, whooped me real good and then driven me down to every practice, game and training session to make sure I went. If it wasn't for my mom standing up to my dad, I'd hate to think where I'd be right now"

Bobby stared at Ricky, unsure of why the sudden rant. "You liked hockey and you quit?" Bobby asked confused.

"Yes, Bobby! I quit! I was so scared of going back to Tommy's house. So I just sucked it up and stuck it out at home after telling my parents I was quitting hockey. I sat there at the table every night letting my dad berate me and call me a quitter. I didn't care about anything anymore, so I took it. Night after night, my dad talked me down, making me feel smaller and smaller each day. I still feel like shit some days. Some days it's so bad, I almost want to die."

"Don't talk like that. I really don't get where you're coming from."

"I didn't know what to do, Bobby, so I quit. I feel the shame in my dad's eyes every time he looks at me from across the room. But quitting hockey was the only option for me. I had only one way out, and I took it!"

Bobby frowned. "Way out of what?" Bobby was bewildered by Ricky's angry outburst. "What the shit are you even talking about?"

"Do you ever remember me going over to Tommy and Jason's house since I quit hockey? No! Not once have I ever been back in that house! Not once!"

Bobby still didn't understand where Ricky was going, but he thought hard about the times the boys had all been together, and it was true. Since he quit playing hockey, Ricky had always made up some excuse when the group met over at Jason and Tommy's.

"Don't you see?" he shouted. "Fuck, you're all so blind and stupid!"

"Don't call me stupid, Ricky," Bobby said back. He was getting angry.

"Well you are. Everyone in this whole town is."

Bobby was visibly upset. "I don't get you! Why are you so upset with me? I don't even know what the heck you are talking about, and I really don't have to listen to this." Bobby got off his chair and moved a step away from Ricky towards the back door.

"Yes, you do have to listen! I've gone this far, and I don't think I can stop talking now. Just sit back down and listen to me!"

Bobby wasn't used to any of his friends talking like this to him, especially Ricky.

"Please, Bobby. Please sit down and listen to what I'm saying. I'm begging you."

Bobby shuffled back and sat down. "This better be good."

"I wish I'd never played hockey."

"Shit, Ricky! Hockey again? What is it with all the hockey?"

"Tim played hockey and I played hockey. We both played hockey. We were good. Real good. And we still wanted to be better. Playing with Tommy and Jason was so great. And there was nothing better than being on a line with Tommy. Tommy was the leading scorer in the league. Everyone wanted to play on Tommy's line, and we'd all do whatever it took to play along with him. You play with

Tommy, you get points, and you get noticed. That's why we both took Mr. Oliver up on his offer for the extra one-on-one training every other evening. You train with Mr. Oliver and suddenly he throws you out there for a couple of shifts with Tommy."

"Uh huh. You and lots of guys took advantage of what he offered. Didn't get to see you guys as much these few past winters with all of the games and extra practices. If you liked bloody hockey so much, then why'd you quit? I don't get it."

Bobby could see Ricky tense up as he spoke again, very softly and very slowly. "Mr. Oliver was doing more than just giving out extra hockey training in his little shop at the back."

Bobby processed what Ricky had just said. Abruptly, a few unexpected pieces from a hell that Bobby never believed existed in his world now came to light.

"We've all heard about guys that do stuff to young kids. I just never expected it would happen to me."

Bobby's mouth dropped open in disbelief of what Ricky had just implied.

"It's true, Bobby. It's true. That's what I'm talking about."

"He was..." Bobby couldn't find any words to properly respond to his friend. "...to you? And Tim?"

Ricky nodded. "Tim too, is what I think. I'm telling you that's why I think Tim killed himself. I got away by quitting hockey. Tim found his own way out."

"No way," Bobby replied in utter disbelief and disgust.

"I feel sick when I think about Tim. Guilty too."

Bobby struggled to listen. He wanted to block the words from his ears, but he couldn't. It just made too much sense, and he forced himself to respond. He looked Ricky up and down from head to toe.

"But it's not your fault. None of it is, if this is true."

"It is true, Bobby. And I know it's not my fault about Tim, but after I quit hockey, I suspected it was happening to others. I didn't do anything about it. I just really didn't want to think about it. Maybe if I had..."

"But you couldn't have known. This is... It's just terrible, Ricky."

"I know. And I only really suspected it was happening to Tim the night before he killed himself. After that basketball game, he was behaving so strangely. Tommy spotted his odd behaviour right away. I wanted to go with Tommy, and I wish I had. I so wish I had, but I was still so ashamed of what I let happen to me that as much as I saw Tim hurting, I couldn't find the words to speak to him about it that night. I went home and cried myself to sleep thinking about how much of a coward I was for not following the two of them."

Bobby's mind drifted to the horror. He shivered as he thought of the violation Ricky endured. He couldn't help but ask.

"What'd he do to you?"

Ricky shook his head. "Not as much as he did to Tim, that I'm sure of."

"But what did he do?" he asked again. He knew he should not have asked, but the words came out of his mouth before he could stifle them. His mind was numb with shock and disbelief.

"What do you think he did? Fuck, Bobby! I'm not telling you the details."

"I'm sorry. I shouldn't have asked. But how could you have known it was happening to Tim?" Bobby asked. He felt deeply ashamed for asking for details.

Ricky looked up into the air. He let the tears run down his cheeks as he continued. "I could so relate to how he was behaving because I had gone through so much myself. I felt so alone and frightened by what was happening to me at the time, and I had no idea where or who to turn to. It's such a shameful feeling. I thought what happened to me was my fault. I still feel that way, like I brought this all on myself just because I wanted to play hockey with Tommy."

"That is so wrong."

"But I knew. I knew what Tim was going through the moment I saw him sitting under that streetlight. He looked so sad. I could relate to it after I let Mr. Oliver have a go at me the second time and understood it wasn't just going to be a one-time thing. I had been getting all of those extra sessions free, but they really weren't free, were they? Nothing is ever free, but I liked playing hockey alongside Tommy and I somehow buried it in the back of my mind. But when he did it again, I just went along because he promised I'd get to play alongside Tommy again if I cooperated, and I did get to play up with him again. I'm so ashamed about the whole thing, and it's all I ever think about now."

Ricky sniffed, wiped his eyes and tried to smile, but he couldn't do it. "And I'd go over for the next one-on-one session, and the whole time I was working out, I worried it would happen again before the session ended, and it always did. Every single time. And then it got worse. I'd show up for the training, and he'd get right into it. There was no more training. Just him doing what he wanted to me, and I'd get to play up with Tommy again the next game. I was glad the season ended and I had time to think. That's when I decided I had to do something. I couldn't stand the thought of the upcoming season and what I'd be put through again."

Bobby could only shake his head about the suffering Ricky had endured.

"And then there's Tim. I knew he was getting the extra sessions, and, of course, I had to suspect that it was happening to him too. But it was an impossible question to ask, wasn't it? But if only I had gone after him."

Bobby shook his head hard. "My God. This is awful, Ricky. No, you couldn't have asked him, and no, you couldn't know what Tim was about to do. Don't you go thinking like that. It's not your fault."

Ricky sighed. "Tommy and Jason must have put it all together after Tim died. That's what I think. I think they found out, and that's why they killed their parents. Well, their dad at least. I'm not sure why they killed their mom. Maybe she knew too, but it was only Mr. Oliver that was coming at me."

Bobby listened to Ricky go on and on. His mouth hung open and a bit of muffin sat on his bottom lip until he finally found his voice. "Shit. I had no idea this was going on. I don't even know what to say."

"You don't need to say anything. I've told someone finally, and it actually feels good." Ricky almost smiled. "Just be my friend. That's all I'm asking for right now."

Bobby nodded. "Anything you need, just say it. My God this is awful!"

Ricky wiped his eyes, and a real smile broke across his face for the first time that morning. "Just be there and don't go on about it. Please don't say a word to anyone. No one can ever know about this. I'd die if anyone ever found out."

Bobby forced a smile back. It was a difficult smile because it felt as if the dirty truth he now held inside made him never want to smile again.

"This is private stuff man. Shit! You know I won't tell a soul." He reached out his right hand to Ricky and Ricky grabbed on. Both boys gripped each other in a bond they both knew was rock solid. They looked at each other teary-eyed, and Bobby could see the weight had lifted from Ricky. There was something in the air that finally felt positive.

"It's just so embarrassing to say it out loud still, but I do trust you, Bobby. I really do. You've always been the one I can say things to that I can't say to anyone else. Telling you gave me the biggest relief I've felt in months. But I really need to talk to Tommy still. I have to talk to him about this. You think he knows about me?"

Bobby shook his head. "I'm pretty sure he doesn't. I think he's wondering why you've never come up to see him or Jason. You going to tell him?"

"I have to. I have no choice."

Bobby could see Ricky's smile weaken.

"Okay then," Bobby said. "We can go in a few hours, if you're up to it."

Ricky nodded in agreement, "I have to, Bobby. While I still feel I can."

CHAPTER 26

Detective Dean Daly was in his cruiser returning from a nuisance call on the outskirts of Bluffington. Simon Pelletier had lodged a complaint against his neighbour Jens Wolfle. A few of Jens cattle had somehow gotten outside the fence and trampled through Simon's front yard destroying the front flower beds and front lawn. Now it looked as if World War Three started there.

Dean knew Jens talked a pile of nonsense. This was another chapter in a feud that went back all the way back to when the Municipality let the landowners break down their land into smaller, three and four acre parcels. Now the city slickers moved into the countryside, complained that it smelled of manure in their backyards and demanded that something be done about it. Numerous civil court actions were filed against the farmers and ranchers who had been on these lands for generations. Where Jens' fourteen hundred acres ended, an explosion of small acreages now lined his property. Simon Pelletier's property was the first one at the northwest corner.

Jens had shrugged, trying to look innocent. He insisted he had no idea how his cattle got outside of the fence. The gate was shut, and there wasn't a break anywhere in the fence.

The last time Dean was called out for a feud between these two, Jens had spread fresh manure out on the strip of property sitting adjacent to Simon's acreage, and only along that section. Dean knew he did it on purpose. Simon had recently submitted a letter to the editorial column complaining about how the ranchers in the area were being disrespectful of their new neighbours. The letter accused the ranchers of letting their cattle graze next to the expensive acreages, which created a foul smelling odour for all of those who lived nearby.

Today's charade was no different. Dean confronted Jens, and Jens willingly had a couple of his hands bring his cattle back, smiling the entire time at Dean. He insisted multiple times that he had no idea how his cattle ended up on the wrong side of the fence.

To complicate the matter, Simon Pelletier was featherweight in stature, especially when compared to the six-foot-two, two-hundred-forty pound Jens. Simon was also very openly gay and owned and operated the Flattened Frog Bistro at the south end of Main Street in Bluffington.

"A bistro?" Jens had said in disbelief. Not only had the little, gay Frenchman built on the land next door, he had the gall to open up what Jens called a "pussy restaurant." Jens was a cattle rancher, and the only true restaurant from his point of view was a steakhouse.

Dean was pissed off about the whole episode. It wasn't over between those two. He would be called out repeatedly as they did their best to provoke each other.

Dean drove away from Jens' property and turned onto the back road to get back to town instead of travelling straight down the same road he took there. Driving down the back roads was part of Dean's patrol routine whenever he was out in the country. Primarily, he did it to show a presence and to keep his eyes open for what was happening just outside of town. It had snowed lightly overnight, and Dean could see that only a few vehicles had travelled down these back roads so far this morning. He had just turned from Battersby Road, which ran up and beyond Jens many acres onto Black Pond Road, when one of the old wooden road signs that displayed the posted speed suddenly burst apart into smithereens right in front of him. The small explosion startled Dean out of his daydream of how to deal with Jens and Simon. He slammed on his brakes and looked about, flabbergasted, as the last of the pieces of the wooden sign fluttered to the ground.

Off to his right, Dean spotted a small side trail that angled off into the forest. A clear set of tire tracks was visible in the light snow. Dean stepped on the gas and turned his cruiser down onto the tiny side road. Dean couldn't believe his eyes as the trees opened up, and he immediately turned on his blue and reds. He gave his siren one short burst as only one hundred yards down the tiny forested trail were none other than Willie Wahnkman and Doogie Fisher. The two boys stood alongside Doogie's old, rusty Ford Bronco and Doogie held what appeared to be a shotgun in his hands. Willie fidgeted with a lit cigarette.

Doogie smiled in disbelief and dropped his head as Dean pulled the car to a stop a few yards away from the two of them, the lights still flashing away on the roof. Willie scrambled behind Doogie. His eyes were open wide and filled with obvious fright.

Dean stepped out of the car and unclipped the holster on his gun, making sure the two boys noticed.

"Put the gun on the roof of the vehicle, Doogie, and step away." Dean said. Doogie did as he was told and placed the gun on top the Bronco. He stepped back slowly with his hands halfway raised in the air. He continued his smug smile. He knew he was caught with his pants down this time. This was a very bad start to a Saturday, and Doogie knew it wasn't going to get any better for him.

Dean motioned both boys over to the cruiser and shuffled Willie into the back seat. He wanted Doogie alone. He hustled Doogie over to his Bronco and had him open up the doors, glove box and rear hatch while he scoured about inside. Doogie produced more goodies than Dean had ever expected to find. Dean cuffed Doogie and Willie and drove them down to the station. Doogie was charged with: possession of two unlicensed firearms, illegal transportation of a firearm, illegal discharge of a firearm, possession of marijuana, driving with expired registration, failure to produce a valid driver's license, damage to public property and a few other minor offences. Willie got off a lot lighter with only a few minor offences against him.

It took most of the afternoon to lay all of the charges against Doogie and Willie. Both were eventually released with a court date set for them to answer to all of the charges.

CHAPTER 27

There were two ways to get up to the furnished apartment Sarah rented on the hillside. One was to follow the road along the bottom of the hill west, about half a block, and then double back onto a small side road that crawled its way up the side of the hill to the back of the small apartment building. The other was to walk up the long staircase from the bottom end of Main Street just below Simon's Flattened Frog Bistro. The apartment block was right above and behind the Bistro and was accessible by the staircase that climbed up from the parking lot.

Sarah told Brandy to pull into the parking lot so they could walk up the long staircase. Sarah still only had the bright red suitcase she took when she had left Gerald. She had since purchased more clothes and accessories, but all still fit inside that small suitcase. Brandy carried the other shopping bag with the rest of Sarah's new life.

"Oh this will be such a lovely place to live," Brandy remarked as she turned around half way up the staircase and looked down across the small town in the valley.

Sarah nodded, and smiled enthusiastically. "It is beautiful isn't it?"

Sarah quickly settled into her new, partially furnished apartment with Brandy's help. It was a long morning, and Sarah followed Brandy out to her car and thanked her again for all she had done.

"Grab a coffee with me before you go?" She looked up at the Bistro. "We can probably grab one right here," she said and motioned to the Bistro above them.

"One coffee, and then I really gotta get back."

Sarah was pleased and led the way into the Bistro. They sat at one of the many windows that fronted the Bistro and looked down Main Street. They noticed the little funny Frenchman immediately. He gestured grandly with his arms and pulled many outrageous facial expressions. They watched with curious interest as he spoke with excitement to someone on the phone in the back corner near the kitchen.

"I don't care who he is! My front garden is in a damn state, and I just can't take anymore of this." There was a short pause as the little man rocked back and forth on his heels and his free hand flapped about in the air. He glanced over, and spotted Sarah and Brandy. He forced a short, tight smile of surprise. He obviously didn't noticed the two of them come in. "I don't care!" he shouted back softly into the phone, now aware of the girls. "I pay you a lot of money, and I want you to see to it that he has my lawn and flower beds fixed up tomorrow!" There was another short pause. "Process? Me pay for it upfront? Oh, you make me so mad. You listen..." There was another short pause. "It wasn't my cows. Why should I have to pay?" He glanced over to the girls again briefly. "No! I don't want to go through insurance. You go out there and sort this out today with him. His cows did this, and I want him to fix this up. I gotta go. I have customers."

Simon flipped his hand in the air towards the girls, grabbed a couple of menus and pranced quickly over. His free hand flapped away with each step.

"Good afternoon ladies," Simon said and smiled. He offered the menus out to each of them. "How are you both doing on this lovely day?"

"Better than you it sounds like," answered Brandy.

Sarah was a bit surprised at the bold response from Brandy.

"Oh, you don't know the half of it," Simon answered back, unabashed by her tart response. He crossed his arms and leaned in to the girls. "My neighbour's cows just tore my front yard to absolute pieces with their hooves. They trampled everything. My dear, dear flower beds are all ruined, and my grass... It was so absolutely perfect and now it's destroyed." He unfolded his arms and gestured grandly again. "I'm in absolute bits about it all."

"I'm so sorry to hear that," Sarah said. She liked Simon immediately. He was open and honest, and his very gay mannerisms were not lost on her.

Simon took their order, and Sarah explained she was new to town and had just taken the apartment out back. The Bistro was very quiet and had only moments ago opened up for the day. Simon soon joined the two girls at the table. He asked how she had come to have the cast on her arm. Sarah shared only a little of the graphic details at first, but soon told the honest truth. She felt immediate comfort when she talked to Simon and felt safe telling him her story about Gerald. It wasn't long before she knew she would be enjoying many coffees at this very window.

CHAPTER 28

"You ready?" Bobby asked.

Ricky said nothing and stared out the side window at the barbed wire-topped fence that surrounded the Spy Hill Correctional Centre.

"It's right in that door there. Just go up to the front and say you are here to see Tommy Oliver. They'll take you the rest of the way." Bobby nudged Ricky and giggled. "Go on, you loser," he said to ease Ricky's nerves.

Ricky smiled back. He punched Bobby hard on the shoulder and scrambled out of the vehicle before Bobby could swing back. He grinned at Bobby and flipped him the finger.

Bobby grabbed onto his sore shoulder and flipped the finger back to him. He nodded to Ricky and urged him forward. He then cranked the volume up on his CD player and laid his seat back. He knew it could be a long time before Ricky returned.

***

Ricky turned toward the large complex, and his grin vanished. The cold December air cut through him as his eyes crawled across the barbwire that separated the inmates from the outside world. He swallowed hard and headed inside to see Tommy.

Inside wasn't what Ricky expected. It seemed more like a hospital than a prison. After going through the security screening, he was quickly ushered into a small empty room that contained only a few tables and chairs. It was brightly lit with soft, lime-green walls. Windows lined the interior wall along the hallway. Ricky sat in a chair at one of the small wooden tables off to the side and waited for Tommy to be brought in.

Tommy strolled in wearing his orange coveralls. He smiled instantly at Ricky and sat across from him. The guard left the room and stood outside the glass door, leaving the boys to talk in private.

"It's about time you came up," Tommy said.

Ricky fidgeted, not sure what to say. "So, what's it like in here?"

"It's okay I guess. They keep us pretty busy."

Ricky looked around uncomfortably.

"How about you?"

Ricky wasn't sure what Tommy meant. "How about me what?"

Tommy laughed and shook his head. "It's not so bad in here. We have a gymnasium, so we can play floor hockey and basketball. There's a weight room. Food's okay, and they have school here too. Both Jason and I are in classes most of the day. I'll graduate in spring if things go well."

Ricky listened and acknowledged Tommy, but he offered little small talk in return.

Tommy carried on and talked about life in Spy Hill. He talked about the dorms and more about the food. He mentioned there were a few bad asses around and, for the most part, life was pretty structured inside. He missed hockey most of all and asked how the team was doing without him and Jason. He purposely ignored the fact that his dad had been the coach of the Triple A team and was also sorely missed.

"Team's not doing great. Big downhill slide since... Well..." Ricky stopped talking and he locked eyes with Tommy. It was time.

"There's a reason I haven't been up to see you or Jason." His discomfort was obvious as he continued. "It's about why you're both in here."

Tommy leaned back in his chair. "I guessed as much after the way Bobby came up yesterday and mentioned you wanted to see me. So what's the big secret anyway? You've been on our visitor list from the start. Why haven't you come up until now?"

"Tell me about Tim," Ricky said abruptly.

"Tim?"

"Yeah. What do you know about why Tim killed himself?"

Tommy let out a heavy groan. He rubbed his hand furiously across his short hair. "I'm not sure I know anything about that."

"Of course you do. You talked to Tim the night before he died. He told you something. I know he did."

Tommy shook his head from side to side. "Tim didn't tell me anything that night. Nothing."

"I don't believe you."

"What do you want me to say? Look around you right now. Where the hell do you think you are? This is a detention centre. What are you expecting me to say? I'm not offering anything up. Not even to you, Ricky." Tommy was highly agitated and glanced over to the guard behind the glass across the room.

The guard opened the door and let in a stressed, middle-aged woman. She looked about uncomfortably and took a seat on the opposite side of the room as she waited for her incarcerated son.

"I think I know why Tim killed himself. And I think it's the same reason you killed you parents," Ricky suggested pointedly.

Tommy suddenly leaned in close to Ricky, and pointed his finger hard at Ricky as he whispered. "Just shut up. Just you shut up for a minute." Tommy looked around the room and took notice of the guard on the other side of the glass door again. Tommy continued to whisper quietly to Ricky. "You don't know anything about what went on. Nothing. And I'm not going to tell you anything, so if that's what you're looking for, then I don't know why you're even here. Me and Jason are just trying to get through this, and we are not saying anything to anybody about what happened. Did somebody put you up to this? Trying to get us to say something?"

Ricky looked back, dumbfounded at Tommy, and he knew what Tommy suspected was at least partially true. His eyes began to water and he wiped at them.

The door to the room opened and another inmate entered and was directed over to the upset, middle-aged woman.

"Okay then," Ricky whispered back and looked momentarily at the two across the room who were already engaged in their own private conversation. "Then I'm going to tell you something that you don't know, and I really hope that you're not going to hate me for what I'm going to tell you." He wiped at his eyes again. "And I think I really do know why Tim killed himself."

Tommy stared back, said nothing and leaned in close.

"I know, Tommy. I know," Ricky said simply.

"What exactly do you know?"

Ricky swallowed hard, and coughed. He was all choked up and trying hard not to implode. "It happened to me too," was all he said and kept his gaze fixed on Tommy.

Tommy stole a glance over to the mother and her son and saw them still highly engrossed in an emotional discussion. He pushed himself away from Ricky and leaned back. Ricky could see Tommy try not to grimace as he turned himself away from Ricky and looked out across the room with a vacant stare. He gazed up to the ceiling and Ricky could only watch as the tears began to run down Tommy's cheeks. He wiped them away quickly.

Tommy began to shake his head in disbelief and kept himself from making any eye contact. He whispered softly in denial. "Not you, Ricky."

Ricky nodded slowly back, understanding immediately that he was right about Tommy. He dropped his head down into his arms on the table, trying to hide his tears. He sniffed and looked up at Tommy nodding again. "Why do you think I quit hockey?"

Tommy shuffled uncomfortably and acknowledged Ricky.

"I found my own way out, Tommy."

Tommy buried his head in his hands and began to weep. Ricky stayed sitting across from Tommy, not sure if Tommy was ever going to stop crying. He wanted to comfort him, but he didn't know how and didn't know if he even should. Tommy eventually stopped and wiped at his runny nose.

"I had no idea."

"You believe me then?" Ricky had to ask.

Tommy raised his head up and down in short bursts. He tried to maintain his composure, but the pain he felt was very clear to Ricky. "If I'd known..."

"So what now?" Ricky asked.

Tommy just shook his head and shrugged. Uneasiness wafted down between the two boys. They both felt the awkwardness that spread between them from a topic neither really wanted to discuss openly. Tommy's eyes shifted rapidly about the room. His discomfort was evident.

"I guess I should be going then. I just thought you should know," Ricky mumbled back through soft tears.

"No! Don't go. Not yet at least." Tommy sniffled some more and wiped his eyes. He tried hard to regain his composure. "Have you told anyone else?"

"Just Bobby."

"Bobby? Bobby knows?"

Ricky nodded. "He knows. I told him about me."

"You haven't told anyone else?"

"No one, Tommy. Never. I'm so ashamed of the whole thing. If it ever got out around town what happened to me, I think I'd probably end up joining Tim. I couldn't..."

"Shush, Ricky! Don't say that! It's not going to get out. I won't let it!" He paused, deep in thought, and suddenly Tommy's expression changed to one of worry. He put his hand to his lips.

"So it is true then, about Tim?" Ricky asked. "You knew. He did tell you what happened?"

Ricky could sense Tommy's thoughts were suddenly very far away as if he was reliving some horrid moment. His eyes crawled over Ricky, leaving Ricky feeling slightly disoriented and uncomfortable.

"No. I didn't know anything. Tim didn't say anything directly to me but just sort of told me that something was going on. I didn't know what. I didn't understand what he was saying until after."

"And your parents?" Ricky asked. It was a tough question, but Ricky really wanted to know.

Tommy just shook his head. "I'm not saying anything about that. Not to you or anybody. You can ask me about other stuff, but not that."

Ricky wasn't about to let up on what he thought was the truth. "I think it was because of Tim. I know the stories went around all over the news and in the papers about him being bullied to death by Doggie and Willie. It is just a bunch of bullcrap. I know it. And you know it too, Tommy."

"Ok, Ricky. Just listen to me then." Tommy's distraction remained. "I hear what you're saying, but I want to ask you a question. It is about my dad, if that's okay."

Ricky sat up straight, amazed by Tommy's change of heart to discuss his parents. "Your dad?"

"Yeah, my dad. In the therapy office out back, during the extra training he gave you."

Ricky shuffled in his seat. "Okay. What about him?"

"Did he… record you at all? I mean the training. You know. Power skating on the fake ice, slap shots, wrist shots, that kind of stuff?"

Ricky frowned and anger set in. "You know he did, Tommy. And don't just beat around the bush with this stuff. What I think you really want to ask me is if he also had the video recording running when he did the other stuff he did. I tried to forget what he did to me, so I don't know. I can't really remember, and I don't want to."

"I'm sorry, but I had to ask."

"Why, Tommy? Why did you have to ask that?" Ricky began to tear up again. "Why do you want to know what he did?" Ricky pushed himself away from the table and stood up. He wiped his tears on the sleeve of his coat.

"I don't want to know. I don't. Honest. It's just..."

"Then why'd you ask me? What difference does it make now anyway? What's done is done." He shifted on his feet from side to side. He was uneasy and agitated. "I hated him so much, Tommy, and I'm glad you killed him!" he suddenly shouted. "I'm so glad he's dead!" The mother and son stopped their debate and turned to watch Ricky's outburst.

"Shh! Sit down, Ricky!" Tommy looked over to the glass. Ricky's eyes followed, and he could see the guard stare in and watch the two closely.

"I'm leaving now. I just can't do this."

"Wait!" Tommy called out as Ricky moved to the exit door, tapped on the glass and prompted the guard to open the locked door.

"Ricky, there's more we need to talk about."

Ricky turned back and nodded, "I just can't do this anymore today."

"But you will come back?"

"I don't know right now. Maybe," Ricky replied and exited the room.

CHAPTER 29

Dean stood in the study of the empty Oliver home. The boy's Aunt Meredith had all the furniture and contents packed up and sold weeks ago with the exception of the boys' personal belongings, which were sent into storage. Cleaning and touch-up crews were readying the house to be sold. The bloody evidence in the hall and study was cleaned away, and the now empty house had a cold, sterile feel to it. Dean's footsteps echoed off the wooden floors and bare walls. The house gave him a chill. Dean thought it was the memory of the horror beset upon this home that eked its way into his bones. It didn't help that the heat was turned down to just warm enough to keep the pipes from freezing.

There were definitely some pieces of the puzzle missing about the boys' motives for killed their parents, and Dean was determined to keep digging until he found something. The charges were laid against both Tommy and Jason for first-degree murder. As young offenders, even if convicted, they would do little more than three to five years inside and another three outside under house arrest or at a halfway home. It didn't bother Dean in the least about the sentence the boys would receive. The justice system worked that way in Canada. He only sought the truth regarding why they committed such an act, and he knew he didn't have the truth.

Dean walked up and set one foot upon the hearth. "Why the hearth?" he questioned aloud. "And why did both of them step up and off?" He set his hand upon the smooth rocks, and he felt the answer lay there in the cold stones. He put his other hand on the rocks and began to feel around. He looked for anything that might have been missed during the original investigation. The rocks were smooth and cleaned of the blood spatter and finger prints. There were no other markings, scuffs or scratches. He wasn't sure what he was looking for, but he again found nothing new.

Dean strolled about the house and recollected the events of that terrible and long day. He recalled where he was when the call about the murders first came in. "Willie Wahnkman," he whispered. He was in the middle of interrogating Willie about Tim's suicide and the beating he and Doogie administered the evening before. Willie was bad news, but Doogie was much worse. Doogie was destined for time behind bars, and it was likely to be sooner rather than later. He thought about the hype that was in the papers. Tim's suicide was provoked by bullying, and the outcry had spread like wildfire. It made the news in every national paper and in many international news outlets overnight. The news vans were everywhere, and the quiet little town of Bluffington highlighted the evening news all around the world. Another town where bullying had gotten out of hand, and it had ended with another horrific suicide. Many months later, the editorials were still written about this sad, unnecessary suicide with bullying as its root cause.

The garage and attached physiotherapy office out back were locked up tight. Dean stared out through the kitchen window and tried to imagine one of the boys smashing the headlights and windshield of the BMW with the axe. That was the first act of rage. The evidence showed that the damage was clearly inflicted by the same axe found with the boys in the study. The garage is where the rage started. But why?

Dean pondered the timelines some more and made a small connection back to Tim. It was just a small link, but it still led back to Tim's suicide. Both boys should not have been home so early from school that day. Tim's suicide occurred early that morning. He believed deeply that the beating and constant physical and emotional abuse from Doogie and Willie prompted Tim's suicide. But maybe, just maybe, there was more to it. Dean knew there was more tidying up to do on both cases. Did anyone check out the time the boys left school that day? Did any one talk to the boys' teachers about that day? Were the boys questioned about Tim's suicide in the course of the murder investigation? Dean didn't recall that they were or at least didn't recall seeing any answers along those lines in any of the officers' reports. Could Tim's suicide be the reason they were home early that day? If so, that still didn't explain the rage in the garage or the sudden horror that resulted in the house. Dean pondered the motive once again and dismissed any direct connection to Tim's suicide.

Maybe it was about the money after all. Maybe after Tim's suicide, the boys thought that this was the perfect time to act. A spur of the moment decision to act at the moment when Tim's suicide would provide some deflection away from their crime. He thought about it some more. He pulled out his note pad and reminded himself to drop by the school in the next few days.

CHAPTER 30

An endless consumption of alcohol numbed Gerald as he recovered from rolling his truck three weeks previously. He had taken off work because he was unable to walk after the incident. His ankle was twisted and very swollen, but he had since recovered nicely, regardless of the amount of alcohol he put back each night. Gerald was now able to move about easily with only minor pain, which was more irritating than painful. The swelling had gone down, and Gerald focused his thoughts on what to do next about Sarah.

Gerald was certainly not finished with Sarah. He was now even more determined to track her down. His little stint in Ratskeller's Bar and the subsequent crash and loss of his truck was just more fuel thrown onto the rage-fire. This was all her fault. The charges laid by the police were her fault too, and he saw this with vivid clarity through the drunken craze he put himself in every night. There was no option but to find Sarah and finish what was necessary.

It was a Sunday, and there was a cool, dry chill in the house. Another light dusting of snow fell overnight, adding to the many inches of snow that now rested on Gerald's driveway and sidewalks. Gerald had not shovelled since he rolled his truck, but not because his ankle was sore. He simply couldn't be bothered to keep the sidewalk clear for others to walk safely. Christmas was only a few days away and Gerald didn't give a shit about it. "The snow can sit and stay right where it fucking wants until spring for all I care, and Christmas can take a fucking giant leap into my ass!" he thought to himself.

Gerald finally discovered Sarah's spare set of keys a few days ago, and he knew he would have to drive her vehicle if he wanted to go anywhere. He wouldn't be happy driving Sarah's foreign vehicle, but it would have to do. Gerald hated all foreign vehicles. "Bloody Korean's and Jap's coming over here taking away all of our automotive jobs," was a common Gerald rant.

Gerald was sober this morning, but the rage that usually only surfaced when he was heavily drunk now seemed to be a semi-permanent state. It lingered just under the surface, ready to break through at the slightest annoyance.

Gerald grabbed the keys to Sarah's car, slipped on his boots and coat and headed out the front door. Sarah's sister's house would be a good place to start. He would make a quick drive by, and maybe he would even sit and watch her place for a while. It had been a long time since he was invited out that way, but he was sure he could remember how to get to her place in the south west part of town. He was only out the door a few steps when his neighbour's sixteen-year-old son, who was out to scrape the snow from their drive, looked over at Gerald and offered some advice.

"You better shovel your walk soon. The city's going to give you a ticket if you don't," young Aaron Phelps said pleasantly. "I saw them go by earlier looking at all the snow on your sidewalk. My mom said that it's the law to keep your sidewalk clear of snow."

The thin layer of reason that kept Gerald's anger at bay suddenly split open. To Gerald, Aaron's words sounded like a threat. A devastating eruption of uncontrolled fury released itself within Gerald. He turned sharply towards young Aaron and stomped headlong through the snow until he stood inches away from him.

"What the fuck did you just say to me?" Gerald shouted at Aaron.

Aaron's mouth dropped open, and he cowered back a step. He let the shovel slip through his fingers to the ground. He couldn't speak and just shook his head from side to side. He desperately wanted to run away. He pointed to Gerald's sidewalk and forced himself to utter a few more words. "The snow. On your sidewalk," he cried out meekly.

Gerald snapped out his left hand, grabbed Aaron by his coat and pulled him forward before he could run away.

Aaron shouted back and tried to free himself from Gerald's grasp. "Let go of me! What's wrong with you?" he shouted, but it was no use. Gerald fist closed tighter, and crushed the fabric tight within his clenched fist. Aaron squirmed and grabbed onto Gerald's hand with both of his hands and tried to break free of Gerald's grip.

Gerald swung his muscular right arm hard. It caught Aaron in the side of the cheek and nose and knocked Aaron sideways off his feet, while he still held Aaron's coat with his left hand. Aaron screamed out in pain, and pulled his hands up to cover his face in case Gerald took another swing.

"Don't you ever fuck with me, you little shit!" Gerald shouted. He let go of Aaron, and dropped him to the ground. He turned and stomped through the snow over to Sarah's car and hopped inside. He started the engine and glared with furious anger at Aaron lying in a heap on the snowy ground next door. Gerald was satisfied to see the little bugger writhing on the ground in agony. He deserved it for provoking him. He quickly drove away and left Aaron to get to his knees on his own. Aaron howled in pain, and as Gerald left, a few drops of blood fell on the snow beneath him.

It wasn't long before Gerald found Carolyn's house. He decided he would stay a while, and parked the car across the street a few doors down so he could watch the front drive of the two story home. He wasn't sure what he was going to do. He studied Carolyn's house, noting especially the

Christmas lights and decorations that embellished the house, trees and hedge so abundantly. He felt his anger rise again at the useless waste of time and effort that went into such decorations. He pushed the thought aside. His purpose for being there was very specific. He searched for Sarah, and he was going to find her. He waited and watched. Hours passed as he sat in the cold. He started the vehicle up periodically to get some heat back. The afternoon wore on, and the soft clouds covering the sky soon darkened. Many vehicles came up and down the street, but none stopped at Carolyn's home.

Gerald put his right hand on his breast to feel through the fabric for something he had completely forgotten about until now. He smiled. He reached his hand into the inside coat pocket and pulled out a Mickey of Whiskey. He often kept one inside his coat pocket these days for occasions such as this. He twisted off the cap and slugged back some of the devil's fever. It felt good, and over the next hour, he pulled out the bottle repeatedly. The burning warmth settled itself deep inside him and brought with it a darkened clarity of his purpose for waiting there.

It was moments after the Christmas lights came on in the darkness that a black Subaru slowed and pulled into Carolyn's drive. Gerald suspected the lights were on a timer. Gerald sat up, eager to see who would soon step out of the vehicle. Would they be alone?

The driver's door opened and Gerald was pleased. Carolyn arrived alone. She reached back inside the car, pulled out a small bag and closed the door. With some quick energy in her gait, she headed up the steps and inside the house, leaving Gerald to wonder exactly when he should make his move.

CHAPTER 31

Nothing new was happening for Tommy and Jason. The Spy Hill routine took over, and the boys politely went along with all the processes and procedures that accompanied nearly every activity. Even going for a whiz in the washroom had its restrictions and routine.

Christmas was only days away, and although Tommy and Jason both felt that longing to be back, huddled around the fireplace and sipping a hot chocolate with their parents, neither let it show. Family members visited other inmates and eagerly shared exciting tidbits of what was happening back at their homes as Christmas drew even closer.

The Oliver boys suffered great internal pain. They deeply missed both their mother and father. While the other boys spoke fondly of their memories of this festive time, the conversations awoke memories that the Olivers had tried hard to suppress. Christmas had always been a special time for the Oliver family. The outside activities waned and being together became the focus. It was about sharing quality time over dinner, playing games, watching movies and socializing. That happy image was forever obliterated for Tommy and Jason. The two remained ensconced behind the firewalls they each erected to protect themselves from collapsing in grief and longing for what they lost. Although the boys appeared to be lacking in compassion, a part of each of them accepted the consequence of having to sever memories in order to survive.

This time was hard for the other inmates who wouldn't be home for Christmas; they each had their own strong attachment to the outside: to home and the hope that everything was alright and was going to still be alright once the time inside was sorted and served. Tommy and Jason could only watch and listen with great angst as the others dreamed of the home to which they would one day return.

Words of promise and a future from those outside the barbed wire walls never came for Tommy and Jason. They had killed their parents, and other than their counsellors and lawyers, they only had the odd visit from Bobby to look forward to. Even Aunt Meredith kept her word, and she was still hoping they had already begun rotting in hell.

The boys hid behind their own walls and kept themselves busy by following the rules with unblemished obedience. The facility offered education, and both boys excelled academically inside just as they had outside. They eagerly participated in the sports offered, worked in the laundry and even volunteered their time in the kitchen making food packages for needy families outside. Both were model prisoners, and it frustrated the counsellors who still sought to discover motivation for the murders. How two such well-behaved, highly educated, gifted boys could fall so far off track as to commit such a heinous crime was a mystery. Even still, they grew on everyone who interacted with them, and soon they were trusted beyond the limits of other inmates. They were granted special privileges normally set aside for those who needed such rewards as part of the rehabilitation and socialization process.

The boys were surprised when they were offered the opportunity to be junior counsellors to some of the other inmates. This was really another part of rehabilitating young offenders: exposing them to the open sharing of thoughts and feelings in a group of their peers. They were in these same group sessions weeks ago, and neither opened up even once about the murders. They limited their discussion and feelings to everything else in their lives and avoided the one thing that the counsellors really wanted to hear.

Tommy was a natural at speaking his mind and comforting others. In a strange way, it was what caused him to commit the crime when he did. Jason, on the other hand, always wanted to be like Tommy, and if Tommy believed hiding the truth this was a good thing, then so did Jason.

Beginning in January, Jason and Tommy would be sitting in on some group sessions with the counsellors and would begin the process of open dialogue to help others come to terms with why they were in the Spy Hill Correctional Centre. These were meant to be informal, mandatory sessions for all of the new arrivals ánd a masked therapy for Tommy and Jason.

CHAPTER 32

Ricky was over at Bobby's again. He stayed for supper, as he often did, and the two boys were now playing a game on the X-Box. It was what the two did every Sunday night now that they seemed to have only each other. Tommy used to be at the centre when the group of boys met, leading them into whatever activity they would be participating in. There was always laughing, teasing and all-around fun. It was much different now. There was a lot less spontaneity without Tommy around and a lot more serious and sometimes solemn talk. Bobby was still the listener, the one the others always went to when they had something serious to discuss. You didn't go to Tommy. Tommy was always eager and wanted to be a part of fixing whatever the problem was, but sometimes things didn't need fixing. Sometimes a good listener was all it took to figure things out on your own. Bobby was that listener.

"I want to go back up," Ricky said as he shot at the approaching zombie on the screen and missed.

"Back up where?" Bobby asked and giggled as he blew the top part of one of the zombie's heads off.

"You know. Up to see Tommy. I think I need to see Tommy again."

"Mmm," Bobby mumbled back. He fired on a couple more zombies.

"You think I should?"

"I know he misses you," Bobby answered. "Jason does too."

Ricky continued to fire away at the zombies on the screen. A beeping sound followed shortly by a thunder crash indicated he had run out of life. He put his controller down and watched Bobby carry on. He still had lots of life left and many options available.

"Can I ask you something?"

"Sure," Bobby answered. He stuck his tongue out to the side as he tried to maneuver his player quickly to the left.

"What do you think I should do about this thing?"

Bobby laughed and glanced over at Ricky. "Thing? What thing? You got something growing on you?"

"No, I'm serious. Will you stop playing for a minute?"

Bobby was still holding a smile as he directed his player over to a safe area and then paused the game.

"Okay, what is it? What's this *thing?*"

"You know. The thing." He gestured with his hands at his whole body. "The thing that happened to me."

Bobby looked back and shrugged. "I'm not sure I follow you," he said, but he knew exactly where the conversation was going. "What do you want to do?"

"It's just... I think about it all the time. I mean *all* the time. I can't even go to the bathroom without having visions of the inside of that training room at the back of the house."

Bobby gave an uncomfortable nod back to Ricky. "Maybe you should go talk to someone."

"A counsellor? No way! I'm not talking to any stranger about this."

"Then what did you have in mind?"

"I don't know. I don't know what to do, but I can't keep thinking like I do or I'm going to go crazy." Ricky got up off the floor, lay back on the couch and stared up at the ceiling.

Bobby stood up and shuffled over next to Ricky. He rubbed his leg the entire way.

Ricky hadn't told Bobby any of the graphic details about what had happened to him, and Bobby hadn't asked. The two friends had become tight these past few months. They shared all kinds of complaints and grief about every day stuff, but they never spoke about the activities that occurred in the back therapy office of the Oliver home. Ricky still had a deep need to release some of his feelings by talking to someone about what happened to him. These things were not easy to talk about; they were uncomfortable, possibly divisive and outside the boundaries of common friendly discussion.

"When do you want to go see Tommy?" Bobby asked. "There's no school for two weeks, so I can take you anytime."

"Tommy knows more about this than he's saying. I'm wondering how much he really knew about me and Tim. He said he didn't know, but it was just the way he acted when I saw him."

"I'm not so sure he knows anything about you, Ricky. If Tommy knew about this long ago, before that terrible day, I don't think he would have snapped that afternoon like he did... well, you know. You know how Tommy is. He's always trying to fix things, and if he knew about you or Tim he would have stepped in long ago. Tommy couldn't have known about Tim. I think he just snapped when he found out. And that's why I don't think he knew about you."

"That's kinda what I was thinking too, but he did ask me some questions about his dad. It bothered me then, and it still does now. I can't get it out of my mind."

"What questions?"

Ricky let out a grunt. He still couldn't believe what Tommy had asked him. "He asked me if his dad recorded me in the back room."

Bobby looked away and began to rub his leg again.

Too much detail maybe, Ricky thought. He could feel the souring of the atmosphere in the room and quickly clarified his last statement. "He asked me if he recorded me when I was power skating, shooting pucks and stuff like that."

Bobby nodded and stole a short glance at Ricky before turning himself away.

"But I know what he really wanted to say. I could feel it in the room. His words suddenly seemed dark and heavy, and when I heard them, it was as if it was in slow motion. The words just hung there, echoing in my head over and over. I knew what he was asking. What he really wanted to know was if his dad ever recorded me he did those things to me."

Bobby continued to rub his leg. He looked up at Ricky and held his gaze. Ricky knew it was an uncomfortable subject for Bobby, but he carried on anyway.

"I don't know why he asked me that. I asked him, and he didn't answer. It really riled me up and I couldn't take it anymore. That's when I had to leave. I need to see him again to find out why he asked me that because it don't make sense to me, Bobby. No sense at all."

The two boys talked on some more, and agreed they would make the trip up to see Tommy some time during the next week after Christmas.

CHAPTER 33

Gerald waited in the car for another half-hour after Carolyn arrived home and finished off the Mickey in the meantime. The liquor helped him focus, and his purpose became very clear as he sat and watched the house. Sarah was in there. He was damn sure she was in that house. Carolyn had come home alone, but Gerald was sure it was just part of her act in case anyone was watching. Gerald grinned and chuckled coldly.

The sun had already receded past the mountains to the west, and the overcast sky turned to blackness leaving most houses on the street lit with multicoloured lights on the trim, rooflines, trees and shrubs. There was a small reindeer in the yard next to Carolyn's made out of tiny amber coloured lights, and the head went up and down slowly. Gerald exited the vehicle, crossed the street and headed for Carolyn's front door. He slowed and raised his middle finger to the nodding reindeer as he passed by.

Gerald rang the doorbell.

Carolyn's startled expression when she opened the door was the opportunity Gerald hoped for. In her moment of hesitation, Gerald threw his shoulder firmly into the partially open door and knocked it inward sending Carolyn reeling backwards. She landed on her backside on the floor in the hall.

"Where is she?" Gerald shouted as he slammed the door closed behind him. "Sarah!" he called out.

Carolyn turned onto her knees and tried to crawl down the hall away from Gerald, but he quickly pounced forward, grabbed her by the arm and jerked her up forcefully until she was standing face to face with him. Gerald continued to scream and shout, and demanded to know where Sarah was hiding.

Carolyn did her best to free herself from Gerald's grasp, but it was no use. He only squeezed harder. He finally grabbed her with both hands and threw her up against the wall.

"She's here isn't she?"

Carolyn shook her head. "I haven't seen Sarah!" she shouted back and still struggled to free herself from Gerald's grasp.

Gerald quickly scanned the house for any evidence of Sarah.

The inside of Carolyn's house screamed participation in the Christmas season. Cedar boughs covered with Christmas cards and dripping with tinsel lined the column from floor to ceiling between the front hall and living room. A beautiful gold and silver decorated tree was the centre attraction in the living room. Dozens of exquisitely wrapped presents were carefully arranged underneath the tree. Stockings hung down beneath the fireplace mantle, and numerous snow-scene-village ceramic houses were scattered about the room.

Gerald grabbed her by the arm and led her into the living room, towards the tree and the presents underneath. "Who are all these for then?" he shouted. He bent down and rifled through the name tags on each of the presents.

"Not for Sarah," Carolyn stated back firmly. "What the hell are you even doing here Gerald?"

Gerald continued to hold firmly onto her arm as he looked through the name tags. He frowned when none had Sarah's name. The presents were all labeled for Carolyn, Carl, Jessie, Mom or Dad.

"I want to know where Sarah is! You tell me where she is!" he demanded.

From outside the room, a familiar noise interrupted them and both Gerald and Carolyn turned their heads sharply towards the sound.   It was the front door.   Gerald spun Carolyn in front of him, crossed one arm around her neck and held her close to his chest.

"Hey Care, were home," Carolyn's husband, Karl, called out.   Young Jessie ran quickly around the corner into the living room and stopped as he spotted a man holding his mother in a half nelson.   The man was familiar, but he didn't quite recognize him.

"Karl!   Gerald's broken in!   Get Jessie out of here!" she shouted.

"What the..." Karl exclaimed as he rounded the corner to see his wife restrained in a wrestling hold by her brother-in-law.   He quickly directed Jessie to stand behind him.   "What the hell is this?" he demanded of Gerald.

"Where's my wife!" Gerald shouted back.

"We haven't seen Sarah, now let Care go right bloody now!" he demanded and stepped towards Gerald slowly.

"You tell me where Sarah is, and I'll be outta here. Where is she hiding?"

Karl was a big, strong man.   He worked out every other day, and even though Gerald was heavy-set and large, Karl could still probably knock Gerald out with one punch. Presently, though, he was concerned about his wife.   As long as Gerald held on to Carolyn, Karl wouldn't do anything to jeopardize her or his son's safety.

"Jessie, go into the other room," he said calmly to his son.   Jessie nodded and backed out of the room, leaving Gerald and Karl in a standoff.

"No one's hiding Sarah.   You let Carolyn go."

Gerald continued to hold tight to Carolyn with his left arm wrapped around her neck.   He drew his right arm across his mouth before he pointed his finger out at Karl.   "You can't fool me. Neither of you. You both are just lying pieces of shit. Sarah's here. She had nowhere else to go." Gerald stood up straight while holding firm on Carolyn. "You tell me where she is, and I'll let your pretty wife here keep her pretty looks. He reached up with his free hand and slowly dragged his fingers through Carolyn's long, blonde hair. He smiled, showing his crooked teeth. Carolyn flipped her head to the side, trying to make him stop. "You wouldn't want anything to happen to your pretty wife now would you?" Gerald asked.

Karl took one more step closer to Gerald and his wife. "Are you drunk, Gerald?" he asked. "You are, aren't you? What the hell are you doing, Gerald; coming into my house drunk like a pig and scaring the shit out of everyone; making demands on me and my wife? You are just a stupid bloody drunk and always have been. If you put one more finger on my wife's hair or body, I will break your God damned neck and beat you down to a pulp, right here, right now! I promise you that! Do you hear me?"

Gerald stared back. He had not expected the response. He also didn't like being called a drunk, but he knew it was true. He remembered the parking lot at Ratskeller's Pub, when he pulled himself up from the snowy ground and stared into the four sets of eyes that challenged him.

Karl took one slow step forward and kept his eyes locked on Gerald's. Gerald shuffled backwards with Carolyn still struggling in his arms, and he stumbled against the coffee table. Carolyn tried to squirm free, but Gerald held on tight as they staggered about. Karl lurched forward as Gerald swayed and tried to regain his balance, and he was suddenly on top of Gerald and Carolyn. The three of them fell sideways into the Christmas tree, and the tree crashed down into the middle of the room. Young Jessie began to scream as he watched the melee from the doorway of the room across the hall.

They thrashed about at each other on top of the fallen tree and presents. Karl pulled his wife free from Gerald's grip and forced himself between them. Suddenly, it was just the two of them. Carolyn crawled out from under Gerald and Karl. She dashed across the room and hugged her distraught and crying son.

Karl was fast and confident. Gerald, in his drunken state, was no match for Karl. Karl turned Gerald over and slugged him once in the face, taking Gerald's fight away immediately. He lifted Gerald out from the fallen tree, manhandled him out the front door and tossed him into the snow on the side of the driveway. He berated Gerald as he rolled about in the snow and tried to stand up. Blood dripped from his nose into the white snow, leaving a crimson trail at every step of his wobbly exit.

Gerald staggered out to the street and cursed himself for not finding Sarah. He looked back towards the house. Karl stood and watched with his arms crossed in front of him as he made sure that Gerald was really leaving. Gerald zigzagged back to the sidewalk and rubbed his arm across his bloody face. He spotted the nodding reindeer once again, stomped angrily up to it and planted his foot swiftly into the reindeer's head as it nodded down one last time. The reindeer would never nod again with its head now mangled and crushed up beneath its underbelly. Gerald forced a grin, and turned back to see Karl glaring at him. He gave Karl the finger and weaved his way across the road to his vehicle while Karl watched from his doorstep utterly disgusted at Gerald's shameful behaviour.

CHAPTER 34

"Ah!" Simon remarked as he set a latte down in front of Sarah. "No cast anymore I see."

Sarah nodded. "I had it taken off two weeks ago. New Year's Eve, actually. Hairy isn't it?" She rubbed the arm over the long dark hair that used to be covered by the cast.

"The hair will go away in a few weeks."

"I hope so," she said as she stared out the front window of the Bistro down upon the snowy cold of Main Street. "I'm thinking about applying for a new job now that I have my cast off."

Simon clasped his hands together. "That's great news. What exactly are you looking for?"

"I'm thinking about applying at the University. They have a counsellor position open."

"Ooh! That would be perfect for you. Delightful!" Simon responded with enthusiasm. Simon and Sarah had become good friends since she moved in, and even though she didn't seen him that often, there was a definite connection between them that began on the very first day they met. It didn't matter that he was effeminate and quirky. Sarah truly cared about the observations and suggestions Simon offered, and she welcomed his feedback and support.

"I think so. The position doesn't start until Fall, if you can believe that. But I can get by until then if I need to."

"You can always help out here if you want," Simon offered. "It wouldn't be full time, but it would be something. You would be helping me, actually."

"Really?" Sarah was surprised by the offer. "I think I'd like that. It would keep my mind off of other things." Sarah continued to stare out along Main Street below.

"By other things, you really mean Gerald."

"You can tell, huh?"

Simon sat down in the seat next to Sarah and stared out the window with her. "You can watch all you want down that street. I see it every time you're in here. He is not out there. And you are not going to see him down there no matter how hard and long you look."

Sarah sighed and knew deep down that Simon was probably right, but she just couldn't help it. Gerald was out there somewhere, and a part of her still felt that Gerald was searching for her. She would be minding her own business doing some everyday task, and she would suddenly hear a sound. A door would slam, a car would suddenly brake or someone would holler in the distance and she would be sure it was Gerald. Her heart would begin to pound hard inside her chest, and she would feel a tremor as she turned to look. But it was never Gerald. As she stared out the window from the Bistro on Main Street below, she always felt safe and secure. She wasn't about to give that up just yet.

"You're probably right," she said.

Simon put his arm over her shoulder and pointed at her. "You, my dear, are going to start work here tomorrow, if just to get your mind off of him."

"Tomorrow? I'm not so sure."

"Tomorrow, and I won't hear another word about it." Simon stood up, bowed gracefully to her and quickly tended to two customers who had just arrived.

CHAPTER 35

Christmas came and went, and the cold winter of January settled in. Bobby and Ricky made numerous visits up to see Tommy and Jason. Ricky had seen Tommy three times since Christmas, but he just couldn't find the words to ask him about what bothered him so much. The talk stayed trivial and always steered clear of the subject that ached in Ricky's mind every day. He found that each time he was face to face with Tommy, he just couldn't broach the subject.

Each time they left the Detention Centre, Bobby could tell Ricky had not asked Tommy about that first visit. Today, he quizzed Ricky on how it went, hoping Ricky had finally gone through with it. Ricky just shrugged and stared out the window.

"So, when are you going to ask him?"

Ricky shrugged again.

"You're just going to make yourself go crazy if you don't get this off your chest."

"Just leave it," Ricky snapped back.

"Look. I'm the one driving you up here every week, and it's my gas. I'm not gonna keep doing this. You have to ask him one of these times."

"I'll pay you for the bloody gas! Just leave me alone!"

Bobby didn't like it when they argued. He knew Ricky was hurting, and it was beginning to show more and more.

"I'm not worried about the gas. I'm just saying, we have been up here three times already. You're going to have to ask him sometime. I can see it's eating you up."

"Just shut up already. I'll ask him when I'm good and ready, okay?"

"You want me to ask him?"

"No!" Ricky shouted and glared at Bobby. "You will say nothing about this! You promised me you'd say nothing. Nobody says anything about this but me! Ever!"

Bobby stared straight ahead and kept his eyes on the road. He could feel Ricky's eyes burn at him. "Okay, okay. I just thought I'd offer. I won't say nothin' to nobody."

The two drove on in silence for a while. Bobby worried about his friend. He wanted to help in any way he could, and believed Ricky knew he would always be there for him, no matter what.

The snow started to fall softly, and Bobby thought about how long it had been since he felt the warmth of the sun. It was cold outside, and it always seemed to Bobby that people became nervous and restless when the cold refused to leave. The cold would burrow its icy roots deep into the valley and leave many thinking it was going to stay forever.

"Is there anything you want me to do then?" Bobby finally asked hoping Ricky would open up.

Ricky said nothing and continued to stare out the window as they drove home through the falling snow. Bobby pondered their friendship. They never used to shout at each other, and it seemed to happen more often lately. Even small talk would cause them to suddenly erupt into a mild disagreement. He didn't like it.

He glanced over to see Ricky still staring out the window. Ricky spun his head towards Bobby and forced a smile. His brow remained furrowed.

"Just... Shut up eh? That's all I really want," Ricky said and lightly punched him on the arm.

Bobby was pleased and returned the smile back with a nod. "Okay, I'll shut it."

Bobby knew Ricky was struggling, but he could also see Ricky rise above the pain that burned inside him. He forced himself to be jovial for Bobby's sake. Bobby wondered if there was some way he could help his troubled friend.

CHAPTER 36

Dean had a lot on his mind as he pulled his police cruiser into the staff parking lot at the high school. He was here just to do a little bit of a background check, that was all. It was about the Oliver murders and, in particular, the whereabouts of Tommy and Jason the afternoon before the murders. As he pulled his car to a stop, he spotted a group of students gathered over in the corner of the student parking lot by the hillside. They were all huddled around one small, beat up four-by-four that was sandwiched in amongst the other vehicles. It was none other than Doogie's Ford Bronco. Now what in blazes was going on over there?

Dean stepped out of his vehicle and tried to discern from across the parking lot who was in the group and what they were doing. He could easily see scrawny Willie Wahnkman and the two usual girls, Patricia Mackie and Sandi Fiestanaugh, who hung out with Willie and Doogie. He knew those two girls well, having cited them with warnings for possession more than once. There were two others girls and one small chubby lad whom he didn't recognize.

He decided he wasn't going to be distracted by this group right now, but he watched for a moment anyway. Sandi pointed with a glove-covered hand towards him and said something to the others. She laughed loudly as he continued to watch the group. Doogie's head suddenly popped up above the group and then disappeared down.

"Oh ya. Something is going on over there," Dean thought to himself. He could see the small plume of smoke rise from the centre of the group.

Dean debated going over to the group to bust them all but quickly decided against it. Doogie's court date for shooting up the sign and for the list of other charges was coming up soon. Nope. It was best to let these things settle themselves out. He knew what headed Doogie's way. Judge Rumpoldt made a point of showing very little tolerance to the wayward youth in town. Maybe one session in front of Judge Rumpoldt would be the lesson Doogie would finally listen to, but that was up to Doogie.

Dean gave a smile and short wave to the group. Patricia was the only one who waved back, and then she ducked her head back inside the scrum and whispered something to Sandi. Dean had seen enough and headed inside.

Bluffington High was typical of any high school with kids crawling everywhere during the noon break. Some leaned against their lockers, and others were scattered about on the floors as they ate their lunches. It was a mad, yet organized, chaos. Dean quickly found himself in the office and, after a few calls by the principal, was directed to the Tommy and Jason's teachers. He quickly discovered both Tommy and Jason abruptly left school upon hearing about Tim's suicide that day, and neither showed up for any classes for the remainder of the day.

It was as Dean suspected. Both boys went to school as usual, but quickly dashed out once they heard the news. Coincidence? Dean doubted it. It was conceivable they texted each other, but that should not have been possible. Cell phones were not allowed in classrooms. No. Each boy must have been upset enough to run out on his own only to arrive at home at the same time and murder both their parents. The odd coincidence bothered him.

Dean learned early on in the investigation that Tim had played Triple A hockey with Tommy and Jason. He had also learned that Tommy's and Jason's dad was the coach of all the boys, and young Tim, a talented hockey player, was getting extra training from Peter Oliver. It didn't fit that anyone with such a dedication to the sport, who was willing to train for an extra hour or more every other night, would be depressed enough to commit suicide. The athletic types were usually well grounded and immune to the taunting of others, or so Dean thought.

The bullying Tim experienced still bothered him a lot, and he wasn't ready to let it rest where it was. His thoughts turned back to the party of teenagers gathered out around Doogie's Ford Bronco. Within the hour, Patricia Mackie sat nervously across from Dean in the counsellor's office. Dean wasn't sure if she was high or not.

"Tell me about Doogie and Willie bullying Tim Guenther."

Patricia shook her head and was clearly uncomfortable. "I don't know anything about any bullying." Patricia was a taut, lean, young girl with jet-black hair. Dean thought she wore too much makeup and could sense her nervousness in the way she sat with one leg crossed over the other. The top leg bounced up and down endlessly.

Dean smiled. "You texted everyone just moments after word spread about Tim's suicide that Doogie and Willie had beat Tim up the night before. Don't tell me you knew nothing about it. Your text is the one that started the entire 'suicide due to bullying' theory."

Patricia started to cry and wiped a tear away with her finger.

"Oh, stop that already," Dean said and offered her a tissue. "You're not in any trouble here, Patricia. I'm just trying to find out more about what happened. So the two of them beat Tim up the night before. Where did this happen, exactly?"

Patricia dabbed at her eyes with the tissue. "Well, it happened just below the hill out in back of the school... in the forest, just off the path that heads back to town. Willie was with Doogie."

Dean nodded. "Go on."

"Doogie just said they had Tim on the ground and they were teasing him. Trying to get him to say something."

"What were they trying to get him to say?"

Patricia stopped bouncing her leg. "Just that he was a faggot. They wanted him to say "*I am a faggot,*" but Tim wouldn't. When he wouldn't, they pushed him down and shoved dirt in his face."

"Uh huh. What else?"

"Nothing really. Just that they kept doing it to Tim. They kept shoving dirt in his face and mouth trying to get him to say it but he wouldn't say it. Ask Willie. He was there too. They shoved him around for a while and then left and headed up to the arcade in town."

"Okay. So Tim wouldn't say it. Then why did they let him go if he wouldn't say it? That doesn't sound like the Doogie I know."

Patricia shifted suddenly with that question and looked away to the floor. Dean could see the wheels turn inside Patricia's brain. She didn't answer.

"Listen Patricia. I'm going to be asking Sandi the same questions. She's sitting in the other room across the hall right now. Your story and hers had better line up. So tell me. Why did they stop bullying him and let him go?"

"I'm not supposed to say," she said and fidgeted with the tissue.

Dean was surprised. He didn't expect such a response. "Who said you're not supposed to say?"

Patricia continued to stare down at the floor. She offered no reply.

"Doogie told you to not say anything. Am I right?"

Patricia nodded.

"And Doogie said to not say anything because..."

Patricia looked up at Dean. "Because Doogie got his face punched in really bad and Doogie doesn't like getting punched by anyone. His bottom lip was split open. He didn't want anyone to know who did it and told us to keep quiet about it."

Dean leaned back in his chair and crossed his arms. He was pleased with the revelation. "So, Tim punched Doogie and split his lip," he replied, nodding.

Patricia shook her head. "No, no! Not Tim. It was Jason Oliver that busted Doogie's lip open."

Dean stared back at Patricia. And there it was. The connection. "Jason Oliver?"

"Uh huh. Doogie said he was kneeling on Tim's back shoving dirt in Tim's face when Jason came out of nowhere and jumped him, punching him in the face and splitting his lip open. Doogie was really upset because Jason blindsided him. He said he didn't see Jason coming at all. The two fought for a bit and that was it."

Dean was still shocked. "Jason Oliver? You're sure it was Jason? Not his brother Tommy?"

"It was Jason. The cute one."

Dean smiled. "The cute one," he repeated. "You like him, don't you?"

Patricia looked up at Dean. "He's okay. Tommy's too much of a jock. Jason's... well, Jason is different. He's kind of shy, and I like the way he peeks out behind his long hair." She smiled briefly.

Dean was pleased with this talk. A lot of new information came out. "So Jason came up on Doogie and Willie beating up Tim. Jason jumps Doogie and busts his lip. The two fight and then Doogie and Willie leave."

"That's what Doogie told me."

Dean thought about his earlier interrogation of both Willie and Doogie, and neither mentioned Jason.

"And Sandi's going to tell me the same story?"

Patricia nodded. "I'm sure she will. She was there when Doogie told me. Willie was there too."

Dean was pleased. There was more to this than he originally thought.

"Okay Patricia. I am going to go speak with Sandi now. I'll be back after I'm done talking to her."

Dean interviewed Sandi, and, after a bit of dancing around the facts, she told Dean the same story. He released both girls back to class and left the school a bit more puzzled over both Tim's suicide and the Oliver murders. There was a connection. Dean now had to figure out what that connection meant, and what it had to do with the murders.

CHAPTER 37

A small group of eight sat in a circle inside Room 116 of the Spy Hill Correctional Centre for Young Offenders. Jason sat uncomfortably in the middle of the group. Three youths sat on each side of him, and the counsellor, Marilyn Sanderson, sat opposite. It was the first session that Jason was asked to lead, and he looked to Marilyn for direction on how to proceed.

"Okay everyone. As you all know, you are each required to participate in these group sessions during your stay here. Today we are joined by Jason Oliver. Jason has been staying here for many months and has offered to help lead these sessions. You all know the rules: Anyone can say anything they want, and I mean *anything*. Once a person has the floor, he is allowed to speak until finished. You can ask questions if you want, or add any comment, but remember there is to be no physical contact or aggression. I ask that you all please remain seated during these sessions."

Marilyn looked about the room of youngsters and could see the discomfort across many faces.

"You don't have to say anything if you don't want to, but you cannot leave until the session is over," Marilyn added and looked about the group once more. "Does anyone have any questions?"

A few shook their heads but most remained still with downcast eyes. They clearly wanting to be anywhere else than in this room.

"Okay then, I'm going to open up the floor to Jason. Jason, you can start."

Jason felt the blood rush to his head and make him dizzy, but he knew it was his time to speak. He brushed his dark bangs out of his eyes and began.

"Uh, hi everyone. My name is Jason Oliver and I've been locked up here for a long time now." He looked around and saw many eyes were now hooked on his. "I guess I'm supposed to talk here about things that you guys can all relate to, but since I don't know any of you, I'm not sure how this is going to go." He forced a smile and snickered nervously, but no one reacted or smiled back. Jason continued. "I'm in here because my brother and I killed our parents in the fall," he said and raised his arms to gestured out to the surrounding walls. "We're both here waiting for the trial, and I know that we will be convicted and be sent away for a long time. We're just trying to get by. Just trying to get through each day. It's not so bad in here, really."

"You killed your parents?" asked a pint-sized, wiry, young kid with a pale complexion and serious acne. He looked like he was about twelve but was actually sixteen.

Jason nodded, "Uh huh. But I'm not going to talk about it at all, so don't ask."

The pock-marked boy, Maurice, leaned back in his chair and looked at the others in the group before he prodded Jason immediately with another question. "Why'd you kill them?"

"I just told you, I am not going to talk about it."

"Jesus, fuck. And I thought I was a bad shit," Maurice said. He smirked and ran his hand backwards through his wavy, blonde hair.

"Anyway, I wanted to say things aren't so bad in here. They treat you well. The food is not so bad and there are lots of things to do. I liked school before landing myself in here, and they have a great program for self-learning." Jason could see he had all of their attention now, but he knew it was because of the murders and not the content of his speech.

"I want to hear more about you and your parents... Jason, isn't it?" Maurice asked.

"It's Jason, but..."

"How bad did you have to hate your parents to kill them? And how'd you do it anyway? Fuck, I hate my parents too, but Jesus... To kill them?"

"I didn't hate my parents. And I said I'm not talking about it." He looked at Marilyn for some direction, but she gave none and continued to watch the group in silence.

"I don't believe you," Maurice replied and smiled while he shook his head. "I'm in here because my effin parents put me in here. I fucking hate them, but I ain't gonna kill them."

Some of the others in the group reacted to the debate. Some smiled, and others simply looked back and forth between Jason and Maurice.

"You're in here because of what you did, not because of your parents. Just like I'm in here because of what I did," Jason retorted.

"What the fuck do you know about me?" Maurice responded, very agitated.

Jason understood more about Maurice than he thought. He could see the arrogance instantly. Maurice was just like all of the other Doogie's in the world who blamed everything that happened to them on others and took no responsibility for themselves when things went wrong.

"I just know that you did something, and you got caught. That's why you're here."

Maurice glared at Jason.

"You got caught, Maurice. I'll tell you now, that's why I'm in here. I did something very wrong and I got caught. I miss my parents every single day. You're lucky you still have yours." Jason looked about the group, and he could see curiosity in all their eyes as they stared back at him. "How about you?" Jason asked as he pointed at a tall, husky, native boy. "What did you do to get in here? Drugs? Breaking and entering? What was it?"

The native boy grimaced at being singled out. He shook his head, clearly uncomfortable about being expected to speak, and said nothing.

"Look. We are all in here for a reason. I killed my parents, and that's why I'm here. Each one of you did something to get in here. It wasn't your parent's or your best friend's fault. It wasn't your brother's or sister's or some stranger's fault. You all did something to end up here. You made your choice. It was probably a bad one, and that's why you are in here with me now. My choice was very wrong, and I'd take it back if I could, but there's nothing I can do about it now. I will be convicted of what I did. I'll miss my parents forever and don't know if I'll ever be able to forgive myself. To never see my parents again? That's my real punishment. I accept that. I have to. I don't know what the rest of you did, but maybe you'll be out of here in a few weeks and stand in front of the judge or your lawyer will cop a plea. Maybe you'll just get a warning or some community service. Whatever way, you are here because you got caught doing something, and you will have to pay the price for what you did."

The boy next to Marilyn raised his hand to get Jason's attention.

"I'm here caus' I got caught liftin' again. Knew't was wrong but..."

Another boy to his left spoke without lifting his eyes from the ground. "I'm in here because of drugs."

The group suddenly came alive, and many offered a piece of their story to the group. A few opted to say nothing, but most at least offered up the reason why they now sat in this cold, uncomfortable room. Jason continued to lead. He answered and commented on what was said by the others. He liked being the centre of attention for once, but it felt very strange to be talking this way to strangers.

Tommy, Jason recalled, was always the leader in any group. It didn't matter where or when, but he always seemed to be the one to rise above. Jason felt surprised when he recognized that he was the one to lead this time.

After the session ended, Marilyn praised Jason for how well he led the group. She said he showed compassion for the inner turmoil that brewed under the surface of many in the group. It was a great experience for him. Jason had no idea coming into the session how he would ever find his way through to the end, but he did. He wished it hadn't had to end. He found himself engaging with each of the other boys' stories. This was another outlet to pass the time away, and he looked forward to the next session. He couldn't wait to tell Tommy all about it as he knew Tommy would also be leading his own group sessions.

CHAPTER 38

Gerald pulled into his driveway and spotted Aaron Phelps dash around the far side of the snow-covered house next door. Gerald had half a mind to go over and bust the kid another bloody nose, but he knew better. Weeks had passed since he left Aaron bleeding on the driveway next-door, and many things happened to Gerald since. He now had a court date for assaulting the boy because the police arrived early the next morning and dragged him down to the station for a long, face-to-face interrogation. His face was still swollen from the fight with Karl, and he was still a bit drunk when they took him to the station. Many hours passed, charges were filed and a court date was set. Gerald was ordered to keep away from the family next door or he would be incarcerated immediately. Gerald knew he had to take this seriously.

Gerald shovelled his walk and driveway before he went into his house. To anyone who watched him, it appeared he had finally started moving forward without Sarah. She had now been gone for months, and he set himself on a track back into what seemed like a normal routine. He kept his walk free of snow, was at work every day and had not had missed or arrived late, but deep inside Gerald still stewed. Gerald liked to control people. Even his periodic drunken behaviour was a tool to control people. When he chose to miss work or arrive late, he controlled his boss and co-workers. His employers tolerated Gerald only because he was good at what he did, and a talented and experienced construction lead was hard to find.

The world was a bad-ass place, and everyone just wanted a piece of him, or so it seemed to Gerald. He didn't realize, nor would he ever admit, that he affected so many people in such a negative way. His co-workers tormented him when he was late, and his boss threatened to fire him many times, but Gerald was used to it. It was all just a bunch of bull, and he expected nothing more.

Gerald had not given up on finding Sarah, but he began to change his ways. He hadn't been on a drinking binge for nearly two weeks. He still drank a few beers on the way home each night, but he didn't overdo it. Gerald certainly had not let go of Sarah; she remained front and centre in his mind. The episode with Carolyn and Karl was the tipping point, and Gerald recognized it. He was dangerously close to losing everything he lived for, and if he crossed over that line, there would be no chance for him with Sarah. It was all about Sarah. The hate still churned deep inside, and the anger refused to settle. Gerald thought he had it under control. He was going to find her, and no matter how angry he was along the way, he swore he would keep it under control until Sarah was once again where she belonged.

Gerald's rage had not abated; it had brewed a new beast inside him. The hate was channeled and ready to be released on anyone who provoked the beast inside him. Through all those years with Sarah, he often berated her, shouted at her and slapped her, but he never beat Sarah before like he had that night. With that one event, Gerald opened the door to darker things... things he never even knew he was capable of. First it was Dustin Toomey, then Aaron Phelps and then Sarah's sister.

It was only a matter of time before Gerald found out how dark and evil he really was and what awful horror he was capable of.

CHAPTER 39

The rich aroma of freshly ground coffee filled the small Bistro on the hillside above Main Street. Sarah sat at the window in her usual spot as she waited for Simon to finish his prep in the kitchen and open the front doors for another day's business.

Sarah stared down the street, cupped her coffee gently between her fingers and brought it to her lips for a small sip. The day was fresh and awash with sunlight as it danced about in the valley below the bistro. She watched the street come alive again as the businesses opened up one by one, and the sidewalks began to fill with activity. She watched the people down on Main Street avidly when Simon came out from the back and got ready to open the front door.

"Great news, I hear," he said cheerfully to Sarah as he walked by.

"Thanks," Sarah said back. She knew Simon was referring her job offer as a counsellor at the University. She accepted the offer and looked forward to working full-time again.

Simon unlocked the front door and turned on the "OPEN" neon sign. "I just knew you'd get the job. You have so much to offer. You're just like a big wad of double bubble and I just want to chew you up!"

Sarah turned to him and giggled. He was so funny all the time and made her laugh. "I am happy about it. I think I told you that I don't have to wait until the fall semester to start? They want me sooner."

Simon stopped in front of her, clasped his hands together at his waist and pursed his lips into a short pout. "Sooner? Does that mean you're leaving me early?" he asked. "You just started here, and I'd shatter if you ran away so quick. It's like you were suddenly dropped from heaven into my midst, and I'd really be shot if you weren't around anymore."

"Oh, Simon," She replied sincerely. "Of course I'm not leaving right away. I could hardly do that. You've been so good to me, and you're probably the only friend I have around here."

"Oh?" Simon responded somewhat surprised but delighted. "What about your friend Brandy? You see her often don't you?"

"Brandy lives in Calgary. She's a good friend and she's been down every other weekend, but it's just not the same, Simon."

"Not the same?" he asked confused. "I'm not following."

She smiled at him again. "Not the same as having someone like you next door all the time. I really like it here. You make me comfortable."

Simon blushed. "You really are delicious." He grabbed her hand and gave it a quick peck. "I'll always be here when you need a friend. Honestly, deary. You need anything, you just ask."

Sarah almost began to cry and nodded. "Thank you, Simon."

Simon disappeared into the kitchen. Sarah stared back out the window at the rooftops of the university in the distance. She was ready to start over and knew the next step was to search for a permanent place to live. Leaving the apartment next to Simon would be difficult, but she really needed to plant permanent roots. She needed to see a realtor and check out properties for sale in the area.

CHAPTER 40

Winter slowly turned into Spring, and Sarah viewed many houses. She finally settled on what she thought was the perfect one, just blocks away from the University and her new job. Simon was pleased and offered to help her move in. The two became very close as they worked side by side at the Bistro. Sarah would miss Simon and his strange ways dearly, but she knew that after she purchased this house and started the new job she would be well on her way to recovery. She promised to keep Simon close and knew she could always rely on him if things ever got tough.

Tommy and Jason each began to bloom in a different way inside of Spy Hill. They both loved leading the group counselling sessions, and the counsellors and staff enjoyed the boy's participation—particularly their enthusiasm and positive attitudes. It became obvious to all that Tommy and Jason were of a different breed than the usual parade of boys detained at Spy Hill. They were incredibly smart and well-socialized individuals. It was difficult for anyone who interacted daily with either of them to believe they could have committed any kind of serious crime. It was especially challenging once the nature of the crime became evident. There was talk of their trial date being set for sometime in early summer. The boys seemed indifferent to any talk or news of the trial and kept their focus on their studies and athletics.

Gerald continued on his own path as the spring thaw arrived in Calgary. He had not given up on his search for Sarah. His anger would periodically erupt, and he would inflict his violent rage upon whomever happened to be in proximity. But given a couple of days of recovery, Gerald would come back to reason and find his self-control. He had eyes for no other woman, and he believed deeply that Sarah would show herself somewhere, sometime. Gerald waited as patiently as he was able. In the meantime, he kept watch.

Back in Bluffington, Dean couldn't find any meaningful connection between the suicide of Tim and the murder of the Olivers. As the winter months slowly ebbed and the signs of spring were budding everywhere, Dean found himself still frustrated without progress on what he thought was the key to answering a number of unexplained questions. The failure to corral the Gardner murderer from last year still bothered him considerably, and to solve this piece of the puzzle in the Oliver murders was tantamount in Dean's mind to forgiveness from the town for that previous fault. He hated that the previous murder went officially unsolved, and he was to blame. He really didn't want the Oliver murders left with any unanswered questions to provide another mark on his record.

There was one good thing Dean saw as the seasons changed. The bad boy, Doogie, finally appeared in court to face the charges from shooting up the speed sign on Black Pond Road. Dean stood silent in the back of the courtroom as Judge Rumpoldt laid out the punishment on Doogie. He was to be detained for a period to reflect on his careless and thoughtless actions. Doogie's mouth dropped open in disbelief. He only expected a small number of community service hours at worst. Doogie was quickly detained and led away by two Officers of the Court. He was to be taken directly up to the Spy Hill Correctional Centre for Young Offenders where he would be incarcerated for a period of no fewer than thirty days. Doogie spotted Dean in the back of the courtroom as he was led away. He screamed obscenities at him and promised him a very manly, face-to-face meeting when he finally got out. Dean just smiled, puffed out his chest and listened to Doogie's empty rant. He was pleased that he had improved the lives of a few citizens of Bluffington for at least a number of weeks with the absence of Doggie.

CHAPTER 41

Bobby sat on the edge of his bed and watched as Ricky tried his best at the Zombie game. He rubbed his leg as Ricky's man ran out of life, and Ricky tossed the game controller across the room in frustration. He began to rant about how tough he found math class this semester. It was only recently that Ricky had begun to struggle at school, and in the past few weeks, he had started to complain and whine about how difficult everything had suddenly become for him.

Bobby slid off the bed, picked up the controller and inspected it for damage. "Why don't you just study more, if you're sucking so bad in math?"

"Study more? I can't focus is the problem. I try to study, but my mind drifts, the numbers start to look all fuzzy and then I don't even know what I'm looking at."

Bobby shrugged and stared at the TV. He tested the controller buttons to make sure they all still worked.

"I used to be real good at math, and now it's just so damned hard," Ricky said.

"Sucks not getting an 'A' doesn't it?" Bobby said and smiled back. Bobby was an average student. The best mark he had ever achieved was a "B".

"It's not funny. I just can't get into it this semester. And it's not just math."

Bobby sat back down on the bed and rubbed his leg again. He was getting tired of Ricky's constant whining these past few days. He stole a glance at Ricky and wondered how much of this was really just the aftermath of what Ricky had been through.

"So?" Ricky asked.

"So what?" Bobby asked back, not sure what Ricky expected from him.

"Jesus, Bobby! My dad is still pissed at me for quitting hockey and now my grades are falling. I'm scared to even see him. The mid-term report card comes out soon and my dad's gonna be even more pissed at me."

"What do you want me to do? You're a grade ahead of me. And your grades are way better than what I ever get."

"Well your mom doesn't care about your grades like my dad does."

Bobby took offence at the comment. "My mom cares a lot about me and my grades. She just doesn't get angry like your dad."

"You don't get it. My dad expects a lot, and I really disappointed him when I quit hockey. And I'm doing it again with my grades. I'm just one big fucking disappointment to everyone!"

Bobby let out a big sigh of frustration. He didn't want to be bogged down by heavy, depressing conversations. He knew what depression was all about because of all he went through with his leg braces. He just wanted Ricky to stop with the negativity. It brought Bobby down with him.

"You're not a disappointment. Your dad just doesn't know you. He'll get over it in time."

"I don't think so. Jesus, I really don't. I guess I'm just fucked up, and I just don't know what to do."

Bobby could see that Ricky was trying very hard not to cry. Bobby had thought about this day for some time. He expected Ricky was either going to get over what happened to him or it was going to eat away and slowly tear him apart. Ricky's cracks were now starting to show.

"You still didn't talked to Tommy about what he asked you about his dad, did you?"

Ricky put his head down. "No, I couldn't ask him about it."

"Jesus! And you wonder why you're acting like you are! Just wait here a minute. I'm getting real tired of all this!" Bobby stormed out of the room with a wobble in his gait from his gimp leg.

Ricky frowned. He was upset that Bobby was angry at him.

Bobby returned carrying two of the leg braces he wore as a child. He dropped them down on the floor in front of Ricky.

"Listen!" he shouted. "I've been listening to you moan about everything day after day. I can't stand it anymore, and you're starting to bring me down too. There's nothing I can do for you!" He sat down and rubbed his leg furiously as he continued to speak. "I can't help you with what's going on. You're gonna have to do this yourself!"

Ricky looked down at the two steel braces. "What am I supposed to do with these?"

"Listen! You've known me for how long now, Ricky?"

"I don't know, maybe six years."

"Exactly! And when you met me, I was wearing those exact braces."

Ricky kept his stare locked on the braces. They were made of stainless steel with multiple pins that protruded inwards with levers and screws on the outside to drive the pins deep into the bones of Bobby's legs. The braces appeared to be more of a device of torture than a medical aide.

"Do you remember when you first met me? I could barely stand up, let alone walk."

"Uh huh, I remember."

"Bionic boy, metal boy, kid curious, Bobby Bracey, Pogo Bobby: I heard it all! I remember every name I was ever called. I hated every day of my life for a time. I had to visit the doctors. You do not know how much it hurt each time I had to go and have the screws tightened in to twist or stretch my legs."

Ricky picked up one of the braces and ran his fingers over a few of the pins. He twisted his head to the side as he looked back at Bobby. He was trying to understand Bobby's point.

"Do you remember me whining or crying? No! I wanted to every single day, but I didn't. Each week it hurt more than the week before. I always hoped that the next week would be better, but it never was. I'd go home each night after the screws were tightened, and I'd cry myself to sleep because of the pain. Just when the pain would ease up a few weeks later, I'd have to go back and have them turned again, bringing back more agony. After many months, I began to accept that the pain was going to be there forever. It hurt so fricking bad. I cried every night."

"And you're telling me this, why?" Ricky asked.

"The pain stayed, Ricky. The pain hurt, and each week it was the same damn pain. And I was letting it happen. Did I believe it was even helping? I'd be lying if I said I did, but I still went to the doctor each week voluntarily. I didn't have to go. I could have kicked up a fuss and screamed and hollered and fought not to go, and I'm sure my mom would have finally backed off and not taken me. But where would I be now if I had done that? I didn't know it then but it was probably the hardest thing I will ever do. I can't even really remember how much pain I had to endure all of those years. Maybe that's why I keep those braces. I had four different sets over the years, but I keep that one set as a reminder to myself if things ever got tough."

"I see," Ricky replied still holding the brace.

"Well, right now things are tough. I can't sit here listening to you talk like you are. You need to get your ass up to Tommy and ask him what you need to ask him. Do you get me?"

Ricky lifted the brace into the air in front of him, and studied all of the pins and turn screws. He nodded at Bobby. "You're right."

"Of course I'm right, you dumb shit!"

Ricky cracked a smile. He laid Bobby's brace onto his lap and nodded again and wiped away at his eyes to keep himself from crying.

"You're right," Ricky said again. "It hurts."

"I know it does, man. I know. But you need to talk it out."

Ricky nodded again. "Talk it out," he repeated. He looked at Bobby, and Bobby could see that Ricky really feared having to face Tommy with questions about Tommy's dad.

"Yeah, talk it out." Bobby moved over and put his arm on his friend's shoulder. "I'll take you. I wish they'd let two of us visit at a time so I could be with you the whole time."

"No, it's alright. I think I need to do this on my own," he said, but Bobby wasn't sure he believed Ricky was up to it just yet.

"But I will still be the one that takes you up there."

"Damn right you will," Ricky said and smiled.

CHAPTER 42

Sarah sat at the window inside the Bistro at her usual spot and listened to Simon go on about his flowerbeds.

"Oh, I've waited long enough. If he thinks he's done and is going to get away with it like this, I'm sorry, because I just won't have it," Simon uttered. He was distraught over Jens response to having finished the repairs to his flowerbed damaged by the cattle.

"But I thought he fixed it months ago," Sarah responded.

"Fixed it? Fixed it? All that Jens did was have his guys come over and spread some dirt over the hoof marks in the lawn and flowerbeds before the snow came down. It looks utterly terrible now that the snow has receded. All lumpy and bumpy. Oooh!"

"I'm so sorry, Simon."

"And he says that's how it was before the cows got in. I am so angry right now."

Sarah wanted to snicker, but she knew how important the garden was to Simon. "So what's your plan?"

"My plan is to see Jens make good on this, that's my plan. Why should my poor plants and lawn have to suffer from the likes of him?"

"That really doesn't sound like a plan."

Simon stopped his prancing about and pointed at Sarah. "Don't you go getting nasty at me."

Sarah laughed. "I'm not getting nasty. I'm just wondering how you can make that Jens guy do anything. It seems he's just trying to provoke you at every chance he gets."

"Well he's doing a smash-darn good job at it, I'd say. I'm provoked, I'm irritated and I'm darn angry, and I won't let him get away with it."

"Well, I wish I could help you. I really do."

"I know you do. And I love you, darling, for caring. But you have your own things to deal with now: the new house and all."

Sarah agreed she had a lot to do with possession of her new home only weeks away, but Simon was a good man, and she wasn't about to let her new life stop her from keeping him close as a friend.

"The new house is all nearly sorted. If there's anything I can help with out at your property, I would be glad to spend some time doing so. I really don't mind getting dirty. Maybe you and I can fix the lawn up ourselves."

Simon moved closer, surprised by such an offer. "You'd do that? Come over and get dirty in the flower beds? Really? I never took you to be an earthy girl."

"Oh, I can be earthy. Just watch me. I'd like nothing better than to get my hands in the dirt with you."

Simon nearly swooned with her response. "Oh! You are a dirty girl," he replied and laughed. Sarah laughed with him. She was pleased that she had such a friend so close.

CHAPTER 43

Ricky sat in the visitor's room and waited for Tommy to enter. He rubbed his hands together and questioned whether he was going to be able to really open up and talk to Tommy this time. This was a big deal, and Ricky had no idea where to start the conversation. How much did Tommy know? Did Tommy really want to hear the sordid details of what went on in the small building in his own back yard? Did he really want to hear what took place so close to where he laid his head each night, all those years?

Ricky almost considered leaving, but Tommy was let into the room right as he shifted to stand.

Tommy lifted his hand and waved. "Ricky. Good to see you again. It's been a while."

Ricky nodded. "It has. Too long."

"Yeah. Been too long in here as well. School's almost out. Maybe once you've graduated you can come up more often?" Tommy asked pleasantly.

Ricky shrugged.

"I'll be graduating inside this place."

"In here? How?"

"Correspondence courses. I'll be done next week."

"Oh, of course. I see," Ricky replied disinterested.

"So what brings you up?"

Ricky studied Tommy's disposition. He looked comfortable, relaxed and almost happy. Ricky fidgeted some more and shuffled in his chair before he spoke. "Listen, Tommy. We really need to talk."

Tommy tensed up and nodded without speaking. He sat down opposite Ricky. "Is this about what you asked me a few months back?" he asked hesitantly.

"You mean, what you asked me. You do remember what you asked me don't you?"

"Oh," Tommy said and began to feel very uncomfortable. He cast his eyes downward.

"You asked me if your dad took videos of me."

Tommy looked back up, and Ricky could see that Tommy would rather not discuss this topic.

"Well he did, Tommy. He always did. The camera was always going every time anyone went in that back office. I know that *is* what you wanted to hear, isn't it?"

Tommy still said nothing and looked away, deep in his own thoughts. Tommy's distance disturbed Ricky.

"Aren't you going to say anything?" Ricky asked.

Tommy's demeanour became very serious, and he stared straight into Ricky's eyes. "I'm not sure what to say. I'm not even sure why I asked you that the first time."

"Bullshit!" Ricky shouted back. "You asked me that for a reason, and I want to know what it is. I've been thinking about why you asked me that question for months now. I came up here every single time since then wanting to ask you, but I was afraid of what the answer might be. I think you know what I'm talking about. So tell me the truth Tommy, why did you ask me that?"

Tommy shook his head despondent. "I can't."

"What? You can't? I've been going absolutely ape-shit crazy thinking about nothing else for months. It's been swallowing me up, and I don't know how much more I can take."

"It's probably best if we both just leave it alone," Tommy said.

"I'm not leaving anything alone today. It was *your* dad, in *your* house, doing these awful things to me. If there's anything else you know, then you gotta tell me, Tommy. You just have to." Ricky wiped his eyes as they began to fill with tears.

Tommy pushed his chair back from the table and stood up. He paced back and forth a few times and glanced at Ricky off and on, deeply distressed, before he finally sat back down at the table.

"Listen, Ricky," he said. The discomfort and pain was etched deep in his eyes. "What I have to say is horrible, and I'm not sure if I can even let it out."

"You have to. I need to know whatever you know. Please!"

Tommy wavered a bit more, put his head down into his hands on the table and groaned.

"C'mon, Tommy," Ricky prodded.

Tommy lifted his head back up. "No one knows this but me, okay? Jason doesn't even know what I am about to tell you, and he was there."

"Go on."

"It's more horrible than anything I could ever dream up. I just don't know if I should say it. It's something that's so bloody terrible..."

"Say it! Dammit, Tommy! Just fricking tell me!"

Tommy took a deep breath and let it out. "There are recordings of what he did. And I know where they are."

Ricky's mouth dropped open. It was what he suspected but hoped he wouldn't hear.

"I don't know how many, but there are recordings of others besides you," Tommy added.

"Who else?"

"Who else," Tommy repeated and nervousness fell over his face. His eyes became cold and stoic and danced about the room. "Tim for one," he said.

"Tim?" Ricky was suddenly furious. "You knew about this? And you did nothing?" he shouted.

"No! No!" Tommy shouted back and raised his hands in the air. "I didn't find out about the recordings until after Tim was already dead. Honest."

Tommy then revealed to Ricky the horrid story of what happened the day of Tim's suicide. He went over every detail and left out nothing. He remained calm and expressionless, as he recapped all of the events to Ricky. He was careful to separate all emotion from the acts he and Jason committed. By the time he finished, Ricky knew all of the events that led up to the death of Tommy's parents and the discovery of the secret room tucked in behind the fireplace where all the recordings remained.

When Tommy was done, he simply stopped talking. Ricky stared at him in angst, and revulsion spread across his face. Ricky turned himself away as tears crawled down his face. He couldn't bring himself to look at Tommy. He didn't know what to do, so for the moment he removed himself from the table and walked about the room to collect his thoughts.

He finally sat back down and wiped his eyes. "So there are recordings of me floating around out there? Damn it, Tommy! Damn it!" He wanted to reach over and slug Tommy, but he knew it wasn't his fault. "What if someone finds them? No one can see them!"

"No one can find them. They're all hidden away in the house."

"You don't know that! Someone might have already found them! Shit Tommy! Shit! Shit! Shit! I'll die if anyone finds them."

"No one is going to. No one knows that hiding place is even there."

"There've been all kinds of people going through that house. It's been up for sale for weeks now. Maybe somebody already found them."

Tommy tried to reach out to Ricky, but Ricky pulled himself away.

"I gotta find them!"

"You can't. The house is all locked up, and there's a security system throughout the house. You won't get in. You and I are the only two who know that room even exists," he said. "Well, Jason too, but he doesn't know about the recordings inside."

"What the hell am I supposed to do then?"

Tommy shrugged. "Do nothing. It's all safe and no one's going to find out."

"I can't just do nothing. As long as those recordings are out there, I won't be able to think of anything else. Shit, Tommy. There must be a way I can get in."

Tommy shook his head from side to side. "No way."

"You have a password! I can use your password!"

"It won't work without a key to the front or back door. The alarm is triggered upon opening the door and you have thirty seconds to disable it, and I don't have a key anymore."

"I'll break a window."

"Same thing. If the front door is not opened with the key and an intruder enters through one of the alarmed windows an alarm is triggered immediately. You'd have to magically pop yourself inside the house without opening any of the doors or windows, and then you'd be able to turn off the alarm. No way in Ricky."

Ricky objected, but he finally agreed to let it rest. He walked out of Spy Hill extremely distraught and promised

Tommy that he would be back up soon. Something had to be done about those recordings.

CHAPTER 44

Jason walked quickly down the hall towards therapy room 117. He looked forward to leading another group session. He felt his self-confidence had grown from having to put himself out front. When he was younger, he would always watch Tommy before he made up his mind about things. He looked up to his big brother and found himself constantly asking himself, "What would Tommy do?" The hesitation and internal query had slowly started to change inside him with the therapy sessions. Interacting with the new boys made him feel like he was respected in his position in the group and that his opinion mattered. Sometimes a few of the boys would lash out at Jason or mock him as he talked, but Jason never saw it as a personal attack. Jason concluded that these boys were simply hiding behind the protective attitudes they wore like shields, and he learned how to respond to them.

Jason's enthusiasm for today's session suddenly diminished when he entered the room and looked at the six boys who were ready to participate. Two of them were new inmates, but one of the new boys caught him completely off guard. It was none other than his nightmare from high school, Doug Fisher, or Doogie. The last time he saw Doogie, he had bust Doogie's lip open in defence of his friend Tim. A long suppressed anger rose in his belly, and he could feel his face flush as he looked at Doogie. He quickly turned away and acknowledged Marilyn with a smile and a nod, and then took his seat amongst the group.

Marilyn quickly went through the usual preamble and released the group to Jason. Jason swallowed hard. He knew this was going to be a difficult session. He glanced over at Doogie to see him grinning and nodding his head as if he was ready to speak.

"Uh, hi everyone. If you don't know me, my name is Jason, and I'm here to lead today's session."

"Well I'll be damned, Jason!" Doogie blurted out. He kept on grinning and followed up with a short laugh. "I thought yous were locked up in some dark pit somewhere."

"I'm right here, just like you are." Not to be bested by Doogie's attempt to control the room, Jason quickly responded with his own demonstrative attitude. "Your lip is looking better than the last time I saw you."

Doogie lurched in his chair; fury etched itself deep into his face. He thrust his finger out towards Jason. "Yous better watch yourself Oliver. Remember what I promised yous last time."

Jason smiled, turned to the rest of the group and responded in a calm, controlled voice. "What Doogie's referring to is a little scrap we had last time I saw him. I actually know Doogie quite well. We went to the same high school. Bust him a split lip the last time we met." He looked over and grinned at Doogie. The rest of the group looked over at Doogie with a bit of awe for Jason's boldness.

"Fuck yous, Jason!" Doogie shouted. He stood up, moved a step towards Jason and clenched his fists. "This is a pretty small building. Not too many places to hide in here."

"Okay everyone!" Marilyn interjected loudly. She would normally let the group talk but sensed the danger of a serious escalation. She stood up and pointed to Doogie's chair. "Remember there is no violence allowed during these sessions. I warn you now that the aggression you are exhibiting will NOT be tolerated. Please sit back down, Doug.

"It's Doogie!"

"Okay, Doogie, if you wish. This is a session for open discussion, but it must remain controlled. You may feel emotional but you cannot act out aggressively according to how you feel." She looked about the group. "Do you all understand? Being here is a privilege, not a punishment. If you will not control yourself, you will be removed, and you will not get credit for being here today. Let's all take a deep breath, sit back and move on in an organized fashion."

The group turned towards her, and one by one nodded. Doogie reluctantly did the same and sat back down. He continued to stare Jason down, visibly infuriated.

"Jason, please continue," Marilyn commanded.

Jason proceeded to lead the group as he would in any other session and simply ignored Doogie and any comment made by Doogie for the rest of the session. Doogie attempted to derail Jason's authority in the group, but even though some comments struck deep inside Jason, he refused to react and didn't let his emotions cause him to respond to Doogie's outbursts. His control, although somewhat weakened by not responding to Doogie's outbursts, soon filtered throughout the room where many of the boys responded to Jason's direction in a positive way. With Doogie, it became a silent war of implied commentary between them. Jason won handily with the support of the group... this time.

CHAPTER 45

Bobby and Rickey were nearly back to Bluffington before Ricky gave up any hint of what happened inside Spy Hill with Tommy. Bobby could see Ricky was terribly upset when he got in the car and knew immediately that Ricky had finally asked what he needed to ask Tommy.

It was a silent drive of forty-five minutes before Ricky let out a huge sigh and began to speak, but his voice came out in a high squeak from the emotional strain. He stopped and started over, but a quiver in his voice remained. "It's not very good, Bobby."

Bobby only nodded and let Ricky say what he needed to say.

"I asked him. I really did ask him this time." He wiped his nose on the back of his sleeve and stared off into the distance out the window.

"Uh huh," Bobby replied.

"It's not very good," he repeated. "I really don't know what to do now."

Bobby sensed the huge burden Ricky now carried. "Is it okay if I ask what Tommy said?"

Ricky remained silent and continued to stare out the window for another kilometer of open highway. They were on the country road just outside of Bluffington. The leaves were beginning to bud on many of the trees creating a soft dust-like coat of green within the grey forest of denuded branches. It was a promise that the rebirth of another cycle of summer was on its way.

"There are tapes. Or maybe not tapes, but recordings of some kind. CDs maybe. I don't know."

"Oh," was all Bobby could offer back.

"Tommy told me where they are."

"The recordings are of you in the… uh..."

"Yes. Recordings of me. Tommy told me there are others too. Tim was one of them."

Bobby was uncomfortable now. Things had suddenly changed a lot. It seemed this story could never just go away, and only continued to simply get worse. "That explains a lot."

"It does, doesn't it."

"Where are the recordings?"

Ricky let out a snicker. "Right in Tommy's old house, just four doors down the road from yours, believe it or not."

"What? I thought the house was empty now. It's up for sale."

"It is empty. But here's the thing. Tommy told me there is a secret room hidden in the study up front on the main floor. It's behind the fireplace. All of the bad stuff is in there."

"No shit?"

"No shit. The recordings are right there, so close, and I can't get my hands on them because there is a security system on that house."

"Wow," Bobby responded. "I guess you want to get those tapes."

Ricky turned to Bobby. "And you said you weren't very smart. Well there's your first 'A' of the year. Of course I want to get those recordings."

"But how are you going to do that if the house is alarmed?"

"I don't know. That's the problem, but I cant let those recordings just sit there for someone to find. No way, uh uh. That's not going to happen. I am going to get them."

"So what are you going to do?" Bobby asked.

Ricky just shook his head and didn't answer. He was thinking about other things. "There's only three of us who know about what's in that secret room. Tommy, you and me. Jason doesn't even know."

"You know me, mum is the word."

"I know, I know. You're solid. I only told you because I might need your help."

"My help?"

"I think I have an idea of how to get to those recordings."

Bobby groaned, took one hand off the wheel and rubbed   his   leg.

CHAPTER 46

It had been many weeks since Dean talked with Patricia Mackie and discovered Jason had bust Doogie's lip open in a fight the night before Tim committed suicide. Dean had been meaning to go talk to Jason, but Spy Hill was all the way down the highway on the other side of Calgary, and he kept putting it off in the name of routine police work. With Doogie now up at Spy Hill too, Dean couldn't find a reason to put it off any longer. He could hit both boys in one shot.

Dean waited patiently for Jason to come into the visitor's room at Spy Hill. He already had his talk with Doogie, and that was, truthfully, a waste of his time. Doogie blamed Dean outright for being locked up and saw no reason to answer any questions that could help Dean on any investigation. It didn't matter if it was about "that little shit, Jason Oliver," Doogie was just not going to help. Dean also had no idea that Doogie would fail to graduate this spring because he was locked up at Spy Hill and was now missing his final exams. He would have to repeat one semester of grade twelve in the fall, and that, of course, was Dean's fault too.

Dean was still thinking about Doogie's self-centred mind when Jason was let into the visitors' room.

"You're looking good, Jason," Dean said. Offering a positive word right away was something he found softened the mood and sometimes worked to loosen the tongue.

"You too," Jason replied politely. He took a seat opposite Dean.

"Been a while since we last spoke."

"Months," Jason said.

"Ayuh. How about if I just get right to it?"

"I wish you would. Everybody always wants to talk in circles up here. You should spend some time up here, Sherriff."

"I'm not a Sherriff. I'm a detective, and it's all these damn PhD people running around in these government buildings that get all of the whirlpools to start turning like they do." He made swirling motions with his hands.

Jason laughed. He felt warmth from Dean today, which was unusual but welcome.

"So, Jason, what I really wanted to talk about has nothing to do with why you're up here, okay?"

Jason frowned and nodded back.

"I wanted to ask you some questions about the night before it all went down. Questions about the night of the girls' basketball game. You were supposed to be at that home opener game, but you never made it. I did some checking, and you were not at the game." Dean watched Jason carefully for any type of reaction, and he caught Jason's eyes darting about for a sec. He knew there was something here.

"You do remember that night, don't you?"

Jason squirmed and sat upright. "Uh, some things yes I, um, do of that night," he stammered.

"I see. Tell me about that night."

"I'm not sure what you want to know." It was obvious to Dean that Jason was stalling as he tried to figure out where the questions were leading.

"Anything. Everything. What you did, who you saw, where you went and who you hung out with. Just give it to me as it happened. How about starting right after you had supper?"

Jason hesitated. Dean could see Jason struggle to put it all together before he spoke. Jason had no idea what Dean knew, and Dean really wanted to see if Jason would be straight up or conceal the fight with Doogie like Doogie and Willie had.

"My guess is you already know where I was, and what really happened that evening. You just want to hear me say it."

Dean was not expecting that. He chuckled and lifted his hands as if he surrendered to being caught in this little game. "Okay then, just go ahead and say it. Your words."

Jason told his story. He recapped the events of the night: how he stumbled upon Doogie and Willie as they beat up his friend, Tim; how he bust Doogie's lip; how Tim ran off afterwards and he gave chase only to finally let Tim go home alone. Dean hadn't heard the entire story in this much detail. It explained a lot. Jason was Tim's close friend. He could sense the degree of agony that Jason must have suffered when word of Tim's suicide got around the next day.

Jason didn't tell Dean the entire story as it actually happened. He left out the part about Tim's confession. He also changed the ending, saying that Tim pleaded with Jason to walk him home after Jason caught up with him in the forest. But Jason refused to walk Tim home, saying he had things to do.

Dean was getting ready to wrap things up when Patricia Mackie came into the visitor's room. Both Dean and Jason looked over, surprised at first to see her, but they both knew she was here to see Doogie. She smiled at Jason. Jason gave a small wave back, and remembered how he had intended to ask her out on the night of the girls' basketball home opener last fall. Patricia took a seat on the opposite side of the room and looked about anxiously.

"Well Jason, that's all I really came up for," Dean said. "Just putting to rest some of the loose ends on Tim's case."

"Tim's case?" Jason said, puzzled. "That's a long time ago now. He's been gone a while. Is that normal to keep a case open that long?"

It was Dean's turn to tell a lie and mislead. "Oh, yea. These cases are always kept open for months after all the work's done. Years sometimes. Nothing to worry about here."

Dean quickly walked out and left Jason sitting at the table alone. Jason looked over at Patricia, smiled and said hello. Patricia smiled back and indicated she was waiting for Doogie. The guard outside the glass door stared in curiously, waiting for Jason to come to the door to be let out.

"Is this your first time up to see him?" Jason asked. "I'm not sure where he is bunked down inside, but he's not in my dorm. Tommy and I are bunked together."

"First time." Patricia replied. She kept staring at Jason.

Jason rose from where he was, crossed the room and pulled up a chair next to Patricia. He brushed his black bangs out of his eyes and smiled. "Doogie will probably be here in a minute or so. They're pretty fast in bringing us out for visitors."

Patricia nodded and smiled back at Jason.

"Graduating soon, huh?" Jason asked to keep the conversation moving.

"Oh yes! Next week is exams! Grad party's out on Wolfle's land. Do you know Michael Wolfle?"

Jason had hit the right string with his question.

"I think so. His dad is the rancher. Jens, I think his name is. Big guy. He's got about a gazillion acres out there on Battersby Road."

"That's the one. It's supposed to be a great party. Michael says his dad is letting everyone tent out there for the whole weekend if they want. Starts Friday night. I can't wait!"

"It would be so awesome to just hang out with friends again for a while. You know Tommy would be out there graduating with you if he wasn't in here. He and I are still going to school here. Tommy's done, I think."

Patricia nodded back to Jason.

Jason was pleased to chat with Patricia. It felt as if he suddenly reconnected to the outside world. His thoughts turned to the night of the girls' basketball game.

"So how's basketball going? I really wanted to watch you play on opening night."

"Basketball's good. We're not at the top, but we're not at the bottom either." Patricia tipped her head to the side, and brushed her hand through her hair unconsciously. "I looked for you that night you know."

"When? What night?"

"The home opener at the school." Patricia giggled and blushed. "I actually thought you were going to ask me out that night after the game."

"Why would you think that?" Jason replied, flustered but thrilled by her disclosure.

"You know. People talk. I heard you liked me, that's all. And I know you watched me from down on the ice at the hockey rink."

It was Jason's turn to blush.

"I saw you looking up at me in the stands," she said. "I could see your eyes peaking through the holes of your mask."

Her flirtatious gestures had not gone unnoticed by Jason, and he remembered them well. "I am an idiot sometimes," he replied and laughed. Patricia laughed too. "I wanted to ask you out so much. I guess it's a little late now. Missed my chance, didn't I?"

"You never know. Everything changes."

"Not everything."

"What do you mean?"

Jason shrugged. "Well, you're still hanging out with Doogie."

"I guess you're right, huh? Here I am, still hanging out with Doogie."

"Yea, why is that? He never really seemed like your type to me. No offence, but you play basketball, you're smart and pretty. Doogie is... well, Doogie."

Patricia giggled. "We aren't going out or anything. I've known him forever it seems. We've lived next door to each other since grade one. We just kinda hang, you know?"

"Shit, yea. I know what you mean," Jason replied, pleased to hear that she and Doogie were not really ever a thing. He hesitated and found himself looking Patricia up and down as if he was seeing her for the first time. She had deep black hair, a delightful, pencil-thin nose and a set of white teeth that gleamed from where they were hidden behind the two softest lips he had ever seen. She was prettier than he remembered. "You should come up and see me sometime."

Jason was really beginning to enjoy himself. He had almost forgotten that he was locked up inside a detention centre when the door suddenly opened and the guard and Doogie both entered.

"Hey, shithead!" Doogie shouted. He moved quickly towards Jason and Patricia. "What the hell yous doing talking to Patricia? She's come up here to see me!"

"Hey, boys! Cool it right now!" the guard shouted and moved up quickly behind Doogie. Jason pushed his chair back and stood up as Doogie raced towards him, ready for an altercation.

"I said stop! Right now, or detention for both of you!"

"I'm not doing anything," Jason replied with his hands raised in the air.

Doogie stopped a foot away from Jason. Anger showed wildly across his flushed face. "I asked yous why you here talking to her?" Doogie demanded again.

Jason pointed to the door. "Detective Daly was just here to see me and..."

"You stay away from her. You hears me?" he shouted and thrust his finger in Jason's direction.

The guard quickly put himself between the two boys and instructed Jason that it was time to leave. Jason gave no objection and headed for the door.

"I will get yous, Oliver! This place ain't so big! You're just lucky yous're in the other wing or yous'd be making a quick trip to the hospital ward later!"

Jason stopped at the door, and turned back towards Doogie and snickered. "Who got the busted lip last time?" He snickered again. "Got a short memory there, hey, Doogie?" Jason looked across to Patricia and smiled. She forced a smile back, but just a tiny one. Jason sensed that she didn't want Doogie to see.

"Yous better watch your back, Oliver! I ain't done with yous."

"Oh, you gots good English too," Jason mocked back to Doogie. "And I guess since you're in here, you won't be graduating next week. You could always use another year to fix your grammar."

He walked out of the room with a smile that felt like it would stay there forever.

CHAPTER 47

Another week slowly passed. It was early Friday afternoon at the Bistro and the lunchtime rush had already died down. Only a few customers remained seated at the window. Simon asked Sarah to go sit by the window and take a load off while she could before the dinner rush came in. He brought her a fresh coffee and let her have a few moments to recoup from the noon rush.

Sarah sat at the window and watched the people as they came and went on the street below. It was a beautiful Friday. The sun was out on a clear, blue, cloudless afternoon, and all the signs of the coming summer were on full display. People dressed accordingly and walked happily about on the streets below as if Bluffington had never seen such a beautiful day.

Sarah was lost in her own world as she watched the people below. She didn't even notice Simon pull up a seat next to her.

"Beautiful day isn't it, darling?" Simon uttered and startled Sarah out of her daydream.

"Oh! It's just you," she said. She released a deep breath. "I was miles away."

"Didn't mean to startle. Just wanted to say I'll miss you. But I'll not miss you staring out the window like this."

Sarah didn't reply as her attention was suddenly diverted by an image below. She was caught in a moment of terror as she stared out on Main Street. She started to shake as she pointed her finger out the window and grunted guttural sounds. Her voice was suddenly gone.

"My dear. What is it?" Simon queried, as he looked at Sarah and then down to street below. He shook his head confused.

Sarah continued to thrust her finger until she finally found her voice. "There!" she shouted. "He's there! That's him!"

Simon gazed out at the street, not sure where he was supposed to look. "Where? To whom are you referring? Is it Gerald?" He frowned.

"Yes! It's Gerald, right there!" She began to shake. "He just climbed out of that truck and is walking this way. He's over there on the left, coming towards us. Just this side of the bank!"

"Are you sure?"

Sarah shoved herself back from the table and spilled her coffee cup over onto its side in the process. "It's him. I'm damn sure it is. That looks like his truck." She went silent and continued to stare out the window. "Please no!"

Simon looked down and spotted the man, ignoring the coffee as it washed across the table, over the side and on to the floor. "The man with the grey top?"

Sarah nodded. "Yes!"

"That's Gerald?" Simon squinted. "How can you really discern details from this far away? I can barely see his face from here."

"It's him, Simon. I'm sure it is. He's finally found me. Oh my God! What am I going to do, Simon?"

Simon shook his head in surprise at the turn of events. He and Sarah both watched in silence as the man on the street walked towards them. He had a wide, purposeful gait and walked with a dark attitude. Systematically, the man moved closer. For the very first time, Simon had finally seen the mysterious figure of the man who taunted Sarah.

"You're absolutely sure? He doesn't seem to be coming up here to the Bistro. He hasn't even looked up here yet."

"I'm sure," she replied, but there was now a small trace of doubt in her voice. "I think... It sure looks like him." Then the man abruptly turned away and walked into the drug store on the corner below.

It wasn't Gerald.

Simon reached over and pulled Sarah close to him until they embraced. "You, my dear, need a break. I mean it. The sooner you stop staring out this window, looking for him, the better off you'll be, I say. That wasn't him and he's not out there. He's probably fifty miles or more away from here right now. I am so happy you are moving into that big house next week. No more of this silliness, staring out this window."

"It's just that sometimes I get so scared, Simon. I know it's been a long time but..."

"A long time?" Simon almost shouted. "It's been nearly a half a year since you arrived. Sheesh! He's probably got himself some new, young filly and has forgotten all about you."

Sarah gazed down the peaceful street again. "I don't know. Maybe you're right," she said, but she wasn't convinced.

"Tell you what. You must come up to my place for the weekend. I will not have you sitting there alone, worrying about this Gerald character any longer. Not this weekend. I'll have Brenda open up the shop alone tomorrow. You will come over, and we will both get our hands dirty fixing up my flowerbeds. Just the two of us. No more being alone, and no talk of Gerald."

"I don't know, Simon."

"Well I do! I won't take no for an answer. You are coming home with me after we close tonight. You can trundle up to your place, grab a few things and off we'll go."

Sarah wanted to rebut, but Simon was persistent and countered all of Sarah's reasons for not going with him until she finally relented.

By the time the busy dinner service was completed, and the bistro was being cleaned and readied for the next day, Sarah realized she was drained and felt relieved at having accepted Simon's offer. When had she last let herself be swept away by anyone spur of the moment? It was certainly not anytime recently with Gerald. The shop would be closing soon, and Sarah found herself excited about going with Simon. Simon always allowed his last seating to be no later than nine o'clock. Today was no exception, and the night was still young.

Simon grabbed Sarah and smiled at her. He told her it was time to go. He let the kitchen staff close up tonight, and he ushered Sarah up to her place to collect some things.

Accepting Simon's offer was a step beyond the boundaries and walls she had built up around herself. She felt something she had not felt for many years.

CHAPTER 48

"I have to make sure everyone sees me, don't I?" Ricky asked Bobby.

"I guess so," Bobby replied. "My mom's gonna be so pissed if she finds out I went to the grad party. I really shouldn't be doing any of this, Ricky. You know how my mom can get."

"C'mon, Bobby. Just start the vehicle and let's go! If this plan is going to work, you have to drive me out to the party and back. Just circle around the field a few times once we get there. I'll talk to a bunch of the other grads to make sure they see me and remember me, and then we'll leave."

"I just don't know. What if something happens? Those grad parties get pretty rowdy."

"We'll be long gone before the party's really even started. Now, c'mon. Let's go."

"There's gotta be a better way," Bobby said. He rubbed his leg and hoped Ricky would agree, but Ricky was persistent in implementing his plan tonight.

"We've hashed this out over and over how many times now? I need an alibi in case things go wrong, and being seen at the grad party is the best option. There'll be so many people out there, and most of them will be drinking to get wasted. No one will even remember what time it was that they saw me."

"Uh huh, I guess," Bobby replied reluctantly.

"And remember, we'll have to go back to the party afterwards as well so everyone sees me after it's all done. There'll be a big bonfire there too, I heard, so maybe I can even throw the tapes or CDs into the fire. Get rid of 'em tonight!"

Bobby looked at his watch. It was nearing ten o'clock and the party would be well under way already. He let out a huge sigh, turned on the ignition and pointed his vehicle in the direction of Michael Wolfle's property on Battersby Road.

CHAPTER 49

Simon stepped out of his vehicle with Sarah and was immediately upset. Wild sounds erupted from the grad party on Jens Wolfle's property directly behind his house.

"I don't believe it!" Simon shouted. "Of all the hundreds of acres he has back there, he has them set that grad party up right behind my house!"

Simon stormed around to the back of the house. Sarah followed close behind. Sure enough, a few hundred yards away in the clearing beyond the dense trees behind Simon's property line, roared a massive bonfire visible through the trees. Simon stared out and bobbed his head back and forth trying to see as much as he could through the thick branches of the evergreens and the leaves of the poplars. There were dozens of vehicles parked haphazardly in amongst the trees that surrounded the clearing where the bonfire blazed. It looked like hundreds of young adults were already mingling around the flames. They screamed and hollered as the rock music blared. They were obviously drinking and having a monstrously good time.

Simon stared at Sarah as if she had an answer to what was going on, but she said nothing. She only watched, alongside Simon at the field full of wild, party-crazed kids and could feel his frustration.

"That bugger did this on purpose! See what I mean? This is exactly what I've been having to put up with living next to him. I heard the party was out on his property, but never in my wildest dreams did I think he would stoop this low."

He looked out at the large fire.

"He must have been planning this for days! Look at the size of that fire! Must've hauled truckloads of lumber in for that."

"Oh, Simon. I'm so sorry," Sarah offered.

"Sorry? It's Jens who is going to be sorry," he replied and stormed off into the house. Sarah knew where he was headed, and by the time she stepped up to the back door, Simon was already on the phone to the police. He demanded that someone get out here to stop this wild party. He paid his taxes and wanted peace and quiet, not a bunch of rowdy kids who screamed and partied all night outside his back door. He stayed on the phone until he finally had the assurance that someone would be out to Battersby road soon.

What Simon didn't know was that the police were already out on Battersby Road down at one of the field entrances to Jens' property. Jens insisted the police be stationed on the road this Friday night to ensure no young graduate would leave his property in a vehicle while intoxicated. It was his sense of civic duty and responsibility, he said, to host this party where the youth who would become tomorrow's great citizens could let loose one final time before leaving home and making their own futures. Hosting this party also meant making sure everyone arrived home safely afterwards, and that meant having the police stationed at the entrance.

CHAPTER 50

"Oh no," Bobby exclaimed. His eyes bugged out as he spotted two police cars at the entrance to Jens' property.

"Cool it," Ricky said. "They're just there looking for drugs and shit. We have nothing, so we'll be okay."

"But they might remember us later when we leave," Bobby replied nervously.

"There're gonna be so many cars and trucks going back and forth. They won't remember shit. Just drive."

Bobby pulled up at the entrance and rolled down the windows. The officers asked them a number of questions. One appeared at each side window, while a third, Constable Heavyhead, walked around the vehicle and shone his flashlight through the windows. They were asked the usual questions: did they had any booze or drugs on board and others along those lines. They didn't and were soon ushered forward onto the property.

The exact location of the party was about a mile and a half from this particular access point to the many acres Jens owned alongside Battersby Road. The path to the party, now worn down by the tires of many vehicles, was easily visible. It started across a grassy slope before it weaved its way into a dense mixture of deciduous and evergreen trees. Once into the trees, the rocky path snaked about through some rises and dips before it emerged into the grassy clearing upon which the blazing bonfire was set. The trip from the entrance took ten long minutes.

"Wow! Look at this!" Bobby shouted in amazement at the number of people that milled about and at the size of the fire.

"No shit," Ricky replied grinning. "This is so cool." Ricky rolled down the window and let the sound of the music and the rumble from the fire enter.

Bobby steered his vehicle slowly around the outside of the circle. Many partygoers waved as they recognized Bobby's vehicle, and some raised a drink in salute to the end of the school year. Bobby waved back and forced a smile. He finally stopped, and the two boys got out.

"Okay, I'm going to go and say hi to a bunch of the guys."

"I'll come with you," Bobby replied. He didn't want to be left alone in the large, disorganized crowd.

"No! You need to stay here. Best if everyone remembers you by yourself and me by myself. Just in case, remember. And no drinking," he added.

Bobby nodded and watched as Ricky disappeared into the crowd. Ricky slowly worked his way around to the far side of bonfire.

Bobby looked about at the festive appearance of his schoolmates. Many were in the process of setting up tents and folding chairs to claim their territory for the next twelve hours of the party.

CHAPTER 51

Dean was at the station when the call came in about the grad party noise down on Battersby Road. He listened from across the room as the dispatcher talked to a very upset citizen on the other end of the line. As soon as Dean heard that Simon Pelletier filed the complaint, he told the dispatcher he would take this one. He knew all about the grad party on Jens' property, and he wondered what the hell was going on between Simon and Jens this time.

Dean jumped into his cruiser and headed out to Battersby Road on the edge of town. He shook his head because he couldn't believe the feud between Simon Pelletier and Jens Wolfle was once again in full motion. Jens was using the graduation to stimulate the conflict this time.

It pissed Dean off immediately that Jens had the gall to involve the Police Department in his little feud with Simon Pelletier. Dean finally understood why Jens had gone through all the effort these last few weeks to convince everyone he acted according to the best interest of the community. He offered up his land as a safe place for the graduates to let loose and go wild, and he insisted on police presence during the entire evening. It wasn't really about the community at all. It was more about irritating the owner of the Flattened Frog Bistro.

CHAPTER 52

Ricky finally reappeared from the crowd that surrounded the humungous fire, and his silhouette was shrouded by an orange glow. He urged Bobby back into the vehicle. "Okay, let's go do this." Ricky had made sure many of his graduating friends would remember seeing him at the party.

Bobby started his vehicle, weaved his CRV slowly around the growing crowd that gathered around the bonfire and carefully edged his way out to the trees and back onto the winding path towards the exit. The going was slower than when they had driven into the party; they had to stop a number of times to let vehicles pass on the narrow path as more and more partygoers continued to arrive.

"It's back to your place first," Ricky instructed.

"I know, I know," Bobby replied, agitated. He really didn't want to participate at all in what Ricky had planned.

"Sorry, but we've got to do this quickly."

Bobby didn't reply. He slowed to a stop at the entrance to the field as Constable Heavyhead raised his arms and motioned for Bobby to roll down the window.

"Been drinking?" he asked.

"Nope," Bobby replied. "Don't drink."

Heavyhead leaned in and asked Bobby to breathe out towards him. Bobby let out a heavy breath toward Heavyhead as instructed. Heavyhead smelled no alcohol on Bobby's breath, nodded and waved the two boys onto Battersby Road towards town.

"See," Ricky said. "No problem."

"You say that now. What if he remembers us leaving?"

"You saw how many cars and people are out there tonight. There's no way he'll remember us."

Bobby wasn't so sure but continued to drive back to his house. He parked in his usual spot in front of the garage behind the house, and the two boys exited the vehicle and made their way across the street on foot to the Dodson property. They snuck carefully through to the backside of the house and onto the path that followed the river.

"Hurry it up, Bobby!" Ricky called out. His anxiety was aggravated by Bobby's slow limp. The houses across the street from Bobby's all backed up to the Highwood River. The boys walked along the path behind the houses downstream towards the Oliver home. Ricky stepped out towards the river and grabbed a rock about the size of his fist as he waited for Bobby to catch up again. "You think this'll do?"

"It's a rock, Ricky. You're throwing it at a window. What do you think?"

"You don't have to be an ass about it," he snapped back. "What's with you all of a sudden?"

They walked on in the darkness. Only the moonlight lit their way along the river path.

"I really don't want to be doing this, that's all. What if we get caught?"

"We won't get caught. That's the point. Tonight of all nights, with the big grad party going on, no one will notice. We couldn't have planned it better. All the police are out on Battersby Road," Ricky said with exuberance in his voice.

Ricky stopped and looked at the big house beyond the trees behind Bobby. "Okay, we're here," he said. The Oliver property loomed eerily in the moonlit night.

"Which window are you going to break?" Bobby asked.

"I don't know yet, but let's go." The boys shuffled through the back gate. Ricky led the way along the narrow path that meandered through the forested backyard towards the back of the house.

"I don't even think anyone can see us here in the back yard," Ricky suggested as he looked at the houses to the left and right. "It's pretty dark, and we have great cover with all of these trees."

"That's great," Bobby said unimpressed.

They walked past the garage and physiotherapy office and looked up to the back door and kitchen windows. The backdoor was four steps up from the patio and had no glass. The kitchen windows were nearly eight feet off the ground.

"Those are too high," Bobby said blankly. "If you break one of those you still won't be able to get in. It's way too high off the ground."

"Hmm," Ricky agreed. "Let's go out front then."

"Out front?"

"Yeah," Ricky said, and he walked around to the front of the house. Bobby followed.

"Are you crazy?"

"No, I'm not. Tonight is the only chance I've got."

Ricky stopped, once he rounded the corner to the front of the house. "See," he said as he lifted his hand towards the house. "That's the one." He pointed to the large living room window where the glass reached nearly down to the floor of the room. The bottom of the window rested a mere five feet above the flowerbed.

"I don't know. This is way too out in the open." Bobby glanced up and down the street. Uneasiness fell over him. "I really think this is a crazy idea. Why don't we just go back to the grad party? Let's just hang out with everyone else for a change? We can find a way to get inside next week."

Ricky moved away from the corner of the house a few steps and searched up and down the moonlit street. "Oh, no!" he suddenly blurted out and began to pace about hysterically.

"It's been sold! Bobby, look!" he said and ran up to the real estate sign in the front lawn. A bright yellow "SOLD" label was stuck across the sign.

Bobby could see the yellow SOLD sticker clearly from where he stood.

"You see, Bobby! It has to be now! Tonight! Once the new people move in, I'll never be able to get inside. Never!"

Before Bobby could respond or say anything to dissuade Ricky, Ricky raced back to towards the front of the house and hurled the rock as hard as he could at the front living room window.

"Jesus, Ricky!" Bobby shouted as the glass showered down. "What the hell?" He was stunned at Ricky's boldness.

"We're doing this right now! Let's go!" Ricky said definitively and moved towards the broken window. "Quick! Hoist me up."

Bobby reluctantly lumbered forward and tried to lift Ricky up to the broken window, but his weak leg repeatedly buckled under the weight and brought both boys down on top of the newly budded tulips in the flowerbed below. After a number of failed attempts, it was obvious to Ricky that he wouldn't get in the house this way. He turned to Bobby and suggested he hoist Bobby in through the window instead.

"Me?"

"Yes! Now let's go! The alarm's been triggered, and we've only got minutes before the call goes to the police and they head this way. Move!" Ricky cupped his hands together for Bobby to step up into.

"I don't hear any alarm," Bobby replied.

"It's silent. It rings down at the security office. Now give me your foot. Hurry up!"

The first attempt was an immediate success as Bobby suddenly found himself looking through the broken living room window. The front window was so large that the safety glass had shattered into an array of pea-sized pieces. He broke away more of the broken glass that sat in the bottom of the sill and then rolled inside onto the living room floor. He quickly stood up. Fear painted its way across his face. "Okay now what?" he asked while he brushed the glass chunks from his pullover.

"The fireplace. Go to the fireplace. Hurry, Bobby!"

CHAPTER 53

Dean arrived at Simon Pelletier's, and to his surprise, Simon wasn't alone. Simon had a woman guest with him tonight. Simon introduced Sarah and Sarah reached out and shook Dean's hand.

"Look here, detective," Simon interrupted. He had a reason for calling Dean, and he got right to it. "Come see what he's done now!" He pointed out towards the back yard. "Come with me!" he demanded.

Dean followed Simon out to the back of the house, and saw through the trees what Simon complained about.

"What is with you two?" Dean asked, after he shook his head in disbelief. "This little thing you and him have going on bothers me. It's not just tonight. This has been going on for some time between you two. You both insist on provoking each other at every chance you get. This is what you get." He removed his hat, looked out at the raging bonfire beyond the trees and scratched his head. "Simon, I'm not sure there is anything I can do about this. You brought this on yourself. You and Jens."

"What? Are you mad?" Simon asked. "Look out there! They're noisy and loud! I'm sure that's a violation!" he screamed.

Dean raised his arms in the air and took a defensive posture. "Look here," he said. "You two have been at it for a long time with each other. That party is on his private property, and he has all the legal right to let those kids have a party."

"C'mon, detective," Simon rebutted. "There are kids out there drinking. Surely, you must know that many are under age. And listen to that noise!"

Dean shook his head. "That's private property, and I really can't go out there."

"Every time I call you, you do nothing. I'm beginning to think he's bought you off or something."

Dean turned red at the suggestion of being corrupt. "Don't you dare suggest I'm taking sides here, Simon."

Sarah suddenly stepped forward. "Simon isn't suggesting any such thing, detective," she said. She looked at Simon and hoped he would just shut up for a moment. "Simon's upset that there's a huge loud party going on behind his property, that's all. He was hoping you could step up and maybe have them cool it a bit." She looked nervously back at Simon and hoped she had not crossed him.

There was something about Sarah that Dean liked. "Okay, okay," Dean replied. "I'll see what I can do, but I'm pretty sure I won't be able to stop the party. I might be able to cut the noise level, but..."

Dean's radio interrupted him as he heard a call for a B&E silent alarm at an address he recognized. He grabbed his radio and called back to dispatch. "Was that call for the Oliver house?" he asked.

"Yes it was, Dean," the dispatcher said.

"Shit! I'm on my way!" he replied.

"You're not leaving!" Simon exclaimed.

"There's been a break in. Gotta go!" Dean said and scurried away.

"What about these animals?" Simon shouted. He pointed to the field behind him.

"Sorry!" Dean shouted back as he ran for his vehicle.

CHAPTER 54

Bobby stumbled around the dark Oliver house, not sure where he was supposed to look. Ricky shouted from somewhere behind him, outside, "The front den! That's where it is Bobby. Go to the front den!"

Bobby wandered about down one dark hall after another. He had been in the Oliver home hundreds of times, but the darkness and his agitated state had him a bit disoriented. He shuffled back to the living room window and stared out towards Ricky. "Where am I supposed to be going?"

"Shit, Bobby! Just go to the front study! That way, to the left!" he said pointing. "Tommy said it's behind the fireplace in the study! Jesus Christ! Just go! Go! Move it!"

Bobby quickly turned and shuffled back down the hallway towards the study. He reached his hands out in the darkness, and felt along the walls to edge himself towards the study. Bobby was scared, and he shuffled as quick as he could, which wasn't very fast at all. He finally emerged in the cold, barren study. It wasn't as he remembered. The walls were bare and the room was empty of all furniture. Even the carpeting was gone. Some of the light that cascaded down upon the street outside stole its way in through the large front window. It allowed just enough light for Bobby to see. He really wanted just to leave and forget about this entire crazy idea until he turned and stared at the fireplace. He knew he had no option but to push on for Ricky's sake and find the hidden room.

Bobby hobbled himself slowly towards the stone-covered wall that surrounded the fireplace. It looked normal. He stared at the stone fireplace. It didn't seem to him that there could actually be a room hidden behind it. He sighed and looked behind him in the darkness. "Ricky?" he called out and waited for a reply, but heard nothing. He called again, "Ricky, I'm in here now. How do I open it?"

Maybe Ricky was too far away to hear him. Bobby shuffled himself back towards to the doorway and popped his head into the hallway so his voice would reach down the hall to the broken living room window where Ricky waited outside. "Hey, Ricky! I'm in here now. Where is it exactly?" he asked. "How do I open it?"

Again there was no answer.

"Ricky!" he shouted even louder. "I'm in here! Tell me where it's supposed to be! I see it, but I'm not sure what to do. Did he tell you how to open it? Where is it exactly?"

It was only a few seconds before a voice suddenly replied. "Where is what exactly?"

It wasn't Ricky's voice. The voice was much deeper and huskier. Bobby felt a sickening feeling crawl through his belly. "Ricky?" he asked and swallowed hard.

"I'm not Ricky," came the reply.

CHAPTER 55

Dean placed his foot down hard on the accelerator. He knew the alarm at the Oliver house was a silent one, and with the home being unoccupied and no one for the security company to call to confirm if this was accidental, the call went straight to the police station. Dean kept his lights and siren off. He really wanted to surprise and apprehend whomever may have entered the house.

"What a night," Dean uttered aloud to himself as he hurried on towards Founders Road. The Oliver house was empty and up for sale. Why in blazes would anyone break into an empty house? "Why?" he said aloud.

Founders Road paralleled the main road that led to the University. Each end of Founders Road turned at a ninety-degree angle to meet up with the main road. Dean turned the corner onto Founders road, and his lights swept across the front of the Oliver home. There in front stood a young, dark-haired, male teenager with his hands up resting in the busted front window. The teenager looked at Dean with an expression of horror as he was caught in the flash of the headlights. He immediately darted away around to the side and back of the house.

"Shit," Dean shouted as pulled the vehicle to an abrupt stop out front and hopped out. The kid was long gone. Dean knew about the river path in the back behind the houses and determined immediately that there was no way he would be catching that one. He walked slowly up to the house and searched the shadows on the way. He saw no one lurking about. As he neared the structure, he was sure he could hear a voice coming from inside the house beyond the broken window. He crept up quietly and listened.

"...in here! Tell me where it's supposed to be," the voice said from deep inside the house's belly.

Dean moved closer to the broken window and leaned his head inside.

More words drifted and echoed from within. "I see it, but I'm not sure what to do. Did he tell you how to open it? Where is it exactly?"

It was definitely another young teenage male by the pitch of the voice. "Where is what exactly?" Dean called out into the broken window. He waited for a reply.

"Ricky?" the voice called out with uncertainty from the darkness.

"I'm not Ricky," Dean said back and waited for an answer.

Silence from inside.

"Okay," Dean began to speak to whoever remained inside the Oliver home. "I am the police, and I think it is best if you come out now. Come out from wherever you're hiding to the front and unlock this front door for me."

Dean waited again for a reply and heard nothing.

"Your friend Ricky ran away." He paused and listened again. "He's long gone, so you come forward young man, and let's talk about this."

Dean waited a moment, and finally heard the shuffle of feet that moved about inside.

"That's it. Come forward, out to the front. Just unlock the door and we can talk about this. You are definitely in a pit full of trouble tonight."

CHAPTER 56

Ricky ran through the backyard as fast as he could in the darkness. He was absolutely sure he was being chased, and the follower was right behind him with an arm outstretched, ready to grasp hold of him. He didn't dare look behind him and bolted straight out across the back yard. He dashed right through the budding cotoneaster bushes that lined the grassy area behind the house. Terror swept through him as the ground suddenly became uneven, and he was forced to dart in and out of a wild array of trees, shrubs, rocks and fallen logs that were left as a natural area behind the row of bushes. He twisted and stumbled about as he edged forward as fast as he dared towards the pathway that followed the river. He had nearly made it all the way when his foot was tangled in a root that waved up from the forest floor. It brought him crashing down headlong into a large Saskatoon berry bush. The thick branches of the bush jutted out like protective spears that stabbed his face and arms as he fell. He threw his hands out in front to break his fall, and an icy pain stabbed through his right wrist as he finally came to rest tangled in amongst the lower branches of the bush.

He breathed heavily as he lay with his face pressed down into the dead leaves and broken branches and listened for any sound of approaching footsteps. He heard nothing but the soft sound of the river as it flowed and gurgled its way past the large rocks that lined the river bottom, just twenty feet away. Slowly he turned himself over onto his back and peaked out towards the house from inside the large bush. He looked down at his hand, but it was much too dark to see anything. His right wrist hurt so bad; he knew he had done something seriously bad to it. He brought it slowly to his lips and tasted the sweet, warm saltiness of his own blood.

His heart continued to thump hard as he tried to discern if the dark shadows that appeared to shift and move in the space between the side of the physiotherapy office and him were real or just his vivid imagination. Minutes passed before he trusted his vision enough to believe that no one was there to follow him down the side of the property.

When he finally calmed down enough to think clearly, his thoughts went immediately to Bobby. "Bobby," he whispered to himself. "Shit." He knew Bobby was a goner. Bobby wouldn't be able to get out the window with his bad leg. He felt terrible and punched himself in the arm, which caused his already sore and bleeding hand to throb even more.

Ricky pushed himself up and out of the bush. He brushed his clothes flat while favouring his aching wrist, and stared again up towards the house. He listened for some sign that Bobby was okay, but he didn't hear a thing. He wasn't sure which way to go at first and turned onto the river path. He stood puzzled for a moment on the path and looked up and down in both directions. He was really worried about his friend, but his first thought was to get as far away from this house as he could. He began to walk downstream towards Head Park at the eastern edge of town.

As he walked, he lifted his injury up into the moonlight, and he could see in the silhouette that there was something very wrong with the way the hand met the wrist. He felt along up the back of his hand and wrist and screamed in agony as his good hand caught the edge of a splintered wrist bone that protruded out from the skin. The intense pain brought immediate tears to his eyes, and his legs buckled underneath him. He let himself fall to the ground and remained kneeling on the moonlit path until the pain abated enough for him to open his eyes once again and look about. He felt so alone and frightened.

Time passed ever so slowly for Ricky as he worked his way along the path to Head Park and out towards the centre of town. He made a right mess of everything tonight, and he was still uncertain about how it would all end. He didn't dare go anywhere near Founders Road where Bobby was currently facing it off with the police and focused only on how to get back home to get his badly broken wrist fixed up. He thought about what excuses he could use that his mom would believe.

Twenty minutes later, Ricky stood on his front steps and stared at his dad's Lexus in the drive. He hesitated and thought about running away into the black of the night. His dad would never sympathize for a broken arm caused by hanging out on the streets at night with friends. He looked down at his dirty and torn clothes from his fight with the forest and feared only the worst from his father. There was blood on his face, hands and tattered clothes. His father would have been proud if he had broken an arm while playing hockey, but an injury caused by running around late at night doing who knows what? He knew his father too well. Thoughts tumbled inside his brain and refused to settle into any logical state.

Ricky opened the front door with his good arm, shoved the door wide open with his shoulder and walked inside. He held his broken and bloodied wrist out in front of him ready to face the wrath of his parents.

CHAPTER 57

"So, you refuse to tell me who this Ricky is?" Dean asked Bobby again.

Bobby and Dean sat in Dean's cruiser. They were parked out in front of the Oliver house. Bobby was in the back seat alone, and he looked uncomfortable.

"I told you already. I'm not saying anything," Bobby replied.

Dean had enough. He had been at it for a while asking questions about what the boys were up to and, more importantly, what they were looking for.

"We weren't looking for anything! Just out being stupid, I guess. We were just looking for something fun to do. Busting the window seemed like a good idea at the time with all you cops down at the grad party," Bobby said.

"Not all of us," Dean corrected him.

Bobby just shrugged and hoped the interrogation would end.

"And what was it you were trying to open?" Dean asked for the third time. Bobby still refused to admit anything. "We weren't opening nothing! I don't know why you keep asking me that. There's nothing to open! Can I go soon?"

After twenty minutes of no progress, Dean relented, drove the few doors down to Bobby's house and escorted Bobby inside where he quickly found out who this other boy, Ricky, was from Bobby's mother. Bobby's mother held her composure like a cement fortress, listening intently to every word uttered by Dean about what happened, and glaring with cold fury at her son. She was also very quick and useful in forcing a proper response from her son. She managed to get Bobby to talk about the reason they broke in to the house.

"I know it was wrong mom, but... But we just wanted to see where they were killed," he finally said with a humbled quiver in his voice. Bobby's mother was horrified that her son got his kicks like this, and she scolded him severely.

"Honest! That's it! It's what all the kids were talking about all summer with the house sitting empty and all. Everyone talked about breaking in there. When we saw the SOLD sign, we figured this would be our last chance."

Bobby's mother apologized multiple times to Dean and clearly couldn't understand how her son could behave this way. She promised him Bobby would be punished.

The new story made a lot more sense to Dean, but he knew there was more to the story yet untold. There always was. Maybe it was simply a dare set out by the other kids to go inside. That sounded exactly like the sort of thing he had seen in the past, but it still didn't quite explain the words he heard as he stood up to the window. For the sake of Bobby's mother, he accepted the story as it was for now.

Dean advised Bobby and his mother before he left that he would be back in the next few days to follow up on this situation after he filed all of his reports. He told them there may be charges and a possible appearance in court.

CHAPTER 58

The smoke from the fire clawed its way into the sky, and the sound of the crackling fire and laughing kids carried across the field and through the trees to where Simon and Sarah sat in the back of Simon's acreage. It was well past midnight, and the party in the grassy field was still going stronger than ever. The music reached over to them in waves as the heat from the fire and the slow breeze caused the sounds to fade in and out. It was quite warm for a late June night, and the heat helped fuel the crowd.

"Look at them out there," Simon uttered with disgust. "Hoodlums. And Jens is the one promoting all of this."

Sarah sighed and sipped more of her iced tea. She was sad Simon insisted on hanging on to his irritation. "They're not hoodlums, Simon. They're just kids."

"Just kids? Look at how they are behaving. They're wild and out of control!"

A rocket suddenly sparkled up in the sky and burst into a chromatic aberration of colours. The crowd roared with excitement.

"See what I mean?" he said and he thrust his thin finger out towards the raging bonfire.

"It's just fireworks. I think they're quite beautiful, actually. You must have forgotten what it was like to be young, Simon."

"When I was young, I didn't behave in such a disruptive way."

"Oh, no?" Sarah laughed sarcastically. "I am betting that when you were young, you had things on your mind other than being publicly wild and untamed."

More fireworks leapt into the sky and showered above in a chaotic dance of bangs and fizzes.

Simon gave Sarah a quizzical stare. "You condone this kind of behaviour?"

"Of course not, but we all need to let it out once in a while." Sarah gazed up, followed more rockets as they rose and smiled as the vibrant colours filled the night sky. "They really are beautiful, aren't they?"

Simon shook his head in despair, "I've had enough. I'm going inside now. You coming?"

Sarah continued to watch the explosions in the sky. They soon became sporadic and consisted of mainly roman candles and sparklers, but it stirred excitement inside her. "In a minute," she replied. Simon rose from his chair and moved into the house, leaving Sarah to her own thoughts. She had not been out late at night like this for many years. As she watched the crowd in the field beyond, memories from when she was younger flooded her thoughts: memories of when she first met Gerald. Back then, she and Gerald would have been in the thick of the party, dancing, drinking and just letting go: living only for the moment. Suddenly she felt old and disconnected as if the part of her youth that chased after excitement and dreamed of the future was severed somewhere along the way. She continued to look out through the trees at the shadows and dark silhouettes as they shifted about the bonfire. She sighed heavily and understood now that maybe it wasn't all Gerald's fault. She let herself be severed and cut off from all that she desired. It was really her own damn fault that she lost so much of her life living in Gerald's shadow.

She watched the fire and listened to the crowd. It was strange, but a part of her suddenly missed Gerald as she used to know him. Maybe it really was her own fault that he treated her the way he did.

Another roar erupted from the crowd across the field, and Sarah wished she were a part of it. She closed her eyes and let her mind drift back to when life was good: back to a time when she laughed with not a care in the world. Gerald was there. Gerald was a part of all of her good memories and her bad ones.

She sighed again heavily, opened her eyes and watched the group for another few minutes before she finally followed Simon inside for the night.

CHAPTER 59

The shower rooms inside Spy Hill consisted of two large, tiled rooms with a half dozen shower heads along the outside wall. The shower rooms were separated by a central area that contained an array of benches and towels at one end where the boys would dry themselves off before getting dressed. The other end of the central section had a number of sinks, urinals and toilets.

A fresh clean set of inmate's underwear, clothing and drying towel was set out on a shelf above a name tag for each of the boys.

Tommy was busy drying himself alongside four other inmates from his dorm when Doogie and boys from the other dorm were escorted inside by a guard. Doogie grinned as he spotted Tommy. The guard stayed momentarily and then left to wait outside.

"I heard about yous friends," Doogie said smartly. "Dumb asses can't even breaks into a house without getting caughts and hurting themselves."

Tommy looked up. "What?"

"Yous friends." Doogie smiled again and began to undress.

Tommy shook his head from side to side. He clearly didn't understand what Doogie was teasing him about.

"Yous friends," Doogie repeated slower this time. It was obvious that Doogie was quite enjoying this moment. "That dumb lame kid Bobby and his side kick Ricky. Those two friends of yous."

"I still don't know what you're talking about."

"Holy shit, Oliver. I guess you hasn't heard. Those two bust into yous house a couple of nights ago. Grad night. Bobby got caughts red handed, and Ricky bust his arm up pretty good trying to gets away." Doogie laughed. "What a bunch of dorks! Can't even breaks into a house!"

Tommy wasn't laughing. "I didn't hear that. What happened?"

Doogie was now fully undressed and stood naked opposite Tommy ready to head into the shower with the others from his dorm. "Yous heard me. They bust a window and broke into yous house." He paused and laughed again. "Oh ya. Let me get this right." He pointed at Tommy, doing his best to provoke some kind of reaction. "They broke in to what *used* to be yous home. Throws a rock at the front window and climbs inside."

"Used to be my home?"

"Shit, Oliver. Yous don't hear nothing does you?" Doogie was pleased to be the bearer of this news. "Your house has been sold. It's not yous anymore." He chuckled again. "Yous homeless, man." He spread his arms out wide. "Take a look around Oliver. This is the only home yous got now. Better get used to it."

Tommy clenched his fists. He wanted to lunge at Doogie but held himself back. He turned away and quickly pulled on his fresh clothes. He couldn't help but wonder what happened inside the house, but Tommy knew why they had broken in.

Doogie continued to amuse himself. He jumped under one of the showers and immediately began a barrage of comments out to Tommy.

"Don't think your friends will be coming back up here to see yous for a while. Ricky's busted up pretty good. Probably still in the hospital. Hey, wait a sec! Maybe yous will see that skinny-ass, wobbly Bobby. He might get thrown in here with yous. Then the two of yous can jack each other's off in here. What do yous say, Oliver? I hear yous'd like that."

Tommy tried to ignore the comments that drifted out from the shower room as he pulled on the final items of clothing, but if what Doogie said was true then he had reason to worry about his friends.

"And ask Ricky how's he's gonna jack himself off now. One bust up arm. Here's hoping it's not the one he uses at night. Let me knows when yous talk to him, hey, Oliver? I wanna knows!" Others in the shower laughed along with Doogie.

Tommy got out as quickly as he could as Doogie continued to rant. He felt his anger rising. If it rose any higher, he knew he wouldn't be able to stop himself from rushing back across the room to tackle Doogie.

"Hey, Oliver! I don't hear yous! Are yous still out there? I really wanna knows about Ricky!" He laughed and hollered. "Is he a lefty or a righty? I really wanna knows!" More giggles and laughter accompanied his voice.

Tommy ran out of the shower room and into the hall. He was relieved to finally escape the plethora of verbal nonsense that spewed from Doogie's mouth. He gave the guard who still stood in the hall outside a quick stare, but the guard just grinned at Tommy. He clearly enjoyed the banter. Tommy needed to find Jason, and he headed towards the common room where Jason would be. Things were escalating.

CHAPTER 60

"It's alright, Sarah," Simon said. "I'm sure everything is going to be fine."

Sarah looked at Detective Dean Daly for assurance.

"It's only the front living room window. It has been boarded up already, and the alarm on the house is still active."

"But I'm supposed to take possession of the house this week! I just closed the deal a few days ago! Oh my goodness, Simon." Simon put his hand on her arm to comfort her.

As the three of them sat next to the window inside the Flattened Frog Bistro, Dean could see that Sarah was quite upset. He did his best to assure her that there was nothing significant about the break in.

"It was just a random act. It's an empty house and a couple of kids got out of hand, that's all. It was grad night. Kids get up to some crazy behaviour during grad night."

"So what did they damage inside? They didn't wreck it or write graffiti all over the walls with paint, I hope?" Sarah asked.

"No damage at all other than the window. I was onsite right away. I don't think they were inside for more than a couple of minutes. With the exception of the front window, nothing else was touched. And I am sure if you call your lawyer they'll have that window replaced before you even move in."

Sarah looked to Simon for support. "You know what I've been through, Simon. I don't know if I can handle anything like this. I mean, what if this had happened next week when I was moved in already?" Sarah shuddered. "I couldn't help but think it was Gerald! Oh my God, Simon. I don't know if I can do this."

"It wasn't Gerald, and like Detective Daly just said, the house was empty. That's why the kids tried to break in. Once you're all settled in that house, things will be fine. You'll see. Gerald's nowhere near Bluffington."

Dean was confused. "Gerald? Who's this Gerald?"

Both Simon and Sarah looked at each other and almost laughed despite the situation.

"Gerald is Sarah's ex," Simon stated simply. "He's not a very nice guy. And he doesn't know that Sarah is here in Bluffington. He's very nasty and lives up in Calgary."

"That's where I want him to stay," Sarah added.

Dean listened intently. "If there's someone bothering you, miss, you just need to let me know. I'll make sure no one bothers you."

"You can call me Sarah," she replied. "I just haven't gotten over the trouble he's caused me yet, that's all."

"Well either way, if there's anything you need, just call me." Dean pulled out a business card and slid it across the table to Sarah. Sarah smiled as she took the card and stuck it into the inside pocket of her purse.

Before Dean left, he turned to Simon. "And this little feud you and Jens have going." He shook his head. "I'd like to see it stop before someone gets hurt. These little games you both play to provoke each other aren't doing either of you any good."

Simon took immediate offence, and he thrust his finger out the window in the direction of where Jens property and his acreage sat. "You talk to him! He's the one who let the cattle loose and destroyed my beautiful flowerbeds! And just last weekend, with the party!" Simon was furious.

Dean raised his hands to calm Simon. "Okay, okay. I hear what you are saying. But if you don't stop, he won't either. That is my point. I am going out to see Jens today to tell him the same thing. I don't want any further trouble from either of you. Understand?"

Simon pulled his hand back down. "If you get him to promise to stop, then I'll see. But I'm not promising anything if   he   starts   up   again."

CHAPTER 61

Tommy found Jason in the common area and led him over to a table in the corner where they could talk privately. He told him about Bobby and Ricky breaking in to their house.

"But why would they break into our house? That's just a shitty thing to do. Don't you think, Tommy? I know we will probably never go back there, but still. That was our home. They had no right." Jason was visibly upset.

Tommy knew it was time to let Jason in on what he knew. He began by reopening the dialogue about Tim's suicide. This brought a deep emotional response from Jason who had not talked about that night for many months now. Tommy's conversation moved from Tim's suicide to the frequent visits from Ricky. Tommy revealed to Jason that Ricky too was a victim of their father, just like Tim. Jason was horrified.

Tommy reluctantly prodded Jason to remember everything he could about the afternoon of the murders, specifically the room behind the fireplace. He then revealed what he heard as he first entered the study and confronted their father and told Jason what now sat undetected in the secret room of their old house.

"Shit! Someone should get that stuff out of there before it's found," Jason said with deep emotion.

Tommy could see Jason getting angry as Jason realized what remained in the house and what significance it held.

"How could you keep that a secret from me, Tommy?"

"I had to, Jason. I didn't know what to do about that room at the time, but I knew for certain that I didn't want anyone to know what was in there. I couldn't talk about it, and I knew how much it would upset you. I cry each night thinking about the horror of it all. It is horrible."

"Why are you telling me this now? Shit! Shit! I thought I was through remembering what happened in that house! I miss them, Tommy! I do! I miss them so much sometimes!

Tommy stared back at Jason with deep sadness. "I miss them too," he replied.

"Tommy, I really just wanted to forget everything." Jason wiped his eyes and tried to go back in time. "Can't we just leave it? No one else even knows it's there. Maybe it'll stay hidden forever. Our secret."

Tommy sighed and shook his head. He wasn't finished telling Jason everything he knew. "We have a problem now, Jason. Things really aren't turning out so well." He paused to make sure he had Jason's full attention. "The reason Ricky and Bobby tried to break into the house was to get to that room."

Jason stared back with an angry denial, and he began to shake his head slowly.

"I told Ricky about the room and what's inside it when he was up here last week."

Jason suddenly slammed his fist against the wall. "Why would you tell Ricky? Shit, your stupid! Jesus! He was probably suffering enough from what happened to him, and you turn a bad thing even worse for him! For all of us! No wonder he tried to break in!"

"I didn't want to tell him. I really didn't. The shit hidden in that room was slowly eating me up, and Ricky could see it. He knew I was holding back something each time he came to visit. He finally broke me down, and I told him everything. And I do mean everything, Jason." Jason turned away from Tommy and stared down at the floor. Distress clearly took over.

"Everything?"

Tommy could see Jason's eyes wander about, and he knew Jason was reliving the murder scene. He could see Jason recall everything that occurred that afternoon.

"Yes, everything. But believe me, I tried to talk him out of going after what is in there. I really did. I told him that the house was alarmed and there was no way to get in. I didn't think he would ever try to break in anyways."

Jason looked up with anger still imbedded deep within his cold stare. "Well they did try, Tommy, and it's your fault! They were caught! That's what you really wanted to tell me, right?"

Jason challenged Tommy's loyalty.

"If you had kept your mouth shut then things would still be the same. Now they got caught, and the tapes or recordings or whatever was in there is now out floating around in public, and everyone knows about everything! Jesus, Tommy!" Jason dropped his head down into his hands in grief, and sobbed and mumbled through his tears. "Everyone will know now, and we will be disgraced."

"No! No! That didn't happen! They got caught before they had a chance to do anything in the house. Ricky got a busted arm, that's all. I'm not sure how bad he is, but that's all that happened," he replied. "Honest."

"How can you know anything about what really happened while you are locked up in here? We should be out there taking care of this!" He lifted his head, gazed about the room and suddenly shouted, "No!" He stood up, pointed at Tommy and clenched his teeth as he spoke. "We should have taken care of this that same day, before we even called the cops on ourselves. That's when we should have taken care of this. But you kept it secret."

"Listen. If that room was discovered, Doogie would have been shouting it from the rooftops. He's the one that told me about the break in. Doogie didn't say a word about it, so I'm damn sure no one else knows about it."

Jason sat back down, mulled over Tommy's words and eventually calmed down. "Okay, let's say you're right, and I believe you about all of this. You're telling me all of this because...?"

Tommy didn't hesitate. "Ricky. That's why. And Tim as well, and any others. Ricky is so torn up about this whole business to risk breaking in while the alarm was activated."

"No shit, Tommy. But I really wish you would have told me this earlier. We should have been the ones to take care of this. We let our friends get molested by our dad right in our back yard, and you let the recordings just sit there. I bet every one of our friends is so scared every time they turn on the internet wondering if they are going to suddenly see their own faces staring out at them in some horrible scene." Jason ran his hands through his thick hair. "This is so bad. We should be taking care of this, Tommy, not Ricky."

"I tried to stop him. I told them there was no way to get in with the alarm on. I really didn't think he would try to break in."

"But there is a way," Jason stated, pointedly.

Tommy frowned. "What?"

"There is a way to get in with the alarm turned on."

"No, there isn't."

"Yes, there is!"

"No, there isn't. You need the front door key."

"No, you don't. I've done it myself many times."

Jason told Tommy how the alarm on his upstairs bedroom window was disabled two years ago when he was sick with a bout of Asian flu. He was flat on his back for nearly three weeks. It was mid August, and Bluffington was experiencing a deep heat wave. The air conditioning system was running all day and night. Their mom believed deeply that air conditioned air wasn't healthy and insisted the window in Jason's room remain open all night so he could have fresh air to recover from his illness. Marie Oliver also insisted the alarm system be set every night and didn't know how to disarm just the one window, so she had the alarm company deactivate Jason's window from the program temporarily. She had forgotten to call them back to have it reactivated once Jason recovered.

"I've snuck in and out of the house a number of times through that window. There aren't even any motion detectors anywhere in the house. Just the windows and doors are alarmed. You know how Mom was at night. We could always go down to grab a drink in the middle of the night while the doors and windows were armed."

Tommy stared at Jason dumbfounded. A smiled momentarily drifted across his face. "You snuck out of the house?"

"Lots of times. It's not easy to get in and out," Jason said. "You have to walk along the ledge around the corner to get on the roof at the back porch. Harder getting back in, but I've done it many times."

"And once back inside, you could just walk to Mom and Dad's room and turn the alarm off if you wanted to?" Tommy asked.

"Uh huh. The second key pad is in their closet. I never had to do that since I always just went back in my own room to bed."

"But what if the window is locked?"

"It can't be locked. I rigged it that way. Unless they fixed it, but I doubt it."

Tommy was deep in thought. "Could you do it again? Get inside?"

"Easily," Jason replied. "Why? What are you thinking?"

"Just that we gotta help Ricky get what's in that house out of there."

Jason chuckled, and couldn't believe what Tommy just said. "We are at Spy Hill, Tommy. Remember? There is barbed wire across the top of the outside walls. How are we going to help Ricky do anything from inside here?"

"Leave that to me. I'll need to think about that one for a while. In the meantime, can you call Bobby to see if he can come up to see us as soon as possible? Ask Ricky to come visit too, if he is able. Doogie made it sound like Ricky's not going anywhere for a while."

"Doogie's an ass," Jason said.

"And he doesn't like you at all, that's for sure."

"That's good. I'll never back down from him, and he knows it. He's such a liar. Ricky's probably just got a bad bruise or something."

"I don't know about that, but just watch yourself around him. Doogie's thirty days are up in a few and I wouldn't put it past him to try something before he leaves."

Jason nodded. He clearly understood his situation with Doogie.

CHAPTER 62

"I'm not supposed to even be here," Ricky said to Bobby. Bobby opened the back door a little wider and quickly ushered Ricky inside.

"Mom's still at work." Bobby looked down at Ricky's right arm. The bright white cast started just below his elbow and covered most of Ricky's hand. Just his fingers protruded out from the end of the cast. "Nice cast," he said and smiled.

"Whatever," Ricky replied, uninterested. "So what is so important that you couldn't tell me on the phone or text me? Why did you have Tommy call me to tell me to come see you?"

"Mom took my phone away. She's so pissed at me."

"Uh huh," Ricky replied. He knew Bobby got caught because of him. "My dad gave me a great big smile and then a great big bear hug when he saw me standing there at the front door with blood dripping on the carpet and my wrist broken real bad."

"Really?" Bobby replied and grinned. He was glad to see his friend again.

"C'mon Bobby. I'm never supposed to talk or hang out with you again. My dad says this is what I get for quitting hockey and hanging out with kids who have no ambition. He says if I'd stayed in hockey none of this would have happened."

"Your dad really is an ass, isn't he? If he knew the truth he wouldn't be saying that. And I do have ambition."

"Well, he'll never know the truth, so let's just drop it okay?"

Bobby shrugged, "If you say so."

"So what's so important anyway? I can't stay long. Gotta get back home before mom or dad gets there."

"This will be quick. I went to see Tommy today. Tommy has a plan to help us get inside the house. He says..."

"Don't be stupid! We'll never get inside again," Ricky interrupted.

"Hang on a sec and listen. Tommy heard at Spy Hill about us trying to break in. Tommy told Jason and guess what?"

"What?"

"Jason's window is not alarmed. It's the only one in the house that isn't. Someone could get in that way. There are no motion detectors, the alarm panel is in the master bedroom closet and he says the window is jimmied so it can't be locked."

Ricky rolled his eyes. "Who is going to get in there that way, Bobby? Jason's room is on the second floor. "You couldn't even lift me up to the front window, let alone climb up to the second floor. And I'm not climbing anywhere with this thing." He shoved his cast towards Bobby's face.

"But at least we now know there is a way in. And a good one." He waited for a positive response from Ricky.

"No. It's not going to work. Neither of us can get in that window up there, and there is no way we are telling anyone else."

"But..."

"No buts! It's over. I really gotta be going."

Ricky brushed himself past Bobby and headed out the back door.

"When can we meet?" Bobby asked.

"Don't know. Call me in a few days. Maybe the old man won't be on my back then. Oh right, you can't call me. You don't have your phone anymore."

"I'll find a way to contact you. Please don't give up, Ricky. We'll figure something out."

"Whatever," he replied flatly. He turned and gave Bobby a weak high five and slumped off down along the side of the house towards home.

CHAPTER 63

"This is so exciting," Simon said to Sarah as he carried in another box. His white teeth almost shimmered as he smiled at her. He almost seemed more excited about the new home than Sarah did.

"It is very exciting, and I can't thank you enough."

"I just love this old house!"

Simon set the box down next to Sarah's bright red suitcase and danced around the room. He purposely pointed out all of the features he loved about the home. Sarah followed him about as he pranced and spewed out his many delightful expressions.

"Ah, look at the lintel above this door. It's so exquisitely crafted."

"Okay already, Simon. It's nice. I get it. You don't have to do that anymore."

"Do what," he feigned surprise.

"I know it's not as nice as yours and it's old. Look at that door there," she said and pointed towards the kitchen. "The hinge is crooked. I don't think that door will even close all the way, but this old house does have the charm I was looking for."

Simon put his hands together with palms touching and laughed again. "You are so sweet." He pointed at her with a limp hand. "I can't fool you, can I? But this is a very nice house."

She nodded, pleased that she had someone as solid as Simon nearby. "It is nice. And it's so close to my new job at the University. That is really why I wanted it."

They unloaded the rest of what Sarah had. She had been on a shopping spree over the last week selecting tables, chairs, cutlery and linens. Simon was with her through most of it and helped to pick out the essentials. Only a few of the larger items had arrived, but it was enough to start to give the home the lived in feel Sarah was looking for.

By the time evening came around, the living room looked almost homey. Sarah asked Simon to stay for dinner and he readily accepted. The two shared a candlelit dinner. It was the first dinner she cooked for anyone since the salmon for Gerald, and it bothered her to think about that.

The two shared a bottle of wine and talked about what the future held, but Sarah couldn't stop the past from creeping in. It was a night like this many years ago when she and Gerald first moved into the house in Calgary. She was so happy that day, and the laughs she shared with Gerald echoed in every conversation with Simon.

CHAPTER 64

Tommy sat in Marilyn Sanderson's office and waited patiently. He was hoping he could sound convincing in the plea he was about to give his counsellor.

Marilyn walked in the room and smiled. She was pleased to see Tommy came to talk to her. He hadn't asked for a one-on-one session before, and he could see the surprise on her face. They exchanged greetings and Tommy got right to the point.

"I wanted to see you about a few things. I passed all of my courses, and I wondered how that works now for me graduating?"

"You did exceptionally well," Marilyn replied with eagerness to engage Tommy's enthusiasm. "You have completed all of the required courses to obtain your General Equivalency Degree. It's not quite the same as graduating with the rest of your class, but it does mean you will receive your high school diploma. Congratulations," she said enthusiastically and reached out her hand to Tommy with another smile.

Tommy smiled back and accepted her handshake. "That is such good news. I know my mom would have loved to see this day."

Marilyn frowned briefly, and Tommy caught her change in attitude. Tommy had kept all of his emotions at bay since he was incarcerated. This was the first emotional response relating to his parents that he had openly disclosed to Marilyn.

"I am sure she would be proud of you, Tommy," Marilyn replied. Tommy could see that Marilyn felt a door was suddenly opened. He had pushed it open purposely, and it was time to seize what he could from that opening.

"I was thinking, Mrs. Sanderson, that the trial will be starting soon."

"Yes, I heard it was coming up."

"Oh, yes," Tommy replied. "Jury selection is next week. I was hoping to ask for something I've never asked for before."

"And what would that be?"

"Well, I think I've been very good holed up in here up until now. I've followed all of the rules and gone to all the classes I was supposed to. I even volunteered in the kitchen preparing the food boxes and meals for the homeless."

"Needy, Tommy. They weren't homeless."

"Okay, needy. And I really think I've stepped up and offered myself up to helping others."

Marilyn simply nodded and let Tommy continue.

"I mean, I've done so much while I've been up here. I even volunteered and helped with the counselling sessions."

"So where are you going with all of this, Tommy? You have been very good and your volunteer efforts are appreciated greatly by everyone involved here."

Tommy heaved a heavy sigh. "It's just that the trial is coming up fast. Once it starts, it's going to be a crazy ride. Especially for Jason. You know what he's like. Always following behind me. I know that once the trial is over we'll only have a few weeks together. I turn eighteen in August. When I'm eighteen, I'm guessing I'll be transferred up to Drumheller to serve out the remainder of my term. Jason will be left here all by himself."

"I still don't understand what you are asking. You both have come a long way during your stay here."

Tommy shrugged. "I guess that's what I am really asking about. I've done a lot. Jason has done a lot. We both miss our parents so very much. Especially Jason. Once I'm gone, he will be all alone. Being locked up hasn't been a fun ride for either of us, and I was hoping that I could ask a favour."

"A favour? That really depends, Tommy. You know everyone up here appreciates how you have both been very cooperative and disciplined. What kind of favour are you looking for?"

"I was really hoping that I could have... well, Jason and me both actually. I was hoping that after all we have been through and how we have both completed our schooling and with the upcoming trial and all... that Jason and I could have one last meal outside of this place."

"Uh, you are asking for a..."

Tommy interrupted. "Jason and I have been locked up here for nearly eight months. Once the trial starts, there will be a circus following us every time we leave this place to go to court. And when it is all over, we both know we are going to jail for a long time. I was hoping we could enjoy one last meal at a regular restaurant before this all kicks off."

Marilyn nodded. "You are asking me for a day pass? I don't think..."

"No, not even a day pass. I was thinking more of just an escorted day out. Just for Jason and me to go out for a pizza. Maybe even to a place we've been before. Marlon's Pizza maybe. Just something to help us keep strong and focused after all we've lost."

Marilyn looked sternly at Tommy and studied him very carefully. He could see she was not expecting such a request.

"An escorted day out?" she repeated.

"Yes. Just one last pizza. You can call it a reward for how well we've listened to you and the others and never gave you any trouble. Or maybe it can be a reward for having graduated. I don't know, maybe it's just a sympathy request because we won't see the outside for a long time. Either way, I really want Jason to have something to hang on to."

Tommy searched Marilyn's eyes. He hoped that he had struck some compassionate chord deep inside her and that some sympathetic vibrations were slowly spreading.

"It's obvious, Tommy, that you have been talking to others about the day escorts. We do offer this as an incentive to some inside here, but your case is much too different. You have been charged with a severe act of murder, and it is not normal for inmates charged with such serious crimes to be allowed passes of any kind outside these walls."

"But you know why we are really in here. Both Jason and I. I mean if we both had parents, relatives or a home to stay in until the trial, I doubt we would even be in here. We'd be under house arrest. We really have nobody. Jason and I have no family left. We only have each other. That's why we are in here," he pleaded, hoping to catch some sympathy.

Marilyn wasn't buying it. "You are in here because you boys killed your parents, Tommy. Of course you have no parents or family to go home to now. You killed them."

Tommy next asked a question caught Marilyn totally off guard.

"But you don't know why we killed them, do you?"

It was the answer everyone, including Marilyn, searched for from both boys since they came to the Spy Hill facility.

"No we don't," she said emphatically. She was clearly perturbed that Tommy was now playing a game, and the truth was the bargaining chip. Tommy could see she was not impressed.

"It is a difficult question to answer," Tommy said and let Marilyn continue to think about what he asked for. "But there is an answer to why we had to do what we did."

He purposely let a little bit of the truth escape for the first time. He could see Marilyn grab hold of his words. She had her first taste at a motive. Tommy could see fear in her eyes, and he knew she wanted to know more.

CHAPTER 65

Jason was looking forward to his regular workout as he walked through the busy hall towards the gym. Out of nowhere, he was suddenly slammed hard against the cinder block wall, and the wind was knocked right out of him. He crumpled to the ground and immediately turned upward to see who blindsided him.

Doogie grinned and bounced lightly from side to side on his feet. He pointed at Jason. "Told you I'd get yous didn't I?" he said proudly.

Jason grabbed hold of his right shoulder and tried to stand up. He could see a number of other inmates stopped to watch and were excited to see if this was going to escalate in to some fiery confrontation.

"That was really fair," Jason said.

Doogie continued to bounce up and down, and he moved about quickly to Jason's left, then right and then back again.

"Who said I was fair?" Doogie laughed. As soon as Jason had finally righted himself, Doogie quickly reached forward and tried to slap Jason on the head, but Jason ducked away at the last moment.

"Ho-ho, Jason. Good move!" He quickly reached forward again, and this time he connected with a slap across the top of the head.

"What is your problem, Doogie?" Jason shouted. "Why are you such an ass hole?"

"Me? I thinks I'm a pretty nice guy." He turned to the crowd that watched eagerly. "Ain't I a nicest guy?" he said to the crowd. A few nodded, but most just stared noncommittally and looked eager to watch the scene unfold.

"I'm not going to fight you. Not in here."

Doogie grinned again. "So what are yous saying?" Doogie stepped in close to Jason's face. "Yous are never getting out of here. I think yous just scared. A coward."

"I'm no coward."

"Well then prove it. Throws a punch at me. C'mons."

"No. A bigger man knows when to fight and this ain't that time Doogie. You aren't worth it."

Doogie stopped his bouncing and put his finger up to Jason nose. "Yous are scared."

"Not of you. Never, Doogie."

"Fights me then." Doogie slapped Jason hard across the face and quickly took a fighter's stance with his fists clenched.

Jason turned his reddening face away and began to slide himself down along the wall and away from Doogie. He refused to be engaged in a fight.

"Where do yous think yous're going?"

"Away from you," Jason replied and continued to move away. Doogie followed him as Jason crept along the wall. The crowd followed the two boys.

Doogie suddenly grabbed Jason by the collar, spun him around and pinned him against the wall.

"Do it!" Jason yelled. "Go ahead, Doogie! Hit me again!"

Fire burned in the back of Doogie's eyes.

"I heard you were supposed to be released soon, Doogie. If you beat me up, I don't think you'll be going anywhere. So go ahead, Doogie. Punch me again!"

Doogie maintained his position and held Jason tight against the wall. He suddenly released his grip and shoved Jason hard onto the floor.

"I am leaving today. Yous'll still be in here rotting always, Jason. But I'll be back outs there living. Yous hear me? Yous'll be rotting! Rotting like the stinking pukes that yous are. Your brother too!"

Jason remained on the floor and stared up at Doogie towering above him. "I will see you again, Doogie," Jason said with conviction. "And when I do, you'll wish you hadn't. And there won't be any audience to witness what's headed your way."

"Yous just try, Jason. I'll see yous coming a long ways afore."

Jason pushed himself to his knees and then stood up and leaned against the wall. "Just like last time with Tim?" he asked smartly.

"That was different."

"Your day is coming."

Doogie took a step closer, put his hand up to Jason's face and tapped him softly on the cheek. "Yous a dead man, Jason. Dead." He smiled and turned away.

CHAPTER 66

Sarah didn't know what was happening when she opened the front door at her new house and a camera and microphone were shoved in her face. She looked around startled and spotted the news van parked at the tip of her driveway. Another one zipped down Founder's Road towards her house.

"Hello! I'm Rich Denton from Channel Five News. I was hoping to ask you a few questions about the upcoming trial."

"Trial?" Sarah asked. She stepped further out onto the front porch and feigned a smile as she tried to understand what was going on.

Rich nodded and extended his hand. "Yes. The trial of Jason and Tommy Oliver."

"Who?" Sarah replied cautiously. She accepted his outstretched hand and shook it.

"The Oliver boys. The ones that killed their parents last year."

Sarah looked past the reporter to the cameraman who attempted to capture every word and image. She watched as another camera crew from the second news station tumbled out of their own van as quickly as they could and dashed up the drive.

"I'm afraid I don't know what you are talking about."

"Peter and Marie Oliver were murdered last fall by their two teenage boys. The trial date was just announced moments ago, and we've come looking for some perspective or comment from the new owner of the home where the murders occurred."

Rich pushed the microphone in Sarah's face and waited for a response.

Sarah placed her hand up to her mouth. "Oh my god," she said. "My house? I didn't know."

"I'm sorry you have to hear it this way." Rich looked over his shoulder defensively as the other news crew raced up towards the house. "I'm wondering if I can have a private word… maybe inside, alone?"

Sarah shook her head. "Uh, no. I really don't have anything to say." She tried to absorb what she had just heard. She remembered the realtor had wanted to tell her about the history of the home. Would she still have bought the house if she knew? She didn't have the time right now to process that thought.

"Please miss. I only want a word or two."

Sarah shook her head, apologized and stepped quickly back inside her house and closed the front door. The reporter rang the doorbell and knocked again, but Sarah refused to answer. She heard about the Oliver murders when they first occurred, but she didn't really followed the story since she had been struggling with her own escape from Gerald at the time. Following the news was the last thing on her mind.

She waited inside until the reporters finally gave up on speaking to her. She moved to the dining room and peeked out the window. Both news vans remained out in front of her home. The reporters stood with their backs to her, while their cameramen captured the reporters with the house behind them. Sarah felt a flutter inside. She suddenly felt should be wary about what had just happened.

CHAPTER 67

Gerald arrived home from work after he stopped for a few drinks at his usual watering hole. He knew he should not have driven, but it had been a rough day at work and he just didn't give a shit tonight. Gerald argued with his foreman at the end of his shift and was told he was close to losing his job. He heard this rant many times over the past few years, but tonight it was different. His boss suddenly stopped yelling, threw his hands in the air in a gesture of complete frustration and told Gerald to report to the big guy first thing in the morning. He was filing a written report against Gerald to have him dismissed.

Gerald slammed the front door and went directly to the half-full bottle of whiskey that waited patiently for him on the counter. He poured himself a strong shot over ice and flung himself on the sofa. He was still irritated over the incident with his foreman. He hated feeling so powerless when he couldn't control a situation! He grabbed the remote and turned on the TV. He flicked mindlessly through the channels while his mind raced madly over what he wanted to do to that chicken-shit boss of his.

It was the supper hour, and most of the local stations were broadcasting the news. As Gerald lifted the whiskey to his lips and flipped from channel to channel, he suddenly jumped up and spilled some of the whiskey across his lap. What he spotted on the screen stunned him. He flipped back a few channels and there she was. Right there on Channel Five News. He only caught her image for a second, but it was Sarah. Sarah was standing with a microphone shoved in her face for a moment before she disappeared behind a closed door. Gerald sat himself up straight and watched as the next image showed a reporter standing out in front of a large Victorian house talking about an upcoming trial. Gerald new about the murder; it was all over the news. Like Sarah, he never paid much attention to the story at the time, but things suddenly changed.

Gerald tried to recall what he knew of the murders, and he quickly remembered they happened in the town of Bluffington, just south of Calgary. Of course, Sarah would run back there to Bluffington. Why not? Bluffington was where he first met her as a striking, young girl when he worked on that job at the University.

"Gotcha," Gerald whispered softly and chugged back the rest of his drink. He let the liquid fuel the fire that burned inside of him. A sinister smile spread across his long face, and he laughed aloud.

"So it's Bluffington where you've been hiding." Gerald nodded. He knew what he was going to do next.

CHAPTER 68

Marilyn called Tommy down to her office and announced that his request for an escorted outing was granted. She repeated what she had suggested to the review board: it was a reasonable request as the boys were really no risk to anyone inside or outside the facility, and with the upcoming trial pending and the boy's futures at stake, the boys could use a short holiday. The review board agreed.

Tommy and Jason were to be escorted out for a few hours on Thursday to share a meal at one of the local restaurants. Tommy suggested the Marlon's Pizza on Crowchild Trail in the northwest. He told Marilyn he and Jason had a lot of good memories at this particular place growing up. His request for this particular location was also approved.

Tommy uttered his many thanks to Marilyn and promised her he would follow all of the rules and not let her down while on the outing.

Moments later, Tommy called Ricky and asked him to find Bobby and have him come up to Spy Hill to see him that night. It was extremely important. When Ricky asked what it was about, Tommy only told him he really needed to speak to Bobby first. It was urgent.

Hours passed while Tommy paced around the facility and waited for Bobby to arrive. He found Jason in the recreation room and repeated the announcement that they were granted the pass. Jason shared Tommy's enthusiasm, but Tommy could see that Jason was filled with worry.

With only a few minutes before visiting hours were over, Bobby finally arrived. He was ushered into the visitor's room where Tommy soon sat across from him and began to lay out his plan in great detail. He made it very clear that Bobby's vehicle was needed if they were going to pull this off.

"You want me to do what?" Bobby was astonished that Tommy had the nerve to ask such a huge favour of him. He wanted nothing to do with it.

"C'mon, Bobby. You know me. I wouldn't be trying this if I didn't think it would work. Think about Ricky and Tim. You were the one who told me what kind of a state Ricky is in these days. Ricky's arm is broken, and you certainly can't do it!"

"And Jason knows what you're planning?" Bobby asked.

Tommy nodded. "Absolutely. He wants this more than I do, actually. He is so upset about all of this, and Ricky certainly can't do this on his own. You'll need to discuss this with him."

"Why don't you talk to Ricky?"

"I'm worried he won't go along with this idea if he doesn't hear it from you first. You have the vehicle. He will need to know you're willing to step up to help him too. You're the best friend he has right now. That's why it needs to come from you."

Bobby scowled because he knew Tommy was pushing their friendship to its limits. He hesitated before he answered Tommy.

"You already know there's no question that Ricky's going to be all in for this with the shit that's going down at home for him right now. I don't think he feels he has anything to lose. He is so upset," Bobby said. He then backtracked a moment. "But I am not sure I really want to be involved in any of this. Not after getting caught the other night."

Tommy grabbed Bobby's hands. "This is the real deal. It's far beyond anything anyone is suspecting, and that's why I think it'll work. It's a big risk for you. I know it is. I don't know who else I could ask. I'll think of a way to make sure you are in the clear. Please, Bobby."

Bobby pulled his hands out from under Tommy's. He hesitated and then reached out a single hand and grabbed one of Tommy's hands in his own and squeezed. He sat quietly and stared at Tommy for a few minutes as he mulled over what Tommy was asking of him. Tommy stared back, biting his lower lip while his eyes pleaded with Bobby to understand how important this was for everyone involved.

"If there is only one thing in my life that I know I should choose to do, Tommy, this is probably it." He sighed heavily. "I shouldn't be doing this. If my mom ever found out..." He shook his head. "If you can find a way to make sure I stay in the clear, I'll be there. But that's my condition. I'm not doing this if there's a chance I will be caught. No way, Tommy. And Bluffington is totally out of the question."

"You'll see, Bobby. You'll see. I'll call Ricky late tonight after you've had a chance to talk to him. I'll figure something out and let him know how we'll keep you both clean in all of this."

"Just so long as I'm clean, I'll start checking things out on my side. And there's no way I'm going anywhere near Bluffington if we do this. That's just too much risk."

"Bluffington is out," Tommy replied.

The two boys agreed to meet one more time to confirm that everything was in place and to finalize the plan. Visiting hours ended, and Bobby was ushered out. He jumped into his vehicle and took a deep breath. He exhaled slowly and rubbed his leg for a few minutes before he drove away. He hated himself for agreeing to go along with what they planned. It was a foolish idea, but there was something about the promise of getting rid of those tapes that made what they were about to do necessary. It was the right thing to do. He thought more about what he had just agreed to, and he was left with a welcomed anxiety. He had a lot to do between now and Thursday.

CHAPTER 69

The Safeway store was only five blocks away from her new house, and Sarah felt a new freedom as she walked the few blocks alone. The sky was lightly overcast and a warm summer breeze wafted slowly through town. She only wanted to grab a few basics for the next few days. She paid for her items and left the Safeway store with her small bag when she looked out across the parking lot and suddenly went dizzy. She spotted what she was sure was her old car from Calgary sitting at the outer edge of the parking lot. She reached out and rested her hand against the building wall to stabilize herself as she stared at it in disbelief.

Was it her car? The one she left behind with Gerald?

Panic filled her chest and made it difficult to breathe. As much as she wanted to look closer, she didn't dare go anywhere near the car. She squinted in the sun and was sure she could even see what looked like the staff parking sticker from Forest Lawn High School, where she used to work, still attached to the windshield. Her heart pumped heavily inside her body. She scanned left and right across the parking lot. She expected to see Gerald charging down angrily towards her, but she didn't see him anywhere. She turned her gaze back to the car. The car was empty. If that was her car, then Gerald was not far away.

Sarah needed to get away.

She walked as quickly as she dared along the front of the building. Her feet wanted to run, but she wouldn't let them. She knew she would immediately attract attention if she ran. She continued to move alongside the building, away from the car, and was careful to keep her head tucked away from the street. She rounded the corner of the building and slipped down the side and out to the back of the store.

Panic continued to rise from deep within her. It brought back memories of the many evenings she sat and waited for Gerald to get home from work. She always let the panic rise, minute after minute, until she finally looked into his angry face when he arrived home.

She breathed a sigh of relief as she spotted the alley that connected the back lot of the Safeway and knew it was the means of escape. She darted as fast she dared from alley to alley until she was safe inside her house on Founders Road. She locked the door, set the alarm and called Simon at the restaurant.

"Simon, Gerald's in town! I just saw him. Please come! Hurry," Sarah pleaded.

"Gerald? You saw him for real?"

"Well, not exactly. But my car... I saw my old car in the parking lot. It has to be Gerald."

Simon quickly reminded Sarah of the last time she thought she saw Gerald in town. He tried to convince her that it was just her wild imagination again, but Sarah was nearly hysterical. Simon finally gave in and told her he would be right over after he gave the staff some directions.

When Simon finally arrived, Sarah was still in a fine state of hysteria. She was convinced that Gerald was in Bluffington. Simon tried to calm her down, but she begged Simon to go to Calgary and see if her car still sat where she left it in the front driveway of her old house.

"Okay, okay! I'll go to Calgary. You'll see," he said. "I'll go up, and I am absolutely positive that I'll see Gerald's truck and your car parked in the back at your old house. Your car is exactly where you left it, sweetie. It probably hasn't been moved for six months now." He smiled at her and tried to reassure her that all was fine.

Sarah sat on the couch and trembled. She shook her head in disbelief that Gerald was really still searching for her. "Not this time. That was my car in the parking lot, Simon," she said. "It was my car. I even saw the parking sticker in the window."

"That could be any sticker. There are a lot of cars like yours about."

Sarah didn't believe him. "I am so scared, Simon."

Simon sat down next to Sarah and cuddled her in close. "I know you are scared. And I am here for you."

Sarah nodded. "I know you are. It's just..."

"Hush now. You just hush and speak no more of this. Tomorrow afternoon I'll head up to Calgary and I won't come back until I am sure that Gerald is up there and not down here looking for you."

Sarah gave Simon the directions to her old place in Calgary with the description of Gerald's truck and her car. Simon promised he would be careful and would come to see her tomorrow night when he returned. Simon stayed with Sarah until late into the night when she was finally sound asleep.

CHAPTER 70

Thursday finally came. The details were finalized, and Bobby fought past his nervous reluctance and stepped outside with his keys. He opened up the back of his CRV and made sure everything Tommy asked for was loaded inside. All looked to be in order.

It was still early in the afternoon, and his mother wouldn't be home until late in the evening. His thought about her and how upset she still was about the break in. He wasn't supposed to be going anywhere, especially with Ricky, so he decided it would be best if he left her a short note. "Gone to Calgary to catch a movie. Hunger Games. Will go see Tommy at Spy Hill afterwards. Might be home late so don't worry about supper." That would satisfy her questions when she arrived home to an empty house.

Ricky was already waiting at the meeting point by Baxter's Garage when Bobby pulled up in the CRV. Ricky quickly hopped inside and grimaced. He anxiously began to pull tiny loose strands of fabric from his cast. "I am so nervous, Bobby."

Bobby smiled. "Me too. This is going to be some ride today. I hope it works out."

"Depends on those two, doesn't it?"

Bobby nodded back. "It does. It really does."

Forty minutes later, Bobby turned the CRV down a common-looking back alley and slowly crept along. He finally stopped beside the back of a cream-coloured, stucco building that was home to Marlon's Pizza. Bobby turned off the ignition. He rubbed his thigh unconsciously with the heel of his palm.

"Now we sit and wait," he said.

"How long?" Ricky asked.

"I don't know," he replied. "We'll just have to see what happens."

Time passed slowly as the boys waited and watched for any sign of Tommy and Jason.

"Is your dad still pissed at you?" Bobby asked.

Ricky rolled his eyes. "You wouldn't believe me if I told you."

"C'mon then. Tell me," Bobby prodded. He could see the consternation on Ricky's face, and he suddenly became very serious. "Your dad scares me sometimes."

Ricky's eyes grew wide in response. "Scares you? You have no idea." He shook his head. "If he finds out what we're up to, I am dead. So dead, Bobby."

"He's not going to find out anything. That's why we have our alibis. We'll both be nowhere near here when this all this goes down later.

"But he'll still suspect I had something to do with it. He'll hear about it on the news, and I'll get the third degree from him as soon as I walk in the door tonight. He doesn't trust me, and he just won't stay out of my face."

"But we have an alibi. That's the great part. It was Tommy's idea. There was no way I'd be doing this if I wasn't so sure it would work. My mom would never understand. I am in trouble so deep with her already."

"Well, I really hope so."

Bobby watched the street that crossed at the end of the alley. The vehicle with Tommy and Jason inside would have to pass across in front of them in order to enter the main parking lot.

"He calls me names all the time now," Ricky said sadly.

"Names?"

"Yeah. He calls me lazy and a slacker. He never used to do that. Still calls me a quitter every chance he gets. I hate going home. I hate it, Bobby. He thinks I quit everything just because I quit hockey. We never even discussed college this year, and now I'm graduated and have nothing planned for my future. I don't think he even cares anymore, and he wants me to fail. I'm thinking about getting a job and moving out."

Bobby understood. Ricky had graduated, and it made sense to do something if he was not going to college.

"Mom wouldn't like it though," Ricky added.

Bobby's thoughts drifted to the reason they were doing what they were doing today. He studied Ricky and tried to sense his sensitivity. Ricky looked very agitated as he picked away unconsciously at the strands of fabric that protruded from the end of his cast.

"There are others out there, you know," Bobby finally suggested.

Ricky didn't answer right away and Bobby wondered if he said too much.

"I try not to think about it," Ricky replied. "It's too weird sometimes. Every one of our friends that I ever played hockey with... I can't help but wonder every time I look at one of them."

"Mmm," Bobby mumbled back.

"I'll see one of them at the school or on the street. Somewhere, anywhere. And when I look at them, I see them so very differently now. I find myself looking beyond their eyes. I study them as they look back at me, and sometimes I feel like they are expecting something from me. It's inside them that I'm really searching, I guess, for any pain inside crying out. I know that pain might be there. And then we go our separate ways, sometimes not having spoken a single word to each other, I just want to turn around and tell them it's okay now. That it's really okay and I understand."

Ricky wiped his eyes.

"How many others do you think there are?" Bobby asked.

Ricky shook his head. "I bet there's more than anyone thinks there is. It's just that there is only a hand full of us who even know what really happened. How many years, Bobby? How long had this been going on?"

Bobby wondered how many there really could be. How many years did Tommy's dad coach hockey in this town? He knew he wouldn't ever be able to understand it from Ricky's point of view, but he felt Ricky's pain. He knew too well what it felt like to feel different from everyone else. He knew what it was like to be stared at.

Several more minutes passed as Bobby and Ricky continued to wait in the alley. Ricky suddenly spotted the large white sedan move slowly past the end of the alley in front of them. Tommy and Jason sat beside each other in the back seat. "There they are!" Ricky shouted.

"I see them," Bobby replied and sat up straight. He glanced in the mirrors and was pleased to see the alley still empty behind them.

Ricky continued to fidget and look anxiously at the stucco building. He pointed to the small window high in the wall above the cardboard recycle bin.

"That's it?" Ricky asked.

"Uh huh. Looks small doesn't it?"

"Sure does!"

Both boys sat quietly and waited. Time seemed to creep slowly along, and Ricky frequently looked at the time on his cell phone. "C'mon already," he whispered.

"They'll come," Bobby replied. "Just be patient."

More minutes passed by and, for a moment, Bobby wondered if his friends had changed their minds. Just then, the small, wooden-framed window was pushed open from the inside.

"Shit! Here they come!" Ricky said excitedly.

The two stared up at the window in awe as Jason slid his lean body out through it with ease. He reached his arms out in front and tumbled, head first, onto the recycle bin in a graceful roll. He then ran madly for Bobby's CRV. Bobby jumped out and had the back hatch open just in time for Jason to jump inside. Bobby quickly tossed an old, unzipped sleeping bag over him and slammed the gate.

"Tommy's coming! He should be right behind me!" Jason said from under the sleeping bag.

Bobby and Ricky stared up at the building looking for Tommy to appear.

"Where is he?" Ricky whispered.

"He was right behind me. He followed me into the washroom as I was climbing out."

The boys went quiet as they waited for Tommy to appear. More minutes passed and Jason thought something had gone wrong. "Do you see him?" Jason's muffled voice called from underneath the sleeping bag. "He should be coming out already! He was right behind me! Do you see him?"

"No," Bobby replied. "He's not coming."

"But he was right behind me!"

Jason was highly agitated.

"Do you think he got caught?" Ricky shouted loudly. He turned away frantically from the window towards Jason. "Maybe we should leave! Bobby?"

"No! I don't think we should leave without him." Bobby replied softly. "We just need to wait a minute."

"Shit, guys!" Jason called out. "We can't just wait here. If Tommy's caught, he's probably trying to buy us some time. You know how Tommy is!"

Bobby reconsidered and nodded in quick agreement. "He's right! We should go."

"You sure?" Ricky asked. "This is not how we planned it."

"Like Jason just said, maybe Tommy's covering for us. I'm not waiting to get caught," Bobby replied. "Done that once already this week. I'm not doing it again. We're leaving."

Bobby started up the CRV and began to pull away down the alley.

Ricky suddenly shouted as he stared back towards the pizzeria. "Stop! Stop, Bobby! Stop! It's Tommy! It's Tommy! Here he comes!"

Bobby slammed on the brakes and turned to look out the rear hatch window. Tommy was slithering his way out of the window as best as he could. Bobby reversed quickly, stopped and rushed out just as Tommy got to his feet after climbing down off the recycle bin.

"Run, Tommy," Bobby whispered and opened the back door. "C'mon!"

Tommy ran as fast as he could and dove into the back seat. Bobby threw a blanket over top of him. "Stay down!" he said.

In seconds, Bobby was back in the front seat with his two escapees safely concealed. He exited the alleyway and headed down Crowchild Trail to the southwest part of Calgary.

"What happened back there? Did they see you?" Ricky asked Tommy. "What took you so long?"

"It's cool, guys!" Tommy hollered and laughed brightly. "We did it!"

Bobby wasn't as confident and continued to drive in silence looking into the rear view and side mirrors every few seconds. His knuckles were white from clenching the wheel so tightly.

Tommy quickly told the others about what happened inside. It really wasn't difficult to escape because they had the full trust of the escorts. Jason simply slipped out to the back to wash up moments before the pizzas came. When the pizzas arrived, Tommy told the escorts to dig in and he would go grab Jason from the washroom.

Tommy and Bobby knew this restaurant well. It was a common stop after the hockey games in northwest Calgary over the years. It was old and run down. None of the newer restaurants have windows in the bathrooms, probably due to the face that the boys could skip out as they just did. Bobby and Ricky came down the night before to check the window out. Bobby was prepared. As expected, the window was secured with a number of screws. Bobby removed the screws and made sure that the window would open when needed the following afternoon.

"Okay, okay, let's just chill for a bit!" Ricky hollered. "We've got to be sure there's no one coming." He turned and stared out the back window for anything suspicious.

Twenty minutes later the boys arrived, undetected, at the large outdoor mall near the southwest corner of Calgary. Bobby parked near the outside edge of the Cineplex Odeon Theatre parking lot, and Ricky ran inside to purchase the two tickets for the five o'clock showing of The Hunger Games. Both boys already saw this movie, but Bobby insisted they needed the alibi. He wanted no chance of being caught.

"Okay, where next?" Ricky asked and slid back into the front passenger seat.

"Just as planned. Down to Sandy McNabb."

"You sure we have enough time?" Ricky asked.

"Checked it out yesterday. The movie runs just over two hours. Sandy McNabb campground is about as far south of the city into the mountains as we can get and still get back before the movie is over."

"How far will it be for Jason and me then?" Tommy asked.

"My guess is about thirty kilometres. It'll take you at least a day to get there on foot. My guess is you'll be there sometime early tomorrow afternoon."

"You bring all of the gear?" Jason asked.

"It's all there. Back packs, pup tent, sleeping bags, matches and food. Water is heavy so I only put two bottles in each pack for you."

"I hope you put a map in there," Tommy laughed. "Be crazy to get this far and get lost in the woods."

"We've ridden those trails on Mick's horses many times," Jason piped up. Mick was another friend from the hockey team. He lived on an acreage just outside of town. The boys often went riding with Mick and his parents on the trails in Kananaskis country.

"Not all of them," Tommy replied from under the blanket in the back seat.

"Quit worrying guys. I got you a book with maps. I even marked the trails inside," Bobby added.

The boys went silent as Bobby hit the open road south towards Turner Valley and the Sandy McNabb Recreational area in the foothills of the Rocky Mountains. It would take another forty minutes to get there and each of the boys reflected on their own reasons for participating in this scheme.

CHAPTER 71

Simon left his cook, Brenda, in charge of the Bistro and announced that he wouldn't be back until Friday morning. As promised, he headed up to Calgary to give Sarah the peace of mind that Gerald wasn't following her and had not been in Bluffington.

Simon released a heavy sigh as he headed up the highway. He honestly believed this was a big waste of his time, but he would do just about anything for Sarah. He had never really met anyone like Sarah and her friendship meant a lot to him.

It wasn't a long drive, and Simon soon found the street in the northeast, just off Fifty Second Street, where Sarah and Gerald once lived together. He drove slowly and scanned the numbers on the houses as he looked for 404. It was barely after five o'clock, and Sarah pointed out numerous times that Gerald always stopped for a drink on the way home so he certainly wouldn't be home when Simon got there.

Simon spotted the small bungalow and could see Sarah's car sitting in the drive, just as he expected. He searched both sides of the street for Gerald's truck but didn't see it anywhere. He was pleased and smiled comfortably. To be sure Gerald was not parked in the back, he drove down to the end of the block, rounded the corner and entered the back lane behind the house. It wasn't there. There was just an empty gravel parking pad in the back where the garage would have been. Sitting on the gravel pad was a boat and some piled up scrap lumber. Simon drove back around to the front and parked across the street, a few doors down.

Simon watched the house for a number of minutes and searched up and down the street. He wasn't entirely sure what he was looking for, but all seemed quiet and orderly. Gerald's truck wasn't around. If what Sarah said was true and Gerald had stopped for a drink, Simon should have a good half-hour before Gerald arrived. It was certainly enough time to do a short walk around the property. Simon considered just staying put in his car and waiting for Gerald to arrive home, but his curiosity finally got the best of him. How bad could this guy really be?

The bungalow was typical of many in the neighbourhood with no attached garage. Most houses in the area had a separate garage erected in the back, but Sarah and Gerald's had a concrete parking pad in the front yard where Sarah's car presently sat.

Simon strolled cautiously up the front drive and peered inside Sarah's car. He could see crumpled fast food bags, empty coffee cups and newspapers inside. This car was driven recently. From what he knew of Sarah, this certainly was not her mess. He wandered up to the house, put his hands on the glass front door and tried to look inside, but it was too dark in the front hall to see much of anything. He considered looking in the front window, but the flowerbed in front was too overgrown. He didn't intend to fight his way through just for a peek.

Simon shuffled his way along the front of the house and raised himself up on his toes as he still tried to get a look inside. His curiosity was still unsatisfied. He could see nothing. He popped his head around the side of the house and quickly decided it would only take a few minutes to check out around the back of the house. He would be safely back inside his car by the time Gerald returned home.

He entered the back yard and wasn't surprised that the grass was long, scruffy and unkempt. He climbed up the three steps to the landing next to the back door and looked around.

"What the hell... might as well give it a try," Simon suggested to himself and grabbed the handle for the screen door at the back of the house. The door released a long squeak as Simon slowly pulled it wide open. It seemed to call out a warning to him to be wary of what he was attempting. Simon next tested the door handle, and to his surprise, it was unlocked.

Simon stood there, dumbfounded for a moment with his hand still on the doorknob. He looked out at the other houses across the lane-way. It was a quiet afternoon and he saw no one. He looked back down to the doorknob and turned it again. He couldn't believe it really was unlocked.

It turned easily.

"I really shouldn't be doing this," he muttered under his breath.

Simon tightened his grip on the doorknob and turned the knob. He only had it open a fraction when he frowned and sensed something wasn't quite right.

Simon did not see anything nor hear any sound, as Gerald slithered silently out from around the corner of the house. He held on tightly to a two by four, raised it high above his shoulders, moved up the few steps and slammed Simon across the back of the head, knocking him instantly unconscious.

CHAPTER 72

By the time they arrived at the Sandy McNabb parking lot, Tommy and Jason had already changed into the clothes Bobby brought for them. They all helped unload the goods from the back of the CRV near the trailhead at the edge of the parking lot. Bobby and Ricky wished them good luck and promised they would see them soon on the other side. Moments later, Tommy and Jason waved goodbye to Bobby and Ricky and disappeared into the bushes on the hiking trail along Wolf Creek.

Bobby dashed as quickly as he was capable over to the outdoor toilets, and dropped Tommy and Jason's prison garb into the bottom of one of them. He returned to the vehicle, and, in minutes, he and Ricky were on their way back towards Calgary.

"Give me those tickets," Bobby demanded.

"Why?" Ricky asked as he handed them over. Bobby tore the top part of the ticket off and threw it out the window. He stuffed one in his shirt pocket and handed the other back to Ricky. "Take this."

"Oh. Good thinking," Ricky replied. A complete ticket wouldn't do as an alibi.

Bobby kept looking down at his watch. He breathed a sigh of relief when they finally arrived at the south end of Calgary. He looked at Ricky and smiled again.

"Right on target. Hunger Games should just be ending," he said as he pointed to his watch. "I did the practice run yesterday just to be sure. Now it's up to Spy Hill."

Thirty minutes passed before Bobby pulled into the parking lot at Spy Hill and parked his CRV.

"Looks quiet," Bobby said to Ricky. He was expecting some obvious activity around the detention centre in light of Tommy and Jason's escape. Ricky nodded nervously, looked about with Bobby and shrugged, unsure what they were supposed to do next.

"They'll only let one of us in at a time. What do you think? Maybe you should go in on this one?" Bobby prompted. He hoped Ricky would have volunteered himself by now.

Ricky quickly raised his arms defensively. "You go. I'm okay just sitting here."

Bobby laughed nervously. "Sure, Ricky. Push me under the bus! I got us this far. I think it's your turn."

"I'm not pushing you under any bus!" Ricky replied apprehensively. "This is your idea remember."

"It was Tommy's idea! And who are we all doing this for?" Bobby asked. "This has nothing to do with me at all! I'm not the one who tried to break into that house once already. You're totally paranoid about what's hidden inside!"

Ricky scowled back. "Screw you, Bobby. Don't start that shit talk with me now. You didn't have to get yourself involved in any of this! You know how it's been for me. It's still better if you go in because you have nothing to gain or lose."

"What?" Bobby laughed. He was surprised by Ricky's interpretation of the events. "Nothing to lose? I just helped two people escape from jail! What do you mean I have nothing to lose? You have done nothing so far. Nothing at all. You just sat in the car the whole time. I'm even the one who went in the bathroom yesterday and jimmied the window so it would be open for them today. I was the one who scrounged up the spare clothes, sleeping bags and all that other stuff for them." It was unusual for Bobby to show any outward anger, but he was extremely disappointed and annoyed at Ricky's inaction. "I really think you ought to step up and do something!"

"I don't drive, Bobby! How could I do any of this?" He furrowed his brow at Bobby.

"Why are you suddenly pissed off at me? I got us this far!"

Ricky's flustered face turned a deep red.

"Lookit!" Bobby added. "No one even knows how you are even involved but me, Tommy, and Jason. And those two are now on the run. You really need to do your part too!" He stared at Ricky and waited for a reasoned response.

Ricky suddenly opened the door and stepped out of the vehicle. He ducked his head back inside and shouted. "Screw you! I thought you were my friend! I will go do this part by myself!" Ricky slammed the door, turned away and strode towards the entrance of the Spy Hill facility.

Bobby sat back, surprised by Ricky's sudden tirade and chuckled. "What an ass." He laughed some more because he was nervous. He watched Ricky walk towards the front entrance and decided it was best just to let him be. He hoped Ricky knew what to say once he was inside the facility.

CHAPTER 73

Simon's head ached ferociously as he slowly opened his eyes and looked around. The darkness confused him and he became immediately flustered when he tried to comprehend where he was. He tried to rub his eyes, but his hands wouldn't move. His nose hurt terribly, and he thought he could taste blood on his lips.

He tugged hard on his arms and realized they were pulled tight and secured behind his back.

Panic set in, and Simon squirmed. He realized he was tied to a wooden chair in the centre of a small living room. He turned his head rapidly to the left and right. He was still too confused and disoriented to realize who had done this to him. His vision remained blurred, and the darkness let show none of its secrets. His mind slowly collected itself, and he remembered that he was up in Calgary looking for Sarah's husband, Gerald.

Simon stopped squirming about. "Oh my god," Simon uttered softly to himself as he realized his situation. A shadow slipped across in front of the drapes that covered the large front window. Simon froze in terror of what was before him. He held his breath and watched as the shadow passed once more between him and the window in front of him.

"Gerald?" Simon asked in a terrified whisper. The shadow stopped abruptly and moved towards him.

The voice spoke in the darkness. It was a guttural sound; dark and deep. "You seem to know who I am," it said.

The room remained eerily quiet. Simon didn't know how to respond. He listened carefully to capture all the sounds he could from the darkened room. He could only pick out the sound of ice cubes swirling around in a glass somewhere in the darkness. He listened to the swirling cubes. A short slurp followed, and then he heard the distinctive rustling of boots on the floor somewhere beside him.

The man shuffled forward towards Simon. With a large hand, he grabbed hold firmly to Simon's cheeks and squeezed.

"Who the hell are you?" he demanded.

"Si... Simon. My name is Simon," Simon cried back and tried to pull his head free from the man's firm grasp, but the hand only squeezed harder.

The man released his grip on Simon's head, and the room went quiet again for a moment. The crisp sound of the swirling ice cubes returned.

"And you've been looking into my car and trying to break into my house. Why?"

Simon stuttered utterly terrified. "I... I wasn't, breaking, not... I wasn't."

"Don't lie to me!" the man screamed and slammed his fist into the side of Simon's head. Simon cried out in agony as the chair flipped over on to its side with him still attached. Simon's head cracked hard against the floor.

He remained on the floor on his side, as the dark shadow towered above him. He was terrified. He listened in fear as the man swirled the ice cubes in the crystal glass around and around. Simon tried to move away but could only kick about in the air with his feet. He was going nowhere.

"I'll ask you again! Who are you and what are you doing here?"

Simon's thoughts went to Sarah. He now understood her terror, and knew he couldn't mention her name under any circumstances. Simon was at an utter loss as to how to answer.

"I asked you a question!" The man shouted. He kicked out with one of his steel-toed work boots hard into Simon's rib cage and broke one rib instantly. Simon gasped, and a horrible screaming pain traveled across his chest. He was unable to breathe.

CHAPTER 74

The sunset was still many hours away as Tommy and Jason headed up the path along Wolf Creek into the mountains. It was late June, and the sky would still be hold a soft glow against the horizon as midnight neared.

The forest was mostly a mixture of pine, poplars and smaller deciduous shrubs. The path was an easy one to follow: wide at the start and reminiscent of an overgrown old road from many decades long gone by. After fording the river just past the trailhead, the path quickly angled up and disappeared into the trees. The trail was choppy and muddy in spots from horses hooves that routinely chewing away at the once solid foundation. The horses were ridden for pleasure up and down the multiple trails that crisscrossed the area.

In some places along the trail, the trees suddenly opened up and exposed small grassy plains before they closed back in close along the path. It eventually climbed further up into the trees where it followed an old cutline for a while before it meandered back and forth along an easier incline to higher ground. The view along the first ridge was breath taking, but neither Jason nor Tommy found any delight in it.

The two boys walked with urgency and thought only about getting as far into the hills and back country as they could as quickly as possible. It was just past the longest day of the year, and Tommy still wanted to set up camp well before the sun disappeared behind the mountains that loomed to the west. Both boys ignored all conversations about the reason for their journey.

"Hold on a sec," Tommy said to Jason as he studied the maps in the back of the trail book Bobby had given him. "Wolf Creek campground is still about three hours or so away, maybe more."

Jason looked up into the sky. He saw only a clear sky with a dusting of cirrus formations in the higher atmosphere. No storm clouds in sight. "Should be able to make it that far pretty easily."

"Uh huh. I was just looking at the map thinking that maybe we should keep on going further if we can... maybe camp deep in the backcountry instead of that campsite.

Jason shrugged. "If you want," he said. He let Tommy make the decision as usual.

Tommy looked down at the path below him. He and Jason walked on the sides of the large path to avoid the muddy section in the middle. "The trail might be sloppier when it gets narrower."

"My feet are wet already from crossing the river. What does it matter now?" He stomped his feet to show Tommy how the water spilled out and down the sides of his shoes.

"Doesn't really," he replied. "It's just that we'll have another eight hours or more tomorrow if we stop at Wolf Creek. The farther we get tonight the better."

"If you think so."

Tommy closed the book, stuffed it into the side pocket of his backpack and started to walk again. He said nothing and remained deep in thought. Jason followed behind close and stared off into the forest.

Hours past as the boys followed the path that meandered up and down, crossed through small valleys and rose up over narrow ridges. The boys had to ford a few small creeks, and in other areas they had to walk through the shrubs along the side because the path was a terrible mess of churned up mud from numerous hoof prints.

"This sucks," Jason said. "Bloody horses!"

Tommy laughed as he struggled on his own through the scrub around this muddy section of the path. "You didn't complain last year, remember? When you were on the horse and passed those hikers who were up to their ankles in mud."

Jason frowned as he lost his footing while he tried to circumnavigate a large shrub on the edge of the muddy trail and stepped deep into a soft muddy section of the path. "Just shut up!" Jason shouted, highly frustrated. He struggled to keep his running shoe attached to his foot as he pulled it slowly out from the deep mud. He succeeded, and continued through the thickets and shrubbery that lined both sides of the path.

Tommy stole glances over at Jason as he fought his way through the bush. He laughed inside and enjoyed seeing Jason in touch with his emotions outside of Spy Hill.

The sun threatened to hide behind the tall mountain to the west. The lower section of the valley descended into the shadows as the boys reached the Wolf Creek Campground. The going had been slower than Tommy hoped, and he decided it would be best if they camped here after all. They would get an early start in the morning instead. Tommy picked a site in the back as far away from the path as possible to set up camp.

CHAPTER 75

Ricky knew he was in for tension by the surprised reaction he received at the reception desk when he asked if he could see Tommy Oliver. Instead of being directed to the visitor's room as he was in the past, he was shunted through a side door and down a hallway to a small tiny room with no windows that contained only four single wooden chairs.

He was only alone for a few minutes before two serious looking officers entered the room. One introduced himself as Seargent Stearn from the Royal Canadian Mounted Police, and the other was a Brian somebody from somewhere Ricky couldn't remember. His mind shuttered with a heavy worry. He felt himself become light headed, and the room swirled around him as the officers pounced on him with many questions about Tommy.

The questions were direct and to the point. Ricky answered as straight as he could, careful to remember Bobby's instructions about what to say.

"And you haven't seen Tommy today?"

Ricky feigned a frown. "I told you, I just got here. No, I haven't seen him today."

"Maybe somewhere else today?"

"Huh?" Ricky forced another frown. "Where else would I see him? He's locked up here. I don't understand."

The officers looked at each other. Both understood Ricky was going to continue to deny seeing Tommy today.

"What about your friend then? The other one who comes up here all the time." He spun his hand around in circles. "What's his name again? Oh yes, Bobby. Have you seen Bobby today?"

Ricky nodded. "Uh huh. He drove me up here. He's outside waiting in the car."

Seargent Stearn looked to the other officer who then quickly left the room. Ricky knew he was off to bring Bobby in for his own questioning.

"Let me ask you this. Where were you this afternoon?"

Ricky responded quickly. "Bobby and I went to see a movie. The Hunger Games. It started at five. Came straight up here after the movie was over."

The officer nodded back. "Hunger Games?"

"Uh huh. The Hunger Games. Down at Westhills."

"Westhills theatre. You wouldn't still have your receipt would you?"

Ricky looked down nervously and shoved his hand into one of the pockets of his jeans. "I think so," he mumbled. He dug deep and pulled out nothing. He stood up and shrugged. "I thought I still had it."

He shoved his other hand into his other pocket and finally pulled up a crumpled piece of paper, and smiled.

"Oh, here it is," he said and quickly unfolded it. He handed the receipt over to the Sergeant.

The Sergeant studied the receipt for a moment and handed it back to Ricky.

"What's going on? Did something happen to Tommy?" Ricky asked as he shoved the receipt back in his pocket. "Is that why you won't let me see him?"

The Sergeant directed Ricky to sit back down. He pulled a chair across from Ricky and sat down himself face to face with Ricky. "Tommy and his brother Jason escaped today."

Ricky knew the Sergeant was looking for a reaction. Ricky lurched up straight in his chair with his eyes wide open in surprise. "Escaped?" he said. He left his mouth open wide in awe. He then let a short smile slip across his face. "Really? Tommy and Jason escaped?" Ricky began to snicker. He started to laugh for show, but as he forced the laugh, he felt his nervousness release and the laughter became genuine. "Escaped? Well what do you know." He continued to hold the smile.

"This is not something to laugh about!" The Sergeant was clearly irate at Ricky's attitude towards the situation. "Those two are in extremely serious trouble now."

"Like they weren't already before," Ricky replied.

"Don't get smart!"

Ricky's smile evaporated. "Oh, I'm not, sir," He replied meekly. "It's just... I never dreamt they would ever try to escape. Not those two. Not if you knew them. Are you sure they aren't just hiding somewhere inside?"

Sergeant Stearn stood up. He breathed heavily and was clearly disappointed with Ricky's lack of information. "You will call us if he tries to contact you?" It was more of a statement than a question.

Ricky nodded fast and hard. "Of course, sir." Ricky knew he had made it through and couldn't wait to meet back with Bobby.

"You will just need to wait here a bit while we talk to your friend, and then you can go. It won't be long." The Sergeant left the room, and Ricky was left with an exhilaration he had not felt in a long while. He was sure now their part of the plan was complete, and tomorrow they would wait eagerly for Tommy and Jason to arrive back in Bluffington.

CHAPTER 76

The sun began to set behind the backdrop of the mountains to the west, and Sarah still had not heard back from Simon. She called him on his cell and then again at home, but the only voice she heard was a recording. It was so unlike Simon not to follow through on his word. He was a very particular character, and the worry she carried since spotting her car at the Safeway sank itself deep within her.

Sarah wanted to cry. She had been trying so hard to start over, but it seemed Gerald couldn't be washed away that easily. She stewed in her own past for a while and paced around the room. She worried about Simon. She thought about her attempts to plant new roots but realized that to grow anything new, even this far away in Bluffington, she had to rid herself of the ghost of Gerald. She accepted the truth that the ghost was there every single day. It was there as she sat at the Bistro and stared out the window day after day. She saw him in every stranger who walked like him or was built like him. She saw him in every white Ford truck that went by, and she often found herself hearing his whispers in amongst crowds. She heard his personal sounds at the most unexpected times.

Would she ever be free? She remembered a few nights ago when she sat out in Simon's back yard. Gerald didn't seemed so terrible that night. She felt foolish for a moment for letting herself waffle. She actually missed Gerald that night.

Now she reflected on previous events and felt a selfish shame for having involved her new friend Simon in her fret. It was unfair to drag him into it. She now worried about his whereabouts. Simon was probably off doing something else for himself. He probably totally forgot about driving into Calgary to check up on the house and Gerald for her. Gerald was probably just getting on as Simon suggested. She felt foolish all over again.

She called Simon again. "Why won't you answer?" she shouted. Her voice echoed eerily off the walls of the empty house. She hated her thoughts and shivered because she felt so very alone and helpless. If there was no Simon to lean on, then who was left?

The sun eventually set behind the mountains, and it left the darkened sky to creep across the valley while Sarah lay curled up under her comforter. She hoped sleep would come soon, but her mind swirled around and around with worry about Simon. It was too late to call Simon again. She settled on trying again in the morning.

CHAPTER 77

Tommy woke Jason as soon as the sun hit the opposite side of the valley. He wanted to get a move on, but trying to rouse his brother was more difficult than he thought.

"Stop it, Tommy," Jason shouted as Tommy shoved his fists into Jason's midsection. He pulled the sleeping bag high over his head attempting to keep his body heat inside.

"Get up, Jason. We gotta move."

"Hmm," Jason moaned and curled up even tighter.

"Jason! We have a long way to go today. C'mon."

Jason ignored him and pulled on the top of his bag again trying to drown out Tommy's demands.

Tommy shoved Jason hard one last time to wake him and slipped outside the tent. He stretched out wide, looked up and reached high into the clear blue sky. He quickly set about starting a small fire and had water boiling for the oatmeal in a short time.

"Jason!" he shouted and he stuck his head back inside the tent. "It's time. Let's move. I've got oatmeal on the go!"

The sun had already snuck down through the trees and onto their tent by the time Jason finally set himself down by the fire. Tommy ate long ago and had most of the gear, with the exception of the tent and breakfast dishes, already packed away into the two backpacks. The fire still burned, and he kept the water hot for Jason's oatmeal.

Jason rubbed his hands through his hair in attempt to make it lay where he preferred. It didn't co-operate and he quickly gave up. He looked down at the bowl of oatmeal Tommy handed him.

Jason grinned. "Mmm, oatmeal!" He laughed. "Just like Spy Hill. Thanks, Tommy. I thought I was done with their food."

"Just eat it. You'll need your energy today," he said and doused the fire.

Jason ate his breakfast and they packed up the tent and the rest of the supplies. They sat and studied the map once more before they headed out on the trail towards Bluffington.

CHAPTER 78

Sarah woke well before her alarm went off. The sun was already up, and she puttered around in the kitchen with a cup of tea in her hands. She studiously watched the kitchen clock and tried to decide what time would be acceptable for her to make her first call to Simon. She knew once she started to call him she would be consumed with Simon's whereabouts. She would be unable to stop her worry and her calls until she found him. The thought of her not being able to reach him kept her from making the call for the moment.

Sarah turned on the news and contemplated not going into work today. She was stressed, and she wouldn't be able to focus on anything else until she spoke with Simon.

She sipped her tea and hoped it would calm her down as she stared at the TV. The top story was one she had not expected. The two boys that had brutally murdered their parents last year in Bluffington had escaped from the Calgary jail yesterday, and there was now a huge manhunt under way to recapture them. The details were scant and the police asked the public for any information about their whereabouts. Photos of the two boys were shown to the viewers, but Sarah had already turned away. The news disturbed her, and she turned the TV off. She knew full well hers was the house where those two boys killed their parents. She didn't need to be reminded of that horrible tragedy at the moment. She had too much on her plate already with Simon suddenly missing. Her big worry was that Gerald loomed out there somewhere, and it left her with mixed emotions. She looked at the clock again and decided it was finally time to place the call to Simon.

She called Simon and felt a nauseous nip in her stomach increase with each ring when he didn't answer. She hung up, waited a number of minutes and told herself maybe he was in the shower. After waiting a number of minutes, she called him again. Simon still didn't answer.

CHAPTER 79

Hours passed as Tommy and Jason slogged forward along the path across Sullivan Creek towards Flat Creek Road. It was going to be a very long day with many kilometers of hiking trail to cover before they arrived at their destination, but if all went well, they would arrive by mid afternoon as planned. Having both Bobby and Ricky waiting for them at the end made the trek a lot easier to accept.

The boys had just crossed over South Sullivan Creek when Jason questioned the outcome of what they were after.

"Are we going to tell anyone?"

Tommy walked ahead of Jason. "Tell anyone what? About this hike you mean?"

"Not about walking through the stupid trees," he replied. He hesitated to clarify and walked awhile before he spoke again.

"Let's say we do this, and it all works out."

"Uh huh."

"Are we going to tell anyone about what we find?"

Tommy only sighed and didn't answer.

"Tommy? Are we going to tell anyone? A lot of our friends have been hurt here."

Tommy still didn't answer.

"Tommy?"

"I don't know!" Tommy shouted and stopped. He turned around and glared at Jason and then softened and shrugged. "I really don't know, Jason. Would you want anyone to know you were molested and abused? I don't think so. I know Ricky doesn't want anyone to ever know. We don't even know what we'll find in there."

Jason was confused. His mouth hung open in disappointment. "No we don't. But don't you think people should know what went on here?"

Tommy turned away. He was beginning to get upset and started to walk again. Jason followed and skipped forward rapidly until he was nearly on top of Tommy.

"Tommy? Don't you really think people should know? Lots of our friends were harmed."

"I heard you," Tommy replied annoyed and kept walking.

"Well?"

Tommy stopped again. "What do you want, Jason? Tim is dead because of our dad. Ricky's life back home is ruined because of him."

Jason shrugged. He didn't understand what Tommy was getting at.

"Ricky's gonna have to live with this every day for the rest of his life. Who are we to tell the entire world what happened to him? And how many others are out there? How many tapes and recordings are we going to find inside that room? I'm not going to look at them and then count them all to find out. I don't think you want to do that either."

Jason just shook his head. "But people should know."

"Really? What do you want?" he asked him again. "You really want everyone to know? This is a funeral mission we are on. We are going to bury this. Not you, nor I, nor anybody else, is ever going to see those who were abused and molested here. Don't you get it?"

Jason attempted to understand what Tommy was saying. His expression remained troubled. He wasn't convinced Tommy could really want to hide these horrible facts.

"If this information gets out, then every friend we ever had will be called out and questioned. It doesn't matter if he was even a victim or not! If he played hockey with you and me, and especially if he played on our line and scored goals with us, then he'll be questioned. No one will believe him even if he denies being abused, and he'll be labeled forever. Anyone we ever played hockey with will be called a faggot. Or worse. Maybe a pedo or a perv! Do you want that? They'll be called all kinds of names. Bad ones. Like cock suckers and fudge packers! Is that what you want?"

Jason began to cry. "Stop it!"

"You can cry if you want! This is serious shit! How many teammates have we had over the years? How many? Every single one of them will automatically become a victim here whether they were abused by our bastard father or not!"

"Stop talking! Just shut up!" Jason shouted and covered his ears with his hands.

Tommy raised his voice higher in response and stuck his face closer to Jason's as Jason turned away. He didn't want to hear any more.

"Anyone our dad ever coached and every kid our dad ever gave extra training to will be looked at as a part of this for the rest of their lives. Forever, Jason. They will be forever looked at for having been a part of some bad shit even if they weren't involved! Do you get it now?"

Jason ran away in to the trees and wiped his eyes as he ran.

"It doesn't matter if there are recordings or not for all those others," Tommy yelled loudly. "If this gets out, they'll still be suspected, labeled and teased. You know it, Jason. And that's why we are here right now doing this!"

Tommy said nothing more, turned away from his brother and looked forward up the path. "Let's just go," he said quietly and started up the path again.

"I'm sorry," Jason shouted from trees where he stood.

Tommy glanced back frustrated. "Sorry? What the hell do you have to be sorry for?"

"For our dad," he whispered through his tears and scurried back on to the path to catch up to Tommy.

"Fuck him!" Tommy shouted. "He's a bastard that deserved to die for what he's done to everyone." He stopped and realized what he just said.

Jason shook his head in disgust as he caught up to Tommy. He walked past Tommy and continued up the trail ahead. A part of him still loved his dad, and all he could do was leave Tommy standing alone with his words.

Neither spoke for a while, and Jason continued to keep his distance ahead of Tommy. If Tommy picked up his pace then so did Jason to keep the distance between them. They still had a very long walk ahead.

Hours passed before the trail exited the trees onto a gravel road. Tommy looked at the map and pointed to the right.

"Flat Creek Road. We follow this road for a few hundred meters and then it's back into the trees."

Jason looked up into the sky as he walked along the gravel road and estimated it would be another two hours before the sun would reach its maximum. It was still only mid morning. He was still upset with Tommy, but he was ready to let it go. He slowed his pace and let Tommy catch up to him.

"We're over half way," Tommy announced. "If we keep this pace we'll be there in good time."

At the end of the gravel road was a wide parking area. Tommy studied the cars briefly. He was pleased to see none were police or forestry vehicles. All were empty. They likely belonged to backpackers out hiking.

"Might see a few people today on the path," Tommy suggested.

Jason walked past the cars and looked inside a couple of them.

"Where does this road lead?" he asked curiously.

"The Highwood Trail highway. Near the Eden Valley Reserve. Why?"

"Just thinking. That's really not very far from Bluffington, that's all. Just up the road actually. These cars probably all came from Bluffington." He looked at Tommy and scratched his head deep in thought.

Tommy knew what Jason was thinking. "Pretty slim chance of seeing anybody on the trail. There are a lot of people in Bluffington. What are the chances of meeting someone we know? Pretty slim I think."

"You're probably right," Jason replied. He was unconvinced. He pointed to the sign at the start of the trail. "This way."

Tommy and Jason walked another forty-five minutes up from the parking lot along the Flat Creek trail to where the valley flattened out and Wileman Creek dumped into Flat Creek.

The junction they needed to take to get on the Wileman Creek trail was just up from where they currently were. It was northwest a little further beyond the grassy meadow they were about to approach. At the junction, the trail turned southward and followed an old exploration road that crossed Flat Creek and backtracked downstream towards Wileman Creek. The Wileman Creek trail would eventually take them up to Grass Pass and down Pack Trail Coulee to the Highwood River and to the backyards of Bluffington.

The valley opened up to large, grassy meadows interlaced with numerous beaver ponds. The scrawny, wind-battered trees in the higher elevations provided evidence of the constant winds that made their home here year round. It left Jason with mixed feelings regarding how unfriendly the valley could be at times. Jason was about to comment on the numerous great camping spots nearby when he spotted movement off to his right amongst the trees at the edge of the meadow.

"People!" Jason whispered to Tommy. He tugged Tommy on his arm and pointed up to his right towards the trees.

Tommy looked to where Jason pointed. Sure enough, there were two people in the distance amongst the trees where the meadow ended.

"It's just backpackers. Keep moving," Tommy replied. He pushed Jason and urged him forward.

Both boys walked on, but they kept a careful eye on the hikers.

"Well, what do wes have here?" a familiar voice called out loudly from their left. Jason groaned, and Tommy grabbed firmly on to Jason's arm.

There was a solid double click. It was the sound of a shotgun being cocked.

Off to Jason and Tommy's left, only a few meters away near Flat Creek, stood none other than Doogie Fisher with a devilish grin etched greedily across his face. He carried a shotgun in his hands. A water jug lay at his feet. He ignored the water jug, stepped slowly towards Tommy and Jason and made sure the shotgun he held was visible in front of him for Tommy and Jason to see.

"What did I tell yous, Jason?" Doogie said. He was very pleased with himself. He raised the gun and pointed it squarely at Jason, then at Tommy and back again. "I told yous you wouldn't see me coming and yous didn't." He laughed triumphantly. "Now gets over here and grab this water jug for me," he demanded of Jason. He kept the gun focused on him. "We's gonna have some fun."

CHAPTER 80

Sarah didn't go into work, but she couldn't stand to stay at home and do nothing except worry constantly about Simon. She grabbed her purse and searched around inside. The detective gave her his card when she saw him at Simon's Bistro the other day.

'Detective Dean Daly' was printed in bold official letters.

She called the detective on his cell phone. He answered immediately.

"Detective Daly? It's Sarah from the other day," she said.

"Sure, sure. I remember you," He replied. "What can I do for you?"

"It's Simon."

"Simon Pelletier?" What about him?"

Sarah tried not to let her emotions break through, but she was sure the detective heard her worry.

"He disappeared, Detective. I've been trying to reach him all day today, and last night and..."

"Calm down, miss," Detective Dean interrupted. "Just take it slow and tell me about Simon."

Sarah told the detective she thought Gerald was in town two days ago with her old car. She also told him she pestered Simon to go to Calgary to make sure her car and Gerald were still in Calgary.

"You didn't actually see Gerald then? In the parking lot?"

"No," she replied. "And I didn't stick around to look for him either. I just saw the car. My car."

"And you didn't see Gerald prowling or lingering, maybe, around your house?"

"No, I didn't see Gerald at all."

"Did you see anyone else, maybe? I mean, prowling around outside your house last night or today?"

"No. No one." The detective's comments scared her. He seemed to be suggesting prowlers may be about outside. She tried not to think about Gerald as a prowler lurking about on her property in the dark.

"Good, good. Then you're probably safe staying right there where you are," he said.

Sarah sensed the detective was trying to put her at ease.

The detective was very polite and promised he would check into Simon's whereabouts this afternoon. He had a few things in the valley to take care of first, and then he would get right to checking out the Bistro and Simon's home.

"And Gerald too," she added at the last minute, before the detective had a chance to hang up.

"Gerald?" he replied confused.

"Yes, Gerald. If Simon really is missing and he went to see Gerald, then you must go up to where Gerald lives. You must!" She was nearly crying.

"Okay, okay," the detective agreed. "I'll go around town, and if I can't find Simon, I'll go up to your old house in Calgary and look in on Gerald."

"Oh thank you, detective. Thank you," Sarah said relieved.

Sarah gave the detective her old address in Calgary, Gerald's full name and a description of the vehicles she and Gerald owned. The detective promised to call her back in a few hours.

CHAPTER 81

Jason and Tommy raised their hands shoulder height into the air as they stared at the shotgun Doogie pointed at Jason.

"C'mon, Jason. Gets over here and pick up the jug for me. And then wes are going to take a little walk."

Jason edged his way slowly towards where Doogie stood and carefully picked up the water jug.

Doogie's expression changed to one of curiosity. "What are yous two doing out here anyways? Yous both were locked up."

"You have a smart phone," Jason replied. "You should know already why we're here."

"Phones don't work up in the back country, stupid," Doogie answered back.

Tommy gave Jason a quick look to say 'zip it'. "They let us out," Tommy said simply. "Not enough evidence."

Doogie frowned and dropped his head to the side confused. "Really? I thought yous admitted it."

Jason shuffled himself back next to his brother. Tommy smiled and shook his head at Doogie's stupidity.

"Don't matter. What matters is yous are here. I don't know whys you are here, and I doesn't really care. You are going to go for a walk with me right now over there." He pointed to the right were Jason saw the other people moments earlier. "And yous see this," he raised the gun a little higher. "It is loaded."

Doogie directed Tommy and Jason to the small camp he set up away from any other hikers who would pass along

286

the trail. Along the way, Tommy asked Doogie what he was doing up here.

Doogie lifted the shotgun up higher. "Target practice," he said and laughed.

When they entered the camp, they were not surprised to find Doogie's friends, Willie, Sandy and Patricia, all seated on small stumps around a fire.

Willie was in the process of trying to cook up some Kraft Dinner over the smoky fire. He looked up with surprise but was confused by the shotgun Doogie had levelled at Jason.

Patricia's eyes sparkled when she spotted Jason. She seemed almost excited to see him and produced a wide smile for him. The excitement faded quickly as her eyes fell on Doogie's shotgun. Sandy said a polite *"hello"* to Tommy and Jason before she looked at Doogie and waited curiously for his explanation.

"Drop your packs, and have a seat, boys. Sandy, there's rope in the side pocket of my backpack in the tent. Tie these guys' hands."

"What?" Sandy replied giggling. "You serious?"

"Get the effin rope, Sandy!" Doogie shouted. "I'm not kiddin here!"

Sandy cowered for moment and then hurried to the tent to grab the rope. Tommy and Jason removed their packs and sat cross-legged on the ground opposite Doogie's gang. They looked at Patricia pleadingly as Doogie continued to wave the gun about.

"What's going on?" Patricia asked. She was utterly confused by the sudden appearance of Tommy and Jason. "I thought they were in Spy Hill still?" She stared at Jason with a puzzled look.

"They are here now. That's all that matters." Doogie paced back and forth in front of Jason and Tommy and continued to wave the gun about. "Where's that rope, Sandy?" he shouted.

Sandy scrambled out of the tent and handed the rope out to Doogie.

"I'm not tying them up. Yous are." Doogie grabbed the rope out of her hand. "Cut off two long pieces!" he shouted. He stretched the rope out to indicate the length he wanted it cut and handed the rope back to Sandy.

Sandy grabbed a knife and quickly cut the rope as directed. She looked back at Doogie in disbelief of what he was asking her to do.

"Now get over theres and tie their hands behind their backs. And I want it good and tight."

Sandy hesitated.

"Go!" Doogie shouted at her.

"Why are we doing this?" Sandy asked as she moved behind Jason and began to bind his hands together. Willie continued to stir the pot by the fire. He enjoyed the scene that unfolded in front of him. Patricia sat next to Willie in fear and confusion.

"Little cock-sucker thinks he can gets one up on me. Who's on top now, Jason! Who?"

Jason grunted and grimaced as Sandy pulled the rope taut and it cut into his wrists.

"Screw you!" Jason called out.

"What did yous say?" Doogie called back. He stepped forward towards Jason and cracked him on the side of the head with the butt end of the shotgun. Patricia let out a little scream and pressed her hand to her lips.

Jason reeled under the pain and a cut opened up near his temple. Blood trickled down the side of his face.

"Nice one, Doogie," Willie said and giggled as he continued to stir his Kraft Dinner.

"Just stop this already," Tommy said calmly. "You really don't want to be doing this."

Doogie turned to Tommy. "Yous don't know what I want at all. Maybe I should bash yous in the head too. What do yous think, eh?"

Tommy shook his head lightly and looked down into the dirt.

Sandy finished tying both boys up, sat down next to Patricia and grabbed hold of her hand. The girls watched in shock and fear of what Doogie was going to do next.

"You two think yous are so effin tough. Why you think I want yous tied up?" Doogie looked back at Willie and the girls. Willie continued to smile.

"Well? I asked yous a question."

"You're trying to prove a point, I guess," Tommy answered. "And you did it very well. You got the gun, and you are in charge. Jason and I have to do what you say."

Doogie frowned and crouched down in front of Tommy. He stuck his face into Tommy's. Tommy winced at the smell of his breath. "You don't seem so tough." He spit in Tommy's face and turned to Jason. "It's yous I want. Thinks you can tackle me and bust me in the face?"

Doogie stood up and paced back and forth with the gun. He pointed the gun at Tommy, then at Jason and back again. Tommy tried to wipe Doogie's spit from his face onto his shoulder, but he couldn't. He looked up and could see the blood veins rising and pulsating on Doogie's forehead as Doogie continued to pace back and forth in front of them. Doogie suddenly stopped and turned angrily towards Jason. He lowered himself down on to his haunches and grinned. "It's payback time," he said as he stared into Jason's terrified eyes.

"What are you doing, Doogie?" Sandy called out. "You just can't go around tying people up like this."

Doogie spun around towards her. "You want to be tied up with them? This little shit here bust my lip. Or did yous forget? And he made me looks like an idiot at Spy Hill, and I ain't gonna let him gets away with it."

Doogie stood up and grabbed firmly onto Jason's arm. "Yous're coming with me!" he shouted and lifted Jason up by the arm until he was standing. He turned Jason around and shoved him in the direction of the forest.

"Doogie! What are you doing?" Patricia called out.

Willie continued to stir his lunch and smiled as he watched, thoroughly enjoying the escalating chaos.

"Shuts it, Patricia. I'm going teach this boy heres a lesson! That's right, Jason Oliver. It's payback time!" he said and shoved Jason again with the barrel of the gun.

"Willie!" Doogie shouted. "Go get my Beretta!"

"The Beretta?" he asked surprised. "Why do you want that for?"

"Just gets it, Willie."

Willie gave the macaroni a quick stir and then hustled over to the tent.

"What are you going to do to him?" Patricia asked.

"We'll see, won't wes, Jason. We'll just see."

Willie scurried back and handed the Beretta to Willie.

"Just purchased the shotgun and this baby," he said and caressed the gun with his fingers. He lifted the black semi-automatic in the air and kissed it. "Seeings how Daly took alls my other guns away." He tucked the Beretta in the front of his pants. "Shotgun's too messy for what this boy's got coming his way," he said and cackled loudly. He grabbed tight to the shotgun and turned back towards Jason.

"Move!" he shouted as he shunted Jason forward once more.

Jason staggered forward, and nearly stumbled as he stepped out of the camp and down into the rocky meadow.

Doogie followed close behind and continued to shove Jason forward every few steps towards the trees.

"Stop it, Doogie! You can't do this!" Tommy called out.

"Tommy?" Jason cried out. "Help me, Tommy!"

Before he had gone very far, Doogie stopped and turned his head slowly back towards Tommy as if a brilliant idea had just come to him. He grinned and bared his teeth at Tommy. "And when I'm done with him, yous can be next."

All Tommy could do was watch Doogie shove Jason further towards the trees. He was terrified. He had no idea of what Doogie was capable of, and he really didn't want to find out.

"Patricia! Sandy! You are not going to let Doogie do this are you?" Tommy called out to them. The girls continued to sit holding tight onto each other with terror etched deep into their young faces. Tommy sensed their discomfort as they looked about frantically, neither sure of what she should be doing.

"Willie!" Tommy called. "For God's sake, do something!"

Willie only continued to stir the pot. He tested the noodles to see if they were fully cooked and licked his lips. He glanced to his left and watched for a moment as Doogie pushed Jason down below the ridge. He watched until they disappeared. "Sorry, Tommy." He smiled. "He's got the gun, and this macaroni ain't done here yet."

Tommy tried to stand up, but fell over without the use of his hands. He tried again to get to his feet but he couldn't get a good footing and fell back down. He lay on his side, and shuffled about some more. "Jesus Christ, you guys! Don't you see what Doogie's about to do?" He stopped squirming, stared at Patricia and pleaded. "You've got to go stop him.

You have to! Doogie's going to shoot him if we don't do something. He's crazy!"

The girls looked at each other and then at Willie.

"He's out of control He's crossed the line!"

"Oh my God, Sandy," Patricia called out as she finally understood what Tommy was suggesting. "I think Tommy is right!"

Tommy rolled his eyes. He couldn't believe it took them this long to come to grips with what Doogie was about to do.

"We should do something!" Patricia shouted to Sandy.

"Untie me." Tommy called out.

The two girls stood up. Sandy pointed at Tommy and ran towards him. "I'll untie him," she said.

"Don't do it, Sandy," Willie said while shaking his head and urging her to sit back down.

Sandy knelt down behind Tommy with her hands on the rope. She hesitated and looked back at Willie to see if he was going to stop her.

Patricia backed slowly away from Willie and the fire. When she was near the edge of the rocky campsite, she turned suddenly and bolted off in the direction Doogie had taken Jason.

"Patricia!" Willie called out. "Damn it, you girls," he said. He stood up and scratched his head. "And leave him be," he said to Sandy.

Sandy shook her head. "No. It's not right, Willie. I'm untying him."

Willie remained standing by the fire. A flustered look crossed his face as he clearly didn't know what to do. "Doogie's gonna be mad when he finds out you let him go, you know."

"Be a man for once, Willie!" Sandy shouted back. "What Doogie is doing is so wrong!"

Sandy just finished untying Tommy's rope when a blood curdling scream erupted from somewhere in the forest. It was Patricia. Her scream coincided with a single shotgun blast that echoed repeatedly off the surrounding mountains.

"No!" Tommy screamed. He couldn't believe Doogie had actually gone through with it.

Willie moved for the first time as if the sound of the shotgun blast finally brought some sense into his little brain. He rushed around the fire, accidentally knocking his pot of Kraft Dinner on its side into the fire. He grabbed Tommy's backpack from the ground and shoved it hard into Tommy's belly. "Run!" he said.

Tommy stared out past Willie to the forest. Willie grabbed hold of Tommy and spun him around. "Just run, Tommy!" he said a little louder and shoved him in the back.

Tommy turned his head again to steal another look to where Doogie took Jason.

"Tommy!" Willie shouted. "Just get the hell out of here now before Doogie gets back!" He shoved Tommy one more time, and Tommy finally began to move.

"Go! Now!" Willie shouted, and he urged Tommy to flee while he could.

Tommy gripped his pack tightly and began shouldering it as he ran. He looked back quickly and caught the site of Willie and Sandy as they ran away from the camp towards the trees where Jason was taken earlier. A cloud of steam rose from the fire.

As fast as his feet would move, Tommy raced out from the few trees that surrounded the camp and down across the meadow. He kept running. His heart pounded fiercely. Once he reached the trail, he followed it northwest as far away from the camp as he could. Tears fell down his cheeks as he thought about his brother. He couldn't believe what just happened. Anger and loss rose inside him.

Why the hell did Doogie have to be up here today?

Tommy ran hard and the adrenalin pumped harder. He soon crossed over the river and was down the switchback and on to the Wileman Creek trail before he felt even remotely safe. He continued to jog up the trail that led to Grass Pass, but the uphill climb quickly depleted what little energy he had left. He eventually stopped and looked further up the trail. It opened up wider and wider into a treeless, grass-covered area. He was tired and needed to find some cover to rest. He scrambled into some bushes well off the trail to his left. He lay in the tall grass, hid beneath the small shrubbery, buried his head under his crossed arms and cried.

CHAPTER 82

Ricky stood on one of the large rocks on the edge of the Highwood River. He was using his good arm to toss small pebbles out into the many pools that rested in this part of the river. His cast, now dirty and scuffed, remained on his other arm. Bobby sat a dozen feet away and watched him from the edge of the riverbank where the grass dropped down a few feet to the rocky shoreline.

"We've been here for hours," Ricky said impatiently. "They should've been here by now."

Bobby nodded. He worried something had happened to his friends, but refused to say it aloud.

"They'll be here soon," he said. "Maybe they lost the trail or something."

Ricky threw another rock as far as he could. It missed its target and bounced off a rock on the other side of the river. He stopped and pointed high up to the mountainside across the river.

"Is that the trail they'll be coming down?" he asked as he pointed to a dark line barely visible in the trees on the mountainside.

Bobby shook his head. "I don't think so. I'm not sure that even is a trail. The trail comes out downstream a ways...down through a coulee not on the side of the mountain like that." He pointed downstream. "Just down past Head Park bridge, I think." He studied the shapes of the mountains where they angled down to the river, and he could see where one mountain dropped off and another rose behind it. Pack Trail Coulee would be tucked in there somewhere.

Ricky looked downstream and could barely see the end of the narrow pedestrian suspension bridge in the distance where it connected to the path along the river on the other side. The path from the bridge only went downstream on that side of the river. The boys had never been very far down that path, but they knew a smaller and less often-used trail climbed its way up along Pack Trail Coulee into the backcountry.

"Oh," Ricky replied. "Why are we waiting here then?"

Bobby shrugged. "Wait here or wait on the bridge. It doesn't really make a difference. Tommy's old house is right there," he said and motioned with his head to the property just a few doors down from where they waited. "They'll see us."

"Well, I'm not waiting here all afternoon. Another hour and then I'm going."

Bobby couldn't remember any conversations they had about them arriving late and what to do if they didn't show up as planned. The plan was for Tommy and Jason to arrive early in the afternoon and sneak into their old house while it was still empty. "I guess that's okay," he said. "I should really hang around longer in case they come."

"Well, you live just over there. It's not far for you to go home. I'm getting hungry and I have to walk all the way across town."

Bobby understood what Ricky was getting at and remembered his mother's words. He wasn't supposed to be anywhere near Ricky. He certainly couldn't take Ricky back to his house for a snack. "How will we meet up later, after Tommy and Jason finally show up, if you leave?"

"Not sure," Ricky replied. He recalled that Bobby no longer had a phone. He gazed down the river towards the bridge.

Bobby sighed and thought about how to do this so they didn't miss Tommy and Jason when they came by.

"How about we do shifts?" Bobby suggested. "You go home now and come back in say… an hour or so. Then I'll go home for an hour, grab something to eat, and then come back. What do you think?"

Ricky smiled and nodded eagerly. "Great idea! We won't miss them that way." He paused and thought some more. "And if I'm here when they come, I'll quickly run over to your house to grab you. I'll try to be discreet in case your mom is home."

Bobby nodded. "And I'll send Jason over to get you if they come while you're gone."

"Perfect! I'll see you in a while," Ricky said. He turned away and jogged down the path towards home.

Bobby wandered up and down the trail, glanced towards the mountain across the river and watched for any sign of his two friends.

CHAPTER 83

Dean sat in the parking lot outside of the Bistro. Sarah was right. Simon didn't show up for work today. The staff confirmed that it was extremely unusual behaviour for Simon. It was so unusual in fact, that none of the staff could ever remember a day when Simon didn't show up in the morning or call if he was delayed.

He was glad Sarah called; not because he was attracted to her, but speaking with her had already been on his list of 'to dos' for today. She made his list because of the furor that was created about town yesterday over the escape of the Oliver boys.

Their escape bothered him as much today as the unanswered questions he had of the murder itself did. He knew there was more to the murders than had yet been revealed and the escape of the boys fit in with his line of thinking. The boys, young offenders, if found guilty of murder, would be released after short incarcerations. The boys most certainly would know by know the legal limits to incarceration for young offenders in Canada.

So why escape days before the trial begins? Dean knew he was correct about there being more to what happened to these boys.

Having Sarah call him before he went to call on her simply saved him some time on a very busy day. He only had a few questions for her following the escape. Had she seen either of the boys? Had she seen anyone lurking around outside the house since yesterday afternoon? The answer he received in her phone call was a solid 'no'.

He started the engine and readied himself to head over to Simon's property.

"Damn it!" he said to himself. He really wanted to spend more time on the Oliver boys case, but he simply had to continue searching for Simon.

It was only a short, ten-minute drive out to Simon's property. The sun was out, and Simon's property looked immaculate. The hedges were nicely trimmed, grass was cut and even the flowerbeds looked fine. Dean chuckled to himself as he thought about Jen's cattle. "Doesn't look so bad to me," he said as he inspected the property.

After ringing the doorbell and knocking on the door a number of times, Dean began to believe that Sarah was right to be concerned. He took a quick walk around to the back of the property and even looked in through the windows. There was no sign of Simon anywhere.

Dean jumped back in his cruiser and ran a check to see if Simon's vehicle had turned up anywhere. After a few minutes, the report came back with nothing.

Simon had disappeared.

Dean looked at the time. It was near dinnertime. He knew he was in for a long night since he agreed to drive into Calgary to check on Gerald. He decided he would grab a quick bite to eat and then head out of town.

CHAPTER 84

Ricky was tired of being on watch for Tommy and Jason. It had been more than two hours since he returned from grabbing a snack and relieved Bobby. He was bored silly. Where the hell was Bobby? He said he was going home to have a quick bite to eat and be right back.

Ricky walked a few hundred yards down the trail and looked across to the far end of the suspension bridge. Nothing.

"This is stupid," he said aloud to himself. He paced up and down the trail once more.

"C'mon Bobby already!" he shouted. "Jesus! Two goddamn hours already!"

Ricky had enough of waiting alone. He had looked forward to this afternoon for days now, but suddenly it turned out to be a great big let down. Tommy and Jason didn't show, and Bobby left him standing out along the river all by himself.

"I'm done here," he mumbled quietly, and wandered down the path, to where he cut across an access path that lay between two properties connecting the river path to Founders Road. He walked out along Founders Roads and ducked into the alley that would lead him down behind Bobby's house.

Ricky moved along the back alley until he was behind Bobby's garage and then shuffled along the side of the garage towards the backyard. He popped his head around the side. He could see Bobby's CRV was still in the drive. Bobby's mother's car was nowhere to be seen. Good.

Ricky slid back out into the alley, picked up a couple of pebbles, and moved back in towards the house. He hid alongside the garage and watched for movement inside any of the windows, hoping to see Bobby. He fiddled with one of the pebbles and got ready to toss it at one of the windows. He watched for a while, saw nothing and decided he wasn't going to wait any longer. Bobby's bedroom was on the second floor. He tossed one of the pebbles towards the window and hit it on the first try. He waited to see if Bobby's face would appear in the window.

CHAPTER 85

When Tommy finally reached the lower end of Pack Trail Coulee and emerged along the Highwood River, he was exhausted. He was worn out from the long hike out along the coulee, but the thought of leaving Jason's body somewhere up in the mountains severed a part of his heart. His grief sucked away some of his life and purpose. The shotgun blast and Patricia's horrid scream convinced Tommy that Jason was dead, and he doubted he would even remember where to look for him if he ever got the chance to go back up into the hills.

Tommy could see the rooftops of Bluffington across the river in the distance and quickly headed for the suspension bridge upstream.

Once on the narrow rope bridge, he stopped and looked up and down along the river path for Bobby or Ricky but saw neither. He was tired and needed to rest. A day and a half of hiking left him extremely wasted. He wanted to stop to give his feet a break, but he knew he couldn't stop completely so he took a short pause on the bridge and leaned against the ropes. His eyes caught the reflection of the sun as it flickered and danced on the ripples on the water, and he glanced down over the edge of the ropes to the surface. He was suddenly mesmerized with how the water flowed and moved rhythmically over and around the many rocks that lay visible under the surface. He stared deep into the water and watched as it passed beneath him.

He gazed into the darkness underneath the surface, and what he saw disturbed him. He was tired and rested himself upon the ropes as he looked deeper into the water.

Underneath the surface, he saw things he had never noticed before. Maybe it was because he was so tired, but he saw things. Terrible things. Rocks of all shapes and sizes worked hard to deliberately divert the water's path. There were eddies, deep pools and sharp sticks that threatened to break the surface. There were fractured boulders, split by centuries of tumbling and rolling about. He saw a terrible place under the surface. He could even see the thin film of slime that collected on the bottom. The slime coated the entire surface. The boulders, rocks, pebbles, sticks and everything else that he could see underneath were covered in slime.

Tommy breathed a sigh and wiped his dry mouth with his sleeve. He knew already what was underneath. He didn't need to look into the water anymore to see it. He saw it himself months ago, and it stole his innocence. It was easy to smile when he was innocent, but he looked beneath the surface at the dark place. Now he couldn't smile. It was impossible to smile, knowing about the slime.

Tommy tore his eyes away from the flowing water, looked up towards the town and scanned up and down the river for Bobby or Ricky. He still didn't see either of his friends. With the last of his strength, he hustled across the bridge and continued up the path until he stood out in back of his old house.

"Damn you guys," he muttered under his breath.

He stood on the path alone and his thoughts turned once again to Jason. Jason was supposed to be here to help him do this. A horrible image crept into his mind of Jason lying broken and twisted amongst trees and rocks, all alone on the cold earth. He felt himself begin to choke up. He breathed in deep and tried desperately to catch himself before he broke out in tears.

Tommy always ran towards trouble, but when Jason needed help this time, he turned and ran the other way. It was all he thought about as he came down from the mountain. But now he forced himself to stop thinking about Jason. He would cry later. He would cry when his task was done.

He stared at the house and rehearsed his next movements in his mind: Climb carefully up the wall. Skirt the outside of the house and crawl through Jason's window. Sneak quietly through the house upstairs to silence the alarm and then slowly edge down the staircase, through the house, to the study. Finally, open the fireplace.

Tommy visualized each step repeatedly. He closed his eyes and focused. He was attempting to rebuild his confidence and push away the fear and apprehension. This was a momentous challenge he had to undertake alone, and he had only one chance to make it happen. His exhaustion made it difficult to focus. Minutes passed as Tommy rolled his movements over in his mind.

Then it came. He felt the small fire begin to smoulder inside. He hadn't felt it for a long time.

Tommy nodded. He recognized the burn. It was what he called his "hockey fire". Tommy felt this burn before every shift of every game of hockey he ever played. Tommy knew that burn well, and he welcomed it now. It was a mixture of fear, nervousness and confidence. When in balance, it would drive Tommy to fight and commit himself when others became indecisive. It was the edge that allowed Tommy to understand the limits of his own emotions.

The fire grew, and Tommy knew he was ready.

Tommy opened his eyes, walked confidently to the back of the property and climbed over the post rail fence that paralleled the river. The back part of the property was a wild, forested area with a narrow pathway that wound its way through the trees to the lawn at the back of the house. He knew this part of his back yard well. He walked slowly through the dense trees and shrubbery and easily kept himself out of the sightline of his house and the others on each side. As he neared the back of the physiotherapy office, he scooted off to the side of the property and edged his way up behind the garage.

He shuffled slowly along the back of the garage to the office and stopped. He listened carefully for any sounds to come from inside the therapy office. It was all quiet. He slowly lifted his eyes up over one on the window ledges and peered inside. The window coverings were gone and the office was dark and empty. It wasn't as he remembered it without all of the furniture, shelves, and training equipment.

Tommy moved around to the side of the building where he could look out at the back of the house. He studied the house carefully for a number of minutes and scoured deep inside each of the windows.

Even though it was late evening, the sun would stay up in the western sky for a few more hours. He didn't like the idea of a daylight break in, but it was the only option.

Tommy saw no movement in any of the windows, but there was one vehicle parked in front of one of the garage doors that concerned him.

He scampered quickly across the backyard to the steps that led up to the back porch and looked up to the roof.

"Shit, Jason," he cursed. "How the hell did you ever figure this one out?" he asked as he looked up at the gable roof that covered the porch with impossible angles.

Tommy dropped his backpack into the shrubs to the side of the porch steps and was soon standing on the flat, wooden porch railing. He used the house to steady himself as he calculated his next move. As he stood on the railing, he reached up as far as he could along the ridge line. He grabbed on as tight as he could with his left hand and pulled his feet up to the side as high as he could until he hooked one foot into the gutter on the side. He wobbled about and scrambled with one hand while he reached up with the other in an attempt to grab any part of the roof to get leverage. He fumbled about, scraped his knuckles on the shingles and somehow managed to pull his lower body up enough to roll his hips onto the small roof and then pull the rest of his body fully on top.

He lay there a moment, stared up into the sky catching his breath again. He silently cursed Jason for having revealed the route.

Tommy stood shakily on the sloping roof and looked next at the narrow skirting board that separated the first and second floors of the house. He followed the skirting with his eyes around the side of the house to Jason's bedroom window.

"You've got to be kidding."

The skirting board protruded out from the wooden siding a mere two inches. He could see where the paint had been scuffed and rubbed off the narrow ledge by Jason's previous excursions and felt an energy boost.

Tommy knew had to move quickly. He grabbed hold of the corner of the house with his left hand and stepped pensively up onto the narrow skirting board to test his balance.

He slid one foot around the corner and awkwardly forced his body around the side of the house. He reached along the wall and grabbed tight into the ridges of the wooden siding for support. Sweat dripped down Tommy's face, and he felt his hands begin to shake from gripping as hard as he could.

He moved his body inch by inch along the skirting, while still holding his body tight to the wall. He shuffled himself as far to his right along the narrow skirting as he could while he held on to the corner, but Jason's window was still out of reach.

He pulled his head back and pressed his chin tight up against the house. His eyes darted back and forth. He trembled, and his fingers began to cramp. He forced himself to look to the right again, and he tried to reach as far as he could to the window. No matter how far he stretched his fingers, they couldn't reach Jason's window. Tommy began to panic.

There was nothing to grab hold of. One hand held on to the corner of the house and the other reached towards Jason's window, and only the rough surface of the siding was there to hold on to.

He closed his eyes. He knew he could only hold on like this for a few minutes more at most, before he would lose his grip. His fingers began to tingle and he could feel the numbness begin to set in. He cursed Jason again for telling him of this dastardly route.

He tried to remember what Jason said about getting in the window this way. He was forgetting something.

He felt his left hand fingers start to slip away from the corner of the house. "Think!" he said to himself, "Think!" He remembered nothing.

Tommy couldn't hold his grip any longer and his fingers slowly slipped off the corner. He tried to dig his fingers in, but there was no grip left and his fingernails scraped along the side of the house. Tommy lost his grip and started to fall. Tommy opened his eyes, terrified, and saw what he had forgotten above him.

"Shit!" Tommy shouted, as he thrust both of his arms to the sky. He reached up desperately and successfully wrapped his fingers tight around a two-inch drainpipe that protruded less than four inches out from the wall above his head.

His feet slipped off the narrow ledge, and he hung in the air and scrambled madly to get his feet back on to the skirting. "Shit!" he said. He cursed himself for forgetting that Jason mentioned the spout. It was a small cast iron drain that protruded from the wall. It drained the water from a hidden valley where the rooflines met.

Tommy waited until he recovered his composure and footing with both hands now gripping tight to the drain spout. He shuffled his feet and carefully reached towards Jason's bedroom window with one hand while the other held tight to the drainpipe. He tugged up on the window, and, to his relief, it lifted easily.

Tommy scrambled inside and sat down on the floor, relieved he had made it. It felt good to be off his feet, and he welcomed the brief luxury. He rubbed his hands across his sweaty face, and listened intently for any sounds from inside the house. All was quiet. Tommy leaned against the wall and looked around Jason's old room. He scanned across all of the walls. The room was now bare and stripped of every sign that Jason had ever existed. It hit him hard as if someone did it deliberately. Tommy rested his head in his hands and quietly sobbed.

CHAPTER 86

Dean found Sarah and Gerald's house easily. Sarah's car wasn't in the drive and the search he had dispatch conduct for him said Gerald's truck had been written off in the accident back in December. The registry showed no new registration from Gerald, so Dean was fairly certain that Gerald had no other car than Sarah's. He concluded that Gerald was not home.

He walked up to the front and rang the bell. Gerald didn't answer. He knocked anyway and still got no response. He drew his hands up around his eyes and pressed his face to the glass, just like Simon the day before, and tried to see inside. It was much too dark inside, and all he could see was a short dark hallway.

Dean shuffled himself away from the front door. He sauntered around the side of the house and then further around to the back yard. The back door had no window. He tried the doorknob. It was locked. He moved across the small landing and leaned over the side, hoping to look in through the kitchen window. He could see the drapes open, so he expected to be able to see something inside the house through this window.

Dean rested his body against the railing and leaned out as far as he could toward the kitchen window. He methodically set about to discern what he saw. The kitchen was a mess with dishes propped up in the sink, and the garbage container overflowed in the far corner. On the counter next to the sink was an empty whiskey bottle. Next to the whiskey bottle was one empty glass tumbler and an assortment of tools and utensils.

"What do we have here?" he whispered. It all seemed normal at first, until he studied each one of the items individually. A butcher knife, a cheese grater and a nutcracker were resting on the counter. Dean also spotted a pair of pliers, a roll of duct tape, pruning shears and dirty rags.

Dirty rags? That wasn't dirt he saw on the rags. He instantly recognized the color, and he tensed up as the adrenalin began to pump hard through his veins. He leaned in closer to the window. He needed to be sure about what he saw. He could see the utensils and tools, and they were covered in blood.

Dean leaned farther over the railing in an attempt to see further into room. Just as he spotted the bloody footprints that criss-crossed a number of times across the floor from the front of the house into the kitchen, the railing gave away. Dean crashed hard onto the ground beneath the kitchen window.

He cursed aloud, as he landed on the busted railing, and he felt a new, unwelcome pain blaze through his shoulder and right leg. He lay on the ground for a moment, but his adrenalin blocked all the pain. He knew he had stumbled onto something far more sinister than anything he had bargained for. Dean rose quickly to his feet and he raced around to the front of the house and towards his cruiser. As he came around the corner, he spotted Simon's SUV parked a few doors down.

"Shit!" Dean said. He checked the plate and verified that it was Simon's. He turned, raced back around the way he came and dashed around back and up the stairs to the back door. He opened the screen and threw his body hard against the door. He heard the doorframe crack. He charged again. The door frame gave away, and the door swung inward and slammed against the inside wall. Dean quickly drew his handgun and stepped inside with gun drawn.

As he looked around the kitchen, his stomach turned. Dark, bloodied footprints led from the kitchen out to the next room. He cautiously moved into the kitchen to follow the footprints.

He peeked around the corner into the next room and a wave of fear and terror like he had never felt before rushed him. He spotted the horror that presented itself there. It was like some bad horror scene from a Ripley's Believe It Or Not exhibit. A single chair sat in the centre of the living room, and fastened in to the chair slumped a body. The body was covered in dried blood. The legs and arms were duct taped to the legs and arms of the chair, and Dean could see many disfigurements that told him that the person in front of him had been savagely tortured.

Dean swallowed hard, moved into the room and stepped closer to the body. Dean new instantly that it was Simon, and he doubted that he was alive, but he needed to check either way. The state of Simon's body repulsed him. He placed his hand on Simon's neck to check for a pulse, but there wasn't one.

As Dean looked at Simon's body, he quickly understood the purpose of the utensils in the kitchen. Simon was missing two of his fingers on his left hand, and he had no fingernails left on two of his right fingers. The bones in his right hand appeared to be broken, from being forced back, one by one. He could see bloody ridges in the skin that he was sure would match the pliers that sat on the counter in the kitchen.

Dean put his fingers under Simon's chin, and lifted his slumped head up high until he could see Simon's face.

It was a gruesome sight. Simon had been beaten severely about the head; both of his eyes were bloody and swollen closed. His jaw looked like it was broken, but he couldn't be sure.

He let Simon's head fall forward and he slowly backed out of the room. There was only one thing that crossed his mind now. Sarah.

CHAPTER 87

Tommy slowly crept out from Jason's old room and into the master bedroom to disable the alarm. He could see the red light indicating it was armed. He reached out his hand to enter his code but stopped as he suddenly realized the code may have been changed. He had not even given any thought to that. He stepped back from the alarm pad and looked around the closet desperately, wondering how to proceed. He had only paused a moment when he spotted the yellow sticky note on the wall to his left. A six-digit number was written on the small piece of paper. Tommy took a deep breath and carefully keyed the six numbers into the pad. He pressed the pound button to enter the code, and to his relief the red light changed to green. The alarm was now disabled.

He then moved into the upstairs hall and danced around the many creaks towards the staircase to the main floor. He had to be very careful because the house was old and had many specific sounds. He advanced slowly down the staircase and stopped to duck down every few steps as he scanned the lower level beyond the bottom of the stairs. He saw no sign of anyone in the house on the lower level and crept down further.

It took Tommy a number of minutes to make his way to the bottom of the staircase on the main floor. He breathed a huge sigh of relief as he was nearly at the study. He was almost certain the house was empty.

Tommy clearly remembered how Jason swung the axe that killed their mother after hearing the creaks in the hallway he was now about to walk down. He took a deep breath, put one foot in front of the other and moved closer to the study. He was extremely aware of where he planted each foot.

The door to the study was wide open, and Tommy leaned his head inside to look around. He saw no one and stepped inside. He scanned across the room; it seemed different from when he had lived there. In front of the fireplace were two large back chairs set at an angle facing the fire. To his left was a long, black leather couch that faced the front window with its back to the centre of the room. The dark shears on the window were pulled closed, and the single lamp that rested on the side table, next to the couch, was turned on. It was late afternoon, and the sun was still high, but the shears blocked most of the light that would normally brighten up the large room.

Tommy reached behind him, put his hand on the door and carefully started to push it closed. He wasn't going to close it tight, just enough so he felt safe. The door was almost completely closed when it gave out its custom squeak.

Tommy froze and stared at the door. He waited for someone to suddenly approach from down the hall. He didn't see Sarah pop her head up from behind the black couch where she had been resting as she read a book, unaware that an intruder had entered her home.

He only heard her terrified scream.

CHAPTER 88

Ricky threw another pebble up at Bobby's window and waited, but Bobby still didn't appear. Frustrated, he crawled out from the shadow of the garage and ran up to the back door. He looked inside the window to see if he could see Bobby inside, but he didn't see anyone.

He tapped lightly on the back door and hoped to see movement inside.

As he stared, disappointed, inside Bobby's darkened house, the sound of a vehicle suddenly rose out of nowhere, and Ricky froze right where he stood. Bobby's mother's car appeared from around the side of the house and stopped a few feet away from him. Bobby sat in the passenger seat and rolled his eyes angrily at Ricky.

Ricky remained standing at the back door as Bobby's mother stepped out of the car and walked up to the back door with a bag of groceries in each arm. She burned her eyes into Ricky letting him know that she wasn't pleased to see him standing there.

"Hi, Mrs. Fornier," Ricky said politely.

She frowned and ignored Ricky.

"He's not supposed to be over here, Bobby!" She shouted. "You can tell him to leave right now, and then you can get in this house. Do you hear me?" She walked past Ricky and entered the house as if he didn't even exist.

Bobby nodded sheepishly back to his mother and stepped up beside Ricky. "What the hell are you doing here?" Bobby whispered in Ricky's ear. He snuck a look back at his mother inside the house as she moved about in the kitchen putting the groceries away. "You're supposed to be watching at the river!"

"I got tired of waiting," Ricky replied. "They're not coming."

"They are so!" Bobby hissed vehemently. "Tommy and Jason are coming, and we need to be there."

"Bobby!" His mother shouted from inside the house. "You tell him to go away now!"

"In a second, Mom!" Bobby shouted back.

Suddenly the back door swung wide open and Bobby's mother stood there furious. "I told you to ask him to leave!"

She looked down at Ricky. "Why are you still here? You're not welcome around here anymore! You hear me? Bobby was a good boy. I don't know what's gotten into you, but I won't have you turning my Bobby into a rascal like you." She burned her eyes into Ricky until he turned away. "Now shoo!"

Ricky stepped back away from Bobby and his mother. He shook his head from side to side and shrugged. He didn't know what to do exactly and looked for some direction from Bobby. Bobby dropped his right hand down by his side where his mother couldn't see it, and ushered him away, down the driveway. "I'll catch you later," he whispered. "By the river."

"What did you just say to him?" Bobby's mother asked as Ricky disappeared around the corner of the house.

"Nothing," Bobby replied.

"I don't want you hanging around with him."

CHAPTER 89

Tommy panicked as he heard Sarah scream out and instinctively rushed towards her to silence her. "Shhhh!" he responded, but Sarah only continued to scream louder. She raised her arms to her face in terror at Tommy's sudden presence.

As Sarah continued to scream, Tommy was at a loss about what to do, but knew he had to shut her up as quickly as he could.

"Please, just shut up!" he shouted. "Be quiet! Please, please." Tommy reached out towards her in desperation. Sarah continued to scream as she pulled herself away from Tommy's reach and he saw no option. He lunged forward, grabbed on tight to her and shoved her hard, backwards onto the couch. He continued to wrestle with her until he was on top of her and forced his hand over her mouth to stifle her scream.

"Please, just be quiet!" he called out. He was terrified by the sudden turn of events.

Sarah squirmed underneath him for a few minutes and then suddenly stopped. Her eyes were wide and full of terror as she looked up at Tommy sitting on top of her.

"Shhh, shhhh. That's better," he said. "I'm not going to harm you. Honest," he said. He didn't remove his hand from her mouth. He kept his body on top of hers while he thought about what he was going to do next.

He really needed to get into that room quickly, but he decided it would probably be impossible if he let her up. He puzzled quickly over his options and finally decided what to do. He searched around the room for anything he could use to tie this woman up and immediately spotted a charger cord for a cell phone plugged into an outlet only a few feet away.

"Okay," he said calmly to her. "Here is what we are going to do..."

Sarah stared back at Tommy, and he could see the fear growing in her eyes. Tommy hated what he was about to do, but decided he had to do this if he wanted to finish what he came for.

"I'm so sorry, but I'm going to have to tie you up."

Sarah started to squirm again.

"Wait a sec! I mean it. Stop moving!" Tommy shouted, and she immediately stopped.

"I promise I'm not going to hurt you. I can't hurt you," he said and hoped she would believe him.

"But you still need to let me do this. Please."

Tommy could see the terror in her eyes.

"I'm going to remove my hand, and you're not going to scream. Okay?"

Sarah nodded back.

"That's good, that's good," he replied. "But I do have to tie you up, and I promise that I will not touch you at all."

Tommy removed his hand from Sarah's mouth, and nodded at her. Sarah remained quiet. He slowly reached one hand over to the small table beside the couch and yanked the charger cord from the wall. He removed himself from the couch, pivoted Sarah to her side and quickly secured her arms behind her back. He repositioned her up on the couch to a seated position and knelt on the floor beneath her.

"I'm not going to touch you at all," he said calmly. "I'm here for another reason, which I will tell you all about in a few minutes, but I need to make sure you won't stop me from what I have to do. Understand?"

318

Sarah shook her head from side to side sheepishly. Her eyes were wet and frightened.

"What do you want?" she asked. Her voice was shallow and nervous.

Tommy got up from his knees without replying and searched about the room. He spotted a tea towel on the coffee table, grabbed it and carefully ripped it into long strips.

"Well, I don't want to hurt you, that's for sure. But I really can't let you stop me from what I have to do here."

Tommy knelt down before her again and used one of the strips to bind her feet together.

"I am so sorry about this, but I really have to do this. I'll let you go when I'm done."

"Why are you doing this? What do you want?" she asked again. Her voice had steadied some, but the fear remained.

"I'll tell you in a sec," he said as he thought about how much he could tell her. He carefully rolled up another strip of the towel and wrapped it around her head and across her mouth to prevent her from screaming again.

"There," he said. He was confident she wouldn't give him any trouble now that she was tied and gagged. Tommy left Sarah sitting on the couch at the front of the room and made his way over to the fireplace. He glanced back to see Sarah strain to follow him with her head twisted around. He nodded back at her and pointed to the fireplace.

"I used to live here," he said. He stopped in front of the fireplace and felt around under the opening for the release lever.

Tommy was about to open the fireplace, then he wondered if he really wanted to have her watch him reveal the secret room. He moved back near Sarah and picked up another strip of cloth.

"It's probably best if you can't see what I am about to do." Tommy wrapped another strip around Sarah's eyes.

"There were some horrible things that happened inside this house," Tommy said as he finished tying the blindfold. "Terrible things. And I am not talking about the murders that happened in this room. There are far worse things than murder."

Sarah, now bound and gagged, could only listen as Tommy spoke.

"I'm so ashamed to even be here, but it's something I have to do."

Tommy stood up, walked over to the fireplace again and found the release mechanism. He slowly pushed the fireplace back and revealed the secret room. He stood there, stared into the darkness and shivered. His memory tortured him. He could again feel the horror that Tim's voice represented as it had drifted out from the darkness on that terrible day.

Tommy felt suddenly all alone, and the terrible truth rose up from the deep and swelled like the behemoth that it was. In that dark room, only a few feet away, was the weight on so many friends' minds and hearts. He wanted no part of that truth. But who else was able to rise up to make sure that there was no more hurt?

"I can't," he said aloud. He turned away from the fireplace and looked over at Sarah on the couch.

"You probably already figured out who I am and know that my brother and I killed our parents in this house."

Tommy saw Sarah jump at his words. "I'm sorry. I thought you knew who I was."

Tommy moved back next to Sarah and knelt down on the floor in front of her again.

"I don't know why, but I am not sure if I can finish this. You weren't supposed to be here and things don't seem so easy anymore."

He reached his arms out to touch Sarah, and then pulled them back. "I don't even know who you are." He crossed his arms across his chest. He felt uncomfortable about having invaded what was now her home. He looked at her and studied her features, looking for a reason.

"Maybe it's best that way," he said finally. He shook his head and wiped his eyes on his sleeve.

Tommy looked up past the couch to the room behind the fireplace and pointed. Sarah couldn't see him point through her blindfold.

"It's all in there… what he did. My dad. It's all there. Right in that room. And how many victims are still in there? I'm scared to find out." Tommy stopped talking and stared into the dark cavity beyond the fireplace.

"He sodomized them, you know? My teammates. My friends. Brought them out back to his shop and did awful things to them, and I feel so very humiliated for not knowing it was even happening. It hurts because he was my dad, and I really loved him so much. I never knew… I just never knew it was happening until it was too late."

Tommy started to cry. He reached up and placed his hand on Sarah's knee. He needed to touch someone to feel human.

Sarah flinched.

"I'm sorry," Tommy responded and pulled his hand away. "It's just everything is so wrong right now." He was hurting inside and needed to explain. "I left my brother up..." He couldn't finish the words. "I ran away. Just when he needed me, I ran away."

Tommy tried not to cry. "I've never ran away before. But I did this time. I ran away and left him up there. And then I come here and I am hurting you now."

He looked about hoping to hear some word of comfort, but Sarah could offer none.

"I am so sorry. So sorry. I shouldn't have tied you up. I don't know what's happening to me. I don't like this at all."

Tommy stood up and stared into the dark room. He could almost see shadows inside, and he shuddered as he was sure he could see them moving around.

"And it's gotta stop. The hurt, I mean. My dad's dead now. He can't hurt anyone anymore, but what's in that room continues to hurt. Until it's all gone, the hurt will stay because they all know it's still out there. Pictures and video recordings of them all, and secretly they cry… they know it still exists."

Sarah grunted in response.

Sarah's phone suddenly began to ring, and Sarah turned her head towards the phone on the end table. Tommy shook his head, "We're not going to answer it."

The two of them listened until the ringing stopped. Tommy sighed and returned his focus to what happened to so many of his friends.

"They don't talk about it at all, you know. None of 'em. But that doesn't mean the hurt's not there. I'm afraid, I really am. I don't even know who they all are, and the truth, is I don't want to know. I am so scared right now, and once I walk inside that room I'll find out who they are. I'd really rather not know. Do you understand?"

Sarah gave a soft nod to Tommy, but he wasn't convinced she understood a word of what he rambled on about.

Tommy sat for a few moments and breathed in the silence. It spoke volumes of the pain he felt. He reached up and removed the blindfold he had just put on her. She looked back at Tommy, and Tommy could see she was very confused. She tried to comprehend what he had just told her. She followed him with her eyes as he stood up and once again, walked over to the fireplace and stared into the dark space beyond.

"My name is Tommy."

CHAPTER 90

Dean rushed out to his cruiser and left Simon's lifeless and mutilated body in the chair inside the darkened living room. He was worried about Sarah now. He called the number Sarah gave him, but there was no answer. The call went to voicemail. He didn't leave a message and instead called his dispatch back in Bluffington to request that a car be sent over to Sarah's house to make sure she was okay. He asked that he be updated immediately after the car arrived at her house.

Dean then called the Calgary City Police and explained the situation with Simon. Simon was dead. He was he killed after being brutally tortured by Gerald. There was only one reason in Dean's mind why Gerald would torture Simon so severely: to find out where Sarah lived.

To say that Gerald was "not a very nice guy" was the biggest understatement Dean had ever heard.

Dean sat in his car and looked at his watch. He knew he would be tied up here with Simon's body until long after the City Police arrived. He wished he could just leave and get down to Sarah's immediately, but he knew he couldn't head back to Bluffington until all the details were captured.

CHAPTER 91

Tommy was still standing at the entrance to the secret room when the doorbell in the front hall rang out. Tommy skipped quickly back over to Sarah and put his hand softly upon the gag he had wrapped around Sarah's mouth. He whispered in her ear.

"Were you expecting someone?"

Sarah shook her head hard from side to side.

The doorbell rang again and a quick, repeated knock on the front door followed.

"Shhh," Tommy instructed Sarah. "Maybe they will go away."

Tommy looked around the room and thought about running up and pulling the fireplace closed, but he didn't dare leave Sarah alone. She had been cooperating up until now, and he wanted it to stay that way. He leaned over to the front window and slipped one hand between the shears to create a small opening so he could see out to the front of the property.

"Shit!" Tommy said softly as he spotted a police car in front of the house. There were no lights flashing on the car. It was parked directly in front of the house, and Tommy could clearly see it was empty.

Tommy looked back at Sarah and decided not to tell her it was the police in case she would scream to raise alarm.

"Let's just be quiet until they leave," he suggested.

More minutes passed by and the doorbell rang once more. Again, it was followed by another set of knocks. The knocks were much more persistent this time.

Tommy wiped at the sweat that had begun to collect on his forehead. He held his breath and kept one hand gently pressed over Sarah's mouth. He looked out the front window again and breathed a sigh of relief as he watched the officer walk away down the sidewalk and climb back inside the police car.

The police car remained in front of the house for what seemed forever to Tommy, but it finally drove off, and he removed his hand from Sarah's mouth. He desperately wanted her to trust that he didn't want to hurt her, but he was unable to let his guard down.

Tommy rechecked her bindings and walked about the room nervously. He knew he should be getting on with finding the tapes in the secret room, but he felt truly ashamed at having tied Sarah up. He was still not sure what he should do about it.

Tommy finally moved back towards Sarah and removed her gag.

"Listen, I just can't do this with you sitting here looking like this. I need to know you're going to be okay."

Sarah nodded back.

"I'm not going to hurt you. I want to know you believe me."

Sarah nodded again. "I believe you," she whispered.

Tommy was not entirely convinced.

"Listen to me," he said. "I'm just trying to protect my friends who were hurt. Abused."

Sarah frowned, and Tommy could see that she was actually listening and attempting to understand what he was trying to say.

"One of my best friends committed suicide a few months ago."

"I am so sorry," Sarah replied. "But, I don't know what that has to do with..."

"My father was molesting him," Tommy said. "And I never knew."

"Oh my," Sarah said. She sounded sincere to Tommy. "But it's really much worse."

Tommy could see Sarah's mood had softened. His own panic level had abated, and he now sensed that she almost seemed to be showing a sincere compassion for him.

Tommy continued to share with Sarah about what he was about to do and what he had already done. Tommy even confessed to Sarah that he was the one stirred up everything and caused her house to be broken into just before she moved in. He apologized deeply, and his anguish increased since he had no intention of ever causing her any harm. Now that he saw Sarah, he knew he committed a terrible violation of her, and Tommy didn't want her to be yet another victim. Sarah seemed to understand. He believed she was no longer completely terrified of him, and he sensed a small sliver of trust as she listened and asked her own questions.

Tommy talked for a while, and Sarah listened. As Tommy shared his pain and his fears regarding what he and his friends had suffered, Sarah spoke up and began to share some of her own pain. She even offered up her real reason for being so terrified when she had first spotted Tommy in the room. She was terrified of Gerald, and even as she looked at Tommy and screamed, it was Gerald whom she feared.

It didn't take long before Tommy was satisfied, and he knew he would be able to continue his task. He again apologized to Sarah for everything he had done up until now, and he told Sarah that he really needed to put the gag back on her. Sarah almost smiled as she told him it was ok. Tommy sensed that she understood.

He secured the gag. Tommy wanted to thank Sarah for understanding, but he couldn't find the words. He could only manage a smile before he moved forward to the secret room to finish what he came for.

CHAPTER 92

All Bobby had wanted to do when he left Ricky on watch out by the river was to go home, grab a quick bite to eat and get back out to the river before Tommy and Jason arrived. His mother had other plans from the moment he stepped in the back door. She was home early and demanded that Bobby go grocery shopping with her.

Bobby was beyond upset when they arrived home to see Ricky standing at the back door. His mother continued to dump on him after Ricky left. She told him he wasn't going anywhere as supper would be ready soon.

The supper amounted to a simple soup and sandwich. On any other day, his mother's beef vegetable soup and tuna sandwich would have made him smile. He loved her soup, but tonight it lacked all flavour. Maybe it was his discomfort from having his mother ban Ricky from ever coming around again. She had no right to tell him who he could keep as a friend!

Bobby watched his mother with disdain. She puttered over at the sink, cleaned up the dishes and wiped down the counter where he sat, before he was even finished eating. It irritated him when she did that; it suggested he was a slow and sloppy eater. She would always give him her funny leer when she picked up his plate and wiped underneath it while he was still eating. Bobby took this as a warning to make no mess now that the counter was clean.

Bobby had always wanted to ask his mother, "Why wipe the counter before I'm done?" but never dared. He knew what the answer would have been. She always wanted to have control, and she always found it, sometimes in the simplest of ways. Today, she stepped it up a notch. She was out to control who he could see and who his friends could be.

The soup tasted awful, and Bobby suddenly pushed it away from him across the counter spilling it over the side. A trail of soggy vegetables lay strewn across the freshly wiped counter. He was sure his mother heard every single vegetable as it hit the surface of the counter. She turned rapidly towards Bobby with the wet and dripping washcloth gripped tightly in her hand.

"I'm not hungry," Bobby said and frowned.

His mother pulled her chin in and scowled.

"Look at that mess!" she chirped. "I just wiped that, Bobby!"

Bobby felt the tension inside of him overflow. He wasn't used to such elevated emotion within himself. He certainly never stood up or responded after his mother picked at all of the little things he did, but tonight she pushed him past his limit.

Bobby spun around on the stool and turned his back towards her. He crossed his arms across his chest and wanted to scream.

"Bobby! I want you to clean that mess up! You hear me?"

Bobby kept his arms crossed and stubbornly refused to acknowledge his mother.

"Bobby!" she shouted again. "It's about that damned boy, Ricky, isn't it?" she demanded.

Bobby just lifted his shoulders and kept his back to her. He was purposely unresponsive.

"That boy is just no good! I don't want him around here anymore. Is that why you are acting like this right now? Well, I want you to stop this nonsense right now. Turn around and finish your soup!"

Bobby couldn't take it anymore.

"No!" he shouted, uncrossed his arms, spun back around and stood up. He stared up at his mother's horrified face and rubbed his leg fiercely with the heel of his hand.

His mother stuttered in surprise at Bobby's sudden outburst. "You... It's soup! Bobby... That Ricky boy. He's just a terrible boy!"

"He's my friend!" Bobby shouted. "Stop talking like he's bad! He's not!"

"Bobby! You listen to me..."

"I'm not listening! Ricky's my friend, and he's not bad! You can't tell me who I can have as a friend!"

Bobby jumped off the chair and moved towards the back door as his mother watched in shock at Bobby's defiance.

"He's the only friend I have left!" Bobby shouted. He slipped out the back door and left his mother staring out the window at a loss for words.

CHAPTER 93

Tommy had just stepped inside the small secret room when he stopped and popped his head back out to see Sarah on the couch still bound up tight. He thought he heard a thumping sound. It was a very loud thumping sound. He studied Sarah, wondering if she was the source, when he heard it again.

"Sarah!" an angry voice suddenly screamed from outside of the house. It was a terrifying voice filled with a dark rage of fury.

"Sarah!" it screamed again. "I know you're in there!"

The thumping and pounding began again. The angry newcomer began to beat his fist firmly on the front door.

Tommy remained half in and half out trying to decide what he should do. He looked across the study to Sarah, and from where he was all the way across the room he could see she was shaking to a point nearing convulsions. She was in absolute terror over the thumping heard coming from the front door. She twisted and turned her head about, looking back toward Tommy. Her eyes were filled with the utmost horror he had ever seen in real life. Although she was gagged, it was as if her terrified eyes screamed and pleaded to Tommy for help.

The thundering sound at the front door returned once more with a fury. Tommy was indecisive as he listened to the pounding of the man thrusting himself at the door to gain entry.

"Jesus Christ!" Tommy whispered.

Tommy froze half in and half out the secret room. Tommy heard another thundering crash and he knew the door was breached. He jumped inside the room, closed the fireplace and locked himself in.

CHAPTER 94

Bobby cried as he shuffled along the front walk down Founders Road. He felt a hurt deep inside from hearing his mother talk that away about Ricky.

"If she only knew what happened to him, then she wouldn't talk that way," he whispered to himself. He knew that wasn't the truth. If his mother knew what horror befell his friend, she might go even farther to suggest that Ricky was dirty and contaminated. This dirty boy, just by being his friend, would taint the pure image of her son.

Bobby ran as best he could down the road and began his search for Ricky. He wasn't just Bobby's friend; Ricky had become Bobby's very best friend. He didn't even look at the Oliver house as he shuffled passed it. Finding Ricky was the only thing on his mind, and he knew Ricky should be out by the river. If he had looked at the Oliver house, he would have seen that the front door was breached and lay askew on its side.

Bobby tried not to cry as he thought about how he talked back to his mother. He had never talked back to her that way before and feared the punishment waiting for him at home. He decided he wouldn't even think about going back home at all until it was dark. He would stay out late tonight if only to make her suffer. But he had to find Ricky first. Once he found Ricky, they were going to wait for Tommy and Jason to arrive, even if it took all night.

As fast he could move with his weak leg, he trundled forward down Founders Road and was soon back onto the river path behind the houses where he immediately spotted Ricky standing out on the suspension bridge.

Bobby smiled and waved to his friend.

CHAPTER 95

Dean's cell phone rang and he picked up immediately. It was dispatch about the officer he sent to check on Sarah.

"No one was home?" Dean asked.

He listened to the response.

"You sure?"

Dispatch repeated to Dean what they found.

"Well that's good, but I am still worried about her."

Dean refrained from telling his dispatch what he found up at Gerald's house, but he did tell them he would be tied up with a situation for a while.

"I should be out of here in a half hour to forty-five minutes. Once I am out of here, I will go straight over to check on Sarah myself."

Dispatch acknowledged his reply.

"I'll call you when I am back in Bluffington."

CHAPTER 96

Gerald threw his shoulder against the front door and was immediately encouraged as he felt the door give.

"Sarah!" he screamed. "I know you're in there!"

He stepped back and charged at the door once again. This time, the door cracked in the middle and the frame buckled and separated in a number of places from the outside wall. He charged at the door again with his entire weight crashing into the door. Splinters of wood flew into the air as the door fell inwards, and Gerald's large body fell with it. He stumbled over the door and landed in a heap on the floor inside.

Gerald lay on his back for only a moment as he reached out and tried to grip his fingers onto anything to right himself into a standing position. There was a small side table in the foyer, and he pulled himself up quickly by it and began to look around the house for Sarah.

It had taken Gerald many months, but he had finally succeeded and he was determined to see this through. It took a very long couple of liquor-filled days to pull Sarah's whereabouts out of Simon, but he succeeded.

Peeling back the layers of another human being was very hard work. Gerald enjoyed the challenge Simon imposed on him. Simon refused to answer why he was searching around Gerald's car and home for a long time. Each time Simon refused to cooperate or disengaged himself from the process, Gerald reengaged Simon with another smash to the side of the head or a punch in the ribs. All the while, he sipped on his whiskey and let the rage of the moment fill his dark desire to release his anger on another victim. There would be no regret later for dealing the dirty side of the deck to Simon as Simon had laid his hand first when he stepped onto Gerald's property. He was trespassing, and Gerald felt truly entitled to act accordingly.

Torturing Simon was almost an exhilarating experience for Gerald because he had never let his anger carry him that far before. It was a slip of the tongue that doomed Simon to a fate he wouldn't escape. A simple request to "go home".

Simon was broken and tired; Gerald had been at him for hours.

"I just want to go home," Simon slurred through his bloodied mouth. His broken teeth made his words almost incoherent.

"Where's home?" Gerald asked not really caring where Simon had come from.

"Bluffington," Simon had answered.

Gerald thought he heard the name Bluffington, but it was so slurred and mumbled that he at first he thought he had imagined it. There was a blister in his brain from where the name Bluffington rubbed repeatedly in his mind as he wondered what to do about Sarah. He asked Simon to repeat what he had just said, and this time it was crystal clear.

"Bluffington."

Gerald immediately upped the ante.

"Sarah," he then whispered to Simon.

Simon winced and lifted his head up to Gerald. He shook his head as best he could and cried. "Not Sarah. Please."

Simon was doomed. The game was on, and Gerald was set to win. He held all the cards and would play them all, one by one, until Simon spilled Sarah's hiding place. Simon fared well to start with. He screamed and cried as Gerald bent his fingers back, one by one, until each one broke. Gerald smashed Simon in the mouth repeatedly until what was left of Simon's teeth lay in his own lap, shattered and crimson. When that didn't get results, Gerald went even farther and used pliers to pull out Simon's fingernails, but he found that too much work. Simply cutting off a finger at the knuckle, one at a time with pruning shears got him the best results.

Gerald stopped his reminiscing about the sessions with Simon and moved into the front living room of Sarah's new home. He called out to Sarah a number of times, but she didn't answer. He moved about slowly from one room to another and finally stopped in the kitchen.

"Sarah?" He whispered. He began to second-guess himself and thought maybe he was at the wrong house. Was it possible that Simon gave him the wrong house number? He moved about the kitchen and, on the counter, he spotted a few items of mail. He picked up the mail and smiled. Sarah's name was printed on the front of the envelopes.

He set the mail back down gently and called out loudly. "You know it's me, and you know you can't hide from me. Just tell me where you are, and we can both get this over with." He said it almost sweetly.

He moved from the kitchen down the far hallway towards the front study and slipped inside. He saw the couch facing towards the front window, and he saw movement. It wasn't much, but enough to cause Gerald to move in for a closer look.

Gerald eased his way along the wall until he could see around the back of the couch. He broke into an evil grin as he saw his beloved Sarah sitting there on the couch, shaking in fear as she stared back at him.

His look suddenly changed to puzzlement when he realized that Sarah was bound and gagged.

"What the hell?" he asked as he scanned the room nervously. He couldn't comprehend how Sarah ended up this way. His thoughts went immediately to Simon. He didn't know why, but he could think of no other answer.

Gerald stepped forward until he was looking down at Sarah. He grinned again. He didn't really care that she was bound up. In fact, this may actually be better than he could have asked for.

"What goes around comes around, eh?"

He laughed, put his hand on the side of Sarah's head and pushed it lightly to the side.

"See?" he asked. "What are you going to do now, Sarah?"

Sarah pulled her head away from his hand. Her eyes were cast downwards, and Gerald grabbed her by the chin and forced her face up towards him. He wanted to see her look him in the eyes.

"You ran out on me, Sarah." He watched her eyes as they darted back and forth.

"You know you can't ever leave me."

Gerald let go of her head and stepped back. He slowly circled the couch. He paced and paced as he thought about what to do.

"I loved you, Sarah!" he shouted. "Why did you run out like that?"

Sarah mumbled back through her gag.

"What? I didn't hear you?" Gerald replied and laughed. He was pleased to see her suffer.

"I tell you what Sarah. I am going to remove your gag, and we are going to have a little chat. I don't know why Simon tied you up like this, but I am glad he did. It's too bad he won't be seeing you anymore."

Sarah squirmed about on the couch and mumbled more incoherent sounds.

Gerald stopped his circling and removed the gag. Sarah coughed and wheezed and grabbed a couple of deep breathes.

"So tell me. What's with that scrawny little shit, Simon? "

Sarah only stared back at Gerald. He saw the anger bubbling up under her fear. Gerald liked that and taunted her more.

"He couldn't even put up any fight. What a weak piece of shit. But I'll say this much about him. I had to remove a few of his parts before he would tell me where you were."

Sarah tried to stand up, but her hands remained bound behind her back. Gerald easily shoved her back down on to the couch.

"What did you do to him, Gerald?" she asked sternly.

Gerald just laughed. He was delighted. "I did what I needed to do. He won't be telling any more secrets, that's for sure."

He watched as Sarah began to cry and shook her head in denial.

"Did you hurt him?" she asked through her tears.

"Hurt him?" Gerald laughed again. He loved that Sarah was suffering. "Oh!" he exclaimed as if he suddenly remembered something important. "By the way. He gave me something to give you."

Gerald continued to laugh even harder and neared hysterics. He reached one hand deep into the pocket of his trousers and closed his hand around the object inside.

"He gave me something," he repeated and slowly pulled his closed fist out of his pocket and lifted it up towards Sarah.

"I'll let you guess what he said when he gave me this." Gerald's fits of hysterical laughter ceased as he slowly opened up his hand.

Sarah screamed at the top of her lungs, as she stared down at Gerald's outstretched hand to see a finger resting in his palm. The finger still had a ring attached. Simon's ring.

"Yup. That's exactly what Simon said," Gerald said as Sarah screamed again.

Gerald dropped the finger on to her lap. Sarah jumped and twisted her body frantically to dislodge the finger, and continued to scream hysterically.

"Hey!" a voice erupted from somewhere within the study. Gerald looked around and was startled to see a teenage boy standing in the room against the fireplace on the far wall. He seemed to appear from nowhere.

"Who the fuck are you?" Gerald shouted at the teenager. He was furious about the interruption and moved away from Sarah towards the teenager.

The teenager mimicked Gerald's movement and stepped forward a few paces towards Gerald. "You leave her alone!" he demanded.

Gerald's severe rage changed to one of curious amusement after he eyed the kid up and down and determined that he was really no contest.

"What the fuck did you just say to me?"

"Tommy, don't," Sarah wheezed out the best she could from the couch behind Gerald.

Gerald stopped when he heard Sarah call the boy by name. He looked back at Sarah and then at Tommy. He nodded as he compiled his thoughts.

"It was you who tied her up. Not Simon," he suggested.

Tommy stood his ground. "I tied her up. And I don't know any Simon. Now you just leave her alone."

Gerald simply laughed at him. "You can't be serious, you little shit. Sarah's my wife. Do you understand me? I'll do what the fuck I want with her." He paused and studied Tommy carefully. "But maybe you need a short lesson before you start mouthing off. I've eaten little shits like you for breakfast. You really want a piece of me?"

Gerald gritted his teeth and readied himself to charge forward. He glared at Tommy with his fists clenched tight.

CHAPTER 97

When Dean finally arrived on Founders Road, his roof lights flashed brightly and lit up the neighbourhood with a blue and red cadence of colours. The flashes reached across both sides of the road and grabbed onto the corners and crevices of every shadow they could find as the afternoon rolled over well past the supper hour. His stomach turned when he spotted a car that matched the description Sarah gave him sitting in front of the Oliver home. He pulled the cruiser to an abrupt stop in front and looked up at the house. He could see from where he sat inside his vehicle the front door was busted and flattened, and the terrible possibility that Sarah may be inside suddenly became very real. He immediately called dispatch and asked for reinforcements.

Dean exited the vehicle and moved slowly up to the house. As he neared the front door, he drew his gun from its holster and crept forward cautiously. He was still a few yards away from the front door when he heard voices and shouts from somewhere deep inside. He listened intently for Sarah's voice but could only discern the voices of two men as they shouted back and forth at each other. He considered handling this himself but decided the risk was too great. Dean didn't want to face Gerald alone after the scene he witnessed at the house in Calgary. He returned to his cruiser, called into dispatch with another update and screamed for his backup to hurry up. He ran the plate from the car he thought might be Sarah's old car, and his suspicion was quickly confirmed. He was sure Gerald was inside the house.

CHAPTER 98

Bobby and Ricky were only waiting a short time on the suspension bridge when Ricky spotted blue and red lights from a police car bouncing off the sides of the houses on Founders Road. He didn't know the police car was racing towards the Oliver home. The boys turned towards the lights and felt the adrenalin rush inside them.

"Do you know where it's stopping?" Bobby asked.

Ricky was already racing across the bridge towards Founders Road.

"It's stopped! It's stopped," he shouted and continued to run up ahead. "I think it's Tommy's house! C'mon, Bobby, run!"

Bobby tried to run, but the best he could do was a fast shuffle. Ricky stopped at the intersection where the river path crossed the access path between the houses onto Founders Road and groaned at Bobby. He wanted Bobby to move faster, but he knew he was moving as fast as possible.

Bobby huffed and puffed when he caught up with Ricky.

"Let's go," Ricky prompted again as soon as Bobby was beside him. Ricky jogged slower this time. He wanted Bobby with him when they finally moved out onto Founders Road.

"It is Tommy's house!" Ricky shouted as he pointed his casted arm towards the police car.

"Oh no," Bobby replied.

Both boys walked cautiously down the road. Two more police cars screamed past them with lights only, no sirens, and the boys watched as these two cars also stopped in front of the Oliver home.

By the time the boys arrived in front of the house, Detective Dean Daly and Officer Heavy Head were busy directing the other officers who had just arrived. Two of the officers had already been instructed where to go and quickly darted between the neighbouring homes, out towards the back of the house. Dean remained out in front of the home in deep discussion with the arriving officers. None of the officers had yet approached the house.

"See! You missed them! I told you to stay at the river," Bobby whispered to Ricky. "I bet Tommy and Jason are in there now. Now what are we going to do?"

Ricky didn't answer and Bobby knew Ricky was thinking about the secret room again. He watched the officers for a moment and was curious as to why none had yet approached the house.

"Something happened," Bobby suddenly said to Ricky.

"No shit!" Ricky replied.

"No. I mean it. Why aren't any of the police going up to the house? Something's wrong here, Ricky."

Ricky grunted to acknowledge Bobby. "What do you think is going on?"

"I really don't know."

Both boys continued to watch as Detective Dean Daly directed his officers. A few of the neighbours started to file out onto the street, and Ricky spotted a number of kids as they ran excitedly down towards them from the end of the block. The crowd was going to get large very quickly.

Officer Heavyhead and two other officers were already ushering everyone back and away from the Oliver house.

"I think you're right. Something bad has happened. Real bad."

Bobby nodded and continued to watch the chaos. There was no real action from the police yet. Detective Daly looked very serious as he spoke with his officers. He pointed up at the house a number of times, which made Bobby even more nervous.

"What should we do?" Bobby asked Ricky. Ricky didn't reply and only stood and stared up at the house. He shifted his weight from foot to foot and a look of consternation crossed his face. Bobby had seen this same expression on Ricky's face before, and he knew that Ricky was about to act on impulse.

"No, Ricky! Don't!" Bobby shouted at Ricky, but it was too late.

Ricky suddenly bolted towards the house.

Two of the officers out in front were focused on the crowd and were attempting to lay out a perimeter as Detective Dean Daly instructed. Neither officer noticed Ricky as he skirted between them. Dean was still engaged with the two other officers when he caught a blur of movement in the background near the house. He looked up just in time to see Ricky as he hustled up the stairs towards the front door. Dean turned and thrust his fist angrily in the air as he knew there was no chance of catching the boy before he entered the house.

Ricky had just reached the top of the front landing when a gunshot rang out from inside the home. The large crowd outside flinched and ducked at the sound. The spectators and police turned towards the house, but by the time all of the officers and most of the gathering crowd looked up, Ricky had already jumped over the busted doorway and was inside the house. Almost no one saw him enter.

"Goddamn it!" Bobby heard Detective Daly shout.

CHAPTER 99

Sarah screamed louder than she had ever screamed before as Gerald dropped Simon's finger onto her lap and her horror reached a new dimension. She knew then that Simon was dead. Gerald said something, but she couldn't hear his words. She stopped her screaming as she grieved for Simon and stared down upon his bloodied finger. She immediately squirmed about and attempted to dislodge the bloody appendage from her lap. She couldn't even breathe.

It was Tommy's shout from across the room that caused Gerald to turn his attention away from Sarah.

Sarah was still staring down at Simon's finger when she heard Tommy yell for Gerald to leave her alone. She couldn't really understand what was happening and the room spun away. Sarah heard herself call out for Tommy to stop, which caused Gerald to hesitate as he looked at both Sarah and Tommy. Gerald realized it was Tommy that tied Sarah up. He began to gesticulate angrily and advanced towards Tommy. Sarah forced her eyes upwards to watch Gerald and Tommy as they shouted at each other and moved a step closer to each other.

Sarah wanted to scream. Tommy was no match for Gerald, and she felt responsible again as if it was her fault that Tommy was about to become another one of Gerald's victims.

The two were only a few feet away from each other, and it appeared as if neither would back down. Sarah didn't understand why Tommy even came out of hiding, and she hated herself for it. Gerald swung first, but Tommy dodged to the side just in time.

Tommy almost lost his balance but managed to rip a right hand into Gerald's right ear as Gerald fell away to the left.

The fight progressed rapidly. Sarah could only watch in hopes that somehow Gerald could be stopped and Tommy would be spared.

Gerald responded by turning quickly around. He grabbed Tommy by the waist and tried to throw him to the ground, but Tommy was much too thin and wiry. Tommy easily slipped out of Gerald's grasp, danced around Gerald and gave him a hard shot to the back of the head. Gerald turned around and managed a grab of Tommy's shirt. He yanked hard, and Tommy's feet slipped out from under him. Tommy flailed his arms about in an attempt to recover his balance, but it was to no avail. Tommy soon found himself lying on the floor.

Gerald spun himself around as Tommy fell and Sarah could see that Gerald's rage ran deep. His eyes burned with a fire that danced about with a crazy hatred that Sarah knew could never be extinguished by the likes of a boy the size of Tommy.

Tommy tried to get to his feet, but Gerald stopped him abruptly with a hard kick into the ribs. Tommy fell over onto his back and grimaced in agony. He clutched the right side of his chest with both hands. Gerald readied to kick again but held his foot back as it was apparent that most of the fight had now gone out of Tommy.

Gerald paused and stared down at Tommy writhing in agony on the floor.

"You really want to mess with me, you fucking punk ass shit?"

Tommy opened his eyes to see Gerald pacing, back and forth, above him.

Gerald glanced around the room, reached over, and picked up a small wooden end table. He lifted the table high above his head and was ready to bring it down on Tommy who still lay on the floor and clutched at his ribs.

Sarah managed to find her voice and screamed, "No! Gerald, no!"

Gerald hesitated for just a second and looked towards Sarah. He grinned. He nodded at her as if to let her know that this was payback, and that this too was her fault.

Gerald raised the small end table as high as he could in the air above Tommy.

Suddenly, a shot rang out from somewhere and Gerald gasped loudly. His body went limp as the bullet struck him in the heart and brought him to an immediate stop. As Gerald's body fell to the ground, the small end table slipped out of his hands and landed hard on top of Tommy. Tommy was instantly knocked unconscious and a huge gash broke open on his forehead.

Sarah was dumbfounded as she looked around and wondered where the shot had come from. Her eyes landed upon another young boy who stood just inside the doorway. The long dark-haired boy stared blankly down to the two bodies on the floor. He held the handgun tightly in his outstretched hands.

Only a moment had passed when yet another young teenager appeared in the doorway.

"Jason!" This latest arrival shouted at the one with the gun. He stepped forward quickly, placed his hand on Jason's shoulder and looked past him to the two bodies on the floor. "Oh no," he exclaimed as he spotted Tommy laying on the floor with blood running down his forehead. He ran over to him and hovered over his limp body.

Jason remained by the doorway and lowered the gun. He let it slip out of his fingers to the floor and then shuffled slowly over to where Tommy lay. "I didn't mean to shoot him, Ricky! I didn't." He began to weep.

"I don't think you did," Ricky replied.

The two boys fussed over their friend and completely ignored Gerald's lifeless body just a few feet away.

Ricky placed his hands all over Tommy's body, as he felt for wounds and checked for blood. "I don't think you shot him, Jason."

Ricky placed his ear on Tommy's chest. "His heart's beating and he is breathing. Look at his head. I think he just got knocked out."

"You sure?" Jason replied. He moved forward next to Jason and stared down upon his brother.

The two boys continued to hover over Tommy's body when Sarah called out from across the room. "What's happened? Is he okay?" she asked. She managed to stand and shuffle around the side of the couch towards the boys with small steps due to the binding around her ankles.

"Huh?" the two boys both said in unison and turned towards her voice. Neither even noticed Sarah in the room.

"Tommy's okay," Jason said. He looked over at Gerald. "He's not so good though," he said as he motioned towards Gerald's body with his hand.

"What do you mean?" Sarah asked.

"I think he's dead," Jason said.

"Yea. He is very dead," Ricky added. He stood up and looked at Gerald once more and then over towards Sarah. His eyes crawled over the bindings on her ankles, and he could see her hands were also bound behind her back. He tilted his head to the side and frowned. Sarah could see the puzzlement in his eyes as they called out to her for an explanation.

Sarah let out a deep sigh. She wasn't sure if it was relief or sadness. A part of her hated Gerald, and she was glad to see he had not succeeded in harming Tommy. But no part of her had ever wished him dead.

With Tommy lying unconscious on the floor, Sarah remembered what Tommy had told her about why he was there and felt it necessary to tell the boys what Tommy had told her. She glanced quickly out to the front window where she could still see the glow of the blue and red lights that lit up the world on the other side of the window coverings.

CHAPTER 100

Dean was furious.

"Did you see that?" he shouted at Constable Heavy Head.

"See what?"

"That kid, for Christ's sake. He ran into the house."

Heavy Head looked up at the house. "What kid?"

"Jesus! A kid just ran into the house there." He put his hands on his hips and stared up at the house. He picked up the radio, called to the officers out back and asked if they were in position. They confirmed they were in position to cover the back of the house and also reported that they saw no one leave the house.

Heavy Head shrugged his shoulders. "I didn't see anyone run into the house. You sure?" he asked.

"Goddamn it, yes! I am sure! And I think it was the same kid who tried to break in there a few weeks ago."

Dean looked around at the gathering crowd and immediately spotted Bobby who had been staring at Dean the entire time. He hustled over to where Bobby was standing.

"Was that your friend who just ran in there?"

Bobby nodded back sheepishly.

"What the hell is going on here? Do you know we have a very serious situation happening in that house?"

Bobby just stared back because he didn't understand what Dean was telling him.

"Your friend is going to get himself killed in there. Now why the hell did he just do that?"

"I don't know!"

"Listen to me, son. I need to know why your friend just ran into a house when it is damned obvious that it was a stupid and dangerous thing to do! Look at that damned front door!"

Bobby simply shrugged. "Ricky does crazy things sometimes."

Dean looked back towards the house. He really needed to get the situation under control.

"You stay right here! You hear me?" Dean shouted at Bobby.

Bobby nodded back timidly.

Dean moved back next to Heavy Head and spoke to his officers. Once Dean was sure the house was secured on all sides, he picked up the radio on his cruiser and turned on the loudspeaker. He called out on the loudspeaker to the house and announced the presence of the police. He asked if everyone was all right inside. He was surprised when the response he received came from the young boy he was sure was Ricky.

"Is that you, Ricky?" Dean called out.

"Uh huh. I'm Ricky," Ricky's voice called back softly from the doorway.

"Is anyone hurt?"

"Yes. There's a dead guy in here."

Dean remembered the two voices he had heard arguing earlier.

"Can you tell me who else is there with you?'

There was a moment of silence in the house.

"There's a lady. Sarah."

"Who else?"

"No one else."

Dean was suddenly puzzled. Something was wrong. He had definitely heard two voices earlier when he first rushed up to the house. With Ricky now inside, that meant three males were in the house. With one dead, there should still be two more. Dean picked up the radio and called the officers out behind the house. They confirmed that no one had exited back there.

"Is Sarah okay?"

"Uh huh. She's tied up though."

Dean felt relief at the news of Sarah.

"How many are dead?" Dean asked.

"Just the one guy. Gerald, I think his name is," Ricky called back.

Dean was agitated. Who the hell shot Gerald?

"Where's the gun now?"

"It's here. I've got it," Ricky replied.

"Don't touch the gun!" Dean shouted to Ricky.

"I've got it here in my hands. I'll bring it out if you want."

"Aw, shit," Dean said quietly to himself. "The boy's fingerprints are all over the gun."

"Can you toss the gun out onto the porch?"

Ricky didn't answer, but in a few moments, the gun flew through the air out the front door and landed on the steps. Dean motioned for one of the officers to retrieve the weapon.

"Any other weapons inside?"

"No."

"Are you sure there is no one else in the house besides you and Sarah?"

"Uh huh. There is no one else in the house."

Dean wasn't so sure. He knew he would have to be quick to secure the house, and he directed a few officers to come with him as he cautiously approached the house. They advanced slowly and entered the house with guns drawn. Dean moved to the study and commanded the others to search every room, every closet, cupboard and possible hiding place. Dean was sure there was someone else still in the house.

355

Dean slipped down the hall towards the study and stopped when he was outside the door.

"You alright in there?"

"Uh huh," Ricky called back.

"I'm coming in now," Dean said, and moved slowly into the study. Gerald's body lay on the floor in a pool of blood, dead from a single gunshot wound to the chest. Ricky stood over by the couch next to Sarah. Dean could see that Sarah was securely bound.

He asked again if Ricky and Sarah were injured and quickly instructed Ricky to untie Sarah, while he kept his gun drawn. He looked at Sarah and asked her directly where the other man was.

"What other man?" she replied. "It was only Gerald who broke in here." Sarah looked like she was about to cry, and Dean asked her to sit. He didn't believe a word of it. "I heard two men arguing earlier. Where did he go, Sarah?"

"I don't know what you're talking about," Sarah insisted. "It was just Gerald who broke in here while I was reading my book."

"Uh huh. So who shot him? You with your hands tied behind your back? I know it wasn't you," he said to Ricky. Ricky nodded his head in agreement.

Sarah looked over at Gerald. "He shot himself."

"Did you see anyone else?" He asked Ricky.

"No. That man was dead when I ran in here. It was just her sitting over there tied up on the couch."

Dean paced around the room and looked at Gerald's body. He noticed the broken end table, but other than that, there wasn't much more to see in the room. He paced and waited. Minutes passed. When the other officers returned, they reported that a full search of the house had turned up no one else. That included the basement and the attic. Dean didn't like it.

Dean turned to Ricky. "Why did you run in here anyway? You know you could have gotten yourself killed."

"I do crazy stuff sometimes."

Dean didn't believe him. "And you kept running inside even after the gunshot. Most people would turn tail and run the other way. That includes me."

Ricky said nothing.

"Listen. I don't know what's going on here, but something just isn't right. I'm going to get this mess cleaned up, and then we'll all have a little talk about just what the hell is really going on."

Sarah looked up at Dean, and he could see she was trying not to cry. He had not yet told her about Simon. He wasn't sure how to tell her.

"About Simon," Dean said.

Sarah dropped her face into her hands and cried heavily. She pulled one hand away just long enough to point to the floor in front of the couch and then turned away. Dean stepped forward to see Simon's finger on the floor.

"I am so sorry," he said and placed his arm across her back.

Dean took both Sarah and Ricky out of the house and into the back of his cruiser. He sent the rest of the team back inside to do the cleanup. It would be hours before they were done, and Dean continued to collect the details of what happened from Sarah and Ricky. Ricky's parents were called and he was eventually sent home. Dean offered to take Sarah to a hotel. Sarah insisted on staying in her home. Even when Dean demanded that she should leave, telling her it was a crime scene, she refused. Dean had no choice but to let Sarah back into her home. He insisted she stay clear of the study until they completed their investigation. The last of the investigators left Sarah's home as the hour neared midnight.

They promised they would be back around 8:00 AM the next morning to continue.

CHAPTER 101

It was black as pitch in the small room behind the fireplace. Jason had been sitting for hours listening to the mumbled voices that slithered through the blackness. Tommy laid outstretched and unconscious on the floor next to him.

Jason could hear Tommy's shallow breathing as the hours passed, and it gave him hope that Tommy would be all right. He didn't dare move around inside the small room. He saw how cluttered it was when the room was first revealed. He couldn't risk making any sound that would attract the interest of the police officers on the other side of the fireplace.

The room was narrow and lined with shelving on both sides. He saw the shelves littered with VHS tapes, CD cases, binders, photos and stationery when they shuffled themselves quickly inside. There was writing on many of the cases, but he had not had time to read any before closing themselves inside.

It was Sarah's idea that they hide until this was over. She repeated to them Tommy's confession about what was inside the room, and she told them she understood. She insisted they see this through. The boys didn't understand why she was helping them, but they didn't have time to argue. Listening to Sarah was the only real option they had.

Jason felt Tommy's leg move against him, and he leaned over Tommy's body.

"Tommy?" he whispered quietly.

"Hnnn," Tommy groaned back.

"Shhhh! Tommy, be quiet," Jason whispered close to his ear.

Jason turned his head towards the back of the fireplace. He could still hear the muffled sounds as people moved about on the other side.

Tommy stirred again and moaned.

"Tommy, you have to be quiet," Jason insisted.

"What?" Tommy replied in a soft, incoherent manner. "Where the hell am I?" He sounded groggy.

"Listen to me. Please, Tommy. You have to be quiet or else we are in deep trouble."

"Oh, my ribs," Tommy replied. His voice was quieter and clearer, and Jason knew Tommy was coming around.

"Tommy, it's me. Jason."

Tommy stirred and his breath became heavy and rapid. Jason suspected he was attempting to sit up.

"Don't move. You've had a bad knock on the head."

"Jason?" Tommy inquired tentatively. He suddenly stopped moving.

"Shhh!" Jason replied again. "Yes, Tommy. It's me, but you have to be quiet."

"Jason?" Tommy whispered back excitedly. "Oh, my God! I thought you were dead!"

"No, no," he whispered.

"But how? I heard Patricia scream and the shot gun go off."

"I was so scared, Tommy. Doogie had me up against a tree in a small clearing. He had the shotgun pointed at me and I was so sure he was going to shoot me. Patricia came out from the trees behind Doogie, jumped on his back and screamed."

"I can't believe it, Jason," Tommy said. Tommy moved and groaned again. He began to cry, but it wasn't due to the pain in his ribs. "I was so sure you were dead. I was so sure. I think I cried all the way here. I am so happy right now. Oh, God. I missed you so much."

He reached out to Jason and Jason reached back. The boys hugged each other in the darkness. Tommy grimaced from the terrible pain in his chest, but it didn't matter. Neither said a word as they shed tears of joy.

"When we heard Patricia's scream come from the trees and the gunshot, we were all sure Doogie killed you. Even Willie thought so," Tommy said. "He shoved me so hard to run away. I've never seen Willie so terrified."

"Patricia's the only reason I'm still here. She screamed and jumped on Doogie's back. That's when the shotgun went off. It hit the trees above my head and knocked branches and shit down on top of me. The two of them fell to the ground with Patricia on his back choking him. She screamed at me to run. I didn't know which way to go, so I just ran past them into the trees. I grabbed Doogie's Beretta that he dropped when Patricia took him down."

"I'm so happy right now," Tommy said again. "My forehead hurts like hell. I think it's cut. And my ribs. I think one or two are broken. It's all kind of a blur. What happened? Where are we?"

Jason's voice saddened as he disclosed the details to Tommy.

"We're in the secret room behind the fireplace. I saw your backpack in the shrubs by the back door, so I knew you were inside already. I was so excited to see you, but I heard you shouting with that crazy guy as I came down the stairs and pulled out Doogie's Beretta."

"Oh, right," Tommy replied. "I totally forgot about that fight. Shit my head hurts."

"The wooden table fell on your head when I shot him, Tommy," Jason said. He sniffed as he tried not to cry. "He was about to smash your head in. He would have killed you. I had to shoot him." He remembered how he had swung his axe in the direction of his mother and killed her. That feeling of pain and loss returned. He sobbed.

"You had no choice. I should thank you."

Jason continued to sob. "What are we doing, Tommy?" he asked.

"We are setting things right. That is what we are doing."

"Are we?" Jason asked.

They hugged each other again. They remained quiet and waited to hear silence from the other room.

CHAPTER 102

Dean tried to sleep, but he kept waking as thoughts about the events of the night danced about in his head. He looked at his bedside clock and groaned. The sun would soon rise. He had been reviewing all of the facts in the case all night. He fluffed his pillow, rolled over and hoped to find sleep, but his thoughts returned to the events of yesterday.

He couldn't help but think that Ricky ran into the house for a reason. He was convinced of it. It was probably the same reason he and Bobby attempted the break-in only a week before. They were definitely after something in the house, but he couldn't think of anything it could possibly be. He remembered Bobby's words: "How do you open it?"

He tossed and turned, and he wondered why Sarah lied to him. There was no mistaking what he had heard when he first approached the house. There were two men inside arguing. "So what the blazes happened to that other man?" he asked himself. "And why would Sarah lie to cover anything up?"

Dean liked Sarah from the moment he met her, but she seemed different last night. She seemed to have far more control over her terror compared to the absolute distress she was in the night before when he agreed to go check on Simon. Both Gerald and Simon died, and she seemed too calm about it. Where was the distress over the deaths of two very close people in her life? Simon especially.

Dean returned his thoughts to the house itself, and the Oliver boys popped into his mind. "Now where the hell did they suddenly vanish to after escaping from their escorted leave?" It's not easy to disappear without a trace without even one reported sighting in a city the size of Calgary.

He remembered how he first felt when the call came in about the murders in the Oliver home. He had felt elated; it was the opportunity he was looking for. It provided him the chance at a bit of personal redemption after failing to provide adequate and accurate evidence in his last murder case: a case that ended with the acquittal of the man who he knew, without a shadow of a doubt, committed the murder. He had not felt that elation since that first phone call. The Oliver murders still made no sense to him at all. He suspected, once again, that the Oliver boys were connected to the events of yesterday, but how?

Dean began to second-guess himself as sleep continued to evade him. He wondered if he really had what it took to be an effective detective. He had not done very well on the only two murders he handled since he came to Bluffington. He knew the questions he would be facing from his bosses over the next few days, and he would again be short of answers. He hated that part of his job.

These thoughts continued to roll through his mind, and soon a different thought surfaced above all others: Sarah's insistence on staying in the house after they took Gerald's body away. It annoyed Dean at the time, but now it bothered him. Gerald was her tormenter, and he just died in her new home. Still, she insisted that she wanted to stay there. Maybe she felt if she left now she'd never be able to face coming back to that house. He should have expected her, at a minimum, to have a friend to stay with her, but she had not even suggested a friend and refused the offer of a hotel. Who was her closest friend in town? That would be Simon, and he too was murdered.

Why did she not show grief? She should have been much more upset than she appeared to be. Could she still have something more important on her mind?

Dean rose out of bed and decided he would head back over to Sarah's as soon as the sun broke the horizon.

CHAPTER 103

It was around 10:00 PM when the coroner finally left with Gerald's body and shortly after midnight when the last investigator left Sarah's house. She forced a smiled as he said goodbye. She thanked the officer and closed and locked the front door. She watched out the window until the vehicle disappeared down the road and immediately rushed over to the fireplace.

She shouted out to the boys and knocked against the metal frame of the fireplace enclosure.

"Everyone is gone. You can come out now."

She listened for sounds from within the room and heard shuffling from the other side.

"Hey! Boys! It's safe to come out. How do you open this?"

Sarah felt the fireplace move and then the right side slipped backwards and revealed Tommy and Jason's worried faces as they poked their heads out from the darkness.

"They're gone?" Tommy asked warily.

"Yes. They are all gone, but they will be back first thing in the morning. You need to get going on this thing of yours right now," she said.

Tommy stepped out of the room. "I need the washroom first," he said and quickly headed up the stairs.

As he passed her, Sarah looked at Tommy's face with dried blood crusted in his hair and smeared down his face.

"Oh, you're going to need something for that cut," she said.

Jason stepped out of the room and thanked Sarah for all she did for them. He looked back into the dark room and paced anxiously outside of it as he waited for Tommy to return. It was obvious to Sarah that he didn't really want to go back into the room alone.

Sarah tried her best to put him at ease.

"Is there anything I can do? Something you need?"

Jason just shook his head. "I don't think so. I'm still wondering why you're helping us. I don't even know who you are."

Sarah felt many emotions rise up at Jason's questions. She thought of Gerald and then Simon. There were many reasons she could offer Jason.

"Tommy told me all about what is inside that room. And my name is Sarah," she said.

"Oh," Jason replied. "I'm, uh… Jason." He dropped his eyes to the floor as he hoped to avoid discussing the details of what Tommy may have said.

"I promise I will not tell a soul about any of this. I don't pretend to know why you think this is up to you and Tommy, but I could see your brother was really upset over this yesterday."

Jason looked up at her. "If not us, then who?"

Jason's commitment surprised her. "But why you?"

Tommy came back in the room as Jason answered. "In that room is bad stuff. My best friend Tim killed himself because of what's inside there and what it all represents. I don't want anyone else to die. It needs to stop, and getting rid of it is the only way we can be sure that it's really over."

Tommy nodded. "He's right you know. We have to get rid of it all." Tommy pushed past Jason, walked into the room and flicked on the light. "Our dad did all of this."

He hesitated for only a moment and then moved over to the shelf on his right. "Oh, Jesus," he said as he flipped over the top photo. It was one of what seemed like hundreds stacked in separate piles. He looked back at Jason and Sarah and wiped his eyes.

"Who was it?" Jason asked coldly.

Tommy could only shake his head.

"Who?" Jason asked again. "Was it Tim?"

Tommy turned away and closed his eyes. He nodded.

Sarah shuddered. She didn't know how she could help them, but she wanted to do something.

"You'll need something to carry this out of here. Wait here. I think I have just the thing," she said.

Sarah hurried out of the room and upstairs to her bedroom. The thought came to her immediately. A few moments later, she stood in front of Jason and passed her bright red suitcase to him.

"Will that be big enough?" she asked.

Jason held the suitcase up for Tommy to see. Tommy nodded back.

"It's real nice," he said.

Sarah smiled and left the study. This was a task for the boys to complete alone. She felt diminished as her own troubles with Gerald paled in comparison to the burden these boys were carrying. She didn't know if they were going to look at the photos of their friends or try not to look at any of them. It troubled her that she couldn't help them. She put on a pot of coffee, gathered up some gauze and bandages for Tommy and sat at the kitchen table.

It started with a little sniffle as Sarah let the fact sink in that she would never see Simon again. She would miss him and his strange ways. Her sniffle soon turned to real tears as she knew what happened to Simon was truly her fault. If only she had not pushed him to check on Gerald, but she knew Simon would have insisted on going anyway.

Sarah let the tears flow for Simon as she waited for the boys to finish. She even cried for Gerald because she remembered the good times they shared in their early days together.

CHAPTER 104

Tommy flipped over the top photo and grimaced in disgust. He could almost taste bile because he felt so deeply sickened by his father's perversions.

"Aw fuck," he said and gazed out at Jason and Sarah. He didn't know if he was going to be able to do this.

"Who was it?" his brother asked. He could see his brother shut out all emotion as best he could.

Tommy wiped his eyes. The image seemed to burn itself into his retinas, and he fought hard to make it go away.

"Who?" Jason prompted him. "Was it Tim?" he asked.

Tommy closed his eyes and turned away from Sarah and Jason. He nodded.

The photo was a simple image of their friend Tim naked and sitting on the training bench in his dad's physiotherapy office. It wasn't that the image was disgusting or even remotely graphic; it was just a simple photo of Tim sitting naked on the bench. He wasn't smiling, but he didn't look sad or uncomfortable. Both boys saw Tim naked many times as they changed and showered after hockey games and practices. They saw Tim naked when they stripped down at the pool to crawl into their swimsuits and even twice when the crew went skinny-dipping in the river. It was the actions and purpose behind the photo; those that made the image such a horrible, revolting trophy of a perverted conquest that repulsed him.

Tommy breathed deeply and slowly opened his eyes. He was terrified of what he was about to see as he moved his eyes across the many shelves. He could see names and dates written on the packages, boxes and cases that littered the shelves. He tried not to read any of the words and names, but his eyes betrayed him. As Tommy opened the bright red suitcase and began to shovel the video tapes and CDs inside, the names began to leap off the labels. Each one screamed at him to never forget them. He recognized some of the names. Some he didn't know at all and many were from years ago. From years before he was in Pee Wee hockey.

Tommy wanted to scream.

"Jason," he called over to his brother who stood just outside the entrance. He sighed heavily and wiped at the tears in his eyes. "Just stay out there, Jason. I'll get this."

Jason stood at the doorway as Tommy continued to fill the red suitcase. Tommy looked up briefly and watched as Jason stole a glance down at the labels stuffed into the suitcase. Jason pulled his eyes away to his left and let them fall on a small, flat-panel TV screen that rested on the shelf inside the room. Below the TV was a small DVD player. Tommy said nothing as Jason stepped inside the room and pressed the eject button on the player. The player churned and grunted in the process of releasing the disc. The voice of Tim from the night of the murders echoed in his head.

"No, Jason!" Tommy shouted as Jason reach for the disc.

It was too late. Jason removed it and held it in his hands. *T G* was written on the label. He stood there staring at it in his hands. Tommy was shouting at him, but Jason didn't hear a word he said. Jason caressed the disc in his hands for a moment, and then slipped it back inside the player, hit the play button and turned on the TV.

"No!" Tommy screamed and scrambled up from the floor. He grimaced as the pain throbbed in his ribs, but it wasn't enough to stop him. He rushed over, swept the TV and

DVD player off the shelf and let them both crash down on the floor.

Tommy grabbed Jason and hugged him tight. "I miss him too, but that's not the Tim we know. We have to let it be. It's over, and we need to remember him the way we always knew him."

Jason squeezed Tommy back and sobbed.

Tommy held his younger brother until he was sure Jason was going to be okay. He led Jason out of the room and instructed him to go see Sarah to get a bag or something for the rest of the stuff while he continued to load it all up. There was too much to fit inside the one suitcase. Jason left the study and Tommy returned to the task of removing all of the images from the room.

As Tommy emptied shelf after shelf, he realized these images were trophies. Each one represented his father's sick power over the young boys entrusted to his care. The violation of each one of his friends and of the many boys he didn't know didn't stop once the victims left this property. Even with his father dead, the violation continued. That was what made these images so vile. In each of the images, a piece of each boy's soul was imprisoned in the digital memory and on to the photographic paper. Every victim knew these images existed, and Tommy realized that they could never heal completely if the images remained.

It was really so much worse than he first understood. His father was a collector. The worst kind of pedophile. Tommy couldn't do anything about what happened to each one of these victims, many of whom were his friends, but he really thought what he was doing here with Jason was important and would somehow stop the hurt from continuing. He knew the victims would want to know that the evidence was destroyed, but he couldn't bear the responsibility of learning the name of each and every victim. For now, his focus was only on ensuring that all evidence was removed and destroyed forever. Once this was done, he promised himself that he would revisit his concern about letting the victims know. He wasn't sure how, but he would find a way.

Tommy looked around the small room and spotted a computer in the corner. A greater fear brought a new darkness over him that he had not even considered before. He wondered if his father had even gone farther than collecting. Was his father also a trader? He didn't want to know the answer.

Tommy stopped loading the suitcase. He stared hard at the computer, and his worry multiplied the longer he looked. He glanced back towards the entrance and was glad to see that Jason had not yet returned. He moved quickly and smashed the computer onto the floor. He used a long, steel screw driver he found sticking out from a small tin filled with a few pens and a pair of scissors and pried the hard drive from the computer. He tossed it in the suitcase with the rest. He zipped the suitcase closed before Jason returned. He wouldn't tell Jason what he thought about the hard drive.

Jason returned with a large, paper, handled gift bag. Tommy filled up the bag until there was nothing left on any of the shelves. Jason remained outside the room and watched from beyond the door. He dropped his eyes often but never looked entirely away. It was necessary that he be part of the process.

It was almost 3:00 AM when Tommy and Jason entered the kitchen and stood behind Sarah. Tommy held the paper bag, and Jason held the bright red suitcase.

Sarah told Tommy to have a seat. They sat in silence as Sarah cleaned up Tommy's cut and bandaged his forehead. She tossed the bloody rags into the sink when she was finished, sat back down and looked at the boys. She couldn't smile.

"It's done?" she asked.

The boys nodded together.

"Well. Let's get you out of here then."

Sarah grabbed her car keys, opened the back door and ushered the boys outside to her car was in front of the garage.

CHAPTER 105

The mountains to the west were washed with a cool, amber glow as the sun rose up on another cloudless Saturday. It promised days of wonderful weather.

Dean waited eagerly on the driveway alongside Sarah's house until Sarah finally pulled up and stopped in front of the garage. He gave a gentle wave to Sarah and walked over to her car as she got out. Dean arrived more than an hour before she arrived home when the sun was first breaking over the horizon in the east, and he was very surprised to find she wasn't at home.

Sarah greeted Dean pleasantly, but he sensed an edginess about her when he peered in the windows of her car.

"Morning to you as well, Sarah," Dean replied. There was nothing of interest in her car.

Sarah walked up the steps towards the back door. Dean followed close behind.

"Bit early for you, isn't it, Dean?" she asked light-heartedly. "I thought you weren't coming back until eight this morning."

Dean paused and looked over at her car in the driveway. "Wouldn't have expected you to be up so early after last night. Any special reason you went for a drive this early in the morning?"

Sarah fumbled with her keys in the lock. "Couldn't sleep. That's all. Come on in," she offered. "I have the coffee on already."

Dean followed Sarah inside to the kitchen, and they sat at the table with coffee. Dean scanned the room out of habit and tucked what he saw in the corners of his mind. He was tired and he hoped the coffee would perk him up.

"It's a bit strong. I made it a few hours ago."

Dean nodded. One sip confirmed that it was definitely not fresh.

"Tell me, Sarah. Where does one go for a drive when one can't sleep after a night like that?" He watched Sarah carefully.

"I just drove out of the city."

Dean purposely withheld any reply, and Sarah fluffed her hair unconsciously. He expected she would offer more if he waited long enough, if only to break the awkward silence, and he was right.

"I just kept driving. Ended up in Calgary. I just drove around thinking. I even drove by the old house before I came back here.

"Hmm," Dean responded. He didn't buy it.

Dean maintained his silence and sipped at his coffee. He wondered where she had really gone.

"You must be tired," Dean suggested.

"I am," Sarah replied and smiled. "Yesterday was such a long day. Then after I went to bed, my mind just went crazy. I tossed and turned and finally had to get up. It was 3:00 AM I think when I put on the coffee, and then I just had to get out of here."

Dean smiled back. "I couldn't sleep either," he said. He sat up and leaned closer to Sarah. "What am I missing, Sarah?"

Sarah shook her head. "I don't know what you mean."

Dean laughed and stood up. He walked over to the kitchen window above the sink and looked out the back to the porch that protruded off to the side.

"Do you own a backpack?" He stared out the window above the kitchen sink.

Sarah shook her head. "No. Why do you ask?"

Dean pointed out the window. "Well, you see right out there, in the shrub next to the back steps, I found a backpack this morning while I was waiting for you."

He turned back and faced Sarah. She looked as though she had no idea what he was talking about.

"I found a backpack. And do you know what was inside?"

Sarah shook her head again.

"There was a small sleeping bag, two empty water bottles, some crackers, two empty porridge pouches, two bowls, matches and a book."

"A book?"

"A trail guide book of the mountains out back. I flipped through the book while I was waiting for you to come home. I've been out there a while." Dean studied Sarah's expression, but she certainly wasn't giving anything away.

"The book looks new, like it was purchased just days ago. There are a number of trails marked in the book. The marked trails lead from the Sandy McNabb Campground up north and come out just yonder over there by the river."

"Oh, wow," Sarah replied. "You found this where?"

Dean laughed again. "I found this by your back steps. In the shrubs. I don't know why anyone would leave a backpack in the shrubs in your backyard. Anyway, it's about these maps. To me, it looks like it's a map that leads from the Sandy McNabb Campground to your back door."

"I don't know anything about any backpack, Dean. Nor any map."

Dean studied Sarah. He almost believed her.

"So who was the other guy?"

"What other guy?"

"Oh, come on, Sarah. When I first ran up here yesterday, I came up to the front door and heard two people arguing. Two men. One, I know for sure, was Gerald. I'd like to know who the other man was."

Sarah remained quiet for a moment. She hesitated, and Dean was convinced she was hiding something.

"I was bound and gagged by Gerald," she said. "There was no one else in the house."

"But I know what I heard."

"We'll, I'll tell you straight out. Only Gerald and I were here yesterday afternoon."

Dean knew he was at a dead end with Sarah.

Dean's cell phone rang, and he answered the call. It was the forensics lab. They had interesting information on the gun that killed Gerald.

"Who?" he yelled into the phone. "Would you say that again?" he demanded. The words made no sense to him.

Dean hung up the phone and looked blankly at Sarah. He was very confused; it really made no sense. The gun used to kill Gerald was purchased just last week by Doogie Fisher's father.

CHAPTER 106

"I am so tired, Tommy. Can't we sit for a bit?"

"No," Tommy replied. "We have to keep walking. Sarah was nice enough to drive us all of the way here, and I want to be sure there is no way anyone can trace our steps back to her."

The two boys continued to walk. Jason looked behind him to the east.

"The suns coming up."

Tommy glanced over his shoulder to catch a peek at the sun rising between the houses.

"Just a few more blocks. We'll make the call at the 7-11 store."

Tommy and Jason walked the streets for more than an hour. They were careful to stick to the alleyways and residential side streets and made sure to avoid any of the main roads with stores that might have video cameras. Sarah dropped the boys off on a residential street in Bridgeland, well over a mile away from the 7-11.

When Sarah left with the two boys, she had no idea where the boys wanted to go. Tommy quickly gave her some directions. The idea was for Sarah to drive up to Calgary and drop the boys off somewhere discreet before she headed home in order to arrive before the police returned at 8:00 AM. The boys would carry on by themselves on foot through the backstreets and alleys until they were somewhere close to Marlon's Pizza, where they escaped two days ago. They were going to turn themselves in. The 7-11 they headed for was just a few doors down from Marlon's.

Both boys were completely exhausted. It had been a long twenty-four hours for both of them. The run-in with Doogie now seemed like days ago.

"I am so tired. Can't we just stop for a few minutes and rest?"

"You'll get lots of rest after we make the call."

Jason grunted his disapproval and plodded on behind Tommy. He brushed his bangs off to the side. Time passed slowly for both boys, and with each block further, the city began to awaken. Dogs barked and the sound of the occasional car a few blocks over on the main road rose to a constant buzz. When Tommy and Jason reached the main intersection near the 7-11, the sun was high and the city was alive with activity.

Tommy nudged Jason forward to the front doors of the 7-11.

"I'll do the talking," he said and stepped inside.

The 7-11 was quiet as Jason and Tommy stepped in line at the counter. They waited patiently as a man dressed in steel-toed boots and khaki coveralls paid for his gas and coffee. The man thanked the young, East-Indian clerk and stepped outside. Tommy stepped up to the counter and smiled at the man.

The man stared back with disinterest.

"I need you to call the police for me?" Tommy said directly.

"Pardon me?" the clerk replied, in his strong, East-Indian accent.

"I want you to call the police."

"What is wrong? Is there a problem?" the clerk replied and looked at the bandage on Tommy's forehead.

"Yes, there is. You probably heard about us on the radio," Tommy said and he pointed at Jason.

The clerk frowned and shook his head. "I don't know what you are talking about. If you want to purchase something, you should do that now, sir."

Tommy grew impatient. "Listen! I want you to call the police. He and I broke out of jail two days ago and now we want to turn ourselves in."

The clerk looked Tommy and Jason up and down.

"Why don't you two just go then? Go away. This is not a police station."

Tommy laughed and Jason snickered.

"There's a reward," Tommy said. He didn't know if there was one or not, but this guy was really being difficult.

"A reward?" he asked.

"Yes," Tommy replied. "You call the police and say you've got the Oliver boys, and they will be here in minutes."

The man nodded up and down quickly. "You are not fooling me?" he asked directly.

"No. Now call the police," Tommy insisted.

The clerk picked up the phone and began to dial. As he dialled, Tommy asked if there was someplace private they could wait until the police arrived. "Maybe in the back," he suggested. At first the clerk refused, but when Tommy told him it would be best if no one else knew about them in case someone else tried to claim the reward, he was all for it, and ushered Tommy and Jason into the tiny office in back. It only took five minutes for the police to arrive. Tommy and Jason were handcuffed, escorted out of the store and shuffled into the back seat of the police car.

"What about my reward?" the clerk called out as he stood in front of the police car. The officer honked his horn twice and waved his hand in an attempt to usher the clerk out of the way.

Tommy and Jason giggled as they listen to the banter of the clerk who insisted he wasn't moving until the police confirmed that he would get a reward. A few words from the police officer had the clerk scrambling off to the side and they were on their way.

Relief swept over Tommy, and he knew his younger brother felt the same way. There was a comfort in having been able to help Ricky and all of the others. Knowing they would soon be back inside Spy Hill in a bed they had become accustomed to was also, strangely, a pleasure they had not expected to feel.

Jason seemed more than content as he finally got to sit down after two long days. He was asleep by the time the police car arrived at the Spy Hill Correctional facility.

CHAPTER 107

Sarah couldn't force her eyes away from the coffin as it was lowered into the ground. She felt the tears crawl down her face, and she shivered. Not even a year had passed since she laid her parents to rest in the cold earth, and now, here she stood again trying to hold it all in as Simon's coffin dropped from view.

The sun was high, and the heat of the afternoon had many wiping their brows as they squirmed under suit jackets, sports coats and dressy shawls. Sarah didn't feel the heat. On the contrary, she only felt the chill a day like this always offered.

Unlike her parent's funeral where everyone was huddled close in a scrum offering comfort to one another, she stood off to the side and very much alone. The scrum was reserved for family and close friends, and although she and Simon had certainly become close, she had not yet come to be known by any member of Simon's family. Even as she stood grieving with everyone else, she saw the glances cast her way followed by whispers asking who she was. She knew what the answer always was; frowns and dirty looks were cast her way. She was the reason Simon was dead.

Sarah asked Brandy to come with her to the funeral. She left the funeral with her and shared her grief with no one from Simon's family. Gerald's funeral was the same day and a part of her wanted to be there if not for any other reason than to put her life with Gerald behind her. She felt double shame: she was the cause of death for two people who were worlds apart from each other.

Sarah wanted to cry, but she wouldn't let herself. Brandy held her close and promised it would get better.

She turned her thoughts to the three boys who entered her house that night three days ago, and she felt a drop of hope linger. The boys reminded her of her own youth when she really believed in the future her mother always talked about. "The future you make yourself," she said. These boys were doing exactly that with the poor hand they were each given. Where they would end up was anyone's guess, but Sarah knew they believed what they believed. Knowing that was enough for Sarah.

CHAPTER 108

Bobby threw another log onto the small fire, sat down and watched the flames crawl up the side of the log. The cool stillness of the night air seemed to emphasize the crackle and snap of the flames as they licked at the fresh log in delight at the present feast.

"Let's do it," Ricky said as he watched the flames lick around a log. The log shifted and brought forth a small eruption of sparks.

"It's not hot enough yet. We need more coals."

Ricky glanced over at Bobby and nodded. Tonight, as he remembered all that they had gone through together, he saw Bobby differently than he ever had before. Bobby may not have good grades in school, but Bobby certainly knew about things. He had very good instincts. Tonight Ricky realized that Bobby was right again. He didn't ask why or how Bobby knew the coals were not hot enough, but there was something about the way Bobby said it; Bobby knew what he was talking about. Ricky smiled at his friend.

Bobby grinned back when he spotted Ricky smiling at him. "What are you smiling at?"

"Just you," Ricky replied. "You've been a good friend, that's all."

Bobby laughed aloud. "You're a dumb fuck, you know?"

Ricky laughed back and nodded. "Yeah, I know."

The two boys laughed and poked at the fire.

The sun soon fell behind the mountains to the west, and the boys huddled in closer to the fire as the temperature began to drop. Even though Cataract Creek was only a few miles out of town, it ran through the thick of the forest reserve, and it could get very cold at night. It was Tuesday, and the campground was empty of campers except for Ricky and Bobby.

Ricky stood up and Bobby nodded at him. It was time. Ricky strolled over to Bobby's CRV and opened the back gate to reveal Sarah's bright red suitcase and paper bag. He pulled both out and sauntered back to the fire.

"That lady really brought those over to you?" Ricky asked. "With everything inside?"

"Uh huh. Sarah did," Bobby replied. "Tommy and Jason were already back in Spy Hill Saturday morning before you and I even woke up. She must have kept them in her trunk the whole time while she watched for me to leave the house. She followed me as I drove to the gas station on Sunday and pulled up behind me."

"What'd she say?'

"Not much really. She just asked if I was Bobby, and then said she had something for me from Tommy and Jason."

"Oh," Ricky interjected.

"Yeah. I knew what she meant immediately. She said I'd know what to do with them. She loaded them into the back and, well… here we are."

"She's a nice lady."

Bobby laughed. "Nice? You don't even know her. You said she was tied up when you saw her!" He laughed again.

Ricky laughed too as he set the bag and suitcase down by the fire.

"I like 'em when they are tied up," he joked.

"You wouldn't know what to do with 'em even if they were tied up." Bobby howled with laughter.

"Just shut up already! I'll get mine someday."

"Oh yea. Keep talking."

Ricky was still smiling when he opened the suitcase, but his smile instantly vanished.

"Jesus!" he said and turned towards Bobby. "This is really it, Bobby."

Bobby grabbed a stick and stirred the fire. "The coals are as hot as they are going to get."

Ricky tried not to look at what was in the suitcase. He reached his hand inside and pulled out some of the discs. He tossed them onto the coals and watched as the plastic curled in on itself. It reminded Ricky of how he had curled himself into the fetal position when he cried at night.

Ricky continued to reach into the suitcase and slowly fed the fire. Bobby sat opposite and remained silent and expressionless. Ricky tossed disc after disc into the fire with many VHS tapes. The flames fed on the plastic and leapt higher into the air as if the content spewed the flames from hell itself.

As much as he tried not to, Ricky looked at what he grabbed. The images in the photographs were barely visible in the dim light cast only by the fire that raged, but the images he glimpsed disturbed Ricky greatly. Ricky looked up to see Bobby had turned away as he fed the multitude of photos into the fire.

When the suitcase was nearly empty, Bobby saw the fire needed another log. He retrieved a number of smaller, split pieces of wood, which he placed into the pit and stared blankly at the fire. The wood instantly erupted into huge flames that quickly climbed into the air.

Ricky spotted the hard drive in the bottom of the red suitcase. He lifted it out and knew immediately where it came from. It felt cold in his hands as if the metal surface was trying to suck a part of his confidence away. He tossed it onto the hot coals and watched the flames quickly envelop the drive. Brown gooey bubbles eked out from the inside through the tiny slots in the metal case and erupted in tiny balls of fire. He watched as the drive slipped deeper into the coals. The shiny silver surface turned black like the hellish contents it carried.

Ricky emptied the last of the photos from the suitcase into the raging fire. He rummaged around the bottom of the suitcase for the last of the discs and then silently pulled his arms in tight around himself and huddled into a ball.

"You okay?" Bobby asked.

Ricky lowered his head down and nodded sheepishly.

"You sure? You don't look okay."

Ricky kept his head down and shook it from side to side. He popped his hand out from where he had it tucked and thrust a disc towards Bobby.

Bobby stared at the disc and slowly reached a hand out towards Ricky. Ricky looked up at Bobby as Bobby pulled it out from between his fingers. He wiped some of his fresh tears away on his sleeve and continued to look at Bobby.

Bobby tilted the disc in his hands until he managed to capture the light from the fire on the surface. Bobby almost dropped the disc when he read the initials.

"This is Tim," he said and looked at Ricky.

Ricky nodded. "I know. I thought it was still in the player at the house, but Tommy must have retrieved it."

Bobby looked back at the disc and his expression changed to one of utter disbelief and disgust. He looked back at Ricky again as if wanting Ricky to explain it to him.

Ricky reached for the disc. Tears fell down his face again.

Bobby held the disc out towards Ricky. His mouth still hung open in shock of how real it was.

Ricky grabbed the disc and squeezed his eyes shut. The tears came quickly. He mumbled, "I'm sorry. I am so sorry, Tim." He repeated those words a number of times and then flung the disc into the fire where it quickly curled in on itself.

Both Bobby and Ricky cried as they watched the disc curl up tighter and tighter. It curled and twisted, and the flames that licked about in delight quickly faded. A dark mass of twisted, black, ashy plastic that continued to curl and twist about on top of the coals remained until the pieces fell away. There was nothing left.

Their task was almost complete.

Both boys reached into the paper bag and fed the fire with the rest of the collection. Neither read the names, nor did they wait patiently. As fast as the fire would accept the items, the boys fed its thirst until everything was gone. Only then did the boys know it was finally over.

As the fire burned down, the boys could feel the temperature in the forest continue to drop considerably. It was going to be a cold night in the forest.

The sky turned dark, and the boys crawled into their sleeping bags inside the small tent after dousing the fire.

"My mom is gonna be really pissed when she finds out I'm out camping with you," Bobby said.

Ricky laughed. It was a genuine laugh.

CHAPTER 109

Tommy and Jason were both already seated in a private room at Spy Hill when Dean walked in alone. It was the same room the officers interrogated Ricky the afternoon the brothers escaped. Dean requested that the boys be brought in together. He assured the staff at the Correctional Centre that he didn't need anyone else present, and he insisted that he wanted to interview these boys in private.

"So, you two made it back okay, I see," Dean said.

The boys both nodded together. Tommy smiled at Dean. Jason kept his eyes down.

Dean looked at the boys. He was fuming inside, but he kept himself calm on the outside. He promised himself he wasn't going to explode on them today. He was going to break this case wide open and reveal the truth.

"It was your photograph in the paper on Monday, Tommy. That's what finally put it all together for me."

"I don't know what you're talking about. Put what together?"

Dean lifted his hand, put his finger to his forehead and tapped twice.

"That cut on your forehead. How many stitches did it need when you finally got up here?"

"Only two. It wasn't so bad."

"Ayuh. I suspected as much, but a cut like that can bleed pretty badly."

Tommy shook his head. "Not really."

"Oh you say that now, but I bet it bled quite a bit on Friday night."

Jason flinched and stole a glance up at Tommy, when Dean mentioned Friday night. Dean pretended not to notice.

"What Friday night?" Tommy replied.

Dean laughed. "You escaped Thursday afternoon and you turned yourselves in on Saturday morning as if it was no big deal. And you returned with one big gash on your forehead and no explanation."

Tommy just shook his head and offered no response.

"Okay, here's the deal. I think I know what you two have been up to. I couldn't figure it out for the life of me at first, but it all came together when I saw your photo in the paper after you turned yourselves in. You had that bloody bandage across your forehead."

Jason sat up and crossed his arms in front of his chest. He frowned and looked up at Tommy, but Tommy ignored him.

"Jason and I just wanted to feel some freedom before the trial. That's it detective. Really," Tommy offered.

"How about I tell you where I think you really were?"

"Go on, then. Where were we?"

Dean nodded and stood up. He clasped his hands together tightly and smiled.

"What puzzled me at first was why your friends Ricky and Bobby tried to break into your house on grad night. I caught Bobby while he was still inside. He was yelling, calling out for some answers, thinking I was Ricky. And do you know what he asked?"

Tommy and Jason both shook their heads.

"He was shouting out to Ricky. 'How do you open it?'" Dean snickered. "I replied back. 'Open what?' Your friend denied ever saying that, but I didn't forget."

Dean moved about the room slowly.

"And then there are your other friends, Doogie and Willie."

"They are not my friends," Tommy said.

"Nor mine," Jason added.

"It doesn't really matter, but what does matter is Doogie's father's gun was used to kill a man in your old house on Friday night. How the hell did Doogie's father's gun, the one he purchased just days before, end up in the hands of a total stranger back in your house? That was a big mystery for me.

"I finally talked to Doogie on Sunday night. Apparently, he was up camping in the backcountry with Willie and two girls. He said his father purchased the gun for him, and he didn't know where he lost it. He swears he had it when he left on Thursday to go camping, but by the time he got to the campsite, the gun was gone."

Dean stared at both boys, but neither gave Dean anything back.

"Strange, wouldn't you say?"

Dean sat back down across from the boys.

"Here's what else. I found a backpack with maps marking out a trail to get from Sandy McNabb Campground to just across the river from your old house." Dean noticed Tommy swallow, and Dean nodded at him.

"Ayuh. I Found the backpack in the back bushes by the steps."

Jason looked at Tommy and frowned.

"Still, I didn't know what was going on. I suspected you two were involved, but I had no idea how exactly you were connected. I figured it must be something very big for you two to risk an escape over it."

"Let's move on to Friday night. After Gerald broke in, I rushed up to the house and I heard two men shouting at each other. One is Gerald, who was later be found dead on the floor of the study. I know what I heard, but I couldn't figure out how you got out of the house when I had it surrounded. I'm still not quite sure how you even got into the house."

Tommy looked at Jason and shifted in his chair uncomfortably.

"What do you want, detective?" Tommy asked him bluntly. "If it's a confession, you are not going to get one."

"I expected you would react this way. But let me go back to that photo in the paper of you. That's what put it together for me."

"I am not following you, detective," Tommy said. "Are you really suggesting we had something to do with the death there on Friday?"

"That's exactly what I am saying. I went back to the house at first light on Saturday morning. I found the backpack in the bushes by the back steps. I still had not figured out how Doogie's gun ended up inside the house.

"The way I see it, Doogie's gun would have to have been picked up in the back country and brought down to the house because I really do not believe Gerald brought the gun with him. It looks to me like Doogie was a part of this too. A big coincidence that he was camping on the very route marked on the map.

"It also bothered me greatly that Sarah wasn't home when I arrived just as the sun was breaking the horizon Saturday morning. She arrived nearly an hour later and told me where she went."

Dean paused and stared at both boys. The room went quiet until Jason broke his silence.

"Where did she say she went?" he asked.

"Calgary. Another coincidence isn't it?" he said. "You turned yourselves in shortly after she was in Calgary."

"So?" Jason countered.

"So?" Dean shouted back at him. He realized he had raised his voice and quickly lowered it back down.

"Sarah invited me in for a coffee after she got back from her little trip to Calgary. The house was the same as we left it the night before, but I did notice something in the kitchen sink as I went to the window to show Sarah where I found the backpack. It was just a couple of bloody rags and such. There was also a pair of scissors sitting by the sink and a roll of gauze. We had just had another bloody murder in the front study, so why not have a bloody rag in the sink?"

Jason let out a sigh and put his head in his hands for a moment. Tommy looked at his little brother and put his arm around his shoulder. "It's okay, Jason. We've done nothing wrong," he said. Jason cried.

Dean continued with his revelation as Tommy continued to comfort Jason.

"When I saw your photo, I at first wondered where you had been for the last thirty-some hours, but as soon as I saw the bloody bandage on your forehead, I thought of the bloody rags in the sink. It was then that it hit me. Why would there be any bloody rags in that sink? Sarah wasn't injured. My team was in there immediately, and Gerald's body was the only one with blood on it. Sarah was certainly not cleaning up Gerald's blood in the middle of the night. So whose blood was on those rags?"

Jason kept his head buried in his hands.

"I have those rags from Sarah's trash back at the precinct in my office, but that's not why I am here."

Jason continued to sob.

"And I haven't even dusted the backpack for finger prints yet."

Jason frowned at Tommy.

"You boys have two very good friends in Ricky and Bobby. Good boys; both of them. I believe those two would do almost anything for you."

Tommy hugged his brother again and looked up at Dean. He nodded in agreement. "They would," he whispered softly.

"I searched for them yesterday, and found out that they went camping Tuesday night. Curiosity got the better of me and I, of course, took a drive out to find their campsite."

Dean placed his hands together on the table.

"It was no accident that Ricky and Bobby tried to break into your house. They were definitely after something inside. When Ricky ran into the house on Friday night, he must have been overwhelmed with fear, fright, terror or something equally powerful to cause him to rush into a scene like that. Now why would he put himself at risk? What could be so damned important to risk getting yourself killed over?"

Dean let the boys think about all he said.

"I can only make a guess here, and you can stop me if I'm wrong or you can say nothing and let me believe what I am about to say.

"I have no doubt that you two were in your house Friday night. You were after something, but for the life of me, I couldn't figure out what it could be."

"You boys were good hockey players. The best this town has seen in a long while."

Dean cleared his throat and spoke directly to both boys. This was a difficult moment.

"Your friend Tim played hockey, and so did your friend Ricky. I did some homework, and Ricky's father was certainly not pleased about him quitting hockey, especially when he was nearly as good as you were, Tommy. So what would make Ricky quit hockey and put himself at odds with his parents? And then your friend Tim? What could be so bad that he would commit suicide, but tell no one why?"

He was done talking, and after regurgitating his theory aloud to these boys, he sensed he needed to change directions.

He felt a lot of pain in the room, and he couldn't hide the fact that it was affecting him. He had intended on speaking to the boys to confirm what he suspected and blow this wide open, but after hearing his own voice repeat what he suspected and seeing their reaction, he began to reconsider what he was about to do.

"Jason, can you please look at me for a minute."

Jason kept his head buried in his hands. Tommy was watching Dean carefully. He looked worried.

"Please, Jason," Dean said softly. "Just for a minute."

Jason lifted his head up and wiped his eyes on his sleeve. He did his best to keep his eyes on Dean.

"Listen you two. All I want to know is one thing. Just one question. A simple yes or no."

Tommy nodded. Jason continued to stare. His eyes darted about uncomfortably.

"This is about your friend Tim. And now that I think about it, maybe your friend Ricky too and maybe many others."

Jason's eyes suddenly stopped their darting around and focused on Dean's intently.

"Your friends had a big fire going out there. A hell of a hot one. I'll ask this one question and please answer this honestly."

The two boys didn't moved a muscle as they waited for Dean's question.

"I found what looked like a hard drive in the ashes. There was a lot more than just wood burning in that fire. Lots of plastic. I have a very good idea of what they were burning, and I really need to ask you this." He hesitated only a moment before he asked the one question that was so important to everyone.

"Did they get rid of it all?" he asked.

Tommy blinked rapidly. He glanced over at Jason and then nodded at Dean. He looked back at his brother who also nodded quickly and then pressed his face back down into the crook of his arm. Jason began to weep once again.

Dean released a heavy sigh, gave a short acknowledgment, pushed his chair back and stood up. Dean was satisfied. He trusted that he knew enough. He believed he understood why the boys killed their father, and though he may not have all the facts, he knew enough about where things stood. As he reasoned it out, he accepted it.

Dean searched for words of comfort to offer the boys, but he had none to give. He smiled softly and removed his hat.

Jason lifted his face to Dean. Tears continued to crawl down his cheeks. "Are you going to say anything?"

Dean looked down at both boys and slowly shook his head from side to side.

"It's not my story tell; is it, son? If it needs to be told, it will be. But not by me."

Dean left the room. Tommy hugged his brother. He held him tight and cried with him.

The End

See next page for all books by R E Swirsky

WISH ME FROM THE WATER
When a young teenage boy commits suicide, the town's people believe it was because of bullying. Two brothers quickly uncover the horrible truth and take matters into their own hands.

EXTREME MALICE
The teenage boy living next door is charged with the crime of strangling Jack's wife. The boy's guitar string was found around her neck. Jack was hundreds of miles away on business.

IN THE MIDST OF A PREDATOR
A very short story.
Young Bobby finds himself alone at the fair and lured by a sexual predator. (This same Bobby, many years later, becomes one of the main characters in Wish Me From the Water).

THE BLUFFINGTON FOUR
A time travel mystery. Four students stumble upon a device hidden away in an attic and are sent through a portal back in time. Their attempts to find their way home takes them to many different dates, but all lead back to one point in time in which a crime was committed. They soon believe the four of them committed the crime and resolve to go take their place in history.

BUMSTEAD'S WELL coming in 2014
It was just a dare to spend 24 hours alone at the bottom of the old well on the abandoned farm. What's the worst that could possibly happen?

Made in the USA
Charleston, SC
29 May 2014